POUL ANDERSON

THE DEVIL'S GAME

PUBLISHED BY POCKET BOOKS NEW YORK

Another *Original* publication of POCKET BOOKS

POCKET BOOKS, a Simon & Schuster division of
GULF & WESTERN CORPORATION
1230 Avenue of the Americas, New York, N.Y. 10020

ISBN: 0-671-83689-7

First Pocket Books printing November, 1980

10 9 8 7 6 5 4 3 2 1

POCKET and colophon are trademarks of Simon & Schuster.

Printed in the U.S.A.

THE CREATURE
IN THE MIRROR

"God in Heaven," he mumbled, "what are you?"

The sacred name did not frighten his visitor. "To explain that, at this stage, would be impossible. Probably it always will be. Perhaps we can discuss it a little, if we form a partnership."

"What do you want?"

"An associate who can act for me and with me in the human world. Again, there is no point in my going any further tonight. Let me assure you that I am no Mephistopheles. I have no desire for your soul, assuming you possess one. Nor do I pose the slightest physical threat to you. How could I?"

Haverner stood for a minute, a hundred rapid heartbeats, while thunder growled and his cheap clock clattered. Finally his face congealed, his hands unclenched, and he said, "Okay, no harm in talking, I guess. But what should I call you?"

"You may as well follow tradition," his visitor answered, "to the extent of calling me Samael."

To
BILL BROXON

THE DEVIL'S
GAME

SAMAEL

The shadow whispered.

It should not have been there at all, in this room which was half antique grace and half modern steel and electronics. Blinds, drawn against noonday, quelled and scattered light, filling space with an ocherous dusk. The old man was not even sure if dimness deepened toward darkness in the corner he faced, or if it was a trick of old eyes or old brain. Nor could he quite tell whether he heard a real voice, or a modulation of the murmur from the air conditioner, or a stirring inside his head. Throughout the years with Samael, and they were now many, he had never known.

"You are ready," it seemed to tell rather than ask him.

Sunderland Haverner nodded. An ache jabbed through him at the motion, reminding of how tense he was. That always happened at first when Samael returned, and went on in lesser degree for the whole time that Samael remained.

"Yes," he said. "In fact, more than ready. I have had to delay matters, waiting for you."

His own words sounded unnaturally loud and as though, impossibly, they echoed. Silence lay heavier on the island than ever at midnight. Among its dwellers went stories about ghosts and other creatures who walk through the sleeping hours of the day.

"Explain."

Haverner frowned, then shrugged. Often Samael's demands made no human kind of sense. Why need he spell out the obvious? Well, just as often the questions, comments, or commands that were omitted had been just as curious. Haverner had long since given up trying to understand Samael. He had—very nearly—given up fearing Samael.

"The preliminaries took months, as I warned they

would," he answered. "Several detective agencies had to search in several different places, especially since you wanted . . . ah . . . 'a broad distribution of types.' Once found, prospective candidates must be investigated in depth and the unsuitable weeded out." He let a somewhat spastic chuckle break from him. "Incidentally, a number of problems and little crises arose along the way. It was not precisely simple for me to conceal the purpose of this expensive effort from men whose profession it is to snoop, especially when I had to work from a distance through two or three sets of intermediaries. Would you like to hear the story?"

"No. It is clear that you coped; it was clear from the beginning that you would. Proceed."

Haverner sighed. "The rest should be, too. I still had a good many reports to study. Since you weren't here [and no use wondering where Samael had been, or why, or if perhaps Samael had been present unbeknownst to him], I had to choose the seven as best I could to match your specifications. Thereafter the subjects must be approached and convinced, and arrangements made to bring them— and when everything was ready and still you hadn't arrived, I had to give them a plausible excuse for the delay."

Weariness dragged him down against the chaise longue where he sat. Surely Samael could have waited to appear until an old man had had his siesta. He resisted, squared his shoulders, forced business into his tone. "I did get them to stand by, and it hasn't been so long that any are likely to have changed their minds or made conflicting commitments. We can doubtless have them here within a few days."

"We will now examine their dossiers," rustled from the shadow.

Did it glide out of its corner, across wall and bookshelves and desk, to hover at his back? Did it look through his eyes, or did Samael have sense organs not manifest in that shadow?

Haverner's hand, gnarly, liver-spotted, not altogether steady, reached for a binder that lay on the desk beside him. It was full to its limit with sheets of typescript, so that it pulled hard in his weak grasp and he was glad to let it fall onto the blanket covering his lap. His heart began to flutter and he needed a moment before he could open the volume. Meanwhile he wondered vaguely if Samael felt carnivore eagerness, or abided in emotionless patience, or if either of those ideas meant anything where Samael was concerned.

He flipped back the front cover. The first few pages were merely letters of transmittal from his agents, but he scanned them through his horn-rimmed reading glasses because he had received no order not to do so. The interesting part began at a synoptic list of the persons he had selected.

Why had Samael spoken of "broad distribution" and then required that all but one be *Yanquis?* Could it have something to do with Haverner's own origins? As it happened, the only native of these parts came alphabetically first:

Orestes Cruz. 25. Ciudad Vizcaya. Born in back country of Santa Ana. Unmarried. Associated with previous government as driver to Colonel Ybarra with rank of sergeant. Arrested last year after overthrow of that government, on suspicious (justified) of connections more subversive than this.

Matthew Aloysius Flagler. 40. Ciudad Vizcaya. Born in Chicago. Married, four children. Reform school and two prison terms in U.S.A. Manager of Casino Flores for four years until the former government closed down such operations; has since been living hand to mouth.

Ellis Erik Nordberg. 47. Minneapolis, Minnesota. Born (as Elias Erik Nordberg) on a farm in South Dakota. Married, two children. Former Army officer, brevetted major at time of discharge, 1960. Founder and owner of Northmount Electronics, a small subcontracting manufacturer.

Julia April Fenn Petrie. 33. Braidwood, Long Island, New York. Born in Arizona. Former psychiatric nurse. Married (to an attorney), one child. At present has no paid employment because of child's illness.

Lauritz Willem Rance (always called *Larry*). 35.

Richmond, California. Born in Los Angeles. Unmarried, two divorces, one child. Air Force service, 1963–65, followed by engineering degree, 1969. Lost several good positions and presently lives by odd jobs.

Byron Latimer Shaddock. 28. New York City. Born in Annapolis, Maryland. Unmarried. B.A., prelaw, Harvard, 1973. His inherited wealth makes employment unnecessary, but he is active in various cultural and humanitarian organizations as well as in sports.

Gayle Jeanine Matlock Robertson Thayer. 26. San Francisco, California. Born (as Gail Jeanine Matlock) in Chillicothe, Ohio. Married but separated, one prior divorce, no children. High school education only. Has been living by a succession of jobs, chiefly as a waitress when not on unemployment compensation.

Haverner paused. "The photographs are attached to the individual reports," he said.

"Go on."

"But this is such a huge lot of material. I . . . am too tired. Let me rest till evening, and, yes, let half of it wait till tomorrow. Unless you want to kill me."

"You are more tough than that, Sunderland Haverner." He barely heard, or thought he heard, laughter. "But be it as you request. I will come to you at nine, and we shall see how toughly you waited."

And he knew he was alone.

His head and eyelids drooped. Abruptly they snapped back up. Breath gusted in between his lips. Damnation, the next hours were indeed going to be hard!

Had he not suffered through enough postponement? He wanted Samael's game to start as much as he had ever wanted anything. Or was that true? At his age, memories themselves were gliding, whispering shadows.

Certain was, that at that age this was his final chance to play God.

Or play Satan. If there was a difference.

Unless his partner could and would prolong his existence, renew his youth—unlikely. The world was full of people who would gladly make the bargain that Haverner had made. How many of them were already partners of Samael?

Regardless, he must sleep, or else he would be unfit to continue at eventide. With the discipline of a lifetime, Haverner settled back and closed his eyes again. Noonday stillness became total, until somewhere afar a dog howled.

THE ISLAND

Who remembers the empire that England lost generations before gaining the empire that Britain lost so lately?

Perhaps "empire" is too strong a word. Along the whole Caribbean littoral and up into the Gulf of Mexico stretched this forgotten aspect of kingdom. It had almost nothing to do with the sugar islands of the Main, and was little known in London even when it was at its full. But for two hundred years and more these hot and musky coasts were speckled with enclaves of English-speaking men who sought not precious metals but precious trees.

Here was a cedar walk and there a mahogany works. Beyond that headland and on this bayshore were stands of rosewood. Past yonder bend grew logwood; when indigo meant blue dye, logwood meant red. In towns that never became cities, black men wielded broadaxes side by side with white, and Indians who learned broken English instead of Spanish went (when they went) not to a Catholic but to a Protestant church.

A strange sail in the sea, the Dons attack, the English hide in the woods. A strange smoke on the coast, the English attack, the Dons flee to the hills. At length someone in London unrolls a map, raises eyebrows, looks in ledgers, shrugs, rolls up the map; someone in Madrid signs a paper, takes snuff, shoves a document into a pigeonhole. Flags come down. Flags go up. Campeche is lost (recovered). The Mosquito Coast is redeemed, (abandoned). Jamaica is safe for the Protestant Succession and six percent on 'Change. The banners of Iberia and Iberia's children (what is a republic, Señor?) fly forever over Bluefields, Providence, Darien, over Utilla and Roatan and San Andres and Braggman's Bluff and Bonacca. The Isle of Tanoa becomes La Isla Tanoa.

Centuries erode the antique English tongue of the dwellers, but never wipe it out. "The Spaniard" rules the mainland and Britannia no longer rules the waves; the Tanoans are no longer British and never so much as consider becoming Spanish. What are they? They are Islandmen. They fish. They smuggle. They 'list under flags—any flags—and man merchant ships into foreign seas—any seas. When they have made their "enough" they return to Tanoa and either repair their fathers' (uncles', brothers') houses or tear them down and build new ones. They fish. They smuggle. They watch the sky, the beach, the tides, and care nothing for any man not an Islandman.

Tanoa is their world, a world clearly created by God for the Islandmen, the English language, and the old-style Methodist religion. (In England they had been "Independents," and, in another sense, they still are.) This territory is not quite fifteen miles long, a trifle over seven miles wide at its greatest breadth. At the North End ("de Nart' Ind") are the Peak and the Crag. Offshore are the Iron Shoals. Around the Bight ("de Boyt") are the Iron Cliffs. A few orchards and groves, pastures and truck gardens may be seen in the Fields: low hills and glades bearing Biblical names. "He haves a 'tater patch in Bet'lehem and a cow pasture in Gilead. No vun goes to any of dese places at noight. Dere be's sperrits in de voods." No, everybody is at home then, and home is the North Port.

Below these regions you find the Creek, and later the Bog, some miles of it, planted, where planted at all, in coconut trees. Offshore here are occasional turtle nets. At last you come to the South End, mangrove swamps and mangrove "bluffs," the latter small upthrusts of land above the muddy water.

And thus you reach a clear channel, across which you can make out the Caye. This is actually divided into several parts, fairy tale islets, two of them joined by a causeway to form the only other hamlet on Tanoa—scoffed at by the sophisticated North Enders. Elsewhere are other cayes, better known if not more frequented by Islandmen: Waterless Monday, the Serpent Church, Got No Bottom, Gehinnom.

As for "de Sponyard"—represented by six squat, sullen mestizo soldiers in exile—he never goes to them. On clear days he can see the dim blue edge of the mainland. On overcast days he can see a gloom where his country must be. Sometimes it rains.

INTRODUCTIONS

The hog plum tree has been unfortunately named.

Islandmen are in the habit not of feeding the fruit to their swine, of which they have a few, but of eating it themselves—green, as they do all local fruit, "else de vurms gits dem." Hog plums are thumb-sized, pale orange to yellow in color, with a thin skin and a stone. The flesh when ripe is sweet and succulent, contended for by birds, ants, and, yes, worms.

The seven who sat just before a particular hog plum tree at the shady west end of a patio behind the big white house had no traditions regarding it. The larger woman, Julia Petrie, turned a fruit over and over in one hand as though it were a feeling-piece, perhaps a jewel, solid throughout. Gayle Thayer held one very tentatively in her palm and looked at it as if it were so alien that anything might be expected of it: a kiss, maybe, a message of some sort, or even a small explosion. Of the men, Byron Shaddock had taken a sample, smiled to register absent-minded enjoyment and refocused his whole attention on the speaker. Lauritz—Larry—Rance had a plum raised to his lips, licked at a hair-thin crack, now and then applied the slightest pressure and licked again. Orestes Cruz had already eaten three; the pits lay at his feet, not wholly gnawed, and whenever a *vivi* ant came scurrying up to them a heel descended on it. Ellis Nordberg and Matthew Flagler sat beneath the tree as if it had never existed.

Slim rattan seats had been given all of them, but Sunderland Haverner was in a sort of Morris chair made of unstained mahogany and lined with an Indio blanket from the Picos Lindos, the distant mainland mountains. Old blood runs cold, and, while the air was tropical, touched by jasmine and roses, a salt breeze drifted off eastward waters. No matter their sweat, the seven newcomers also looked, in their seven different ways, as if they felt scant warmth.

"The sum in question," Haverner was saying in a high but precise tone, "is a most traditional figure. The means of getting it are not in the least traditional. However, the sum in question is not really in question." This seemed to amuse him a little. "One million United States dollars, on which the tax is one dollar per annum, payable to the Republic of Santa Ana." His lips parted in a brief, withered smile as he nodded. That gesture traveled west across the highlands and the sea beyond them, to the capital city from which the seven had flown this morning in an airplane of his and mostly in wary silence.

"Two weeks or less from tomorrow," he went on after a moment, "the winners of the game you are going to play will sign certain papers which make this arrangement perfectly legal in both nations, and elsewhere for that matter. Or, of course, there may be only a single signature, if there has been a single winner. However many or few, they divide the prize equally. My staff will help in arranging any desired discretion. I urge you to take advantage of this, knowing from long experience what nuisances—even dangers—swarm around one whose sudden good fortune becomes widely known."

The fruit she had been handling popped between Julia Petrie's fingers. "Get to the point!" broke from her. Eyes swung in that direction. Haverner raised his brows. She swallowed, glanced away, then back again at him. "I'm sorry." Her tone ran down from shrillness to a near mumble. "But please."

Still Haverner waited. Did he smile anew? It was hard to tell in this play of shade and sun-flecks against light whose intensity drained color from the sky itself. The breeze rattled leaves. Cruising up from the beach, a gull mewed.

Julia straightened her shoulders. "Well, look, Mr., ah, Haverner," she got out. As she talked, her voice regained its normal huskiness, if not much steadiness. "Look, I guess I'm typical, from what bits and pieces we've told each other. Your agents, somehow they found out I need money, lots of money, desperately. They proved they were from Haverner Enterprises; they offered me a flat million dollars if I could do . . . do exactly right . . . a job they didn't describe. . . . They gave me an airline ticket and a hotel reservation in Ciudad Vizcaya, some pocket cash, instructions to meet your pilot this morning—and that's all! That's all!"

She bit her lip, fumbled in the purse on the flagstone deck beside her, found a handkerchief and dabbed at the sweat that ran down her forehead to sting her eyes, at the juice that had stained her plain white dress.

"Indeed," Haverner replied. "My representatives made clear to you—did they not, Mrs. Petrie?—this is an experiment in psychology. It is not the first conducted here, though it will probably be the most interesting." He raised a hand. "No, of course you have not read about the earlier ones. I have not published, and my volunteer subjects have not been the sort of people who run to the news media with accounts of their experiences. Nothing sensational, anyhow; please understand that. Simply the unorthodoxy of a lay researcher.

"Still"—he leaned forward, making the Morris chair creak—"you must realize, ladies and gentlemen, under stress as you are, that stress is what the present experiment is about."

Ellis Nordberg cleared his throat. "Well, yes," he said, "but you must realize in your turn, Mr. Haverner, we aren't going to play your game for nothing. I hired a few investigators myself after I'd been approached."

"And?" the old man responded quietly.

"And so, sure, Haverner Enterprises owns most of the business in this country, and a lot of the land, and enough of the government." (Orestes Cruz sucked breath between teeth, half rose, sank down and shivered.) "You can shell out a million, plus incidental expenses, and feel no pain.

17

But your, uh, hobby hasn't taken anything like this form before. You've paid people pretty good wages—nevertheless, straight wages—to go through assorted odd tests; and that was that, as far as they were concerned.

"Now, though . . . we seven are supposed to compete, somehow, for a million dollars you claim you can make tax free. I was willing to come this far, Mr. Haverner, but now, by heaven," Ellis Nordberg said, "I need details."

Their gazes—in some cases, their glares—were upon him as he spoke. He was no unusual sight: of medium stature, lean except for the encroaching paunch of middle age, his long skull bearing angular features which had begun to wrinkle and sag a trifle, thinning nondescript hair, wan blue eyes. He wore bifocal glasses and an expensive, conservative tropical suit.

Haverner nodded. "True, sir, true," he answered. "This is why you were brought directly from the landing strip to me. Your curiosities shall soon be satisfied. The reason for the secrecy to date is merely to control this experiment and to save it from bothersome public attention." Again he raised a skeletal hand. "Don't be afraid. You will shortly get the whole story. If anyone declines to play—well, it was agreed beforehand you'll stay here while the game lasts. But you're free to quit at any stage. In fact, the game is an elimination contest."

Larry Rance's look strayed to Julia Petrie. No conventional beauty, she could be called striking: high cheekbones, prominent straight nose, wide mouth, hazel irises under heavy brows, dark brown hair worn fairly short. Tall and rangy, she could also be called stacked. Her age was obviously in the earlier thirties, which would have been less obvious were it not for the marks of strain carved upon each of the seven.

She caught his appraisal and gave him an angry return. He grinned at her. The biggest person there—though Haverner had once been physically impressive—Larry Rance stood six feet two and amply broad to match. Muscles bulged under the short sleeves of his flamboyant shirt, under the gold pelt on his forearms. They had shrunken somewhat, however, and his own belly had grown in spite of his being not much older than she. His face was square and hook-nosed, with small blue yellow-thatched eyes. Sun-bleached, his hair was cut at the same length as hers, but in an age of triumphant beards he, like the other men present, had stayed smooth-shaven.

Because they were side by side, he could murmur in his hoarse baritone, "Relax. Let them use up their energy." She jerked her stare toward Haverner. Larry shrugged, drew forth pipe and tobacco pouch, readied a smoke.

Matt Flagler, who had already gone through half a pack of cigarettes today, started a new one from the butt of the last, which he tossed into a flowerbed along the south edge of the patio. "Sure," he said. Chicago's West Side had never quite left his speech. He was forty, in reasonably good shape, handsome in a tilt-nosed, long-lipped, blue-chinned fashion, his eyes gray-green and slanty, his hair black and stiff, his clothes retaining a threadbare nattiness. "Sure. I know about you, Mr. Haverner. Been living in Vizcaya these past six years, haven't I? We can trust you."

"Thank you, Mr. Flagler," Haverner replied. "Yet you may as well satisfy yourselves at once that payment will be forthcoming to the winners and that no government can lay a finger on it." He turned his head, which was bald and resembled that of the mummy of Ramses. Two men stood behind his chair. To him on the left he said, "Captain, bring me the papers bound in red on my desk."

"Yis, sir." That attendant was slight but wiry. The Indian share of his genes dominated his features, save for the alert pale eyes. Neatly clad, he affected a brass-buttoned blue nautical jacket over tropical white. He was off at once.

"My factotum here," Haverner remarked of him. "Evans York. Not that that is specific on Tanoa. One might as well say 'William Jones' in Cardiff, and as for the title, most Islandmen are or have been captains, even if only of a fishing boat. But don't consider him a menial or underestimate his intelligence, ladies and gentlemen. By and large, you will have the freedom of this house, these grounds during your stay. But Captain York has the keys to my study. . . . To be sure, the only full set of keys is mine."

He sighed. "Forgive an old man's wordiness," he continued in a tone that, without bothering to be sarcastic, asked no pardon. "While we are on the subject, let me introduce Anselmo, Anselmo Gomez, since you'll have more to do with him." He nodded backward at the man who stood behind him on his right. "He'll be my chief representative, my referee and reporter, while you play out your games."

He thought a moment. "Games," he said. "Anselmo will see to it that the rules are observed. You may appeal his decisions to me. Be warned, I'll probably back him. Anselmo and I have worked together for quite a few years, and he has my total confidence"—he grimaced—"as far as does any member of our mongrel species."

" 'Ow do you do," said the man bespoken. He didn't seem to mind his employer's reference to mongrels, perhaps because he was nearly pure mainland Indio, bearing no resemblance to Orestes Cruz in looks or behavior. He didn't reach upward to snatch yet another plum, or shift about or crush yet another ant. Instead, he stood as if he could stand forever, growing no more tired and no less supple than the tree. White open-necked shirt, trousers, deck shoes stretched immaculate over his stocky frame; the 9-mm Smith & Wesson automatic belted at his hip was somehow not conspicuous. His face, broad, flat, brown, bore a mustache in lieu of expression.

"We 'ave studièd your records, ladies and gentlemen, the detecteeves sent us." His English, fluent and not unduly accented, sounded almost casual. "You 'ave been chosen out of many. We theenk you do well. I am 'ere to 'elp you. Please feel free you call on me." He bowed slightly. *"Y Usted también, naturalmente, Sr. Cruz."*

"You had best omit the Spanish, in *this* company," snapped the man thus singled out. Orestes Cruz was lean and very dark; his features were smooth, part Negro, part Indian, tinged fractionally Visigothic; but his hair was a black bush and his clothes—no, they did not bespeak poverty; they were too plainly given him a day or so before the airplane fetched him. He talked harshly, his accent dissimilar to Anselmo's. A certain jerkiness of movement suggested a bout of chorea or the like during his mainland childhood.

The breeze was dropping as noontide neared. With less noise in the leaves, people heard surf out on those skerries that sheltered the little bay. They had heard nothing from the electric generator that supplied the establishment. It worked in an insulated vault beneath the service building near the landing strip. This house and its satellites kept the width of Tanoa between themselves and the North Port, almost the entire length of the island between themselves and the Caye. From the servants' quarters, a domestic called to a child, "You dere, Sam?" It was a peculiarly lonely sound. Insects droned. A native rankness crept out from among the flower perfumes.

"Well, then." Haverner nodded. "Let's get on to business, and afterward to lunch, eh? I said the object of the next two weeks, as far as I am concerned, will be to test how a variety of individuals react to stress—to challenge, if you prefer. I admit, Mrs. Petrie, this requires me to explain the terms under which you seven will create that challenge for yourselves."

They waited, knowing they must. Gayle Thayer took up her purse in search of a cigarette. The plum she had been holding rolled from her.

"What you will do—those of you who remain willing and, ah, qualified—is simple," Haverner told them. "You must all know the children's game of Follow the Leader. *Seguid el Conductor*." (Oerstes Cruz scowled.) "Leaders are chosen in turn. Whatever the leader does, the rest must imitate. Those who cannot, drop out, losing their chance to lead if they have not already done so. Ideally, one alone is left at the end."

He paused for a moment before adding slowly, "I have a personal preference for a version I recall from very long ago, by the name of Simon Says. The leader cries, 'Simon says jump up and down!' or whatever action he has chosen, and performs it. Again, the others must do likewise or fail. However, if he calls the order and performs the action, but did not begin his words with 'Simon says,' then anyone who does copy him is a loser. Many a child has thus been betrayed by his own overeagerness.

"I mention this touch of subtlety in order to remind you at the outset that you are not asked to engage in a merely physical contest. At least, it would disappoint me if that is what you do. No, stratagems, quick-wittedness, the out-thinking of your rivals are not only allowed but encouraged in this game of Follow the Leader you are going to play—for the prize of a million dollars."

Gayle Thayer's large, ornate purse dropped and spilled its contents. They were numerous and, here, foolish.

"Oh!" Her voice, inherently high, went thin and wavered. She herself was plump, verging on stout, and short, with a fair complexion, curly light brown hair, snub nose, pouty lips. Her eyes, in contrast, were big and gray, bright and long-lashed, her best feature emphasized by careful makeup. She wore a flowered maxi-length gown and, on a massive necklace, a peace symbol. "Oh, I . . . I . . . I'm sorry. Please go on."

"Quite all right, Mrs. Thayer," Haverner said. "Or do you prefer Miss, or even this ridiculous new Ms. I hear about? Your dossier isn't clear about that. About which you use, that is."

"Anything, anything," she whispered, scrambling about on hands and knees to recover her possessions.

"No, wait, surely not anything goes," Byron Shaddock put in. "I mean . . . this comes suddenly, and no doubt we'll spend the rest of the day arguing over details, but, . . . well, . . . rules, the law, not to mention individual capability . . ."

Now it was he whom they regarded. He flushed and snapped, "Listen, I'm not afraid. Some of you will've heard of me. Nevertheless, I agree with Mr., ah, Mr. Nordberg?—I agree the rules will have to be spelled out beforehand."

"That's what Mr. Haverner's gonna do, you," Matt Flagler said. His look was insulting, but when countered it vanished at once and was replaced by a pleasant enough grin.

Byron Shaddock straightened in his chair and met their glances. He hardly seemed the surfer, water skier, auto racer, stunt pilot that the newspapers reported. Rather, he resembled the tennis player, the attender of important opening nights, the server of numerous worthy causes and generally conscientious scion of a distinguished family, that the newspapers also, less prominently, reported. His body was tall and thin, his nose cragged, his mouth traplike, his chin interminable, accompanied by vaguely brown flat hair and vaguely brown flat eyes, archetypal New England. His clothes were reasonable for the environment, and one felt that they always would be, whatever the surroundings.

"At ease, at ease," Haverner murmured.

Captain York returned bearing a crimson-covered

document, gave it to him, and resumed his stance behind the master. "Ah, yes," Haverner said. "Here we are. As you can see, this is a long and complicated instrument. But in front is a one-page précis. I imagine everybody will wish to examine that, at least. Perhaps right away?"

"If you please." Ellis Nordberg rose, stretched out an arm, took the codex and resettled himself. "Go on, Mr. Haverner. I'm used to reading legal papers, reports, that kind of thing, during the conferences they're relevant to."

Gayle appeared surprised that a Midwestern business-man should know the word "relevant."

"Good." Haverner clicked his tongue. "How I wish I could smoke! At my age . . . Would anybody care for a drink? Not yet?"

His tone grew stern. "Yes, Mr. Shaddock, certainly we'll put common-sense restrictions on what game the day's leader may call on the rest to play. Otherwise the game becomes meaningless. You, for instance, given your Ivy-League education, could demand that Sr. Cruz parse Greek verbs; he could demand you do likewise for a mountain Indio dialect. Who shall say which knowledge is better to have? Mr. Rance appears able to lift, say, three hundred pounds; the ladies presumably cannot.

"No, everything must be within the limitations of every-one." He paused to let this sink in. "In case of dispute, Anselmo is the lower court, I the final. Believe me, neither of us cares who wins or who loses. We . . . I am concerned only with observing the psychology of the interplay."

He bridged his fingers. His desiccated cheeks creased in another smile of sorts. "One million dollars tax free, to spend or invest as you choose . . . and my investigators verified that you each have compelling reason to want it."

Did somebody whimper far down in his or her throat? "The game," Haverner said. "Follow the Leader. You will cut cards today to decide the order of precedence. Play begins the day after tomorrow, so the first leaders can have a chance to devise their strategies. Each turn lasts from sunrise to sunrise. We'll post the schedule in the living room. Between turns there'll be twenty-four hours for rest, recreation, preparation, whatever you wish.

"The leader—the day's leader—will call on you to do that which he or she chooses—as I said, within your physical and mental capacity. Anselmo will judge its fairness. If necessary he'll ask me via a walkie-talkie radio he'll carry. Or you can approach me directly by appointment. You must be satisfied that your judges are impartial. If you are not, or if you are otherwise discomfited, you're free to drop out, though your contract does require you to stay here until the game is finished."

He paused, probably for breath. "Of course," he said, "the leader must perform personally. He can stop or modify or completely change his demand at any instant, subject only to the rule of fairness. His object will naturally be to force you out of competition. If you meet his challenge, then when your turn comes, your object will be to force *him* out. Because only those who last the full two weeks will share the prize money. The rest get nothing except transportation back to Ciudad Vizcaya. Those who are from the States have already been given their return tickets.

"Mr. Shaddock mentioned the law. Well,"—his smile flickered—"in effect, here we are beyond the law. I assure you that no authorities in the sovereign Republic of Santa Ana will pay attention to any charges that anyone may bring in connection with this episode. As for the press, when you have returned home—" He chuckled. "Go ahead. Tell what you like. That too should make an interesting study. However, for your personal sakes, I do recommend you keep quiet."

He said into faces bewildered, appalled, uncertain, thoughtful, "Calm, calm. You have the rest of today and the whole of tomorrow before you start. Those who draw high cards, early leadership, will have less time to plan. On the other hand, they'll be less tired, more alert and resourceful. What you do in your leisure will be your own business. Think of this as a cutthroat but not necessarily unfriendly game—for a pot of one million dollars.

"Maybe ideas will come up that require special equipment. In that case, ask me, in strict soundproofed confidence. I have various things here in storage . . . material for past experiments, contemplated experiments, cancelled experiments. . . . Anyone who can't think up a challenge may read the inventory in the hope of inspiration. Or, if you need something not on hand, you may order what you like, free of charge, within reason, and 'reason' really means little more than 'feasibility.' We're not far by air from many large cities. I have agents in most of them, and radiophone connections."

He lifted a gristly finger. "Now no doubt you'll have questions, plus you'll want to get settled in. I'm not strong these days, and, besides, I have other affairs. Let's go to lunch. We'll cut a new deck of cards immediately afterward. Then I must retire from your company. I'll be available for discussions, open or private as you wish, this evening and parts of every following day. Anselmo will always be available."

He rose, a slow process, assisted by his men at either elbow. He shaped a tiny laugh. "Good luck, ladies and gentlemen," said Sunderland Haverner.

INTERVAL ONE

The lunch was excellent. Two white-clad Islandwomen waited faultlessly on table in a long and graciously furnished chamber whose French doors, now Venetian-blinded, gave on the patio and the lawn and flowerbeds beyond. It was a shame that none of the diners paid much attention to the bonito almondine or the hearts of palm salad—except the host, and he doubtless had limited capacity left for sensory pleasure.

He raised his glass of Chablis. "To your health and fortune," he toasted.

Larry Rance grinned in a strained fashion. "Mine, at least," he said.

Matt Flagler regarded him with what was at the moment honest hate. "Go ahead, crack wise while you can," the Chicagoan growled. "Want to make a side bet? I say you won't last half the course."

Gayle Thayer, who chanced to be seated by Larry, winced away from him as if expecting violence. The big blond man shrugged. Byron Shaddock urged, "Let's stay cool. As Mr. Haverner remarked, we're in competition, but it needn't be, ah, unsporting."

"Why shouldn't it be?" Orestes Cruz demanded. "Sport, that's a thing the white man invented to pass the time." He glared around the table. "How many here really *need* a million dollars?"

"I do," Julia Petrie said, voice low but clear. "A goodly share, anyhow. My God—my child's life—"

"Sympathy pitch, eh?" Ellis Nordberg muttered. Eyebrows raised, he looked away from her and around at everybody else.

She started up from her seat, then subsided, breath audible and uneven. Blood flew across her face and withdrew. Haverner sipped his wine, watching.

"We might get acquainted," Byron suggested. "What do we do for our livings? Why are we here?"

Ellis turned to Haverner. "Sir," he exclaimed, "isn't your idea to . . . Well, you know . . . You must have some rule against collusion. I mean, splitting the pot seven ways. That's better than one hundred and forty thousand dollars apiece. Not bad for two weeks spent in a tropical paradise! You don't want *that,* so—"

"I want to see what you do," the Ramses head answered on a note of such calm as to sound above all wants. "My detectives' reports, which are more thorough than you probably realize, make me deem a seven-way collusion impossible. You personally, for example . . . But no, I mustn't give out information that might put one player at a disadvantage."

Julia spoke slowly. "Suppose everybody tell why they came."

"Might's well, seeing you've already let your reason out," Matt said from behind a smile that could have meant wry compassion.

"Have I?" Her features were taut but her tone most soft.

Silence stretched. Gayle broke it, perhaps in desperation. "Mr. Haverner, I can't read law and contract language." A nervous titter. "I can't even balance a checkbook. If a leader in the game tells me I got to do figures, I'll holler, 'Unfair!' Could you please explain how that whatsie about the prize money works?"

The old man took another sip. "I went to considerable

trouble there," he replied. "In order to keep a million dollars after taxes, if given them in a straightforward way, a North American would have to receive an amount that would strain even my resources." A sardonic note: "When a nation elects to be simultaneously the Empire and the Welfare State, it must expect to pay for its amusements. Sr. Cruz, being a Santa Anan, would theoretically be taxed at a lower rate. But in fact he's in such disfavor with his current government—"

"Not mine!" Orestes flared.

Haverner was not annoyed. "In any event," he said, "I feel sure you too would prefer a hard currency, Sr. Cruz. Certain items are most readily purchased in the United States . . . Well, my problem was how to eliminate income tax.

"The method is simple in principle, though much high-powered talent was needed for the execution of it. Santa Ana is among the many countries with which the United States has a treaty forbidding double taxation. If you pay taxes to one government, you do not pay them to the other. Most such treaties limit the exemption, but not this one—an oversight with which I had a little something to do, years ago. From Washington's viewpoint, it encourages Yankee technicians to accept work in friendly underdeveloped nations."

"Yankee agents," Orestes said.

Blandly, Haverner ignored him. "Now the law of Santa Ana, in order to attract philanthropies, provides that foreign nationals employed as directors—full or associate—as directors of such organizations here, . . . that these people pay minimal income taxes. In fact, this is graduated inversely to the amount of capital invested by their groups in Santa Ana.

"Some of you may have heard of the Haverner Foundation. It's a perfectly lawful nonprofit organization, recognized as such by all governments concerned, which carries out both scientific and humanitarian projects. For example, it's provided housing for mainland workers who used to live in hovels; it's undertaken medical and psychological studies, which include today's affair. . . . Do you follow me?"

"Yes, sir!" Matt whooped. "You're a great man, Mr. Haverner!"

"I do follow you in truth," Orestes said. "You get more out of the workers if they live in better kennels; your genetic research produces trees that wear out the soil faster than ever before— Oh, yes."

Gayle's breath hissed. Larry barely smiled. Byron took some wine, looking embarrassed. Ellis and Julia flickered glances back and forth from host to guest. Matt managed to say, "I know your kind, Cruz—" and Orestes frigidly to answer, "So does Mr. Haverner. I was only explaining to the rest of you—" before the unruffled old man interrupted them.

"In your case, Sr. Cruz, any monies due you will be paid in the Republic of Hidalgo, where the Foundation also operates under similar rules and whose government has no interest in you . . . or a mildly favorable one, considering which party is in power there. But the payment will be in Swiss francs, just as for every other winner." He nodded. "Swiss francs, as specified in your contracts, because the dollar does not look very durable of late, does it? Winners may leave their winnings in Zurich, or convert them piecemeal to any other currency, or all at once, whichever they prefer. The amount will, however, be the exact equivalent of one million United States dollars, at the rate on the day your game ends."

He leaned back, contemplated his fingernails on the table, and continued, "A million dollars hardly ever means 'a million dollars' these days. Winners will be appointed to the board of directors of the Haverner Foundation for a ten-year period at salaries which, over that ten years, add up to whatever sums they have won. They will, though, draw the entire amounts due them at once, as a nonreturnable advance; and they'll be given no duties. The Santa Anan tax on such income, under such circumstances, will be approximately one dollar per year —a total of ten dollars, and not one cent owed to the United States . . . or, of course, Hidalgo."

"That could raise a big stink," Byron murmured.

"I do advise discretion," Haverner said. "Conceivably this will cause amendment of the treaty. But that can't affect those who've already, quite legally, earned their money and paid their tribute. And as for myself, I don't care if a loophole of mine gets plugged. I can always find more or—likelier at my age—die and be done."

He spared them whatever protestations they might have felt were called for by blinking at Ellis and proceeding. "You have studied the contract and the attached legal information, Mr. Nordberg. Do you agree the instrument is safe and sound? That, once signed, it will be irrevocable, independent of my own death, disability or change of heart?"

Hesitation dwelt for an instant behind the bifocal lenses, until: "Yes. sir. I don't know why I should give my competitors free advice, though."

"You've just done that," Julia said dryly. "You'll play the game, won't you?"

After a while Gayle seemed once more to feel she must end silence. Midday flamed beyond the blinds. Air-conditioned, the room was cool, a shadowiness of hardwood floors and mahogany furniture in Colonial style. On one pale plaster wall hung a faded painting of a boy, a girl, and a scroll that read *"Arturo Principe de Galles y su Esposa la Infanta Catalina de Aragon"*—a legend as dim, failing, forgotten as their hopes. Outside, a mockingbird fluted.

"We . . . we talked about . . . telling each other why we're here, why we want—need—money," Gayle said. "It'd make things kind of friendlier, wouldn't it?"

Haverner showed faint mirth. Matt was noncommittal, Ellis totally impassive, Julia more tense than before. Orestes frowned. Byron nodded slowly. Larry smiled. It was he who drawled, "I daresay we overlap, some of us. Like, we're broke. I don't mind admitting I am—and, worse, I've got an expensive ambition." He cocked an eye at Orestes. "Maybe not as expensive as what I suspect yours is, Sr. Cruz. But still, it wants a lot of bucks."

"What is it?" asked the Santa Anan, word by word.

Larry shrugged. "Call me a boat bum. I want to build my own schooner, and take aboard the right crews—in succession, I suppose, because this is for the rest of my life." Some would have called his grin boyish, some childish. "Broad-minded broads among 'em, yes."

"What will you do thereafter?" Orestes inquired.

"Cruise the world."

"Nothing else—for a lifetime?"

"Well, I've got ideas about shipping occasional ocean-

29

ographers and marine biologists and such, and trying my own hand at science."

"We should have a talk about that, Mr. Rance," Ellis proposed.

Anger broke through Matt's shell. "Behind everybody's back? Oh, no, you don't!"

"And how would you figure to stop us, Flagler?" Larry responded in genial contempt. "For your information, I hold a black belt in karate." To Ellis: "However, I kind of doubt we'd find a lot in common, Mr. Nordberg. What do you care about the oceans?"

"We can discuss that later," said the man from Minnesota.

"No," said Larry. "I'm not taking orders"—a prickly look at Matt—"but I'm not after trouble either, like what comes from rousing everybody else's suspicions. We'll discuss things right here or not at all."

Ellis's gaze darted around the table. "Very well," he clipped. "Shall we state our reasons, then? Is that agreed?"

The right side of Julia's mouth tugged upward. "Why not? We can't spend two weeks totally fenced off from each other. And the biographies, the motives—data to take into account, in planning our challenges, hm?"

"You start, baby, if that's how you feel," Matt said.

Julia considered the old man. *"You* know about us, Mr. Haverner. Will you hold us to the truth?"

"I fear not," he answered softly, and regarded them one by one. "You see, the game has already commenced."

There was another stillness.

Julia sighed, before lifting her spine in defiance. "Never mind," she said. "I guess I have let my own cat out of the bag. Okay."

Staring into the luminous blankness of the blinds she went on, flat-voiced: "I'm married. We live on Long Island. My husband's a very new lawyer, doesn't earn much yet, has a long commute—but Manhattan's no place to raise a kid nowadays. We have one. A girl. Name of Kilby. Six years old. Three years ago, her kidneys failed." She paused, as if gathering strength. "A transplant—from an accidentally dead child, because Malcolm, my husband, Malcolm and I weren't suitable—a transplant didn't take, and left her so frail that a second attempt would probably kill her. So she's kept alive by regular treatments on a dialysis machine. Not one of those new portable units, nor a standard sort owned by us and used at home, which would have made the expense bearable. The complications following that transplant would make it too dangerous. She goes to the hospital three times a week, and already once it was only the equipment there for emergencies that saved her. The cost is well over thirty thousand dollars a year. It may go higher if she comes to require additional therapies. In that case, we're helpless. We've used up our resources by now: insurance, savings, borrowings, charities, begs. Yet we don't count as paupers whom the government would underwrite. Her head lifted together with her voice. "And that's not going to happen, either. We've been through enough as is."

Byron registered distress. Larry gnawed his lip. Matt flushed with a somehow offended expression. Ellis frowned. The scowl on Orestes might have been aimed at a personal enemy.

"Oh, God," Gayle said into the emptiness, "I'm sorry. If I win—alone I mean—Julia, I'll help. You dig?"

"I do," Ellis told her. "You're fishing for a collaborator."

"I am *not!*" Tears came forth. Gayle rubbed them. Julia reached out to pat her hand.

Byron Shaddock turned reflective. "Hm. I imagine secret agreements. Well, since presumably you've no way to prevent them, Mr. Haverner, doubtless you have no rule against them." The host barely nodded.

It was a diversion from the awkwardness of a minute earlier. Likewise was it when Larry squeezed Gayle's shoulder and asked, "So what're you after? Just a life of ease?"

"A life, anyhow." Her words were barely to be heard. "I . . . I . . . I'm sick of being poor." She clenched fists on lap and plunged ahead. "Okay, I've got no talents, except maybe I could be a good artist if I wasn't always tired from what grubby jobs I can find. . . . When I remarried, my alimony stopped, and my second husband, that bum, you might as well try getting blood from a banker, after we split up—" She forced a smile. "Your boat, Larry, *that* sounds exciting."

He held his peace.

Matt Flagler stirred. "Sure, Gayle, I understand." He

beamed while she fished a handkerchief from her purse and sniffled into it. "Me, I'm out of a job myself, and I've gotten tired of always being somebody else's man, you know what I mean? Six years I spent in that pisspot—uh, 'scuse me—that dump Vizcaya, managing a casino . . . belonged to the Family, my wife's in the Family, know what I mean? . . . The Family had this here casino. Then came the goddamn stupid revolution, the goddamn colonels—" His excitement was waxing. "They got reform like pimples; they closed us down in 1977, and then what could I do? Hang on, that's all, hang on. Yeah, try raising an American family anywhere on—" His fist thumped the table; the fork rattled on his plate. "The restoration last year, the sensible people back in power, yeah, sure, now the casino could open again. Only Papa —Papa Delvecchio, my father-in-law—he dropped dead back in the States, and had no sons to stick up for his daughter, and the Family picked somebody else. Me with a wife and four kids! You call that loyalty? Gratitude?"

He jerked to a halt, glowered around, took forth his pack of cigarettes and lit one. As the ashes developed, he dropped them on the remnants of his meal. "Okay," he said, subdued. "Okay. I told *you*. You tell *me*. Be fair, huh?"

"You did not tell us why you stayed in Santa Ana during the reign of the junta," Byron observed. "Possibly the U.S.A. is still too hot for you?"

"Shuddup," Matt retorted. "Shuddup. Why're you here?"

"Yes, I've heard of you, Mr. Shaddock," Ellis said. "You're independently rich, besides being the son of a Senator and . . . What's a million to you?"

"The game," Byron admitted. A waitress arrived to refill his glass. He tasted. "A fine vintage, Mr. Haverner. Too bad we drink it distracted like this. . . . Yes. The game. I wasn't told the details in advance, of course. But I was given to understand a no-holds-barred—hardly-any-holds-barred—competition was being arranged down here." He bowed and smiled toward his host as he sat. "It's more fascinating than I hoped."

A tic danced in Orestes's cheek. "And how will you spend your prize, should you win?" he asked.

"Oh, I don't know," Byron answered. "Put it into a genuine charity, perhaps."

"Like mine?" Julia's smile came and went. "I warn you, I have no shame."

"Yeah, real charity's a thing between man and man," Larry said, "not a check you write to some outfit whose president makes more money than you do, because that way you can take a cut off your income tax. If I win, well, I can do without their Christing or their off-key trumpets at Christmas and Easter, but I'll pass a few bucks on to the Salvation Army. That's real. It doesn't help Humanity; it helps Joe and Bill and Jane when they're down on their luck. The rest of the organizations can go whistle."

"You quite through with the sermon?" Matt said.

"What's your aim, Sr. Cruz?" Byron asked politely.

"You may as well know. The revolution." Orestes used thumb and forefinger to pull lips back from teeth. He pointed to the gaps where several had been. In the same level tone as before, he continued, "Two of those rotted in my jaw when I was a boy. How was I to afford dental care? Where I was, I had never heard of it! The rest were knocked out in prison, when I was being interrogated after the so-called restoration." To Haverner: "I am not grateful to you. The old families that have come back to what they think is power are your puppets, and your CIA's. You got me sent to Tanoa as a 'condition of probation,' for me to entertain you. Eh? Meanwhile my brothers are being shot, flogged, clubbed in the testicles, left starving among lice and cockroaches. I am going to win this game, Mr. Haverner, and I am going to spend the money on guns and propaganda and liaison with my brothers in Cuba, Africa, around the world."

Having got where it was bound, the matter-of-fact explanation stopped.

"To be sure, to be sure." The old man seemed, again, mildly amused. "You can trust me to honor my commitment if you win, though you may need a cover story for the Foundation's regular administrators. Why not? After all, supposing your glorious revolution succeeds, which it possibly may, and stays incorruptible, which is beyond possibility—I won't live long enough to be affected."

Orestes gulped air. Ellis Nordberg stared at him, and when he himself spoke his own breath was uneven. "You

33

mean, you really mean you . . . you'd give that kind of money . . . to support terrorism? By all that's holy, then I've got to be the winner!"

"And what is your purpose?" Julia demanded.

"A business investment," Ellis told them. "What makes you liberals think business is a zero-sum game? We create jobs, don't we? We mine minerals that'd otherwise lie unused till the sun grows cold. We, hell, you, Mr. Haverner, you plant fruit trees where nothing but jungle was before. . . ." He put a hatch cover on his vehemence. "Rance, you mentioned being interested in oceanography. All right. So am I. It's the coming thing. The next frontier. Oil, metals, tide motors, scientific fisheries . . . food, plastics from plankton, seaweed . . . A clear million today, put into the right shares and the right people, could be a clear billion in another ten years. You might ask me for a job if I win."

"Looks like I'll have to win," Larry said. "I prefer breathing."

"Huh?"

"Phytoplankton supply fifty percent of the earth's oxygen, and already they're contaminated. I don't care for oil slicks either. And I do like whales and elbow room."

Ellis's face bore a short-lived regret before he laughed. "Oh. An eco-freak. I'm disappointed. I thought you had more imagination, Rance. I really did."

Larry's own restraint broke. "Could be you were right the first time. Because you know, Nordberg, I may just apply that imagination. Come my turn, I may just figure out a game that will kill you."

The pack was new; the cellophane crackled as it was torn; Anselmo shuffled skillfully before his master started the cards withershins around the table. He reshuffled after each cut. Aces were high, suits ranked as in bridge.

Julia Petrie: deuce of diamonds. Triumph flared in her eyes; she was virtually certain to be the last, thus to have the most time for preparing her scheme. On the other hand, she would have the maximum chance to be eliminated before her turn came. She blanked expression out of her face.

Byron Shaddock: ten of hearts. "Rather a Charlie Brown card, eh?"

Ellis Nordberg: five of hearts. No comment.

Matt Flagler: deuce of clubs. "Hey, look! Last! . . . No? No? Just wait one minute. . . . Okay, Mr. Haverner, okay, sir, whatever you say."

Orestes Cruz: seven of clubs. "Well, well. Do you expect me to club you to death, white people? Relax. I'll simply bury you," with a smile that got scant response.

Larry Rance: king of spades. "Oh-ho! Want to try for an ace, Gayle?"

Gayle Thayer: jack of diamonds. "Where does this put me?"

Sunderland Haverner was assisted to his feet. Pronouncing a courtly dismissal, he left the room. His guests were conducted to their own quarters and informed that dinner would be at eight.

The house had been built well over a hundred years earlier. "Villiam Valker slept dere vunce," the Islandmen said, unconscious in their echo of the claim so often made concerning a prior, more famous, and more fortunate revolutionary. The builder was an ancestral Captain York —himself descended from "Captain Yark oz heist de English flag ower Isle o' Tanoa, yis, sir"—who had done well in the copra trade. Eventually this person retired to his homeland, where labor was cheap and (given its siestas, individual attention by the master to events like birthdays or christenings, and similar time-honored perquisites) conscientious. He did not pick the more or less Georgian style of the house; it picked him without his knowing. This deeply does the Island hold its past. He did overdo the size, having acquired a mainland wife who dreamed of restoring the social glories of her own Castilian forebears.

That was a vain wish. Later generations, increasingly impoverished, used ever smaller portions of the mansion. At last they abandoned it altogether. Good materials and honest craftsmanship resisted sun, rain, hurricane, termite, fungi of mold and dry rot. When Sunderland Haverner bought the place, he found it needed little repair, and he had the taste to order minimal remodeling.

The grounds were another story. It took years to displace crab grass, Bermuda grass, saw grass, aloe, fever flower, palmetto, bamboo, viper- and tick-sheltering liana, huge treelike thistle, in favor of sweeping lawns shaded by oak and tropical cedar, with orderly blossoms along graveled paths. The enemy would always prowl the marches, watching for a chance to return. As if for homeopathic protection, somewhat north of the house was an enclosed botanical garden, featuring desert plants as well as natives.

On the east–west axis of the house, a great L-shaped living room-cum-library overlooked land that curved down to a lagoon. That water, shark-netted for the benefit of swimmers, lapped on a wide white beach where stood a summerhouse. Immediately south of it was a spit of land on whose farther side clustered a pier, a boathouse, and a shed, of frame and shingle weathered silvery. Northeastward the strand narrowed and the terrain rose sharply, until it broke in the black grandeur of the Iron Cliffs, miles distant. Behind these, hills tumbled upward, unutterably green, to the naked Crag, beyond which in turn the Peak could be seen looming on clear days.

East of the mansion, a row of neat cottages were homes for the staff. They were backed by a concrete-and-tile storehouse with attached garage. Not far north of it was the service building—from which, among other items, ran power lines, esthetically underground like their generator—and north of that the paved landing strip and a hangar that could hold several executive airplanes. Narrow roads of crushed pipeshank connected all these. A larger one snaked off toward the North Port, biweekly goal of a truck that brought back supplies and, when the packet-boat came in, surface mail.

But as for the Big House: it had white walls, a green tile roof, and pleasing red-brick chimneys. The aerials for television and radiotelephone had not been allowed to spoil it; their hideousness was at the airstrip, with cables to pass the signals here. Around the north and east sides stretched a covered and screened veranda, complete with porch swings; on the north side lay the patio.

The living room occupied the entire eastern interior. Like everything else, it had a structure and décor basically Colonial. The library part thrust westward from its northern end and held an astonishing number and variety of books in different languages. Beyond came a luxurious bath, Haverner's study, and his austere bed-chamber. Across the hall, past the living room, were the dining room, the kitchen, a utility cubicle ancillary to the cellars, and—directly opposite Haverner's—the chamber occupied by Anselmo Gomez.

Upstairs, a bathroom opened on the landing at either end, and eight bedrooms lined the corridor. The southeast one was permanently used by the present Captain York. The rest often held guests. Although the principal offices of Haverner Enterprises were in New Orleans and Ciudad Vizcaya, with branches around the globe, he did do occasional business while on Tanoa, as well as the experiments he had begun in his later years. Those were pleasant lodgings, each spacious, breezy through a pair of windows, handsomely decorated. Each held two chairs, an escritoire (pens and stationery in the drawer), a bureau, a closet complete with chamber pot (changed every morning regardless), a radio on a stand, and a double bed (*cama matrimonial,* as the Spanish demurely has it).

At the east end, the corridor gave onto a frame balcony that ran the width of the house. From there one could see how surf smashed fire-white against a thousand blues and greens and purples on the line of reefs that sheltered the lagoon. A couple of miles further out lay the stark caye named Gehinnom.

The baggage of the newcomers had been taken to their quarters. Captain York explained that room assignments were at random and the ladies and gentlemen were free to swap. Nobody did. On the north, from east to west, the order was: Larry, Ellis, Byron, Julia; on the south, beyond York: Matt, Orestes, Gayle. Nothing in the manner of the permanent resident indicated that he thought of himself as a chaperon. However good a Methodist, he would have had to acquire the art of turning a blind eye on some of Haverner's visitors.

The present group unpacked. Afterward they were not sociable. Larry and Orestes vanished on long separate walks around the territory. Byron explored the library till the sun was low, then went for a swim. He found Julia already in the water—she had spent the hot hours in her room, whether napping or planning she did not say—and they exchanged cautious amenities. Ellis rested awhile before he got Anselmo to give him a guided tour of the area. Gayle stayed upstairs, soothing her nerves with her radio and a thin joint of pot. Matt likewise remained indoors, but had a servant bring him soda, ice, and a fifth of bourbon.

Having asked about companionship and been deferentially told that he must make his own arrangements, he knocked on Gayle's door and suggested he come in. When she pleaded the conventional headache he muttered a mild obscenity and settled down to pass the time as best he might. The bourbon was far superior to the cheap *aguardiente*, which was all he had for a long time been able to afford.

The atmosphere at dinner was constrained.

Over the port (after a superb flan, which followed an unimpeachable prime rib, et cetera) Larry tried to brighten matters. "Here, let me take care of that, Julia," he said. He had maneuvered to be seated by her. Paying no heed to the nutcracker that was part of each service, he started cracking walnuts in his hands, two by two. The noise was slight but conspicuous against an insect stridency and a remote booming of breakers, both of which drifted in from the breathless odorous warmth outside.

"Why, thank you." She smiled mechanically. Her chief attention had been directed at Byron, who sat on her right. After a minute or two: "Take some yourself."

"I, uh, I don't care for nuts," Larry said.

"Including us, who must've been nuts to come here?" Gayle snickered. In haste: "No offense, Mr. Haverner."

"None taken," their host replied rather wearily.

"Of course not," Orestes said, his own tone almost impersonal. "Don't worry about that, people. You cannot insult Mr. Haverner. You see, he does not regard us as human. We are more like chickens, who produce eggs for him till we're cooked—and first, maybe, some entertainment, when he pours us full of gin to see how we stagger."

He smiled into several dismayed stares and Haverner's imperturbability. "Anybody care for a game of cards after dinner?" Byron said across the hush.

"Sure," Larry answered. "Poker, that is. Nickel-dime. I can't play for more." He attempted a laugh. "Till I've won that million."

"Nickel-dime?" Matt's voice was slurred and loud. "That's not poker, that's tiddlywinks." He drained his goblet. "How 'bout some whiskey 'stead'a this Portugee horse piss?" Abruptly, almost dropping the glass: "Uh, uh, a joke, Mr. Haverner. It's real good, this wine. Real good."

"I prefer bridge," Ellis said, "and we have two foursomes."

"Real good," Matt said. "Delicious." His eyes flickered anxiously.

"I only play whist," Haverner said, "and not tonight in any event. I shall retire early."

"What kind of television can you get here?" Gayle wondered.

"I don't know wine," Matt said. "Not like you, Mr. Haverner. I do know what's good, though, and when it's real good, like here, I kind of joke about it. Get me? I pretend like it's lousy. The better it is, the worse I call it." Seeing no response, he gave up and slumped back in his chair.

Ellis watched.

"Any thoughts about what game you'll decide on, Larry?" Byron asked. "Game of Follow the Leader, I mean." Julia's gaze swung at once to the man on her left.

He grinned. "Let's not discuss that at mealtimes. Maybe not at all. Okay? You know, in Zen there's no bow, no arrow, no archer; there's just the shooting. I believe in letting the world happen."

Byron smiled back. "Or, as they likewise say in Zen, if you have a pile of dirty dishes to wash, you need not wash them twice."

Larry leaned toward him, which brought his arm against Julia's, both being more than half bare. She did not draw hers back. "Hey," Larry said, "you're into that yourself?"

"Not really," Byron admitted. "But I've read, talked to disciples and even masters." He shrugged. "I'm not a committed type. Mainly, I'm an observer."

"Like Mr. Haverner?" Gayle suggested timidly.

"Oh, no," Byron said. "Mr. Haverner is a man of action. It's no cliché to call him a mover and shaker."

"You shouldn't need to suck up to him," Matt said. "Tha's whudd they're doing, sir."

"In a way, that is true," Orestes said. "We dance to his pipe. I also, yes, I also."

"You doubtless know a good bit more than I do about our host, Sr. Cruz," Byron replied in amiable wise. "However, given my connections—a considerable sum of my family's money is invested in these parts, and my father takes special interest in U.S. Central American policy—naturally I've heard about Sunderland Haverner. Today, among the books, I found out more. Not that our host keeps a brag shelf. But he does have many reference works dealing with the area. They're bound to contain mention of him." He nodded at the head of the table. "In short, sir, I imagine your reputation is great enough to make you immune to flattery or"—a glance back at Orestes—"vilification."

"I like to think so." Haverner signaled. Two servants were immediately there to help him rise. He smiled at the assembly. "Don't get up. No, I wouldn't be embarrassed by anything you said about me, good or bad. You might be, though, in my company. I want you to feel free to interact. That's the whole purpose of this project. Therefore, if you will excuse me, I bid you a very good night."

When he was gone, with a single exception the group visibly relaxed. The waitresses poured more wine and offered cigarettes and Havana cigars. Matt lit one of the latter. Larry, after seeing Julia wrinkle her nose, tucked his in his shirt pocket. She and Byron were the nonsmokers.

The one who did not ease off at least a little was Orestes. For a few minutes after Haverner's departure he sat amidst the small talk, his dark features and thin frame quivering with the effort to stay quiet. At last the words broke from him, an explosion that shocked everyone back into tension.

"Freedom to interact? *¡Mierde!* I bet he goes to listen in. Each corner of this house is . . . is bugged. It must be."

"The servants?" Glancing at the door through which

the neat white-clad women had passed, Gayle shivered.

Julia responded with a grimace. "I doubt that," she said. "But think about electronic eavesdropping, friends. Like microminiaturized audio pickups, tiny battery-powered TV cameras, infrared snooperscopes for nighttime, everywhere around the place, inside, outside, hanging from trees, wedged between rocks, planted in shrubbery—"

"No matter now," said Ellis. "When we agreed to go through with this thing, we gave up our privacy for the duration. So we might as well talk openly."

"What about?" Matt mumbled.

"Well," Ellis said, "how about you gentlemen who know it, Mr. Shaddock, Mr. Cruz, how about you filling the rest of us in on Mr. Haverner's background?"

"Why should we?" Orestes retorted.

"O-oh," Ellis told him, "I might have something to contribute. After I'd first been approached, I ordered some checkups of my own. Shall we three go off together and exchange information?"

"No." Drink barely tinged Byron's tongue. "Outrageous it may be to both of you—Nordberg, Cruz—the idea of playing by sporting rules. But I intend to. Besides, in spite of being in competition, we do have common interests, like survival." He paused to choose words. "Not that I believe Haverner wants to do us in, or will renege on his part of the bargain. But he is a strange man, and this is an uncanny situation, and the more truth we can get about him, the better for everybody."

"I've been down in these parts before," Larry said. "I have a few stories and such to pass on, if you want."

"I don't," Julia added, "but I do have experience in . . . applied psychology. Maybe I can throw some light on the matter."

Ellis pondered. "Flagler? Mrs. Thayer?" They gaped at him, the first muzzily, the second fearfully. "Well, why not include you two?" he decided. "The fact that an opponent in a game has certain information is, itself, information a player can use. Okay. Let's pool our knowledge and our guesses. If nothing else, we all need an estimate of how honest a game this is."

Byron and Larry each started to speak, stopped, gestured the other on. It was Matt who broke the silence.

Staring ahead at no one, his tone a mixture of wonder and hunger, he crooned, "A million dollars cash. A *million* dollars cash."

SUNDERLAND HAVERNER

Although he had never sought publicity, but rather always shunned it, much information about Sunderland Haverner was inevitably in the public domain. Persons with occasion to study his career believed they knew fairly well what he was. They were mistaken. They knew what he had been. No human being knew what he *was*—saving perhaps himself, and perhaps not—since that day long ago when his own face in the mirror had spoken to him.

As for what he had been, that was the scion of an old New England family, less affluent than in earlier generations but still well respected and well connected. He was born just too late to be eligible for the draft while his country was engaged in the war to end wars, a fact which he said pained him until such feelings ceased to be expected. Soon after democracy became safe throughout the world, he entered the college that sons of the Haverners always entered. For four years he studied Latin, Greek, English, French, history, a gentlemanly amount of science. The latter included one course in psychology (Descartes, Leibniz, Locke, Charcot, Binet, embarrassed mention of that, you know, Freud fellow). Upon his graduation, with acceptable marks though no special honors, his family gave him the European tour that was also traditional.

This exhausted the financial resources available for him. His father inquired among connections and got him a position with a large firm based in New Orleans and dealing in tropical fruit. It was a good enough position for a beginner—nowadays it would be called "junior executive"—and he could expect that faithful service would in due course win him promotions until he was well-off by the time they gave him a gold watch and retired him. To be sure, New Orleans society did not exactly take yet another young Yankee to its bosom. However, there were establishments less exclusive and not too expensive. There was the companionship of one's officemates. There was the occasional dinner invitation from a superior who wished to size up the employee, or show himself as genial beneath the businesslike exterior, or sometimes provide a break in the loneliness for a daughter of his guest's age.

Sunderland Haverner was preparing himself for such an evening when his own face spoke to him.

First it smiled. Always observant, he nevertheless failed to notice change at once, so gradually did the thing happen. Then he saw that the image was not brushing its hair. As the smile in the glass began to show teeth, the brush clattered out of his fingers to the dresser top.

"Oh, no," broke from him.

"Oh, yes," whispered back.

He stood for a time that felt very long and very short. Strange how aware he became of everything else. Glare of electric bulb on faded wallpaper, threadbare rug, armless chairs, narrow brass bedstead. Dusk in the window, street noises, air still sullen with the day's heat and mugginess. From down the hall of the rooming house, Mr. Durant's old Victrola giving forth "Let Me Call You Sweetheart" for the—hundredth?—time. Yet it all seemed infinitely far away.

"You need not be afraid," murmured his image, as if it used the whirr of his small fan to form words. "Not unless you choose to be. You have not gone insane."

"So *you* say," he heard himself reply, which struck him as an insane thing to say.

A hand lifted into view in the mirror to make a reassuring gesture across white shirtfront and brown vest. "You would be mad if you were not astounded, not bewildered and dismayed. But consider yourself, your surroundings, the state of your own mind. Think back to whatever you recall of your dreams, and to the fever that had you delirious when you were sixteen, and to those few times when you let alcohol get the better of you. Compare. After you are satisfied, consider the possibility that this is real—if you have the manhood."

Haverner clenched his fists. He stood unmoving for a while that his tin-plated alarm clock agreed was long. Finally he breathed, "Who are you? What are you?"

"That comes later," the face told him, and grinned. "No time now. You have an engagement soon, remember?"

"What do you want of me?"

"Nothing to your harm. On the contrary, any agreement we may reach should be to your enormous advantage. I have no power to compel or hurt, only to advise and persuade."

"And . . . you . . . you gain . . . ?"

"I said we must carry this matter on, if you are willing, later. Not in one piece, either. You will need time to learn, think, understand, decide." The face, which had taken on a serious expression, smiled anew. "As far as that goes," it whispered in marvelously ordinary Americanisms, "I'll want a chance to size you up before I decide what sort of partners we'd make. Meanwhile, for a sample, I'll tell you: act natural tonight, and when Mr. Fielding brings up the Central American and Caribbean areas in talk, act real interested. Be interested. You could build yourself quite a future in those parts."

Sweat that was not from the sultriness stung Haverner's eyes and drenched his armpits. As if out of the small white Congregational church of his boyhood Sundays, he mumbled, " '—all the kingdoms of the world—' "

"Oh, no," answered the face. "Let us not get above ourselves, you and I." It paused. "You have had a shock. Give yourself a chance to think. If, after that, you want to know more, be here at this hour, alone, in eight days. If you aren't, have no fears; you will never see me again. Good evening, Sunderland Haverner."

It did not vanish in a puff of smoke or anything like that. It simply resumed being his reflection.

Somehow he went through the motions, walked down the hall to the bathroom and scrubbed the reek from his torso, changed his shirt, made his way to the home of his superior, was a deferential but brisk dinner guest who, over cigars and port (from the best bootlegger in New Orleans), listened closely to his host's discourse on the commercial possibilities of the Central American–Caribbean region, and offered a few shrewd responses of his own.

By the date of rendezvous, the episode of the mirror naturally seemed unreal. Haverner told himself that it must have been a dream his memory had displaced. He would keep its appointment merely out of a certain curiosity about how his own psyche worked, and to show he was not afraid, and, well, to make sure nothing was going wrong in his head. He disliked admitting what comfort lay in the fact that this was the Lord's day, and that that morning he found a bit more than expediency in attending services as usual at his boss's church. He was not mired in medieval superstition, after all; he knew his Channing, Huxley, Spencer, yes, a bit of his Nietzsche.

Thus he stood before his bureau mirror at the deeper dusk of an aging season while thunder boomed off Lake Pontchartrain, lightning flickered, a breeze flapped drapes, and down the hall Mr. Durant was playing "You Made Me Love You." He decided he might allow as much as half an hour before he went to a movie.

"Here I am, Sunderland Haverner."

The mirror showed him only himself agape. He whirled about, his heartbeat suddenly fast and thick. The whisper, if it was a whisper, was well-nigh directionless, but—but the left drape by the window no longer stirred in random fashion. The shabby cloth rippled around what might have been a human form standing against the wall behind it.

The whisper laughed. "I have a variety of manifestations," it said.

Stiff-legged, Haverner approached. "You are welcome to touch," the voice in the wind invited. When he poked, his finger met no resistance other than fabric and plaster; and the vague outline did not reappear until he stepped back.

After several attempts he was able to croak, "Who are you? What do you want? And why me?"

"You are promising material," was the reply.

"Material for what?"

"The acquisition of wealth and power. The doing of mighty deeds. Are those not your dreams? Are you really content to serve other men until you are so old that they shrug you off? You will, you know, without the special advantages I can give you."

"Such as?"

"Information, to start. For example . . ." and the voice told Haverner, in detail, of matters he had believed were secret to himself alone.

"God in Heaven," he mumbled, "what are you?"

The sacred name did not frighten his visitor. "To explain that, at this stage, would be impossible. Probably it always will be. Perhaps later we can discuss it a little, if we form a partnership."

"What do you want?" Haverner repeated.

"An associate who can act for me and with me in the human world. Again, there is no point in my going any further tonight. Let me simply assure you that I am no Mephistopheles. I have no desire for your soul, assuming you possess one, and you shall always be free to take any precautions against that that you wish. Nor do I pose the slightest physical threat to you. How could I?"

Haverner stood for a minute, a hundred rapid heartbeats, while thunder growled and his cheap clock clattered and the Victrola began "There's A Long, Long Trail A-winding." Finally his face congealed, his hands unclenched and he said, "Okay, no harm in talking, I guess. But what should I call you?"

"You may as well follow tradition," his visitor answered, "to the extent of calling me Samael."

Sunderland Haverner surprised and pleased his superiors by angling for transfer south. Not many young men would willingly forsake the delights of New Orleans for those unkempt and fever-ridden shores.

Soon after his arrival there, Samael pointed out three soft spots in the Company's way of operating, and suggested that Haverner call his employers' attention to two of them. Repeatedly and with proper respectfulness, he did.

One was its policy of buying only the absolute best of the tropical fruit available. This hurt numerous independent producers who had no other foreign market. Haverner's reports argued for purchasing not the bad, but simply the slightly less than top-grade fruit, and marketing it more cheaply, more quickly, under a different brand name. Even if this would bring little additional profit, it could yield much good will.

Then there was the Company's policy of planting, or buying, just a single specific variety of any given fruit. Many more kinds existed. Should a blight or pest strike the favored crop, it would prove worthwhile to have other sorts growing in reserve areas.

Certain further matters, he wrote, he would not raise at this point unless encouraged to do so, since he judged these two as being of primary importance.

The Company's home office assured him that his recommendations would receive due consideration.

Persisting, he was at last informed that the regional superintendent would take the business up with him when next in port on his long annual round of inspections. This august official did not normally hold interviews with employees in Haverner's pay grade. "However," the superintendent said, "we regard you as a coming man, and we like your helpful spirit. So I'm going to take the time to make things clear to you."

The whole picture, as unfolded, included the Company's policy of buying (and selling) only the very, very best of tropical fruit. It did not matter what happened to the rest of the crop. As for the independent producers, it was not thought desirable that they be more than nominally independent. The Company was aware that they had no alternative foreign market. The Company preferred this. It kept them on their toes. As for the chance of disease or devourers attacking a Staple Variety, well, the Company retained some of the best agricultural scientists in the world. The Staple Variety had come to mean "tropical fruit" to the American and North European housewife; "tropical fruit" meant the Staple Variety.

"We've spent fifty years educating them to expect the

fat yellow bananas, for instance, and nothing else," said the regional superintendent. "Why confuse them?"

He invited Haverner to join him in a drink at the Club, the equivalent of a king on tour bestowing a decoration. Of course Haverner accepted.

And, after a while, he requested a leave of absence to try out his ideas on his own time and with his own funds, in hopes that if he succeeded, the Company would like to take over the program. He needed a year of argument, and marriage to a slightly withered virgin of appropriate family during a visit to New York, before he was condescendingly given permission and paternally invited to reconsider.

"You'll lose your belly button, boy," the port captain said to him on his return. "If there was money to be made your way, the Company would be making it right now."

Sunderland Haverner did not care what became of his belly button, which had long ceased to be of any special use or interest to him. His chief concern was the *Sindicado Registrado Centroamericano,* etc., etc., a corporate person that had lain on a shelf in a lawyer's office for better than a decade.

Abruptly it found itself taken down and dusted off, injected with money and expanded by several shareholders. These included the past president of one neighboring republic; the present president of another; the brothers-in-law of the chief of the Supreme Court of Santa Ana; sundry large landowners, all of pure Castilian stock; a Captain-General of the military, who was not Castilian but who spoke the tribal language of eleven thousand intensely armed little brown soldiers; one Chinese and three Levantine businessmen—

—plus, naturally, Sunderland Haverner.

Samael was no constant companion. In fact, the apparitions were infrequent, often months apart, and seemingly capricious. Nor were they apt to be of long duration. At critical periods Samael might be revealed, off and on, for days, even two or three weeks in a stretch. Ordinarily, though, it appeared sufficient for Samael to ask a few leading questions, give some valuable information and advice, all interspersed with sardonic remarks, and be gone again.

Once his business had Haverner riding alone on a forest trail. As a rule he would have considered that unwise, in spite of being expert in the use of the revolver at his hip. Today he had reasons for not giving gossip a chance to spread, and the gentleman whom he was going to see had so thoroughly pacified the area of late that local people were calling it *el cementerio*.

A slow wind broke the hot green silence of the trees and made the flecks of sunlight that fell on the mould beneath them dance. As his horse bore him onward, Haverner got the illusion that those spots blended into a flickery shape that trotted among the boles on his left hand. The soughing formed words that proposed he enact a profitable treachery upon the man he was to meet.

"Are you really a demon, Samael?" he asked at the end of the suggestion. "I don't have to believe your denial that your aim is to make me damn myself. Naturally, you'd be a liar."

"If you think that," the other pointed out, "your logical course would be to break off our relationship and become a good churchman. You show no signs of intending either."

"No. Still, it doesn't follow from the fact that there is no God, that there is no hell. Or you could be a ghost, or an astral projection, or one of those elves or witches that . . . m-m . . . lure men in the old ballads and stories."

"You have done some rather wide reading, I see."

"Yeah, I took time for it while I was Stateside. I wanted ideas. Read some of H. G. Wells and his imitators, too. You know about him?"

"I do now." Afterward Haverner realized how ambiguous a reply that had been.

"Well, suppose you don't belong here on Earth at all. Suppose you're a being from Mars, or maybe a different solar system. You might not be here in your body. You might communicate with me by telepathy."

"It is obvious that I have knowledge of the minds as well as the doings of men," said Samael almost merrily.

"Well—" Eagerness stormed through Haverner. "Have I guessed right? Are you an extraterrestrial being? Or a superman from the future, come back in a time machine? Or are you a, a magical creature?"

"To you," gibed Samael, "what difference does it make?"

The light among shadows became scattered sunshine, and Haverner rode silently on toward the man he would betray.

This case was somewhat exceptional. By and large, his syndicate functioned smoothly.

Take a bunch of tropical fruit that through, say, Latin or Indian impetuosity has been cut two days before it should have been. Allow it somewhat more jostle on muleback than has been accepted treatment. See it refused by the Company's buyer. Immediately purchase it at a far lower price. Move it to the United States or northern Europe by a freighter that, unscheduled, is fast because of having few stops to make. Sell it when it looks its best, looks as good as any Company article, and sell it at a slightly lower price. Multiply this by the millions.

It adds up to a great deal of money.

To be sure, the housewife might theoretically observe that your fruit does not keep as long. But this remains theoretical, since she did not buy it to keep, she bought it to eat. If faster ripened, it goes faster onto the table. Afterward she buys more, preferably at the same low cost.

Before long the *sindicado* began to encourage the planting of non-Staple varieties in Santa Ana and adjacent countries. It is remarkable how persuasive eleven thousand soldiers can be. But they were not always necessary. For example, the few cents apiece that the new crops fetched locally were a few cents more than their planters would otherwise have had.

Meanwhile, as Haverner had warned, disease did strike more than one Staple plantation. He was not prescient. Samael had urged he acquaint himself in depth with the findings of such impractical professors as Thomas Hunt Morgan. Thus he had realized that mutations must inevitably happen. The effort to combat the resultant sicknesses was costly, and forced up the price of the product. This caused more housewives to patronize the competition.

Over the years, the Company had developed short ways of dealing with dissenters. But in the present case it had tied its own hands. Being headed by realists, it bought the dissenters out. A number of aristocratic families moved en masse to Paris. New villas were built in the suburbs of Beirut, Aleppo, and Canton. A Captain-General of the military obtained considerable land holdings and married the daughter of a Castilian family in reduced circumstances. She never had the pleasure of meeting Augusta Haverner, née Van Horn, who after her own wedding had spent several puzzled, wistful, lonely years before succumbing to the unfortunately unsuitable climate.

She had requested burial "at home." It meant an ancestral plot in upstate New York. Haverner did the decent thing and accompanied the sealed coffin by chartered steam launch to Miami, thence by Pullman (she in the freight car) to New York City, thence by hearse (he in a limousine) to the old village on the Hudson. He was overdue for certain conferences in Manhattan offices anyway.

His in-laws asked him to spend a few days as their house guest after the funeral. He was as charming as a bereaved man properly could be, with many an anecdote from the exotic countries of his work. Other in-laws were among those he would be seeing in the city. When at last he could depart, he bade the chauffeur stop first at a florist's shop, where he obtained a large bouquet of roses, then at the ancestral plot, where he went by himself to lay them on his wife's grave and meditate awhile. Her kinfolk would hear about it and be appreciative.

The wind was cool. Cloud shadows swept across rolling, verdant land and the mercury gleam of the river. That play of light seemed almost to make the headstones—whether blurred and lichenous, or sharp-edged as the one before which he set the flowers down—grow tense, like soldiers waiting for a command. Or like faces waiting to speak. . . . He was hardly surprised when her inscribed name somehow hinted at brows above the eyes, that were the years of her birth and death, above a graven cross that was like a nose above a red bouquet that fluttered as if lips moved.

"You proceed well, Sunderland Haverner," Samael complimented him.

"It's been a long spell," he said.

"You had no need for me. However, when you want to negotiate a substantial loan—"

"Yes, I know. Competition for money. I could use some leverage against those bankers. I was hoping you'd show."

"Actually, you should only take out the bare minimum necessary to finance your immediate future operations. I have a few ideas about how to do that. Soon, though, money, like men, will go begging."

Haverner stroked his chin. "You expect a crash? I've thought, more and more, I saw one coming."

"Yes. Then the opportunities for the right kind of manipulations will approach the limitless."

Haverner stood for a space in the noisy wind and the blowing shadows before he said, "You know, there are times when I think you don't exist outside my own skull. Have you ever actually told me anything I couldn't have figured out for myself? Oh, yes, often unconsciously, by intuition—but you could be the other half of my split personality, Samael."

"Or you could be a dream of mine," laughed the voice. "I have asked you before what difference it makes."

"None, I suppose. All right, let's hear your ideas."

Having listened, he said, "Yes, that's pretty much what I had in mind already, except . . ." and went into detail.

"Good," Samael declared. "You have learned. You will continue to learn. Proceed."

"What happens when I don't need you anymore?" he wondered.

"Maybe you never did," Samael replied.

Sunderland Haverner moved on.

What he moved on to was those "further matters" he had mentioned in his reports of an earlier time but had never been invited to specify. Not that he had courted any such invitation. Honor had been served by a hint. The "further matters" concerned *los otros derechos*.

To purchase land in Santa Ana, Hidalgo, or Caribbea —to name but three of several republics of that region —involved to this day certain complexities. During a long history, many rights, claims, customs, and usages have developed, some dating back to pre-Columbian ages, and they are attached to that piece of real estate whereon they evolved.

When land changes owners, the buyer may include "the other rights" in the transaction if he chooses. As a rule he does not, because they would raise the price by, ordinarily, a twentieth. Thus someone else retains the lawful privilege of grazing sheep there, or driving cattle through, or seining for fish, or whatever tradition has created for the particular parcel.

Should the buyer elect to include those rights, a *licenciado* is then briefed to acquire and/or extinguish them on his behalf. In short, he pays people to exercise them no more.

Formerly the phrase *"los otros derechos"* was taken to mean, chiefly, a sum to dispose of ghostly claims if the land had belonged to the Church before the nineteenth-century expropriations. In every capital city of these republics, in a small and stuffy office, sits a clerical gentleman whose task is to wear a melancholy expression, take snuff, speak with an Italian accent, and note in a crumbling ledger the rare payments still made on this account by the pious.

By customs always complex and frequently tedious, included among *los otros derechos* are what Yankees think of as "mineral rights."

The Company had never bought "other rights." It simply and flatly forbade on its lands any practices it wished forbidden. Never mind native archaisms; one has armed guards patrolling anyway, doesn't one? As for ecclesiastical demands, tut-tut. Wall between church and state, no?

Doubtless somebody in the legal department occasionally chanced to reflect upon the matter of mineral rights. But this was in the days when, say, a glue company thought only about making and selling glue, not about diversifying into, say, ribbons, dried puddings, book publishing, and inland marine insurance. Reflection was brief.

Thus in theory *los otros derechos* to the Company's lands remained available for purchase—cheap.

Sunderland Haverner bought them—cheap.

And so, not overnight, but in due course, the Company was forced to confront two exceedingly new thoughts. (a) It played billy-be-damned with operations when Haverner's surveyors, protected by the full majesty of a law now cooperative with *him,* crossed fields newly cleared for planting, or when his prospectors started drilling for oil. (b) There is a lot of money to be made from oil. A hell of a lot of money.

The Board ran in circles, and likewise the legal department, but neither grew too dizzy to understand that the handwriting was on the wall and was signed "Sunderland Haverner." Quite a few Company officials retired that year who hadn't been intending to.

Under the terms of the agreement reached, Haverner became able to work virtually at will on Company lands; to draw upon Company employees for labor; to house his own men in Company barracks or cottages, treat them in Company hospitals, educate them in Company schools; to travel on Company roads, Company trains, Company ships; to use Company materials as if they were his personal property. All this was done at Company expense. He kept half the profits.

In time he found it convenient to make the Company his in name. By then it was a relatively minor interest.

Through forty years he played with oil wells and oil refineries and oil outlets, mines, smelters, factories, timber plantations and similarly lucrative enterprises throughout the region—in regions elsewhere, too, though he seldom let his left-hand executives know what the right-hand ones were doing. He rode the Depression, the Second World War, the Cold War, the Korean War, the Second Industrial Revolution, the crumbling of empires, the Vietnam War, the assassination of an American President and the self-destruction of his successors, the brief glory and decline of the dollar, the brief glory and decline of

man beyond Earth, the age of sinking expectations—
he rode those like a surfer on huge waves, the kind
of combers that break the backs of men less adept. Aristotle once said that money cannot breed; but Aristotle is
not listed on the Stock Exchange.

Yet Sunderland Haverner was by no means a narrow
man. Quite apart from his curious relationship with
Samael, he had a mind inquisitive as well as acquisitive.
In particular—more and more as he grew older, as his
physical powers waned, as the progress of expanding
his domain tended to become routine—he grew intrigued
by psychology.

His interest was not, at first, obsessive. He had too
many different concerns. After a hard day's work, he
required relaxation more than stimulation. Generally
he would retire to his bedroom of the moment at nine;
at nine-thirty the little Indian girl of the moment
knocked shyly on his door; at ten she shyly slipped
away; at one minute after ten the light went out. Ordinarily, between nine and nine-thirty, he was reading a
detective thriller. He preferred the kind that told of
criminals who were not so much fiendishly clever as
plain, down and out, rotten, stupid bad. Far more plausible.

Nevertheless, he did maintain an awareness of the
progress of psychological research. A particular incident,
rather early on, triggered this in him.

When the regional superintendent, he who had formerly tried to make everything clear to neophyte Sunderland Haverner, found himself confronting instant,
compulsory retirement, years before his plans or his
savings or his pride were ready for it, he took a massive
Army revolver and put a bullet through his head. Blood
and brains spattered partly onto the mirror by which he
had aligned the barrel, partly over the starched shirt
collar which always came high around his throat. When
Haverner was informed of this, the bearers of the news
felt he ought to be, if not conscience-stricken, at least
discomfited.

Instead, he frowned, sat thoughtful and uncommunica-
tive for the next hour, and then ordered that his yacht
be made ready for a cruise to the island of Tanoa. Some

business there had been awaiting him for some time, and he might as well take care of it now.

He had no more patience with sail than he did with any other romanticism. Smoothly snoring Diesels bore him across the waters. He stood at the after rail alone in the dark and heard engines and waves surging and imagined he could make out a face in the wake that swirled moon-white behind.

"I thought you would come," he said.

"What made you think that?" Occasionally, unpredictably, Samael did not behave like one who could read minds. Perhaps, in fact, Samael could not.

"This problem I've got. Why did Goodhue kill himself? I can't see any rhyme or reason to it."

"You are not his sort."

"No." The end of Haverner's cigarette waxed and waned, a red variable star beneath the thronging tropical stars, as he puffed. "That's why you chose me, isn't it, Samael? I'm the kind of instrument you need to . . . to make the things happen that you want. I often think you're a scientist, performing experiments to try to learn what makes us humans tick."

"Well, I do suggest you order texts on psychology, bring your knowledge of it up to date, and thereafter follow along. For instance, subscribe to the principal journals in the field."

"Oh, yes, I'll do that. I've gotten interested too." Haverner twitched a smile nightward. "Even when the experiments include vivisection."

"That may come later."

"Of course," Haverner said, "you may not be a scientist. You may just be idly poking the anthill."

There was no response. He finished his cigarette and tossed it overboard. The wake engulfed the tiny glow in water and moonlight.

Thus Haverner made himself somewhat of an authority on this newest science. It took years, considering the variety of demands on his attention. Also, the science itself was in a less than satisfactory state, and made less than satisfactory progress. When news of what the Nazis had been up to emerged around 1945, he wished that—if they were going to be so cruel anyway—they had carried out genuine research, rather than mere exercises in sadism.

His studiousness increased with his advancing years. Less and less did the little Indian girls, or his empire, come at his behest; his need for the first, the need of the second for him, declined imperceptibly but inexorably. His mind, though, remained active as ever. The postwar upheaval in psychology, as in every other empirical discipline, dazzled him: feedback, psychotomimetic drugs, ethology, Olds pleasure center, computer analog, operant conditioning— Matters such as these claimed him until the rest of what he did was done almost casually.

Meanwhile he had acquired that house on the Isle of Tanoa where William Walker once slept. By then he was so rich that nobody thereabouts believed how rich he was. Never mind what the Latins said, when you happened to meet one. "De Sponyard love to loy," the Islandmen assured each other. "De Sponyard is a fool. A man have more den a t'ousand dollar, first t'ing, de Sponyard say he be a millionaire! . . . Oh, Mr. Sunderland, he be wery comfortable off, yis."

Perhaps their assurance trembled a bit when, aged, largely if not completely retired, spending most of his days here on Tanoa, Haverner began to import outsiders and put them through strange paces.

Or perhaps not. Your Islandman has seen, or has heard of and accepted, many things beyond explaining. Masterman York, who has the sawmill, is known with certainty to be descended from a mermaid.

On his mother's side.

She was a Philpotts.

INTERVAL TWO

This part of the world has no absolute distinction between seasons; but a comparatively dry one follows the
"hurricane months," August through October. A mid-
January night is magical.

Not everyone cared to savor it. In the living room,
Matt Flagler watched a television program relayed from
Panama, catering to the *norteamericano*, and sighed for
that dear lost world of skyscrapers, pool halls, chrome
and plastic taverns, automotive hordes, while he smoked
and drank continuously. In its library arm, Ellis Nordberg went through reference works, now and then entering a suggestive detail about geography or people in
his notebook. Distant in easy chairs—the room was big
indeed—Orestes Cruz and Evans York talked. The
former exerted himself to charm the latter, and may
have succeeded. Eventually they left together.

But Larry Rance settled down with a cigar and
brandy in a porch swing on the veranda. To him came
Gayle Thayer, who asked hesitantly if he wanted company. He made a moderately gallant response; she joined
him and worked to strike up a conversation.

When Julia Petrie and Byron Shaddock strolled out at
the suggestion of the former, they overheard a fragment
of this talk.

"Richmond, Larry? Jesus, I'm from San Francisco!
And we had to come all this way to meet!"

"Well, I prob'ly wouldn't've stayed a lot longer, so it's
just coincidence. To tell the truth, I've about decided I
like Seattle better. I was making up my mind to go back
there and see, when Haverner's boys found me."

"You sound like a free soul. What do you do?"

"For a living? Odd jobs, these days."

"Same. Waitress sometimes, only I never last long,

my feet and that horrible greasy air, same reason I didn't make it as a, you know, dancer. Or maybe I'm a cocktail waitress in a better class of place, but in a way that's even worse. I'm really an artist. Or I'd like to try to be. Do you enjoy what you usually do?"

"M-m-m, it's not bad, mostly outdoor stuff, carpentering, running a back hoe, maintenance on yachts . . . those long beautiful craft that could *fly* to the South Seas, tied where they are year after year because the owners are busy making money—"

The screen door closed behind the voices. They faded away as Julia's and Byron's feet scrunched gravel.

"Oh!" Her hand caught his arm. "Wonderful—no, they haven't got words for this."

The moon had not yet appeared to brighten that sharp, high westward blackness named the Crag. But stars blossomed beyond counting, crowding the sky till its own crystal dark seemed to come alive and, in some way that never touched the great peace, ring beneath their lightfall. They flaunted their colors, blue-white Rigel, golden Capella, ember Betelgeuse. The Milky Way cascaded among them, in knife-edge clarity, quietly and argently ablaze. A planet newly risen glowed so lamplike that it cast a glade over the sea, which reached in polished ebony and flickering pale streaks down past the foot of the steeply descending land.

Trees blocked off most yellow windows, but there was ample illumination to bring the white pathway clearly forth, to tinge flowers and deepen the shadowiness within shrubs. And above the almost gleaming lawn there danced, flickered, blinked, and dazzled hundreds of enormous fireflies.

The air was mild but rich with the scent of the blooms. An odor of harsher native growth, breeze-borne from as far as the rank Bog, only heightened that sweetness. The sighing among leaves blended into the *hush-hush-hush* of the surf.

"I haven't seen anything like this . . . since I was last home . . . to visit my parents, that is," Julia breathed. "And that—Arizona—isn't like this anyway. How low the Dipper is!"

"Yes." Byron pointed. "Look yonder. The Southern Cross."

"I've really seen it now. Cloudy in Vizcaya. . . . I've really seen the Southern Cross."

"And there, that bright one," Byron added. "Alpha Centauri. The nearest sun to ours."

They walked awhile slowly, in silence.

"You must have been hereabouts often before," Julia finally said.

"Never this precise place," Byron answered. "But yes, of course I've toured. The skin diving off, oh, Martinique, is unbelievable." He paused. "I'd like to know how it is here. I asked, but the majordomo—York, is that his name? Yes, York—he told me nobody's tried, for fear of sharks and 'cuda."

"Would *you?* Carrying maybe a harpoon gun?"

He gave her a surprised look. The dimness softened the cameo quality of her face. "What makes you ask?"

"Curiosity, I guess. I've heard about you, read about you. Byron Shaddock, most eligible bachelor on the whole East Coast. Why have you come? You've got ample money."

"I said before, for me this is a sporting proposition. The kind I never could turn down."

"Right. I've read about your nearly getting killed, again and again, motorcycling, auto racing, skiing, surfing. . . . They call you a playboy. I wouldn't. You're terribly serious and strenuous, aren't you, Byron?"

They had halted. "Why do you ask?" he demanded, roughly this time.

Julia dropped her lashes. "I won't pretend to have been any secret worshiper of yours," she said. "But it was interesting, when I happened on something in the paper or *Newsweek*. There's not much to do when a person's quit her job, moved from Manhattan to Long Island. New neighbors turn out to be boring and old friends aren't readily reachable anymore. I read a lot." She raised her eyes again. They caught the starlight. "Only, how old are you—twenty-seven, twenty-eight? And you've already had all this experience and excitement."

"Enough of me," he said, as if counterattacking. "What about you, Julia? You mentioned Arizona. Born there?"

She nodded. "Dad's a professor at a small-town

college in the Flagstaff area. But he met my mother while he was in grad school back east, and she's always been a little homesick. So she took for granted I'd attend her alma mater, and that's where I met my own husband."

"Curious that you came here and not he," Byron remarked.

Her lips tightened. "I was the one invited. I don't know why. Evidently I fit whatever pattern that . . . that mad old man is trying to create." Her tone sank. She stared back at the ground and dug a toe through the gravel. "Besides . . . well, our situation lately, it's made for a difficult marriage. Scary though it is, this trip may well be a very good thing for Malcolm and me both."

"You are scared, then?"

"Hell, yes. And making no bones about searching for help, any help, for my daughter." Julia caught his hands. "I won't give you a sob story, Byron. But you said none of us need to become enemies."

"N-no." He disengaged himself with a tactful casualness and resumed strolling. She paced him. He kept fingers twined behind his back and eyes mostly aimed downward.

Presently they came to the split-bamboo wall that, man-high, enclosed the acre of botanical garden. Its gate was shut, though not locked, for the night. Julia seized on the chance to restore a measure of coolness to the talk. "I must have a look in there. Remember, Larry Rance mentioned at dinner he'd gone in today? The most fascinating plants, flowers, cactuses especially. Cactuses ought to make a desert girl like me feel right at home."

"No doubt," Byron said. "Frankly, I've never liked them much, or Joshua trees, or any of that kind of thing. Too alien. Like invaders from outer space. Don't get me wrong, I don't have a phobia about them, I recognize their value to the ecology and so forth. It's just a slight creepy feeling."

After a moment he continued, "Here especially. This is such a strange affair to begin with. The weirdness of it is only starting to show. We'd better make no solid promises, none of us, before we know more."

Julia touched his shoulder. "All right, enough. I can

see you don't want to discuss it now. So let's just be in the night. In all this beauty."

They hardly spoke further, but wandered about for a not uncompanionable hour. When they returned, a non-descript man—among other jobs, one of their stewards—accosted them on the veranda steps. "Please excuse, mistress, sir. You have been for a valk? I vas vorried you gone into de hills."

"Snakes?" Julia asked sharply, and Byron: "Scorpions?"

"Not so bad, dose, special in de cool dark, sir," the Islandman said. "But you be careful, dawn and dusk, please. Don't be in de hills den. Bat caves dere, hold t'ousands dat come out, and some got de rabies. Bat vit' rabies bites you, he bites in de face, and dat's too close to de brain. No medicines help, no, sir."

Breakfast was ad libitum, toast with ham, eggs, or fried fish being brought in from the kitchen according to a guest's order, sideboard loaded with ice-packed juices, fruits, cheeses, sausages, sweets, and pastries. A servant confided that Mr. Haverner's morning meal was strictly Continental and was taken to him, together with assorted pills, in his bed. Thereafter Mr. Haverner went to his study for dictation, radiophone conferences, and planlaying.

Anselmo Gomez and Evans York were always up betimes, which in the tropics means sunrise or earlier, but they ate with "de vidow Robinson, charvoman, sir" and her brood in one of the cottages. Thus Ellis Nordberg was first in the dining room. He had nearly completed a methodical refueling when Larry Rance sauntered in.

"Good morning," Ellis said.

Larry considered him before repeating the formula. "I hope you slept well," Ellis went on.

"Sure." Larry poured coffee for himself and chose a slice of papaya, pierced it with his fork here and there, squeezed lime juice onto it.

"Even though you start our game tomorrow?"

"Zen," Larry said. "You'd be surprised how much better a few koans are than sleeping pills, if you know how to use them."

"What do you mean to have us do, if I may ask?" Larry sat down, giving Ellis a hard look. "What do *you* have in mind, come your turn?" He began to eat his papaya.

Orestes Cruz had entered meanwhile. He stood regarding the two Americans until they were compelled to meet his eyes. "Yes," he said, "this will be a long, long day for everyone. Correct?" Gaunt and awkward, his legs bore him to the sideboard, where he loaded cream into his coffee till his fingers, seen above the cup, appeared not chocolate brown but deeply black, the nails a startling pink.

"Haverner's forethought, of course," he added after a bit. "Part of the torture."

A waitress interrupted, requesting his and Larry's orders. When she had gone, Ellis wanted to know what he had meant.

Orestes shrugged. "Isn't it obvious? This is no scientific laboratory we are in, it is a torture chamber." He spoke calmly.

"Where we skin each other?" Ellis stroked his chin. "Test to destruction, actually? Hm."

"Typical fascism." Orestes's gaze brooded upon them. "I do not wish to destroy any of the players, personally. Including you, Mr. Nordberg. You are as much a victim in your way as I in mine. Please do not force me to destroy you."

"If you last that long," Ellis said dryly.

"Uh, Ore—Sr. Cruz," Larry said in haste, "you speak damned good English. Makes me ashamed of my few words of pidgin Mexican Spanish. Where did you learn?"

The Santa Anan seated himself, lit a powerful tawny cigarette, and answered, voice gradually growing slow and tender. "Well, there was a cobbler in our village. He let me sleep in his hut. You see, my foster mother, after my own abandoned me, she married a man who did not want me, another mouth to feed which did not even testify to his *machismo*. I must . . . scrounge? . . . yes, earn, beg, steal what I could. But Enrico Brunner, now, he had tramped the whole world before he ended up in our village. He had only one leg, but he had books. He thought he saw more in this boy than simply another caneworker. He made me learn reading and writing—

and good English too. I already knew the Negro Creole English, but he made me acquire the real thing. For days on end, he would only talk proper English with me. He also wanted to keep me a Christian. That finally helped drive me away. I was sorry, but—" He shook himself, as if to cast off the hold of memory. "Well, when I arrived in Ciudad Vizcaya, age fifteen, I believe it must have been fifteen, ten years ago . . . I saw how right he had been about literacy and English."

"Did you read Marx in English?" Ellis asked, crook-mouthed.

Orestes ignored the tone. "No. But Lenin and others, yes."

Ellis visibly bristled. "Now hold on," Larry said. "Take it easy, Nordberg. We were starting to get friendly."

Pale, bespectacled eyes dwelt upon him. "Were we?" Ellis inquired. "Wouldn't you like to win the whole stake? I'll be frank; it's hardly worth my while to try for less. And, ah, Sr. Cruz here, he's playing a much bigger game, with the rule of the world for first prize."

"The liberation of the world," Orestes snapped. Then, unexpectedly, he chuckled, and that was an unexpectedly mellow sound. "Words, words. I'm not going to waste this gorgeous morning on more of them. Captain York has two small nieces and a nephew. Last night, when he took me to the cottage where they live, I promised them 'Sponyard' fairy tales. Also I saw in the library a copy of Cervantes's *Galatea,* which is good reading for the shade this afternoon. And first I think I shall have a piece of that excellent-looking melon." He rose to get it.

Ellis was still for half a minute before he bent his lips upward and said, "You're both right, gentlemen, and I apologize. We can certainly try to keep this thing civilized. Melon reminds me, Larry—okay to call you that?—the coconut cake is superb. Be sure to save room for a slice."

"I don't care for any kind of nut meat," Larry replied.

"This'll change your mind. It sure will. Here, I'm through eating, let me fetch—"

"No, God damn it!"

The other two stared at Larry and each other. When

the waitress returned, the rest of the meal proceeded in strained silence.

Not long afterward, Larry spoke at length with Haverner's intended referee, Anselmo Gomez. Finally they went down to the pier and took out one of the boats. They were gone till midday.

Upon coming back, Larry asked about Julia Petrie and found that she had gotten a picnic lunch packed and had set off on a hike with Byron Shaddock. He indicated disappointment, and when Gayle Thayer sought his company told her that he felt like a siesta. In the cooler part of the afternoon, he left the house by the back door to go for a swim. By that time she was watching television. Much of the rest of her day went in writing letters.

Ellis visited Haverner during the permissible hours. They spoke of this and that, nothing germane to the contest or even to the universe of finance. (Does a firecracker talk shop with a hydrogen bomb?) Later Ellis systematically scouted all territory within reasonable walking distance.

Orestes spent the day much as he had said he would, except that toward evening he told his stories to the children—virtually every child of the estate's prolific servants, no few of them towheaded as well as dark-skinned —following a fishing trip with Captain York. He sat against a huge old ceiba, or silk cotton tree, they in a half circle before him. Besides yarning, he strummed a borrowed guitar and sang.

Matt Flagler, still nursing a hangover, drifted thither and watched for some while. His gaze was not on Orestes; it flickered among the women, the girls, and a couple of boys who were just turning twelve or thirteen. As last he grunted and went inside for the free drinks.

While the first wine was poured at dinner, Haverner asked, "Do you care to make any announcement about tomorrow, Mr. Rance?"

Larry's head snapped up and he glanced around. He had arrived a bit late and so missed his seat by Julia, who now sat between Byron and, as it happened, Ellis. The hiking pair had explained how they waited out the heat of midday in a wood above the Iron Cliffs. They called the scenery magnificent but volunteered no further gossip. Larry himself had Orestes on his left, Gayle on his right. "I saved this for you," she had whispered as he took the chair.

"Well." He flushed beneath the color laid on him by the sun, grinned in partly abashed fashion, tossed back his longish yellow hair. "Yeah, I'm the leadoff big bad wolf. To tell the truth, I, uh, I haven't thought of anything fancy. I tried, but—well, I checked with Anselmo, who's been given this kind of information about us, and he told me everybody's a pretty good swimmer. So we'll take a boat out tomorrow morning, I guess, and swim a couple of miles from it to that Gehinnom rock."

"¡Santa Maria!" broke from Orestes. Matt spelled it out: "The sharks."

"And barracuda," Byron added slowly. Then, faster, smiling: "They eat us, we eat them. Sometimes they poison us. I wonder if we ever poison them."

Larry kept his own grin in place, though it had no real life. "You can drop out right now if you want," he reminded the group.

"The surf . . . that's probably more dangerous," Julia said. Byron nodded; his movement looked eager.

"Sorry 'bout that." Larry didn't quite meet her gaze. "We'll have a boat close by, of course, ready to haul out whoever gets in trouble. I don't want to kill anybody"—his glance touched Ellis—"after all."

"But I *can't!*" Gayle wailed. She swung toward Haverner. "I, I, I protest! It's, uh, uh, physically impossible for me. You *said*—"

"Yeah, I'm no swimmer, I'm not in that kinda shape. What kinda shit is this?" Matt put in.

Orestes tapped fork on glass. The clear small noise brought quiet as no gavel might have done. "I side with Mr. Rance," he told them. "Any person who keeps his wits about him can stay afloat for kilometers. This is not a race, remember. The object, as I understand it, is simply to cover that distance and climb ashore. Save your energy, go slow, float and paddle. You can do it."

"The surf may rough you up," Larry said, "but I checked it out today and it's not too bad, if you don't mind cuts and bruises, as long as the lifeboat's standing by with a couple of strong swimmers, flotation collars, and such.

In fact, we'll have two boats, so one of them can stay near the slow people."

"I approve too," Byron said. "Are we in competition or are we not? This doesn't test bodily strength beyond anyone's limitations. It tests nerve, self-control, endurance of exertion and discomfort and, maybe, pain. If you feel yourself sinking, you need only call for help and be taken back aboard."

"And lose out?" Matt's voice was high. Sweat stood forth on his blue cheeks.

"Of course," Orestes said.

"The sharks, though," Gayle whispered.

"That's the chance we take," Ellis stated. "Larry right along with the rest of us." He barked a scrap of laughter. "In fact, Larry, do you realize you've decreed a game which the leader can flunk?"

"By God," the blond man said, astounded, "I have."

"Want to cancel it, then?"

"No . . . no."

"The odds favor us," Byron observed. "No waters can be packed solid with predators, and any that may be nearby aren't necessarily going to rush at every stray piece of long pig. The hazard's just a, hm, a fillip."

"All right!" Julia snapped. "You needn't emphasize—"

Still shamefaced, Larry said, "Anselmo okayed the idea. And it seems like everybody's willing. I hoped—frankly, I hoped one or two would refuse. Sure you don't want to?"

They sat mute in their various ways.

"It is legitimate, Mr. Haverner?" Larry asked.

"Indeed," their host told them. Throughout the rest of that unpleasantly subdued meal, he appeared very satisfied.

When alone in his bedroom, he did not retire immediately. Otherwise old-fashioned and austere, the chamber held a large television set with unusual capabilities. He settled down in an armchair before this and operated a hand-held remote-control unit. Cameras hidden throughout the mansion showed his guests merely proceeding quietly, piecemeal but within a short interval, to their separate quarters. What they did before turning out their lights varied, but none of it was spectacular.

His satisfaction faded. Restless, he tuned in the pickups concealed at strategic points outside. Necessarily limited in numbers and scope, they had vouchsafed him only glimpses during the day. Simple microphones, though more numerous, had not enabled him to follow events anywhere nearly as closely as he had hoped. At this hour, of course, his instruments gave him back nothing but the island night.

The darkling view in the screen blurred into the hint of a face. Sounds of breeze and sea, out of several speakers, modulated into low words: "You appear displeased, Sunderland Haverner."

"I am," he said.

"Why? You were quite fascinated when I proposed this experiment. You worked on the preparations with more energy than you had displayed in years."

"Yes. I thought—if ever people could be stripped bare of, of everything except their real selves—this would do it."

"While you peered."

"Damn it," Haverner cried, "the tests we ran beforehand I could watch in person! And they were trivial compared to what'll be going on in the next two weeks. But except for what the apparatus happens to detect, all I'll get is second hand. It's not fair!"

"What else did you expect?"

"More cooperation from you. You can glide everywhere, see and hear everything—" Haverner paused. "Can't you?"

Samael made no reply.

Haverner curbed himself. "Tomorrow's contest should be possible for me to follow along with pretty well," he said, "and I daresay after it's done, the subjects will be too exhausted to move around at random over the landscape. Later, however . . . Can't you help me devise how to make them stay in range of observation? Most of the time, anyway?"

"The object of the experiment is to let them interact freely," Samael reminded, "not to cater to your voyeurism."

Haverner stared at the screen, as if eyes were there to meet his. "How free have *I* ever been, since you came?" he grated.

"That is for you to decide," Samael answered with undiminished good cheer.

"I've thought about it a great deal. More and more as time went on." Haverner leaned forward. "See here. What do we mean by freedom? It must include the freedom to choose between courses of action. But how can anybody pick a course he doesn't know about? He may not realize it's possible, or it may never have occurred to him, or . . . If we, you and I, if we can develop, oh, hints for me to drop, or ways to steer a conversation, that sort of thing—"

"It could be interesting to try," Samael conceded, "though you must admit that the probability of success in any given instance will be small. Humans maintain such complicated personalities, as long as circumstances permit."

Haverner sighed. "What do they do when they're out of sight? I have to infer it from the views I get and otherwise from reports by Anselmo and the rest. My guesses may be wrong; I'll never know. At best, it's all so abstract."

"At your age, most of life is abstract."

"Yes," said Haverner starkly. "That's why I agreed to this in the first place."

LARRY RANCE

Ten in the morning (who wants to get up too goddamn early, dawn's a beautiful way to end a night, except at sea, of course, at sea) but the sun's still low enough to turn the eastward waters molten. Light bounces off white sands on the left, under brushy bluffs, in a blaze that hurts my eyes. I should've allowed dark glasses. No, whoever isn't as used to squinting across waves as I am will be handicapped. Good thing I didn't wait longer before calling a start, though. I feel those rays lick around my torso, which hasn't been out of a shirt during my home's rainy winter, and down my bleached legs.

Air and ground are warming fast, but coolness blows off the sea, smells of salt and kelp and distance. The breakers boom that we're going to meet. A gull makes a thin jeering overhead. (Which would you rather be at your death, full fathom five, down in infinite peace and eternal stirring, or washed onto a man-empty beach for gulls and weather to clean your bones? . . . No matter now, me lad. You've got a lot of wandering to do first!)

The path is gritty under my sandals. Boats rock at the pier ahead. From each juts a television camera on a well-secured tripod. The crews stand alert. I daresay one member of either has been trained to use the foreign apparatus and record whatever happens this day. They are four slim Islandmen for the first boat, three for the second. Its fourth hand will doubtless be Anselmo Gomez, who cat-paces alongside me and asks with his disinterested (uninterested?) politeness, " 'Ave you further eenstructions before we leave, Meester Rance?"

"No. Uh, no, thanks." My heart stutters. Damnation, it shouldn't. Don't get excited; don't wear yourself out fighting yourself; leave that to your opponents. Nice theory, hey? "Unless you, uh, have a suggestion?"

"No, sir, I theenk we said everytheeng yesterday." Does that amber-brown face ever show an emotion? When he's off duty in a *cantina,* maybe, or with a woman? Or is he entirely an arm of Sunderland Haverner, who, let's admit it between us, scares the piss out of me?

What fun it sounded like, when his agents and I first talked! A chance, at least, to visit the Caribbean again, expenses paid, a chance, maybe, to win *Morgana le Fay.* But now, I don't know. Haverner's got to have quite a few screws loose to dream of something like this. And the power he's got . . . !

What do the others think? What's this begun doing to them? Stand by on the pier, let them pass you, going aboard, and watch, watch.

Nobody's spoken a word among us our whole way down from the house.

Ellis Nordberg's locked his face as much as Anselmo; it gives him a prim look. Bathing trunks show he hasn't too bad a body for a middle-aged desk jockey. No doubt he invests an exact number of minutes per day in exercises, and the routine leaves him free to think about his operations meanwhile. However, his arms and legs are skinny; he does have a pot; could be I'll eliminate him.

Matt Flagler—Judas priest, the man's a walking rug, isn't he?—doesn't seem in a lot better shape, and hangover-shaky to boot. He gives me the same kind of stare I've seen in the eyes of muzzled dogs that want nothing except to bite. A grin and a V sign to him. . . . He slouches on past.

Orestes Cruz. He has a jerky, arm-swinging gait, but if the muscles under that chocolate skin are ropy, it's the best and toughest nylon rope to be gotten. He surprises me by a grin of his own. As he passes, I see his back is crisscrossed with narrow scars, not completely healed.

Byron Shaddock seems downright eager. He won't have any trouble. Hell, his condition is better than mine, and not just because he's younger. I know, I know, I booze too much sometimes, spend too many hours other times sitting around drinking coffee or blowing pot, swapping clichés with friends or bragging about the great things I've done, the great things I will do. I know my body's begun to slump. The land's no good for me. I've got to get away to sea, and soon, before it's too late. How did Heyerdahl, Chichester, Slocum, any of those guys manage it? They weren't rich either, were they? And how old this thought is, how old all of my thoughts are. There's a whole wide planet out yonder, Larry Rance. What have you been waiting for?

Answer: for a million dollars cash.

Byron pays me no attention, and I don't pay him much, because the lucky bastard's walking hand in hand with Julia Petrie. Her figure's even more beautiful, in a bikini, than her face. Oh, Christ, those boobs, those long arms and legs, that long belly, flat except where it rounds a little between the hips, the way a woman's should! I know some'd say she doesn't have enough ass, but it's plenty for me, exactly right to grab while I go into her. . . . Does she notice me? She doesn't. She's got eyes only for Byron; she's begun talking to him, too low for me to hear. Well, why not? He probably is her best ally if she can charm him. Should I try to make a deal of my own with somebody? I don't need the whole million either. . . . Too bad, yeah, about her little girl.

I suppose I've got a built-in weakness for tall women

with good bone structure. Both my wives were like that, of course, and I suppose most of what others I've managed to get in the sack.

(Julia ought to be a safe lay, no interest in domesticating me; only trouble is I might fall in love with her, and what the hell, that's a thing a man learns to outlive. . . . Domestication? No, I'm being unfair to my wives. Mary worked hard to help me through college. How proud she was when I got my engineering degree and my job at Boeing! Later, when I started feeling more and more hemmed in, she tried just as hard to cover for my drinking, my goofing off; when they finally fired me, it was me who told her she should leave. And Vivian, well, what'd *she* have to gain when she met me, this deckhand on the charter schooner down in these romantic waters? She had to fight that well-off family of hers to marry me. And afterward they too were decent enough. That management job her dad wangled me really would've had a future if I'd hung on. It wasn't anybody's fault but mine that the old pattern repeated, especially after the baby came, poor innocent yowling wet chaining-me-down son of my loins. True, Vivian left after less than three years, when Mary'd stuck it out for better than four, and Vivian did it on her own initiative, but then she had, she has, the cooler head of the two, and neither of them asked me for alimony or child support, though naturally I've made myself send Vivian something for Jerry whenever I've had something to spare, and it was a hell of a relief to learn she'll soon remarry—

Gayle Thayer has trailed the parade and stops. She's got the same idea as Julia, plain to see. Why couldn't they have chosen opposite targets? Because Julia's got better sense and Byron more to offer, that's why. "Oh, Larry," Gayle murmurs. Her skin, bulging from her own two-piecer, is bedsheet white. Blue veins show here and there. "I'm scared."

Trying not to hurt her, I say, "You can quit whenever you want, remember. Right this minute if that's your wish." I smile. "So sit back, enjoy your vacation, watch the rest of us make fools of ourselves."

She stands a minute before me, staring down. I see a pulse flutter in her throat. Odd how moving it is to know that her heartbeat is as skippy as mine. Suddenly she straightens, throws me a look and says, "No, I'm sick of copping out. I'll give this thing the best try I can."

Her eyes are lovely. I've only seen a finer gray in the eyes of Tammy McManus, when we lived together on that houseboat in Seattle (always excepting the gray of winter seas, or of clouds flying above them like smoke on a sunset wind). And it isn't quite fair to call her thighs and stomach flabby. Call her, instead, wudgy. I'll bet she sure knows her way around in bed. It could be fun.

Only I've got to make clear that fun is where it will stop. Julia's kid, well, maybe I can see my way to some kind of grant, if *Morgana* doesn't turn out to be too expensive. But Gayle—why the devil should I support a perfectly healthy young childless woman in idleness, when I don't want more than a romp with her at most? I'll have to make her understand . . . if things go that far. "Well, good luck to you, lassie."

"Thank you." She squeezes my hand. "You're real, Larry, you know?"

One of her problems with me is that I've met her too often before, in too many not-very-different bodies and beds.

Ha! You're already playing God in your own skull, are you, Lauritz Rance? How about first getting through this day? (What *can* I do, demand, in the rest of it, after we've finished here? I've knocked myself out trying to think, and nothing seems worthwhile.) The rest have boarded. They're staring at me.

I jump in. The sailors cast off. Outboards cough to life, blow stink in my nose, and settle down to a steady, pushing roar. The land falls aft.

I saw sails aplenty when I helped cruise tourists between Massachusetts and the Spanish Main. Aren't there any around Tanoa? Not at *Schloss* Haverner, for sure. Well, the old monster wouldn't be interested; no money in sail. And the Islandmen may be colorful, uncorrupted, religious, superstitious, close to nature, so ethnic that Joan Baez wouldn't have it; nevertheless they're the practical folk and I, the robot from Dollar Land, I'm the dreamer.

(*Morgana le Fay*. I name you this, O beloved who has never existed, because she was a sea queen and a sorceress too, sister of Arthur in whose memory banners fly and bugles blow down the sharp winds off Land's End, leman of wander-footed Ogier the Dane, beautiful, magicful, laughterful beyond humanness.

(I know you, *Morgana*. I make my women, but you I will build, *Morgana*, with these my hands. And you will live forever.

(I have been in the yards and shops, to pick your timbers balk by balk and select each plank that shall be yours; in northern forests I have seen the trees for your masts, which I will fell, trim, season, and shape myself; a sailmaker it is not given me to be, but I know a master of the craft—the last of the black arts—to whom I will entrust the suiting of you, my darling, and he shall have the finest of fabrics for his work, and when he is done, I and no other will take the maidenhead of your sail tracks. I and no other will name you and launch you, and captain you until forever ends with the darkening of my eyes.

(It's a filthy world we'll leave behind, the very waters always more crowded, evil-smelling, smeared, littered, and sick beneath poisonous dusty vapors. Less and less am I able to understand what they're doing ashore, more and more do I doubt that they understand it either. I have less and less luck at my jobs, too, and this makes me angry and the anger spills off onto women who therefore put up with me for shorter and shorter times. Oh, I've got my friends, and they're amusing; one or two are actually interesting, but what do we ever do, what are we for? And I have *Kwannon*, sloop-rigged, a whole fifteen feet LOA, to take out on the Bay: better than nothing, no doubt, and not really to be blamed for age and crankiness, when I can't afford to get her the care she needs. . . .)

"Meester Rance. Meester Rance!"

"Huh? Oh. Oh, yeah. Sorry."

" 'Ere ees the place we decided on, Meester Rance."

"Sure. It is." I blink around.

The second boat has also idled its motor at Anselmo's signal. We rock on station, a long easy swing in waves that have marched from the Antilles. When scant freeboard separates you and them, they take you into themselves; you see how lesser waves, ripples, diffractions and interference patterns dance over their flanks until lost in the jewel-dazzle where sunlight breaks; you see living indigo, azure, emerald, white in arabesques; your bones hear them chuckle and rumble, feel them prance and stride; their changing airs and odors fill you, and spindrift kisses your lips.

No, I have got to get down to business.

Gehinnom lies a pair of miles to the north. Behind it sweeps the curve of Tanoa, the Bight an impossibly green jut of forested upland, walled by the Iron Cliffs and roofed by the sky where a few clouds sail. The islet, or skerry or whatever you want to call it, is jagged-backed, bare and dark except for a silvery layer of dune grass, a few wind-crippled palms. It's surrounded by reefs. The surf is snowy violence on them. Its drumfire reaches me louder than it ought to.

I rise in the bows, clear a dry throat, point and say, "Please pay attention. I was out here before, and none of you were, and I don't want to take advantage."

They listen. In this craft are Gayle, Orestes and Ellis; in the other are Matt, Byron and, damn it, Julia. The two hulls lie side by side, crewmen skillfully fending off with boat hooks, and words carry quite well.

"The object of the game," I say, "is to reach that rock. It's doubtless further than any of us are used to swimming, but we're all fairly good swimmers and the boats will stand by for rescue work. Yell if you think you're in trouble. Otherwise keep your cool. Remember, this is warm water, reasonably calm till you get close inshore. It won't drain your energy fast. Whenever you get tired, you can float with very little effort, resting. The real danger, besides sharks or barracuda, is from the surf when you come near land. It can haul you under or throw you on some mighty sharp-edged rock. So . . . look close. Does everybody see that break in the surf? That's the reason we're on this side. A safe channel. Steer for it and you'll be okay. The boats will follow and take us off." I stop for breath. "Questions? Arguments?"

Ellis shakes his head; he's taped his glasses securely on. Does he, inside, believe what he wants most in the world is not to rape the sea but, like me, in his perverted way— love her?

And me? Is this really happening to Lauritz Willem Rance, that everybody but his half-homesick Dutch mother calls Larry? Who am I that it should? Who do you have to be?

(Born and raised in the Los Angeles area. Only child,

maybe technically somewhat neglected—Dad in school on GI the first years of my life, then an underpaid young engineer in a recession, and meanwhile Mom working to bring in extra money; when he began earning pretty well, she didn't want to quit and turn into just a housekeeper, but I enjoyed the independence; I like them both to this day and am often sorry I'm such a disappointment to them; they gave me a boat to keep in San Pedro and let me single-hand her out to Catalina or the Channel Islands whenever I wanted. I am nobody that wild things happen to!

(Well, true, I did get into scrapes in high school. I was lucky that pregnancy case, back when abortion was unthinkable, got settled by a quiet adoption. Nonetheless I joined the Air Force at age eighteen to get away for three years, and was lucky in being sent to Japan. . . . Bells and pure gardens in Kyoto, curve of Fuji against a moonlit heaven, cute little bodies climbing over me in whorehouses and later Suiko, oh, Suiko, maybe I should've stayed. . . . Did my luck run out with my youth, the way strength and senses do?)

A trivial discussion. Then, "I theenk you can start, ladies and gentlemen," says Anselmo. The cameramen get busy. Enjoy at the far end, Haverner, enjoy, enjoy.

I dive. The water takes me, flowing around in a million million cool caresses, such as Suiko could only try to give. It's tawny green down below. I glimpse a fish dart off, can't identify it but it's brightly colored and has an extravagant tail. I break the surface and sunlight pours across my head.

To do this in a thousand waters for the next fifty years!

(Fifty? I am thirty-five, closer to thirty-six. Keep moving, son.)

I strike out for the goal, an easy crawl soon joined in rhythm to the waves. Byron passes, laughs and flaps a hand at me. The rest—I look back and see Orestes swim with skill, Julia with grace, Ellis with competence. Just Matt and Gayle are actually toiling.

Those last two may not make it, but seems like everybody else will. What then? I have till tomorrow daybreak. I've got to find another challenge! Why can't I? Well, keep 'em in suspense, hey?

Or save my energy. I can't hope to eliminate the lot by

myself, and some nasty surprises could lie ahead. I must last out the course. Here in the brute and subtle honesty of the sea, I understand that this is my final chance.

(*Morgana*, I have so much to show you on our honeymoon. The Santa Barbara Channel, where porpoises will still come rolling and tumbling to play with you, where as we lie in a hushed young morning, waiting for a breeze, maybe barely ghosting, a pair of seals or a pod of killer whales will travel by, stick their heads out and bid us a polite hello. Victory over fogs and crosstides down the Straits of Juan de Fuca, till we round Cape Flattery and meet the heavy, shuddering strength beyond. Lost little bays in New England. Bermuda afloat before us like a dream at dusk. The black bulk of Diamond Head at midnight, made starry by lights. The Ryukyus rising from the horizon at dawn, pink as that incredibly early brightness. Hokusai's Fuji.)

The growl from ahead is suddenly louder. I feel a savage playfulness in the currents that wrap me. Am I so close? It hasn't seemed a long time. I peer about. Anselmo's boat is quite near, a crescent moon on patrol, between me and Shaddock in this area, Cruz and Julia to rearward. Further back, Captain York's craft watches over Gayle, Nordberg, and (why?) Flagler.

(Oh, but we have many more discoveries to make together, *Morgana*. I have seen them in my mind, how often, but now I will see them with you. Distant, distant yellow Kerguelen, halfway from Africa to Australia, off in the middle of Kipling's "excellent loneliness"; swart escarpments of Tristan da Cunha, velvet-green hillsides of Fernando Noronha, those twin legacies of Henry the Navigator with the whole South Atlantic between them; ragged sails of the pearl-shell fishers off the almost unknown palm-studded coast where Thailand reaches Buddhist into that Moslem peninsula which at last becomes Malaysia; sheer cliffs and rushing falls along Hardanger Fjord, whence the vikings rowed; cloud-crowned mountains of New Zealand, whither the mightier Maoris paddled; Rio de Janeiro, Buenos Aires, Valparaiso, the names make a song; the Inside Passage to Alaska, loveliest of channels on this overwhelmingly lovely globe; but afterward open water again, *Morgana*, a thousand miles of sea room and the wind a-boom in your sails, outward bound, my darling, to wherever the hell you and I may choose!)

Surf spouts and bawls around me. I am slapped across the eyes, tumbled, hauled about. In a faraway fashion, I feel my left shin slashed by an edge. The slot between the reefs isn't near as easy as Anselmo led me to believe.

I make it okay, though, wade through the shallows, flop down on hot volcanic rock beside Byron, who's already there. As the wetness steams off me, I feel salt crusts itchily forming, I taste them on my lips. Light flames.

He grins. "Well," he says, "thanks for a refreshing trip. What's next on your agenda?"

"Let's see how the others do," I mutter. For I find that I am worried. That really is a dangerous approach, if you're less of a swimmer than I am.

Suppose Julia gets cracked into a reef and drowned, suppose I see her afterward, eyes abulge and teeth gleaming through a cheek torn open? How could I ever explain to her little girl?

Byron seeks what shade he can find under one of the twisted screw palms. That's wise, when you're in nothing except a pair of trunks. But I have to see what's happening at the barrier.

The coral of the outer ridges extends an arm clear to the islet. I pick my way out on that: slowly and carefully, because not only is the stuff jagged, thick waves often break across the lower parts and can knock you over. I glimpse anemones and tiny crabs in a tide pool, outrageously peaceful. Finally I reach a vantage point.

Orestes is coming in. Julia isn't far behind. A crosscurrent grabs her, whirls her against the channel side. She isn't too badly cut, but her blood comes out with weird fluorescent brilliance, and she yells and goes under. I see her flounder; I start, unthinking, to scramble down after her. Orestes has stopped; he treads water, turns his head, sees her drawn below. He darts back—afloat, he's smooth, quick, easy—gets a grip just beneath her breasts. Through the roar and whoosh I can't hear what he tells her nor see very well what happens through the tossed-up spume. I do make out that she's in full control of herself, she doesn't struggle but cooperates. He hauls her free of the churning and lets her go. They swim slowly to shore.

Byron rises to greet her. She turns instead to Orestes

(in that direction their figures are small but clear) and I can guess how she tries to thank him without letting on to Byron that there's been what I may claim is a violation of my rules. Neither has noticed me where I am. I suppose he asks Byron about that, however, since the rich man points at me. The three of them stare my way. After a moment Orestes turns his head and spits.

Sickness rises in me. I send my gaze back seaward. Anselmo's boat is standing offshore, York's trailing the last players. (Neither can have seen what happened between the reefs.) Nobody's far off now except for Gayle. Ellis, swimming stoutly, is ahead of Matt, who appears to have difficulties.

And then Gayle screams. I don't understand how I hear it, when she's such a ways from me. Maybe I only know it. I see her go wild, flail away her strength, and I see what brought on that panic, the tall swift fin.

Shark? Barracuda? I can't quite make out across this glare. It vanishes—dives?—for the attack? I leap about, not caring what I may do to my feet, I wigwag and bellow and shriek.

(I have seen a film where sharks ate a dead whale. They come in fast; there's that monstrous ripping snap; the skin and blubber and flesh are peeled off to leave a pit; fragments befoul the water, and then comes the next pass and the next. Silly little Gayle, who meant no harm to anybody, who offered to help Julia if she—pathetic hope —happened to win!)

Probably I do no good, am not noticed. Possibly the creature has no hostile intentions at all. The fact is, York slams his outboard around, roars up the scale of revs, and is there inside a couple of million microseconds. A man reaches overside, grabs Gayle and drags her aboard.

As I stumble back onto the islet, I'm crying. I'm out of practice at that, and it doesn't come easy.

"Something wrong?" Byron demands.

"She, she, she's all right." I'm damn near strangled by my own breath. "She's all right, I tell you. They reached her in time. They did."

"Who?" Julia seizes my arm. Blood trickles down hers from the gash across her right shoulder.

"Mrs. Thayer, who else?" Orestes says. Again he spits.

"Well, if she had to be rescued, you eliminated her, no? And others, perhaps?"

I can't squint coolly into his eyes and drawl a remark that only he and Julia and I will understand. I'm too busy wrestling myself. Even this minute I know that inside an hour I'll start to have afterthoughts, regrets, had-I-buts. God damn it, though, right now I've got to wash *Morgana* clean!

"N-no." I push the words out somehow. "Nobody . . . eliminated. I . . . I . . . declare th' game ended . . . ever'body in free . . . as of time I . . . myself . . . landed. And'll be no more games today. You got the rest of the goddamn day—and tomorrow—you got it off. Be my witnesses . . . when the rest get here . . . you be my witnesses, I am not a murderer!"

I sit down, knees drawn high, arms across them, face buried, and gasp. Ellis joins us; he didn't let the fish terrify him into quitting, then, but from the way he shudders, that cost. By now I can raise my head. Byron explains, low-voiced. Ellis gives me a look of contempt.

INTERVAL THREE

Larry absented himself as soon as they got back, and nobody saw him till evening. He clumped into the living room at the cocktail hour, clothes muddy; sweat had made canals in the grime on his skin, plastered down his hair, and surrounded him with a sour odor. For a moment the others, who were presentable and cool, gaped. Julia was the first to move. She set down her martini, ran to him and caught his hands.

"Where've you been?" she cried. "We were going crazy!"

Ellis snorted. Matt said, "The hell I was." Orestes smiled enigmatically into his tequila sour. But Byron joined the woman.

"Why should you?" Larry croaked. He met none of their eyes.

"We supposed you'd made for the hills," Byron said.

"Uh-huh. I took a hike. I . . . I . . ."

"Weren't you warned about the bats there?" Julia asked. "Rabies. Nobody goes into the hills at dawn or dusk."

"Oh. Yeah. Yeah, I guess I was told. Forgot." Larry looked around the serene walls and furnishings. "Where's Gayle?"

"Asleep," Julia said. "She developed a terrible migraine this afternoon. Understandable."

Larry swallowed. "Better go clean up," he mumbled.

"A minute," Byron said. "You feel guilty, don't you? Why? Me, I'd call you quixotic."

As if heavily weighted, Larry's arm rose till he pointed at Julia's shoulder. She was in a low-cut blouse, and the bandage showed conspicuously. "You wouldn't say that, would you, Mrs. Petrie?" The words came harshly. "Be honest."

"I would, I would." She threw arms about his neck and kissed him. Immediately afterward she whispered in his ear, "I think you know something you aren't telling. About me and Orestes. We'll talk later." Stepping back, speaking aloud: "Larry, dear, you've given us hope we won't turn into a pack of cannibal dogs."

"You must certainly plan to stay in competition," Byron added. "I warn you, I don't intend to be that chivalrous."

Julia glanced downward and laughed. "But do go wash before dinner. I've got to change my own outfit."

Larry returned a shaken echo of her mirth. "Okay! Only first, damn it, I need about a quart of cold beer."

When he and she were gone—he had talked, or babbled, of the wildlife he saw that afternoon, parrots, toucans, woodpeckers, Fabergé hummingbirds, lizards, snakes, an iguana, butterflies, ants, spiders—Matt turned on Byron. "What kinda shithead are you, anyway?" he barked. "You and her—didn'tcha see he was ready to quit? You could'a leaned on him and gotten him right out of the contest!"

Byron studied him over the rim of his glass before replying, "You know, Flagler, I'm tempted to throw this in your face, except that'd be a waste of good liquor."

Matt reddened, gobbled, fell silent and drank deep.

"You've got your inheritance and your father the senator, Shaddock," Ellis said. "You can afford to make a game of it. But what about the rest of us, eh?"

"A game, by definition, needs rules," Byron answered in a tone too mild for the words. "However, I grant you, for us the Queensberry rules are insufficient. Once he gets over his colic of conscience, friend Rance will bitterly regret that he didn't see this before he threw away his chance. I predict he'll play it tough from here on in." He smiled. "So . . . maybe I kept him active because he'll be a useful tool for me to eliminate some of you others."

Ellis glanced at Orestes. "What do you think, Sr. Cruz?"

The Santa Anan fleered. "Why should I tell you my thoughts? You might gain an advantage. Certainly Haverner would gain part of his end, to vivisect our psyches."

Nobody said more until dinner.

"An interesting start," the old man declared from the head of the table. "Yes, indeed, most interesting." The servants flitted about, setting forth bowls of iced gazpacho followed by a chicken escabeche. The six paid the food less attention than it deserved. Their seating arrangement had tacitly fallen into a pattern: opposite Haverner, Ellis; on the host's left, in order, Julia, Byron, Orestes; on his right, Gayle, Larry, Matt. Gayle's place being vacant now, Larry had moved into it to make an emptiness between him and the man from Chicago.

"Tomorrow, appropriately, is the Sabbath," Haverner reminded them. "Yes, they still call Sunday the Sabbath here, and are strict about its observance. Those who wish to rise at about six o'clock in the morning may join my staff for the ride to chapel in the North Port. Unless your appetite for folkways is unappeasable, insist on seats in the two automobiles. The trucks are less than luxurious, especially on a primitive road that winds over the spine of the Island: only six miles as the crow claims to fly, but fifteen on that road, and easily an hour's uneasy drive. The view from the top is spectacular and, on the farther side, the cultivated fields and orchards are picturesque. I fear you will find little to divert you in town, if town it may be called. But you can return with those who only stay for the morning service."

"Thank you," Byron said. "You're . . . most gracious."

"My pleasure. Pity Mrs. Thayer is incapacitated. I assume she has no scheme that requires special equipment. Let me repeat, if you want something like that, it can probably be fetched by my airplane pilot, but you had better allow time if it's an unusual item."

"Whad'yuh mean, unusual?" Matt asked. "S'pose it's, uh, illegal?"

"I have connections," Haverner replied blandly, "and, as remarked earlier, on this property I am the law."

Byron chuckled. *"La loi, c'est moi."* Haverner alone seemed the faintest bit amused, and silence stretched.

At length the old man said, "We could perhaps have a livelier conversation, don't you think? One senses a certain awkwardness. Would somebody care to discuss a particular interest of his or hers?"

Matt poured his wineglass full again. "Yeah," he said, "let Orestes, there, preach at us."

Julia winced. "No. Please. This much conflict already—"

"Conflict is what we're here for," Ellis said. "However, I admit I don't care to be ranted at by a Communist."

"Don't worry, I will not," Orestes told him. "In your turn, kindly spare me."

Larry glared at Haverner. "We really ought to repay our host by being the sort of entertaining company he wants," he said with thick sarcasm.

"To act as his Scheherazades, eh?" Byron responded. "Well, why not?"

Ellis appeared to be seized by a thought.

"In fact," Byron went on, "we could make a rule, if Mr. Haverner is agreeable, that someone has to tell a story or anecdote each evening in turn, preferably out of his own experience."

"Mr. Haverner has complete dossiers on us," Orestes said.

The man at the head of the table smiled, a dusty expression. "They are not totally complete. Besides, if the period of your life concerned is known to me, I shall be interested to observe the degree of your truthfulness."

"How about it, then?" Byron urged. "Who wants to start? Larry?"

The blond mane shook. "No. Not tonight, anyhow."

Byron's glance traversed the table and came to rest on Ellis. "You, Mr. Nordberg?" he suggested. "You've been the most reticent of us all. I don't even know where you're from."

"Minneapolis," The answer was sour.

"Anything further to tell?"

"No. Your notion is ridiculous." Ellis sank again into his brown study.

Matt hauled him back with a start by saying, after a high-pitched laugh, "Oh, I can tell yuh something. I know about him, a few facts, anyway, seeing as how I lived in Chicago and, uh, business took me to Minneapolis once in a while. He heads Northmount Electronics. Transistorized stuff for computers and missiles and such, mainly, only they're branching out, same as you did, Mr. Haverner, except they're mighty small potatoes."

Ellis flushed, half opened his mouth, snapped it shut. Matt smirked at him and continued, "They say you got your start when you married a girl whose old man backed you. I saw her picture on a society page and sure can't see any other reason for marrying her."

Ellis seemed to reflect, then confronted them with the appearance and tone of indignation. "That's not true! I've nothing to tell that you bright moderns won't find too obsolete to do anything but snicker at. Nothing more than hard work, business sense, service to the community, faith in God." He drew breath. "Born on a South Dakota farm, one of six children. It was an endless struggle to keep that land during the Depression, yes, during World War Two also, when price controls on what we produced didn't match those on feed and fertilizer. I earned us a few extra dollars by working for local merchants after school and farm chores. When I graduated from high school, there was no money for college, so I was drafted into the Army. I did manage to convince them I had brains, and if you think that's easy, think again. They taught me electronics, and by the time I got to Korea to help man the radars, the fighting was over. I was approached about stealing parts to sell on the black market, and notified my superiors, and cooperated with them in getting the evidence that broke the crime ring. For that, I was made an officer. When I left the service, naturally I used the knowledge I'd gained in civilian life. But my country needs what I produce. I'm the father of two fine boys and take an active part in civic affairs.

"There! Are you satisfied? Have I utterly condemned myself in your eyes, Cruz, and become a total square to the rest of you? Funny, wasn't it?"

After a stillness wherein nobody looked straight at anybody else, Byron said softly, "Thanks. Maybe my idea isn't so good after all. I didn't mean to see people goaded. . . . If you wish, I could spin a reminiscence or two, incidents that I at least thought were comical."

"Oh, do," Julia breathed. Larry nodded vigorously. Matt lifted his lip but made no comment. Ellis returned gradually to his introspection. Orestes listened with the same alertness as Haverner.

"For example," Byron said, smiling a bit at the Santa Anan, "a friend and I were walking about in Leningrad a few years back. We grew hungry, and even though we had no Russian worth mentioning, hoped we could make a passer-by understand that we wanted a restaurant and draw us directions on a notepad. The fellow we buttonholed didn't know any foreign language we did. So my friend looked up "restaurant" in his pocket dictionary and automatically read out to our poor native, '*Pectopah? Pectopah?*' "

He spoke on, rapidly and wittily. It was plain to see that the day had exhilarated him. At length he drew some laughs, and the meal ended in a reasonably relaxed atmosphere.

"Bridge, anyone?" Byron inquired.

"No, I think I'll take a small drink and a big book upstairs, read myself early to sleep," Larry replied. "I'd enjoy that North Port trip."

"Same here," Julia said.

Ellis approached Haverner as the latter was being assisted to his feet. "Sir," he asked, as inconspicuously as possible, "may I have a word with you alone?"

The study was misnamed; "office" would have been better. It had kept the original graceful proportions and spaciousness, burnished hardwood floors, tall windows and cream-colored walls. But filing cabinets lined it, reference shelves, functional modern chairs, a bloc of the latest equipment for sending orders and retrieving information around the globe. An air conditioner hummed and, in this especial room, seemed somehow to have drained out every last wisp of odor.

Amidst this, like a damning or saving touch of lunacy, stood Sunderland Haverner's century-old rolltop desk.

He sat, legs blanketed, in the chaise longue to which his men had brought him before they withdrew. Ellis poised on the edge of a smaller seat, fingers squeezed together on his lap till the nails went white. Haverner bridged his own knobby digits, considered them gravely and said with care:

"Yes, I see no reason not to grant your requests. I will ring for Anselmo and tell him. You and he can work out the details."

The wind puffed from Ellis. "Th-th-thank you, sir. Thank you. You're very generous. I . . . I wasn't sure, you realize . . . under the rules—"

"The rules are flexible, Mr. Nordberg. If no one else has the mother wit to apply to me, why, that's their misfortune. I must confess to being a little astonished that you ever expected I might refuse. Yes, just a little astonished."

"Why?" Ellis forced stiffness into his back.

Haverner arched his tufted gray brows. "Why? Come, come, my good man. I might go so far as to say, 'Tut-tut.' That was a most eloquent lecture you gave at table. But don't you imagine I know better? Matthew Flagler does —you might be well advised to buy his silence—and his acquaintance with the facts is casual. My detectives spent weeks intensively investigating you seven, once the tentative choices had been made. You too have had occasion to have lives pried into, correct? Well, imagine what thoroughness *I* can hire if I wish. And I did wish. This experiment is a keystone of my psychological study."

Ellis squirmed. "Sir, you may have been told vicious rumors, but the truth—"

Haverner checked him by raising a hand. "No, no. Spare your pains. I am tired and must soon go for my rest. Besides, I have heard every form of hypocrisy known to man, and am weary unto death of them. One important purpose of this contest is to strip away that habit, to watch what happens when people are compelled to stop lying to *themselves.*"

Braced on his chair, Ellis waited.

Haverner chuckled. "But please don't suppose I condemn you, Mr. Nordberg," he continued amiably. "In fact, we are much alike, you and I. It's true that your marriage was for pecuniary reasons. Well, likewise mine."

"And why not?" Ellis said in an encouraged voice. "That was always the reason for marriage, before this trash came along about 'love' "—his tone pronounced the quotation marks—"having anything to do with it. Love is adolescent mopery. Marriage is, used to be, ought to be real, honest, a contract entered into for the good of the country or the family."

"Or for oneself, Mr. Nordberg. Oneself. I do not mean to play favorites; that would contradict my objective. But I will earnestly recommend to you, and try to find ways to give your competitors the same hard-bought wisdom—use hypocrisy outside, and only outside, your skin. It is an indispensable lubricant. However, imagine a machine controlled by a computer. The machine must have oil. Let any get into the computer, though, and the results are disastrous."

Somewhere a macaw, startled out of sleep, screeched. "I . . . appreciate your advice, Mr. Haverner," Ellis said in a low voice.

The old man grinned. "But can you take it? Have you sufficient guts—no, integrity—to recognize what you are and live by that?

"I know you, I tell you, I know you. I can reconstruct with certainty your boyhood's calculating, bustling sycophancy before those local merchants and the almighty banker. In the Korean episode, when you got wind of the thieving, you deemed it would pay you best to lure the ring into co-opting you, and report what was going on. What the military investigators never learned was that you covered up for the leader of the ring, who thus escaped suspicion. He paid you well for that, didn't he?

"You were rewarded with officer training and assignment to Japan. There you did a competent job and earned successive promotions; but your best energies went to establishing personal connections that would be useful after you left the Army.

"You take an active interest in politics, oh, yes. In that way, you have been a powerful force toward getting various bills passed that, in effect, give you fat subsidies— after which you speak before civic groups on the virtues of free enterprise. At the same time, you were shrewd enough to recognize that the catchwords of the '60s were not those of the '50s. You destroyed an academician who was asking some inconvenient questions by rousing the militant students against him. He was in fact helping young black people learn what they needed to know in order to enter the bourgeois professions, and helping them get such positions after they graduated. You quietly pointed out that this was depriving the black revolution of potential leaders, and the nonrenewal of his contract became a nonnegotiable demand. Very clever, Nordberg, my congratulations. The following decade was more, ah, pragmatic, but you adapted equally well. Among other intelligent policies, the legislators for whom you do favors that are not mentioned in public never belong to your own state. Excellent thinking!"

"No, honestly, sir," Ellis whispered, "you don't understand—"

Haverner ignored him. "I could go on, but no need. Either you do or you do not have a capacity for self-examination. Let me ring for Anselmo."

When the business was concluded and Ellis had departed, Haverner sat awhile amidst his thoughts. A smile played across his lips. Presently, almost impulsively, he picked up the telephone.

The dial tone hummed with Samael's voice. "Ah, yes. I expected you to want a little conversation. Are you feeling better about this affair?"

"It is becoming more interesting," Haverner said.

"We can look for steady improvement as the game progresses, as the players erode away each other's defenses, and their own. You wanted them manipulable, to suit your convenience. Well, without compromising the scientific aspect too much, this should increasingly become the case. In fact, you will recall my remark, when first we were laying our plans, that among other things we would like to see how much human complexity the situation would strip from them, to what extent they would cease playing the game and the game would begin playing them."

Haverner nodded. "Yes, I remember."

"The process is under way, my friend, and not only in the obvious persons. Tomorrow morning you may find some lively matter on your tapes. Good evening, Sunderland Haverner." Samael chuckled; the sound faded back into the electronic hum.

The man decided he would observe directly, at least for a while, from his bedroom. He wouldn't be able to sleep soon anyway.

The click of latch as his door was opened, of fluffy blue mules on his floor, brought Larry awake. He sat up in bed. The book over which he had fallen asleep thudded off. The glow from his reading lamp limned Gayle against a darkened hallway. She wore a short, lacy nightgown whose filminess fluttered in the breeze, still warm and sweet-scented, which blew in the open windows.

"Oh!" Her hand fluttered to her mouth. The large gray eyes grew larger. "I'm terribly sorry. I saw the light under your door and thought—"

"'Sokay." He brought his wrist across his shaggy breast and looked at the watch thereon. "I must've dozed off an hour or so back. How are you, Gayle?"

"I'm fine now. Woke feeling fine but hungry, went down for a raid on the icebox, and coming back I saw—well, I'm sorry I disturbed you. I'll go." She half turned.

"No, wait. Please." With full wakefulness came a stammer. "I, I'm the one who has to, to beg your humble pardon. I tried to, after . . . right after . . . but you were like in a state of shock, and since then—" His fist punished the mattress.

"What?" She closed the door and came near. "What're you getting at, Larry?"

"You know. It's no thanks to me you aren't dead."

"That!" She smiled very brightly, gave a rippling laugh, and sat down on the edge of the bed. "Why, you poor darling. You've been remorseful this whole day?"

"What else should I be?"

His head was bent. She rumpled the hair. "Larry, you

told me yourself, I didn't have to play. It was a straight game, and . . . and I met that guard type, what's his name, Anselmo. He'd heard me in the kitchen and come to see; he scared me at first, but—well, he told me what you'd done, how you called everybody a winner. And besides, it was probably a false alarm, because nobody really did get attacked, did they? My silly fault. Here, look at me."

He did. She embraced him. The kiss grew long, with much play of tongues and hands. When they broke, both were breathing harder and blood beat in their faces.

"*That's* how mad I am at you, Larry," she murmured.

"Uh . . . I should offer you a chair and . . . but I don't sleep in pajamas."

Gayle giggled. "Think that bothers me?"

"—I guess not." However, he made no move to come out from under his thin blanket, simply fluffed a pillow against the headboard and leaned back on it.

"You could give me a cigarette." Reaching, she helped herself from the cedarwood box that had been placed in the chamber, and snapped the silver lighter beside it. With a slantwise look at him: "You too?" He nodded. She lit a fresh one from the end of hers and put it between his lips.

They smoked in wind-sough, surf-song, insect-creak. Finally, not quite steadily, glance averted, she stubbed out her cigarette and said, "If you, well, if you do feel you owe me some amends, Larry . . ."

His features stiffened and half a minute passed.

"I was no player for you to worry about," she said in that small voice. "I don't know why I was tapped. What chance have I got? I saw I was doomed, the first day here. And you, Larry, you did wash me out. The next guy's not going to be gallant about it."

"You've got the next turn."

"You needn't remind me. I'm going out of my gourd. What can I *do*? How can I beat any of them at *any*thing? I'm not strong or clever or—or ruthless, Larry. I guess I'm not even as highly motivated as some. Like, sure, I want my independence in the worst way. I've had it with dragging around from man to man or those nasty little jobs between times. But I don't want a whole million the way guys like Orestes and Ellis Nordberg do."

She stopped until, abruptly cool, she added, "You don't either. You proved that."

"I could use a goodly part of it."

"Understood. I don't need an awful lot myself. I figured out—a hundred thousand, ten lousy percent of a million, put in safe tax-free bonds, and I can live well enough to suit me till I die."

Larry sat forward. His voice roughened. "Are you proposing we go in cahoots?"

"Yes. I am." She took the cigarette stub from between his fingers, laid it in the ashtray, and then put both hands on his shoulders. Her mouth drew close to his. Her lips began swelling. "You'd pay off whatever moral debt you feel—"

"Do I feel any, after what you've just said? You waited for this chance to catch me here, didn't you?"

She nodded, drooping her lashes. "Uh-huh. I would've regardless. You're a mighty big piece of man, and a sweetheart on top of it. But Larry, don't you see, I can help you also? Two heads are better than one. I may see something, learn something you never would. And if —well, *when*—when I wash out, in spite of what help you can sneak to me . . . I'll be officially out of the game, but that means nobody'll pay much attention to me, and maybe I can—"

"Hm." He pondered; but his pulse was visibly quickening. "The rules . . . Still, these're stakes for a lifetime, and Haverner never said we could not use somebody who's been scrubbed, and it looks like becoming a mean game anyway. . . . Hm."

"What should I call for, day after tomorrow?" She took his hand to see his watch. "No, tomorrow, by now. I'll tell you what I thought of. I've got a nice big stash along. I'll make us blow grass. You and me, we're used to it; the rest'll pass out before we do."

"I dunno. I'm not a steady user myself. And besides, pot has a kind of reverse tolerance, didn't you know? Heavy smokers get high quicker than most, uh, neophytes, they say. . . . Wait. How could you prove your rivals were inhaling? And Orestes, at least, is probably . . . Well. No. I don't think it's a good idea."

Briefly crestfallen, she rallied as fast, locked fingers behind his neck so that the hair fell over them, and exclaimed, "There! You see how you've helped me? Now I'll help you. Between us, we'll plan a game for me that'll beat some of those pigs. Larry, it's like you got a whole extra turn!"

"Maybe . . ." He ran a hand over her back. She arched it and made purring noises.

"Other alliances may form," he said. "In self-defense, we—"

"Right on, darling! We can trust each other!"

The second kiss was longer than the first, but then it had its interruptions, such as getting her nightgown off and her into the bed.

"Love," she crooned, thrusting a nipple against his palm. "Love and trust. Lovers can trust each other." Her right hand slid downward. "Oh, my, oh, my. You *are* a big piece of man. I really have lucked out."

He entered the dining room yawning hugely. Dawn was orange and blue in its glass; jays racketed. Byron happened to trail him. They found Julia already there, eating, and Ellis, though the latter had obviously finished his meal some time before.

"Hi," Julia greeted. "Is this the whole North Port party?"

"Presumably," Byron replied. "Can you see dear Matt Flagler rising at daybreak to broaden his culture? And Orestes, being a mainlander, might well fear hostility. . . . No, wait, he's gotten thick as thieves with the help around here. He can doubtless ride in on the supply truck, any off-game day he wants, at a more convenient hour. Gayle?"

"Definitely not." Larry could not strain all the smugness out of his response.

"You surprise me, frankly," Byron said to Ellis.

"Of course I do," was the answer. "In liberal mythology, no businessman has interests beyond the next quarter's profit. Not that I'll attend divine service just so I can feel amused and superior."

"Aw, let's not fight." Larry went to the sideboard. A waitress entered and raised eyebrows politely for his breakfast order. "Ham, two eggs, sunny side up, please. Lots of fries, too."

"Same for me," Byron put in.

"Wait," Ellis said. "Have your eggs scrambled. Tremendous."

"With the appetite I've got?" Larry replied. "No, thanks. I want something heavier-feeling."

The waitress, about to go, stopped when Ellis crooked a finger. "I do wish you'd try the scrambled eggs," he said. "Make it a double order if you want. I . . . Give me a chance to prove I care about a few of the same things as you, even if only—"

"Huh?" Larry blinked. "Oh, okay. Four scrambled eggs. It's a great world except for morning coming too goddamn early, and I'll take your advice about what's extra good in it." His new yawn threatened to dislocate his jaw. "U-u-u-uh-u-u-u-uh! What I will insist on is coffee."

"I'll go along," Byron said. "Scrambled, since I notice that's what you've been having, Julia."

"They are superb," she agreed. "I asked, and it's a matter of turmeric, chives, cream, and beating the bejesus out of them."

The newcomers sat down, flanking her. "Byron," she said, "before I forget, could you later today go over that contract with me? I can't quite unravel the legalese. Is it really ironclad?"

"I'm no lawyer, but yes, I can try," he nodded. "Should've done it before for myself." His eyes lingered on the glory waxing in the French doors. "I wish this room faced due east."

Ellis seemed hurt. "Don't you trust me? I told you it's okay."

"Well, we do need to know the details in any event," Julia said.

Ellis leaned over his cup of long-cold coffee. "Look, I want to be civilized, same as you do. Things were getting out of hand last night. Suppose I take you both, and you, Larry, or whoever's interested, suppose I take you through the material, point by point. You can check words in the dictionary as we go if you suspect my definitions. Otherwise, really, law really is just logic. Contracts like this one get complicated simply because they have to cover a lot of contingencies."

Larry, falling asleep over his orange juice, jerked awake.

"I can start in a general way at once, and we'll study the document later." Ellis rose. "Excuse me if I prowl around meanwhile. I'm a pacer-talker."

Nobody cared to say him nay, and he ignored the fact that their concentration on him was less than complete. Soon the two breakfast entrées came in.

"There!" Ellis interrupted himself when the first mouthfuls were taken. "Wasn't I right about the eggs? Wasn't Julia?" He came around the table, stood behind, bent over and gesticulated above the plates.

"We-ell, yes. Yes, you were," Byron said.

Ellis's companionable hands, straddling the woman to squeeze each man's shoulder, tightened. "Hey!" he exclaimed. "What's that?"

"Huh?" She and Byron squinted outward, Larry blinked.

"That way—don't you see—no, God help us, can't be!"

They stared as hard as they were able. "What?" Julia wondered. "I see dew on the lawn, and long sun rays and shadows mixed together, and—"

"A shape. Go. To the doors. Please." Ellis urged them from their chairs. He stayed. "Don't let me prejudice you. Look for yourselves."

They did. "Maybe I'm too drowsy yet," Larry said.

Ellis sighed. "All right. I'm sorry. I must have been mistaken. I could have sworn I saw a . . . something like an . . . an odd-looking animal running toward the house. . . . Do they have tapirs on this island? Do on the mainland. . . . Please excuse me. It was a trick of light, I guess, and maybe those damned specks in my vision that bother me worse and worse as I get older." He took off his glasses, held them aloft, blew on them and polished them with his handkerchief. "I am sorry."

Julia gave him a long and careful regard before she sat down again. He resumed his précis of their contract.

The excursion was delayed soon after it started, when Larry Rance grew quite ill and had to be taken back to the house. He lay in his room, behind drawn blinds, in a rank sweat, sneezing and struggling for air, throughout most of the day. After he had vomited his stomach empty, he broke into a rash. His pulse was frantic and thready.

Haverner, who could have specialists flown quickly in from the mainland for himself, kept no physician on his staff, though he was believed to subsidize the only one on the Island, in the North Port. That person could not be located by the tenuous telephone connections available. Larry rallied enough to wheeze a request for antihistamine. What pills were on hand gave some relief.

Gayle Thayer tended his needs. Toward evening the symptoms faded and he fell into a normal sleep.

Matt Flagler woke late. In the afternoon he ambled around to the servants' quarters. The children were back from chapel. He fell into simple conversation with Captain York's thirteen-year-old nephew Billy. His Spanish, while serviceable after his years in Ciudad Vizcaya, was of no great use here, and his English fell strangely on the boy's ears, used to the antique local version. But he had gotten to the point of proposing a long walk in the woods when Orestes Cruz came upon them, drew him aside and muttered in Spanish:

"Stop this. They'll kill you if anything happens. Not that that is undesirable, but the child is worth more. Go."

"I wasn't . . ." Matt protested in English. "I didn't . . . Holy mother, what're you talking about, I was only trying to be nice."

"Go." Orestes chopped the blade of his right hand across his left wrist. Matt went, speaking bad words to himself, to drink and watch television. Orestes turned to Billy and a couple of small sisters who had stood half-comprehendingly nearby. "Hey!" he beamed. "Who knows that funny Belize Creole song, 'Captain Foot's Money Gone'?"

The excursionists came back, inquired about Larry's health, were assured that he was recovering rapidly and must simply have encountered something that disagreed with him. Perhaps on yesterday's ramble through the hills? "We talked awhile before he corked off," Gayle told them at dinner. "He says he'll be in shape to play tomorrow. I'm sure he will, myself. In fact, this may give him a better chance in my game than anybody else."

"What is it?" Matt asked through the sudden quiet.

She tittered. "Be in the living room at eight sharp tomorrow morning and I'll tell you."

GAYLE THAYER

It's going to be a real scorcher today, I guess. Already the brightness outside hurts me to look at. (I asked Captain York and he told me, "Veadder like dis come before de rain. And ven de rain come from de nart', raise de fever." He's sweet. I don't see how he can work for that awful Haverner. That Anselmo now, that goon, *he* could be a San Francisco pig, wouldn't he just love it clubbing students? No, wait, Anselmo's pretty much Indian, isn't he, his people've been oppressed. . . .) Lucky this is my day to be leader. Nobody can drag me outside. "Put down the blinds," I say. "Draw the curtains. Turn up the air conditioner."

Oh, shit, I forgot to say "please" to that little dark man. Bad vibes getting to me.

I feel the tension; they stare and stare, waiting for my orders in this long dim room. Well, Larry's hanging loose, of course. (After all we did together, he should be plenty loose!) He knows what to expect; he ate an extra big breakfast and didn't take much liquid and went to the can right before now. He's looking good. I wish we could have fucked, once anyway, last night or early this morning, but I guess he needed the sleep more, and anyway remember how the guru last year always said sex restraint helps meditation, and Christ but I'd better be able to meditate good today!

I smile at Larry. He frowns and shakes his head, the tiniest bit. Oh, yes, what a dope I am. We can't let on we're partners. No smiles, then, no holding hands, no hugs or kisses where somebody else might see. But a stolen look once in a while, and we can know what we mean when we say, "Good morning, Larry/Gayle, how are you this fine day?" There's a bed waiting for us, and Christ but secrecy makes it exciting!

"Well, Miss Thayer, eight o'clock," Ellis Nordberg says. He would. The clockwork man. Wind him up and he ruins the environment.

I try to, what's the word, take their measure. Eyes, eyes. Nordberg shivers underneath the machinery; I can feel that; I do have some ESP, I know I do. Matt Flagler's in a bad way; I can't help feeling sorry for him; maybe I should offer him a few joints later on; he's killing himself with booze. Byron's excited; he's really into this game. And the son of a bitch doesn't need the money! Though he's kind of nice; and restless, the way he seems to be, maybe he'll be one I overcome. Julia hangs on to his arm. Do I see a film of sweat on her forehead? Her eyes (green today and pretty, but mine're prettier, dear) are like a cat's. That poor little kid of hers. Think of having to spend your life hooking into a machine. I wonder, supposing Larry and I win—I mean, he's the technical winner, though with my help right down the line—could he spare the bread she needs? I couldn't. Sorry, Julia, sorrier, Kilby, but those hundred thousand skins are *my* life. I'll have to talk with Larry about it. . . . Orestes, he's cool. I'd like to know him better. I heard him sing to the children; he's lovely, no Belafonte but he's real. Wonder how he'd be as a lover. Strictly between me and myself, I admit the three (**niggers**) black men I've laid weren't all that great; Rog was downright disappointing, and if he hadn't been black I wouldn't ever have given him another night— Well, I've got my Larry, and what a romp we had!

Shouldn't be. He's a Taurus (that's right on, a big horny bull) but I'm a Scorpio and . . . Got to be something extra, like maybe if there is reincarnation, he and I used to be . . .

"It's to my advantage not to remind you, perhaps, Gayle," Julia says, "but your time is running on." How can her voice be that cool? She still holds Byron's arm in both hands. Wonder if she's laid him yet? (Those bedrooms sure got good soundproofing.) Watch out for those two.

"Yeah," Matt says, "you're having your period." He guffaws.

My heart stumbles and goes sick. Oh, Christ, what if I do have my period while the contest's going on? I get such cramps . . . I shouldn't have it, but it's always been irregular and . . . Oh, Jesus, sweet Jesus, I pray to you, don't let it happen. I really do think the Jesus people are onto something, I really do, Jesus.

Anselmo, he's sat down; he watches us out of his mask. Can't the devil even grin while we suffer?

I'm too dizzy to stand; I sit down too. "Gimme a cigarette, please," I say. Larry forgets his own advice and obliges. A couple of drags steady me a little. (Matt, my friend, the rate you smoke at, you're in trouble today.)

"Okay," I tell them. "Okay. My game's quite simple. You see the kind of chair I'm in." It's a period (that word again) piece (again) like most everything else in this haunted house: mahogany, arms, straight scrollwork back, seat cover embroidered with Georgette Heyer bouquets. "You may've noticed, I've ordered more brought in. We've got one for each of you. Okay, let's put them in a circle, here in the middle of the rug."

Larry calls the rug deep-sea blue. It's thick and soft. I kick off my shoes, real unobtrusive like, and feel it under my stocking feet. Larry's wearing zori.

The chairs don't quite touch. He sits across from me. Good, I'll be able to look at him and he (oh, I hope) at me. On my right are Orestes and Ellis, on my left Julia, Byron and Matt. I'm glad Orestes sits by me, so he can know I'm not a racist.

"Now find a comfortable position." My voice sounds high and weak in my ears. "I mean, more or less upright, like me, but comfortable. You dig? I want to be fair." ("Don't mention shoes," Larry said. "Feet will swell during the day.")

"Okay." I throw it at them. "This is the game. To sit perfectly still. You can breathe, of course, and I guess it's not your fault if you get a nervous tic or something. But anybody who makes any real, uh, uh, voluntary movement is out."

"What?" Ellis exclaims. "This is ridiculous!"

Orestes, beside me, rolls forth that grand deep chuckle he's got.

"You should be used to sitting, Nordberg," I crow. I am!

Matt rises. "Well, lemme go take a leak," he says.

"The game starts in thirty seconds," I answer.

Christ, what a look! It scares me out of my gourd. I get faint again and barely hear him protesting to Anselmo.

"The game ees good," Anselmo says. "You better seet."

(I checked with him yesterday, after Larry and I'd worked the idea out. He must've checked with old Haverner, because he came back after a while and said okay.)

Larry laughs. "Tough shit."

"We, we . . . begin . . . when I . . ." I tug at a fold of my dress that's gotten between my buttocks. "When I stop, stop, stop talking." I settle myself, I hope, I pray, arms on chair arms. "Begin!"

Everybody's in place. Now comes the long wait.

"If you break first," Larry told me, "you won't lose. You're the leader, and you can elect a break. You can tell them to start right over. But it's best if you don't. I really can't see all of them sitting motionless for, mm, eight till six or thereabouts . . . twenty-two solid hours."

Can I see myself doing it? Here's where we learn.

Too bad, what horrible luck, he had to get sick yesterday. If he'd been well, his head perfectly clear, we could have thought of a better gimmick.

(He almost wondered aloud if he'd been poisoned, then zipped his lips and wouldn't say more. Doesn't he trust me either? But Larry, big cheerful royally screwing again-and-again Larry, I'm honest, honest I am.)

I hear somebody breathing hard. Who? I can't turn my head to see. Larry's in my field of view, and—more or less—Matt on his right, Ellis Nordberg on his left. Larry's not looking at me, however. His eyes are turned past me, over me.

"Relax," he said. "That'll be the important thing. If you get tense, you'll fight yourself, you'll wear yourself out. Pretty soon then, positive feedback sets in and you get the shakes."

So relax, damn it. But why doesn't he look at me? If I

saw him getting a hard on under those white duck pants, I'd sure not call him on it.

I won't call anybody on eye movements. Let my own switch around. Yes, there's Orestes, half visible. I know you, handsome Orestes; San Francisco and Berkeley are full of you.

Or are they? My revolutionary friends used to talk a good job of overthrowing the establishment. But even the Panthers . . . What have you done actually, Orestes? I hear you were busted after the fascists got back to power in Santa Ana. I've seen your missing teeth, the whip marks on your back. They must've had reason to hate you that much.

Well, naturally they hate everybody who threatens their privileges. Bourgeoisie yields capitalism yields imperialism. . . . Are big estate owners bourgeoisie? Oh . . . not that I'm a Communist or anything like that. I'm just an ordinary person who'd like to know why we can't all love one another.

How I tried to explain to Daddy and Mom, Christmas before last!

I didn't want to go back. Gayle Thayer—Dennis Thayer's woman—who had been Gail Robertson—what had she to do with Gail Matlock and Chillicothe, Ohio? It's not only not my scene anymore, it's a bad scene, and I bleed for my parents who'll never get out. . . . Yes, I can, I'll bleed for Ruth, too.

(In bed, before our final fuck, me cuddled into the curve and muscles of Larry's left arm, his right hand between my thighs, the sweet sweaty hairiness of him, I cried while I told it like it was.

(My father the druggist, not poor, not rich, lukewarm Christian, lukewarm Republican . . . he and Mom, besides his bowling team and her bridge club, that kind of thing, what'd they care about except my sister? Ruth, she's two years older, beautiful, yeah, I got to admit she's beautiful, and bright and pleasing, oh, Daddy worshiped her, nothing was ever too good for Ruth. Me, I was the plain one, the dull one, never had any dates, Ruth went to college but me, why, I was talked into . . . well, Daddy had this friend who needed a file clerk and I . . . right out of high school . . .

("You mean your parents were cruel to you?" he

asked. And I had to admit, after we talked awhile, no, they meant well, they just didn't see my potential. Mother was always nagging me: "You only *sit* there . . . all you do is *sit* . . . hour after hour, like a bump on a log! You might as well get a job in an office, where at least you'll get *paid* for *sitting* . . . my land!"

(Sure, I was too passive, I accepted being the ugly duckling; it was easier than trying to compete or strike out on my own. Marriage would bring me everything good. . . . Poor Tim! We met at a church social and he was as desperate as I was.

(It might've helped if I'd gotten pregnant. When the doctor found out that stuff with my Fallopian tubes, though, I felt mainly relieved that I wouldn't have to keep trying to remember my pills and failing. Someday I'd get the repair operation, but right now we couldn't afford it, and since then it isn't just the population explosion and all. I wonder if I really do want the work of raising a baby. I wonder if I'd be a fit mother even by my own sloppy standards.

(I sighed to Larry, "When you come right down to it, there's only one thing I'm really good at, and that's sitting on my ass." And then, oh, then, the big doll, he grabbed me to him and laughed aloud: "Uh-uh. You're wrong. One more thing, at least. You're damn good at lying on your back!" And off we went, till stars exploded in me.

(But here, now, alone in my head, I remember how I tried to pick up some money in porno movies, and couldn't stand some of the things they wanted me to do; oh, sure, there's no such thing as sinful sex, but raw eggs always did make me gag, and that—thinking about the hoods and crazies I'd meet—killed off any idea about whoring, so haven't I had my failures here, too?)

Ellis crosses eyes with me. I know you, Ellis Nordberg, you are the enemy and you despise me, but you were always chasing the dollar, always uptight; you never learned how to relax. Today I'll show you. How suddenly happy it feels to hate! It shouldn't, but—

Anselmo passes by. I barely keep myself from jerking where I sit. He scares me. Not as bad as old Haverner does, but bad enough. *Are* the rooms bugged? Did old Haverner sit listening or, worse, play back tapes of Larry and me? Music to jack off by. No, I suppose he's too old; he's not even that human any longer. Brr!

Anselmo takes a cigarette, paces back and forth, disappears from my line of sight. Probably he's bored. Or does he listen with his boss? I've got to warn Larry.

Why? Does it matter? I've made the all-of-us-together scene. But that was good; that was with people you could groove on.

Love. I did try to explain to Mom and Daddy. (Not about the orgy bit or anything like that, of course. What a drag it was, always having to remind myself not to speak honest.) "Why'd I come here, clear across the continent, for Christmas, leaving my husband [and he was, he was, we worked out such a beautiful wedding service with the Universal Life minister] if you didn't write and ask me to? Loving is giving."

Why did Daddy have to go mean right that minute and say, "Tim Robertson was mighty happy when you let him stop giving." I guess it was those drinks he'd had. But Jesus, how unfair! Mom told him so, too, and we had a real fine night before Christmas, didn't we, them yelling back and forth. Why shouldn't Tim pay me alimony till I remarried? What was I supposed to do, starve?

My neck hurts. I've got to relax. What time is it? Why didn't I bring a clock in where I could see it? Me with no wristwatch, too poor even for a cheap Timex, and everybody else's out of my view.

I should've had a joint before we began here. Then I could've relaxed. Or some acid, yes, acid's better yet; I could've spent this time exploring inner space. No, I guess that wouldn't have been wise. Under these conditions here, it might be a real bad trip. Anyhow, no telling what shit they put in acid these days. *Why* won't the establishment legalize drugs and inspect them? They do it with liquor, don't they? Well, I guess Haverner could've gotten me the pure stuff if I'd asked. Too late now.

Larry's finally moved his eyes. They meet mine. He winks. I declare that was a blink and doesn't count. Imagine, Larry, you were right across the Bay when I was getting suckered by Dennis Thayer!

No, let's be fair. Dennis is what he is. Poor Tim Robertson, he is what he is. We all are what we are. Yoga,

Jesus, drugs, everything transcendental, aren't they because we try, want, need, scream to escape from that?

Some won't try. Tim'll always be a gawky bookkeeper in Chillicothe, Ohio. He'll marry again, and she'll be a good housekeeper like I wasn't, a good enough cook like I wasn't, maybe even a good lay like (let's face it) I wasn't either, then. He'll imagine he's happy.

Why, the poor fool may feel sorry for *me*, who used his alimony to go live in San Francisco among a lot of dirty hippies!

"The hippies are dead," I tried to explain to him that strained afternoon during my Christmas visit. "They died the day the establishment press discovered the word. There really weren't any of them left by the time I got out there. I mostly just heard about the activism, even, from people who'd been in it. [How I envied them!] Nothing's been happening, really, till just lately, and we've got to protest against the nukes and all that, don't we?" That satisfies a little bit, but something is still missing, and what might it be, and how to search for it?

What's the time?

I've got an itch between my shoulderblades. I could rub against the chairback. I could ask Larry to scratch it, and let his fingers search around till they found the right spot. No. The rest must be itching too. They must be getting neckaches too.

Really? I don't think Ellis Nordberg has itches. No, his computer has glitches. Funny. I'll tell Larry tonight and we'll laugh. Someone'll quit before night! Has the sun moved since we sat down?

I guess I won't beat you out after all, Byron Shaddock. You're too fanatic a gameplayer. Nor Orestes. If he could be flogged and clubbed for his revolution, he can sit still for it. (Suppose—he does seem to have nervous-muscular trouble—suppose he couldn't help himself; his foot kicked or something. Would I count him out? He'd appeal to Anselmo, who . . .) And Julia will last, soap-opera Julia. Wouldn't it be too awful if Larry flunked? Well, I could do the same as he did, declare that the game ended just before he failed it. That'd be a give-away, but how much secrecy can we hope for when Haverner doesn't even allow us privacy?

Matt's eyes are red, though, and rolling. I see his chest

rise and fall, he's breathing noisy, I do believe—*thr-r-rill!*
—we can force him out. I'll concentrate my ESP on
you, Matthew Flagler. You're going to quit, you're going
to quit, you're going to quit, you're going to quitquitquit,
quitquitquitquitquit. . . .

The chair edge is digging into my legs. They tingle.
I think my right foot's going to sleep. Both arms are
numb. That's because of cut-off circulation, isn't it? How
long do I dare let my arms and legs get less blood than
they ought to? Bad enough, all the chemicals in the food.

I have to get my mind off the fear track. I'll move
my eyes around. This is my game. I can give myself
any relief I want. Julia's long slim calf . . . Wonder
how she is in bed? Not that I'm a lez—those experiments
didn't count, kind of fun but not like the real thing—
still, here I sit and can't help thinking. . . . I guess Larry's got me excited. It was a while, quite a while, since
the last man before him.

The wild San Francisco scene, ha!

Well, it sure as hell beats Chillicothe. But if they
think, back there, I'm getting banged by four different
studs every night in my artistic pad, I've got news for
them.

Larry complimented me. He said I really knew what I
was doing with him. And San Francisco did teach me a
lot, once I got up the nerve to go there, once I got up
the far bigger nerve to let people get acquainted with me
in the little bars and the huge espresso houses. (Oh, God,
I was scared, the first couple of times! Even afterward, when they'd been so sweet, VD. . . . Well, they
know me now at the clinic, and who am I hurting?
Maybe I am helping build penicillin-resistant strains of
bugs, but I support everything that'll help the ecology,
and anyway I've only got this one life, Jesus, don't I?
Unless the Eastern mystics . . . reincarnation. . . .)

I want a smoke. Grass for choice, no, tobacco, damn it,
tobacco, my mouth's gone itchy and dry.

Why haven't I told Orestes I play the guitar? Not as
good as him, but I'm not bad either. Him and Larry and
me, we're the real people here, we three should be in
love with each other, not that they'd be gay about it, of
course. I guess we could include Julia too, though
she holds back so much except for sucking up to that

Byron parasite. I don't mind if Orestes is a Communist. I've heard that one reason the Afghans rebelled against the Communists was that they didn't want women to get equal rights.

("Oh, I s'pose I'd call myself a libertarian, if I must have a label," Larry said. "Dunno how you'd ever get rid of the state—seems as if next thing you knew, you'd be under the boot of your friendly neighborhood warlord— but, sure I'd *like* to get rid of it, or at least trim it down a lot. That's how come I cast my first presidential vote for Nixon, in '68." Nixon! I damn near jumped out of bed and ran down the hall screaming, but then he started stroking my breasts and admitted he'd been mistaken and laughed, "Since then, I don't vote. It only encourages them.")

Quit, Matt. Quit. Quit. You're getting sleepy. You've got a headache. You have to piss. If you do it on the floor, you lose, and if you don't do it, your bladder will explode and you'll die. Quit. Quit. Quit.

Same to you, Ellis. And you, Byron.

I'm hungry. Has it really been that long? Impossible. Somebody would've had to move by lunchtime.

Or would they? They were chosen for endurance, I guess, but was I? What is old Haverner trying to make happen here?

Dennis would never have lasted this long. (Five hours, six, eight? No, the direction of sunlight, as far as I can tell through the blinds—I can't tell.) He never could, never can sit still five minutes running.

Beautiful Dennis Thayer. Young (three years younger than me, and how that made him the more exciting!), slim, sharp-featured, shoulder-length wavy red-brown hair and silky beard, cloak and lace-trimmed blouse and ivory cigarette holder, his book learning, his genuine sensitivity to music, and so virile (how well I know) he never worried about getting taken for a (**fairy**) gay. Dennis, Dennis, Dennis.

Brave Is the Cry. A novel by János Ferenczi. How we talked about it (or rather, I've seen afterward, how he did) in the corners of parties, alone later in a coffeeshop or on a park bench, finally (when he'd gotten rid of his roommate for a weekend) in that dusty, grimy, sinkful-of-dirty-dishes, hair-gummed-into-the-ring-in-the-bathtub pad (though who am I to sneer at such things?) where first he made me!

I believed, Christ, I believed. I still do, in a way, I guess. There are some great passages there. He can write a wonderful sentence. "Baby," and the beard tickled my cheek, "it's going to be beautiful. I'm going to tell it like it is. And I don't want to sound commercial, but they want the truth nowadays. Look at Tolkien. Look at *Stranger*. I've got a fortune here. Maybe a Nobel. And I'm already planning *The Kingdom and the Power*."

"But why the pen name?" I asked, and he explained how you need a name they'll remember.

(My gut rumbles; my stomach hurts. I never could stand to go hungry. My right foot is asleep. I've got to keep my neck muscles quiet.)

I wonder. Am I in love with you yet, Dennis? We did have some way-out times. Was I ever in love with you, Dennis? I'd gotten tired of my own grubby room, grubby jobs, grubby groping around from one man to the next, tired till my bones were ready to dissolve.

Shriek!

I catch my breath, half twitch out of my seat. No, it was only a parrot. Ellis sees. He changes his own position a little. His glassed-in eyes defy me to do anything about it. Where's Larry? He's off again in his own *satori* or wherever it is he goes.

I settle back. I wish I'd never moved. Now a million new aches and tingles and throbs are everywhere in me. My empty stomach belches acid into my throat. Air conditioning or no, sweat prickles my skin and I smell the harsh stink of it.

"Hang tough," Larry told me from his sickbed yesterday evening. "It's for the rest of your life, girl."

He calls himself a boat bum, but he's too modest. He was an engineer till he found out there's more to life than commuting and office politics and the military-industrial complex. He's been a sailor, a carpenter, a machinist, all kinds of things. A universal man, sort of. Even nowadays, down on his luck, just another Point Richmond character, he pays his own freight. I could live with somebody like that. He's no Dennis, but—

A sudden pain in my chest. A wave of dizziness. Am I

having a heart attack? No, can't be, no, dear Jesus, not yet, not this day! . . . Somehow it passes. I'm only agonizingly hungry. What time is it?

("I did two more paragraphs today," Dennis said when I got back from my job that supported us. "Look. Here. Aren't they beautiful?" I was too dragged out to appreciate them. He'd still be asleep when I left for work. At least, however, on days like that he had his two paragraphs. Mostly he was off gathering inspiration, or helping organize a protest march, or down to Los Angeles for a week because he'd been offered a ride. A lot of times he would stay home and put in a lot of work, and very proudly show me the result. And, yes, those were real elegant letters to the *Barb* or our Congressman; now and then they'd be real lovely or funny little poems, but who'd pay for them, who'd pay for them?

(After I asked that too often, he began calling me a prostitute. At last I left. Official divorces cost money.)

I've had it. Had it up to here, with hunger (it hurts, it hurts, I'm getting dizzy again), with squalor, with dependence, with the whole shit scene. Larry's right: get away, make a clean break. Not that I want to be on his permanent cruise, I think. . . .

Not that he wants me, either. Or does he? What am I to him? A tool that offered itself? Well, he has had the decency not to say, "I love you." I've really had it up to here with charming men.

O Jesus, I'm sick of being used!

Noonday simmers outside. Or afternoon? Where's the sun? I want a smoke in the worst way. Why hasn't Matt, anyhow, stirred? He just sits there like a cancer.

What about Haverner, where he squats? I always used to like spiders; they control pests without disturbing the ecology; now I see why so many people do have a horror of them. We're flies in his web—I've *got* to eat. Don't the rest of them? Do they ever eat? Are they human? Has Haverner rung in a set of robots on me? Is everybody in the world a robot, and I the only conscious being? It buzzes in my ears. Darknesses come and go. Daddy, help, help.

I can't stand it. Fuck the whole scene. Let me eat and rest and cry a lot. I guess Larry'll comfort me if he ever comes out of that *satori* he's in, I can't try anything else, not today, they've beaten me, the bastards, the bastards, I rise and curse them and

n
  i
   g
    h
     t
      w h
         i
          r
           l
            s
             d
              o
               w
                n
                 n
                  n
                   n
                    n

INTERVAL FOUR

"Should you be here in my room?" she wondered. "Taking care of me like this? I mean, isn't it giving away our secret?"

"When you came out of your faint and went into your hysterics," he replied grimly, "you blew that."

Gayle sank back upon her pillow. "I'm sorry, darling, I'm sorry."

"What's done is done," Larry said. "Now listen. It's not much past sundown; you have the whole night and you've had some sleep. We—you'll call a new game. I've been thinking and—"

"No. No. I can't."

He stood over her, fists on hips, and glared. "What is this farce? Of course you can!"

"No!" She huddled away from him. Her chamber was curtained and closed off. Assorted clothes and feminine paraphernalia lay strewn about on floor and bureau top. There was a smell of lilac-scented talcum powder.

"No," she begged, "I can't, I simply can't. I've got to rest and . . . Would you bring me another sandwich, Larry?"

"Can't you even holler for a maid, you chickenhead?" He turned to go.

She caught his wrist. "Larry, darling," wavered out through the tears and hiccoughy sobs, "Larry, I love you, don't leave me, I need you. W-w-we're both in the running still. Aren't we? We can still cooperate—"

He yanked loose from her. "I'm going down to dinner," he said. "Somewhere along the line I've got a storm to ride out, and the sooner the better. I'll tell 'em to bring you a tray."

"Will you come here tonight? I want you, Larry, I love you, need you."

He made no reply, but left her weeping loudly into her pillow.

In the hall below, his footsteps thudded. When he entered the dining room, he saw the rest at table. Through the French doors that gave on the patio, he saw leaf masses black and motionless under a crooked moon and a sky where the very stars felt hot. Again he took Gayle's usual seat on Haverner's right.

"Good evening," his host greeted. "Is Miss Thayer indisposed?"

Larry nodded. "Could her food be taken to her?"

"Yis, sir," said the woman who put his lemon soup before him.

"I suppose she won't call any further game," Ellis said.

"Yeah, ask Larry Rance, he knows," Matt put in. He thrust his face partly across the table to get a straight look at its head. "Mr. Haverner, sir, that bitch let out she's in cahoots with this here son of a bitch Rance. Isn't that against the rules? Isn't it? They cheated, they're out. Right, sir?"

Larry flushed. "I gave her a suggestion or two."

"That's not all you gave her."

"Jealous, Matt?" Orestes scoffed.

"Shit, no! But fair's fair, and Mr. Haverner—" Matt broke off. His forefinger stabbed at Byron and Julia. "How 'bout them two, while we're at it? They've been pretty damn close. What're they cooking up to squeeze everybody else out?"

"As I understand the rules," Ellis said in a tone clipped and calm, "they don't set any restrictions on what we do between events. This has to include exchanging of ideas, information, and moral support"—he quirked a smile—"or immoral support, if anybody wants to be that foolish. But the leader each time around has to operate strictly on his own."

"That is correct," Haverner said. "I saw no violation in today's game."

Matt sank back. His eyes roved the table, found no comfort.

Now it was Orestes who smiled, an oddly gentle curve of the full lips. "Actually," he said, "I feel pity for the . . . collusionists. If nothing more formidable comes out of such plots, why should we mind?"

Larry bit his lip.

Conversation around the board became desultory. Immediately after supper, Larry ostentatiously returned to Gayle's room. His lovemaking that night was fierce and frequent.

Haverner nodded, a slow metronome movement, there amidst his electronics and beside his rolltop desk. "Yes," he rustled, "a most interesting idea, Mrs. Petrie. I shall be happy to plan and arrange the details."

"Thank you, . . . sir," Julia said, barely audible.

"Mind you, this is not favoritism." He wagged a finger. "I will make this as fair as I possibly can, which is to say as hard on you, especially allowing for your background and knowledge of psychiatric nursing and the advantage it confers—as hard on you as on your rivals. That will be as hard as intensive study of the dossiers and intensive observation of the group itself enable me to devise."

"I realize that."

"Remember, you are last on the list, Mrs. Petrie. If you are eliminated before your turn, I'll regret missing what could be the most fascinating struggle of the lot. But I will not intervene to save you."

She wet her lips. "Mr. Havener, . . . supposing I do fail—my daughter—you'd never notice the cost."

The mummy head shook, back and forth, back and forth. "No, no, Mrs. Petrie. What incentive would you have, if you knew your wish would be granted regardless? To be blunt, from a standpoint of racial fitness you ought not to save your child. You should breed others instead, since your chromosomes are evidently first class. This one regrettable genetic accident is taking far too much of your potential reproductive time, not to speak of resources that could be better spent on more promising human material."

Julia sprang to her feet. Her fingers bent like claws. "Oh, my God! How can—"

"Quiet, please," Havener interrupted imperturbably. While she stood and gulped for air: "I wasn't condemning you. It was only an obiter dictum of mine. In candor, I expect Homo sapiens will have a shorter course than the dinosaurs did—I give him another hundred years at absolute maximum—and whether or not I'm wrong about this, his future is no concern of mine. By all means, try to keep that child alive if you want.

"In fact," he continued, seeing her partly soothed, "let me give you some advice. Again, it's no favoritism, because what I'll say is obvious, but often the obvious is the hardest to see. You are in a cutthroat situation, Mrs. Petrie. I do not believe any partnerships consisting of more than two persons can form—three, perhaps, under extraordinary circumstances—and all combinations will be unstable. This is one basis on which the players have been chosen. I am testing certain theories of mine by checking the predictions they make against practice.

"Well, you have studied psychology yourself, have worked among professionals. You should be able to estimate the personality factors and project how hatred will arise to add its dynamic to the original greed.

"Play ruthless, Mrs. Petrie. Do others before they do you. It's your only chance of lasting till the end.

"And now, if you will excuse an old man, I bid you a very good night."

When she was gone, Haverner called softly, "Are you here, Samael?"

A buzz snapped his attention around. Muttering a curse, he climbed painfully to his feet and hobbled over to the unit that had signaled. It was for written messages, but no mere teletype. Though it would print out if desired, it could also display on a screen, make a record in the molecules of a disc, and decode according to any of the numerous ciphers for which its computer was programmed. Haverner punched for display. Words formed on the screen.

YES, OF COURSE I FOLLOWED THE INTERVIEW. THAT WOMAN HAS DEPTHS OF FIENDISHNESS IN HER THAT SHE HERSELF CANNOT HAVE SUSPECTED UNTIL NOW.

He settled into the chair before the console. "You approve her plan, then?"

CERTAINLY.

Haverner rubbed his chin; the wattles beneath it swayed. "I really don't know anything about such matters. Never went in for it myself, you remember, and always despised those who did. Can you inform me about it in detail—just what stuff would work best, for instance?"

YOU HAVE AMPLE MEANS FOR HAVING ANY FACT THAT YOU MAY WANT.

Haverner narrowed his eyes. "So you don't know either."

THAT IS A LOGICAL NON SEQUITUR. I COULD SIMPLY WISH TO OBSERVE YOUR RESEARCH FACILITIES IN ACTION.

"Or you could not exist, Samael, except in a hidden part of my own brain, and be unwilling to admit it," Haverner said slowly.

IF MY WORDS TONIGHT COME FROM OUTSIDE YOURSELF, THEY ARE BEING RECORDED. YOU CAN PLAY THEM BACK. YOU CAN HAVE A PRINTOUT MADE. DO YOU WISH TO? THINK ABOUT IT, SUNDERLAND HAVERNER.

The screen blanked.

The man sat alone for minutes, until with a savage gesture he pressed a button labeled ERASE. If there had been anything on the disc currently in circuit, it was gone. He would never know if there had been.

Thunderheads massed during the following day until they loomed blue-black and enormous above the Crag. More and more, clouds torn off from those heights blew over the sky, but scant breeze touched the ground to relieve steam-bath heat. The North Americans took shelter behind the cooling machinery in the house. Their tempers were frayed, and after a couple of spats they tended to avoid contact.

Larry and Gayle did stay together, mostly upstairs. She told him that everything they did or said was surely eavesdropped on, doubtless visually as well. Devices could easily be concealed in the molding around the high ceiling. He grinned and answered, "So if that's how he gets his kicks, maybe he'll learn something new. Or would you really rather go out in the saw grass?"

Byron took some books to his own room and remained there. Ellis, likewise secluded, worked with symbols on paper. Matt watched television till he drank himself asleep on a sofa.

Julia, unable to rest, wandered out after lunch—a buffet which did not require people to eat in company—and found Orestes in a porch swing on the veranda, reading. "Hi," she said tentatively.

"*Salud*," he answered, lowering the volume onto his lap. "I am surprised that you venture forth." The air clung to the skin. It smelled of rankness and wetness. Thunder muttered.

"I was going for a walk, but—mind if I join you?"

"Do." His pleasure seemed unfeigned. She wore sandals, a halter, and exiguous shorts. He could get by with the last of these. The perspiration filming his lean dark frame did not appear to bother him, nor did it smell sour.

She sat down on his left. "I thought tropical storms came fast and went fast," she said.

"As a rule, yes. A slow development is exceptional. I predict violent weather tonight and high winds continuing through tomorrow."

She touched the book he held. *"Galatea, par Miquel de Cervantes Saavedra,"* she read off the title. "Is that *the* Cervantes?"

"Yes. A potboiler. But his potboilers are worth more than most writers' masterpieces. I like to reread this occasionally, savoring the fine lines he could not help let . . . crop? . . . yes crop out, in the middle of the banalities."

She regarded him. "You really are a complicated man, aren't you, Ores—Sr. Cruz?"

"Orestes, if you wish."

"Julia, then. But how—excuse me, I don't want to pry, but we are in the same boat and—well, I know you had a hard time, came from a background of grinding poverty and illiteracy. And nevertheless you read Cervantes, I suppose in the original, ah, sixteenth? seventeenth? century Spanish. . . ."

"That is not difficult. Spanish has changed less than English. I have had my trouble trying to read Shakespeare."

"But your English is almost flawless, Orestes. Accented, yes, but fluent, grammatical, large vocabulary. How did you do it?"

"Persistence. It helps, by the way, to read a great deal of inherently entertaining material. I learned much more English from paperback mysteries and science fiction than from any text, or any classics except Mark Twain and Jack London."

"But surely it didn't just happen that way. You must have had a reason."

His affability was lost in sudden harshness. "Many Americans have acquired a good command of Russian," he said.

"What? I'm afraid I don't follow."

"It is well to know the language of the enemy. Especially when one must deal with him daily. Your folk are everywhere in my country and her neighbors. I feel certain the Maccabees learned Greek!"

If he expected her to be shocked, he was mistaken. She nodded and said, "Yes, that's right, you are a Communist, aren't you?"

"You may label me as you desire."

She looked past him. "I know. There are Communists

and Communists, same as there are Christians and Christians. And you were with the junta while it lasted, weren't you?"

"I had the rank of sergeant and was driver for Colonel Ybarra, yes."

"Too bad they lost out. I mean, well, I'm not exactly familiar with happenings down here; I was a faraway suburban housewife with problems of my own, but before then we'd lived in the city and had intellectual friends and— Anyway, it seemed as if the colonels in Santa Ana were trying to reform things. Your country could've gone the route of, well, Mexico, couldn't it have? Maybe it will yet."

"Not while your CIA exists—"

Julia flushed and snapped, "Congress cut its balls off a few years ago, unfortunately for the Afghans and a good many million other people!"

He ignored the interruption. "—Or Haverner, or a number of such monstrosities." His tone became matter-of-fact. "To be frank, the way of the junta was a blind alley, the same as the way of Mexico. One gives the masses precisely enough to make them forget the need for demolishing the whole rotten structure." His smile was rueful. "It is ghastly easy to be corrupted. Look at China."

"So you're on the Soviet side? Well, I guess that figures, what with Cuba being in this part of the world. All right, look at the Gulag, for openers."

"Exaggerated. And a nation under siege cannot afford dissent, it must have unity. The Soviet Union has been under siege by the imperialists from its very founding. Oh, I grant you, security measures have sometimes been unnecessarily harsh." A flicker of fury: "However, madame, you would know what harshness truly means if you had been born with a black or a brown skin."

After a silence, Orestes relaxed and smiled. "Well, well, let us not quarrel," he said. "You are quite a well-informed and liberal woman, I believe, . . . Julia. What are your political views?"

"Not liberal!" she laughed to show she too was anxious to avoid giving offense. "That is, not knee-jerk liberal, I hope. My husband and I—we've always tried to vote for the candidate, not the party. We've been registered Republicans—what else could you be in New York lately?—but I did vote Conservative last few times around. Does that make me the enemy?"

"Not you," he said, grave once more. "I hope with my entire heart you and I shall never have to shoot at each other, Julia. The enemy is the system that forces you to come down here to save your child's life at the whim of a senile lunatic, because he in his time used the people and the land for no ends except his own."

"I don't want to believe, on the other hand, that the future is the anthill you collectivists strive for," she told him. "I'll fight that as hard as I can."

"Suppose," he said, "you could wave a . . . wand? . . . a magic wand, and bring true socialism to your United States overnight. Never mind if you consider it tyranny. Simply admit that it does provide universal medical care. Suppose that socialist government and nothing else could save your daughter. Suppose this, for argument's sake. What would you do?"

Her features writhed. She looked away from him. "I don't know. Please, Orestes."

He patted her hand. "I am sorry, Julia. I did not wish to hurt you. But millions are being hurt around the world. . . . Well. Let us speak of matters more pleasant."

She exerted herself to win his liking.

Matt Flagler woke, blinked, sat with head in hands, shouted, "Hey! Coffee here! Black!" When it came, accompanied by an unfriendly look from a maid who avoided his grope for her bottom, he took a noisy taste and said he wanted some bourbon to flavor it.

Ellis Nordberg entered the living room as Matt was finishing. "Did you have a good nap?" he asked politely.

"Yeah, okay, I guess. What time's it? Sheest, half past five awready!"

"It's smart to stock up on sleep," Ellis said. "Tomorrow Shaddock's bound to put us to something strenuous. And dangerous, I suspect."

Matt peered at the slender white-suited figure which stood above him. "What's your game, Nordberg?"

"As for what my game will be, come my turn, no comment. But as for what I have in mind right now— would you care to join me in my room for a quiet talk?"

"H'm. Bugged."

"Sure. So is this one. Haverner won't blab."

Matt considered the other man awhile. "Okay. Why not?" He did not altogether keep his voice empty of interest.

"We can use your room if you prefer," Ellis said. "I don't have a bottle in mine."

"Naw, yours will do. What kind of juicehead d'you think I am? I'm bored, that's all, bored till I could climb on the ceiling. What a bunch'a pricks they are!" Carefully: "I guess not you, El—Ellis. I haven't had a chance to get to know you, that's all."

"Or I you." They went side by side up the lovely staircase.

Ellis's quarters were predictably ordered and disciplined. (The chambermaid cleaned every morning, but otherwise did not venture to touch a guest's arrangements.) He waved Matt to a chair, took one facing it, and extended the cigarette box. Through closed windows could be seen how the sky thickened. Occasional lightning winked. The trees sounded like surf.

"Well." Matt took a deep pull of smoke, crossed and uncrossed and recrossed his legs, sat back and traded look for look. "I don't guess you invited me here for my Irish eyes."

"No. Not that I'm hostile. Neither do I have any definite offer in mind. I only thought we might do some mutual sounding out."

"Because we already got a team, maybe two, against us? Yeah. But you said you couldn't be bothered with less than the whole million, which is small enough potatoes in business these days."

Ellis pinched forth a smile. "I was right," he said. "You're far from being the oafish simpleton you pretend. . . . Yes, I am after the entire sum. But I want it to invest, not spend, and the rewarding of service is an important investment."

"You mean," Matt responded slowly, "if I help you win, taking a dive myself, you'll give me a few peanuts? No, thanks. I'm hungry for that bread myself."

"Certainly. But imagine you are beaten. It could happen, you know. Afterward I might want an outside assistant."

"If you're not scrubbed first."

"True. True. I suggest it could be to your advantage that I stay in the game, at least through most of it. Insurance for yourself? Maybe. It depends. I repeat, I make no promises, and I ask for none from you. What I do ask is for a better acquaintance with you. You know a fair amount of my history, I almost nothing of yours."

"Why should I tell you?"

"What harm can it do? And it may do good. Listen, suppose you wash out. Then, with no friends here, you'll have nothing, and you did admit you're out of a job. Well, it could be that I—whether I win or lose—I could have well-paid, interesting work for a man who'd taken this chance to prove himself to me."

"Go ahead," Matt agreed after thinking. "Ask me what you want. I might or might not answer. But I won't get mad."

"You're a native Chicagoan, right?" (A nod.) "How old?"

A reluctant: "Forty."

"I have an impression you've, ah, served time."

"Yeah." Matt thought further. "Probation, reform school, three years and later five at Joliet."

"What for?"

"Different. Numbers, armed robbery, but I was a punk kid then. Later I got smart. Drugs. And ask that sweet little Gayle Thayer chick if I wasn't doing a public service."

"Nevertheless, you lost more than eight years."

"Not really. I got along, inside."

"And outside. You married into the . . . Family, correct? And when the States grew too hot for you—I won't ask why—the Family found you a job managing a casino it owned in Vizcaya. The colonels got reform-happy and closed it down. You dared not go home; you had to scrape along as best you could, which was poorly if I know anything about these banana republics. When the old regime was restored, your influential father-in-law had died and you did not get your position back. That's when Haverner's people found you."

Matt squinted at the angular visage. "You've learned a lot, haven't you?"

"You spilled most of it the first evening. The rest is deduction. How are you with a gun, Matt?"

"Damn good. You better believe. Not that I ever cooled anybody, never did that, but I've practiced, pistol, rifle, shotgun, Tommy gun, you name it. I *like* guns."

"M-hm. You interest me more and more."

With the clouds, twilight was gathering in the room. Matt's cigarette end pulsed crimson.

"We have—we could have—a common cause till the final playoff," Ellis said. "Or, if you fail earlier, all the way. Not if I fail before you; that looks pretty clear, aside from a possibility that I might hire you afterward. But here, on this island, it could be worth my while to help you keep in play longer than you might otherwise be able, and the same for you as regards me."

"It could be." The red coal quivered.

"Your turn follows mine," Ellis said. "If we each set tasks the other can perform . . . Do you see? What have you in mind?"

"You go first, so you tell me first."

"I'm still developing my plan. Essentially, it involves solving problems. If I coached you—or got you off the hook if you did fail, like Rance did the Thayer slut—"

"By God!" Matt's palm slapped his knee. "Holy shit!"

"I thought you'd like the idea." Ellis doled out another smile, barely visible on the pale blur of his countenance. "Of course, I give you no promises yet. This is a very, very conditional offer. Show good faith of your own."

"M-m-m . . . well, okay. Maybe you can even help me, Ellis. I haven't figured out the details. I thought—now don't get me wrong, nothing queer about me, but this is for a million bucks and I'm a, you know, unprejudiced person—I thought I might set something that most of them would be bound to object to, more than a million bucks' worth. Get me?"

"For instance?"

"Well, okay, let's say everybody has to bugger everybody else. In public. I don't think the men could do it."

Ellis recoiled a tiny bit, then laughed. "Nor could the women. I'm afraid that proposal would be ruled out on the grounds of physical impossibility."

"Well," Matt said, taken aback, "it was just a sample idea, get me? I'm working on details."

"The basic notion is excellent," Ellis said. "Something unbearably loathsome. But not to me, eh? I don't go for that kind of stuff either; besides, it's against my religion. But we might agree on something—coprophagy?—well, let's discuss it further."

"What'd you say?" Matt didn't pursue his question at once. His jaw thrust forth. "Suppose I do get an idea you can't follow through on."

"That's the chance I take," Ellis answered. "I'll hope I can talk you out of it. However, for the prize on hand —I don't imagine there's much you or I would not do."

Byron took supper in his room, sending down word that contestants could sleep late if they wished, since his game would not start till two hours after an early lunch. At that time they should be dressed for a hike. Somehow this provoked wild merriment around the table, a schoolboy gallows humor shared by everyone except Haverner and Ellis.

About ten in the evening the freakishly leisured storm finally broke over the Island. First the sky above that house where William Walker had slept was taken by absolute night, then the initial hot heavy drops landed, raising puffs of dust where they struck bare soil, then, after a preliminary monstrous sigh, the wind howled itself to full velocity and the rain came solid.

Larry and Gayle were in his room. An outside observer could have seen him at an open window, watching the weather while she waited forlornly in bed. Matt played solitaire in the living room while Ellis read— or, rather, obviously reread—a translation of *Beyond Good and Evil*. They were careful not to speak. Orestes was visiting in the servants' quarters.

Byron came downstairs and, by way of a rear porch, onto the veranda. He stopped outside Haverner's chamber, which was darkened and blinded. Light from the right-hand end of the house fell distant, a somehow bleached yellow, not important to the night that encompassed them. It quickly gulped down all light.

Rain roared, smote and hissed off the ground, dashed itself against the screens. They smelled of wet iron. The wind brawled among trees, hooted over earth, wailed far out to sea. This was no chilly air, it was rushingly welcome after the sullen day, but one felt a deeper cold in it, that absolute zero of empty space which had whistled those energies out of the sun. The house creaked to the violence of the wind; there went a quiver through the veranda planks.

A step, a hand on his arm, a voice: "You too."

He turned his head. She was silhouetted against the window-glow and the rain-spears it touched. "Julia."

"No other." She smiled. "I thought you'd come here to watch."

"Awesome, isn't it?" At close range, normal speech barely won through. Was that why she leaned her cheek against his shoulder?

"Yes. Makes us realize how little we are—oh, damn the clichés." Julia squeezed his arm. For evening she had changed to a low-cut lacy white dress. The skirt flapped around her knees and molded itself to her groins. "Why've you been hiding the whole day, Byron?"

"I didn't want to be pestered." He stared straight before him.

"I sympathize. Don't worry, I won't ask what you'll make us do tomorrow."

"I—" He cleared his throat while maintaining his absorption in the storm. "Julia, I'm sorry we have to be in competition. If . . ." His words trailed off.

"Yes?" She leaned as close as might be.

"Never mind. Fair warning: I've never thrown a bout, and I don't plan to start now."

"Of course. Same here."

"Afterward—"

"We'll go on being friends. You'll come see us, Malcolm and me, at our place, won't you?"

His mouth drew taut. "And Kilby, don't forget Kilby."

"I haven't. Not for one second. . . . You'll enjoy her, Bryon. Don't think of her as a—what's that sticky-sentimental book I read as a kid?—Birds' Christmas Carol. No, she's loaded with life. Used to come stumping to me, arms out, laughing like a maniac, every day when I came home from work. Since the trouble hit her she's been quieter, naturally; she's frail; but she stays bright, she keeps her sense of humor. I was fixing her breakfast and asked her, jokingly, if she wanted a piece of fried plastic. And she looked at me like a judge and said in the most precise tone you can dream of, 'Man has never eaten plastic.' "

"You've told me quite a bit about her," he said.

"I hope I haven't bored you with the subject."

"No."

A flaw of wind went *whoo-oo*.

"All right." She released him and stood a few inches aside. He could no longer decently avoid meeting her gaze. It was veiled anyway in the rainstormy night. "Why insult your intelligence?" she said. "I want to get you interested in the case so that, whatever happens—" Her lids dropped, her fingers twisted.

"I don't have that much money," he said with extreme care. "Or, well, yes, I do, but it's committed. Look, a peasant in India might think you were rich enough to do or buy anything you chose. But you know better. Well, believe me, it's the same for people above your bracket. For instance, besides working on the board of the Helping Hand Foundation, I contribute—"

"Oh, yes, oh, yes." She looked back at him, and he saw the teeth in her smile. "Byron, dear, I am five years older than you. I know maybe a tad more about how complicated life can get. How scrambled and blurred our motives, our hopes always are. It's plain I'm grabbing at whatever handhold I see for Kilby—but it's for our standard of living too, Malcolm's and mine. We don't want to become paupers or wage slaves. Call it selfishness if you will. Only then all but the saints are selfish. You, Byron, you could raise an extra child—let's say one of Orestes Cruz's starveling caneworker children—for what a ski trip to Gstaad costs you. Isn't that true?"

"Yes, . . . in a way, . . . though if you took my trust fund and split it among four billion people—"

"Sure. Let me finish, though. I only wanted to remind you, you aren't in any simple either-or situation yourself. So can't you accept, never mind what happens, can't you accept that I sincerely like you? As I like Orestes, in spite of our agreeing we might someday have to shoot at each other. You and I don't even have an ideology separating us, Byron."

Rain flew on the wind and drummed. He was in her arms.

"Byron," she said after time and no time had gone by,

"my dear, it's been hard for Malcolm and me. Worry and sorrow and—oh, doubtless I've not been what I should be for him, forever thinking about Kilby the way I did, but— he stays away a lot of nights, pleading business. I think he's found another woman. And half the few times when we do come together, he himself is too tired and anxious. ... Byron—"

"What're you *doing?*" He tried to pull free. Her right hand stayed on his neck but her left roved down under his belt.

"We're having a vacation from reality, aren't we?" she said.

He slapped her across the mouth. "Bitch!" he yelled.

She stepped back. "Byron—" A hand went to the place which hurt.

"Get me into bed! Su-ure. A more effective Larry Rance. You might even have fun, right? And it's guaranteed pure because you're saving your little girl. She-wolf Julia! Well, I say bitch and I say to hell with you!"

He fled from her astonishment, inside and upstairs. The wind, the rain went ramping.

BYRON SHADDOCK

Today's weather is more conventionally tropical-wet. The air blows hard, dances about, often makes a brief leap in strength. It plays with trees and bamboos and quickly bursting showers like a cat with a ball. Clouds race across heaven. Sometimes they cover it altogether in wild gray— then the water brawls down—and sometimes, tinged by sun and rainbows, they fly singly across its incredible blue.

The sea is full of waves. Gunmetal, green, white, they tumble out yonder, rumble in onto the beach, explode, withdraw in a huge hollow roar for the next attack. (What a chance to repeat that test of Rance's which he botched so miserably! But Haverner, via Anselmo, said no, it's too rough now, most of us could absolutely not do it. A drowned person can no longer scuttle through your rat maze, eh, Haverner?) Several gulls are aloft, planing, gliding, veering, most beautiful of birds above this planet. How often have I wished to be, for a while, a gull!

Inland, to my left, I see a vulture, who likewise rides the wind, though his sea is the gold-and-emerald raindrop-jeweled shouting jungle. The Crag was invisible when we left the house, obscured by vapors, but as we move north its dim bulk begins to emerge.

The trail is muddy between stiff grasses and luxuriant shrubs. Water gurgles along it, for the blufftops over which it snakes are gradually turning into the Iron Cliffs. That southern scarp of the Bight looms ahead, black as a robber baron's castle walls, but above stands a fragrance of cedar trees where Julia and I . . .

"Anselmo!" I call back over my shoulder.

"Yes?" He, imperturbably striding at the end of the parade, trots toward me, past my single-file rivals.

What can I ask him? "I, well, that is . . ." Walking at my back, he waits.

"Do you really think we'll have clear skies by sundown?"

He must know I am asinine, for not alone did he reassure me on this point in the morning. Captain York did, and afterward a call to the meteorological office in Ciudad Vizcaya. But he keeps his sang-froid. "Yes, we will, I am sure."

"Thank you," I said. "It's . . . important to my plan."

"Ees that what you weeshéd to know?"

"Yes. Yes, thanks."

He returns to his station. Does he suspect what I intend? (I may be courting a humiliating prohibition, but somehow I could not bring myself to discuss it beforehand.) He made no inquiry, merely nodded, when I recommended that, along with the drinking water he's backpacking for us, he discreetly stow thick gloves and whatever he could find to serve as a face mask for himself.

Does *he* know what was in the package for Ellis Nordberg, which the plane delivered (from where?) shortly before we left today? (Actually flying in this weather! I'd have loved to be the pilot. . . . What does Nordberg have in mind? Beware of him. Cold devils are the worst kind. Well, the more pleasure in besting them.)

Matt Flagler says, in his hard-flat Chicago voice, "Okay, what is your plan, Shaddock? Wanna walk us into the ground? I don't think that'd be allowed."

"No," Gayle Thayer whimpers. "It wouldn't be fair. I'm not a long-distance hiker or mountain climber or, or anything."

I make myself stop and confront them. They stop likewise. The order of march has worked out to: Orestes, Matt, Ellis, Gayle, Larry, Julia. (Thank you, Julia, for your tact, or are you brooding on hatred of me?) Everyone has donned the outdoor garb that was thoughtfully brought to each room, in the proper size, on our first day. In chin-strapped solar helmets, light long-sleeved shirts, chino pants, stout shoes, sopping wet and smeared with clay in spite of the ponchos rolled up under their arms, they look strangely interchangeable. Or is it that, to me, all humans are interchangeable? I do my duty, but I am not a passionate man.

"Have no fears," I tell them. "Not of being required to exceed your strength, anyhow. Your nerve will be tested. We'll soon reach the first spot." I turn about and resume my pace.

My feet squelch. The mud sucks at them. My garments are heavy too. Wind smites, blood-warm. On my left is a gloom of jungle, on my right, quite far down by now, dashes the sea. Somewhere a woodpecker drums, a flock of parrots make buzz-saw shrieks. It reminds me of Brazil, where I swam in the great brown river they warned me held piranhas. What a letdown to learn a year afterward, from that naturalist in New York, piranhas have never in provable fact been known to kill a man!

Vietnam was perhaps not unlike this Tanoa. I did want to serve, I did, unchic though it would be. Never mind the rights and wrongs; combat must be some kind of ultimate experience. But my draft number never came up (I can't prove my suspicions as to precisely why; it could be chance) and, of course, given Father's constituency, I couldn't volunteer. I couldn't do that to him.

Here we are!

I say this aloud. They cluster close. I must shift position a trifle to cut Julia out of my direct view. I point. "Look that way." We are about at the commencement of what may correctly be designated the Iron Cliffs. The beach beneath has pinched out to a boulder-strewn striplet of sand over which the breakers crash. The descent is steep, cragged, cracked, here and there a talus slope, everything of a murky hue that deepens while the sky closes for another shower. Wind hoots.

"We climb down to the bottom and back," I say.

Gayle utters a parrot-squawk. "Hey, wait," Matt exclaims. "Wait a goddamn minute!" Ellis, cool and precise: "We are not experienced mountaineers like you. This is unfair."

I shake my head. "No. I've been the route myself. It requires no special skill. A real climber would call it a Sunday stroll. I'll lead, and you can follow my way if you choose, or take an alternate if that looks better to you. You needn't hurry; find your own speed."

"But if I slip!" Gayle wails. "I could be killed!"

"You could." I regard her. A tingle goes through me. "You'll have to take care. The rocks are slippery from rain and some are loose. Down below, you can lose your footing and be swept out by an undertow. But any person in normal health, which we all are, can make it if he keeps his wits about him. And it's not compulsory, remember. You can resign."

She stares at Anselmo, finding no mercy, before she appeals: "Larry!" The big man thinks a few seconds, then says, "No, it's a proper challenge." It is as if he struck her in the face.

As I did Julia— Quickly, quickly: "I assume Anselmo will come along, ready to help whoever gets into difficulties. Am I right?"

"Yes," the Indian says.

"Let's go!" I toss my poncho aside, drop to hands and knees, feel for the initial solidity, and commence my descent.

Orestes comes after me. He uses those long awkward limbs of his to better effect than I would have imagined. Larry is right behind him. The spider and the bear. And the woman—Julia—do I see how she studies precisely what we forerunners do before she imitates? She would.

Matt, obscenely cursing, next picks his path. Ellis is slow and cautious but, stiffly, he comes. Gayle goes last, shivering, blubbering, sometimes yelling the name of Larry, who ignores her. No, the last one is Anselmo. Spider, bear, woman, ape, machine, sheep, wolfhound. ... What is Byron Shaddock? Man?

Man, Byron Shaddock?

The world glides from beneath me. I barely recover. The dislodged rock clatters and bounds down through skirling wind to cannonading surf.

All right, Julia, damn you, I enjoyed your company as much as I've enjoyed any woman's, till you shoved your genitalia at me. That's when you wrecked the relationship. I do not propose to repeat those episodes in college and shortly after. ("Can't get it up?" asked the first. "Fainting at the threshold," giggled the second. The third—) Not that I mind staying celibate—it took me two otherwise useless psychiatrists to realize that I don't really mind —but the fact is nobody else's business. I have my sense of privacy. Hence I squire the young ladies whom I am expected to squire, and everybody says what a perfect gentleman I am. What is this ludicrous Hugh Hefner notion that incessant sexuality is as necessary to a man as it is to a buck rabbit?

It's reverse Puritanism; that's what it is. It sells a lot of magazines and other products; that's what it does. And I pay it its tribute, I too, in sly hints and sniggers directed at the appropriate acquaintances, oh, yes, I have my women but I don't choose to make a public display of them; frankly, I don't care much for American (English, French, Italian, Yugoslav) girls after having been in Rio, Morocco, the South Seas. . . .

Bad spot here. Breath comes heavy. Fingers strain. How hard and wet-cold the rock is, how beautiful. Bones of the planet. "The solid and enduring bone." I am quick to read every fashionable book, but Housman I always return to when I am by myself. He staves off the silent screams.

Blue-blackness boils overhead. The rain comes galloping. Its million lances strike home; it halloos and laughs, under bugles of wind. Easy, easy. *Festina lente.* However great the temptation to play mountain goat, remember, you too can err, you (like Larry before you) can throw the game you called (he did). A broken leg could be used against you, day after tomorrow, and force you out of this evilly fascinating strife.

You've snapped enough bones in the past, Byron Shaddock, skiing, motorcycling, climbing; it's more luck than skill that that Cape buffalo dropped dead of your bullets before he reached you; nobody doubts Byron Shaddock's courage. But today, have a care.

Wind howls. No, that's human terror! I cling to the ribs of the world and peer desperately upward. I don't want to cause anyone's death. Truly I don't!

Gayle, of course. The poor little sloven put her feet on a loose rock that spun off from beneath her and left her sliding toward yonder sheer dropoff. She's dead! . . . Unless—

Anselmo pounces. No wolfhound in this moment, he's jaguar, how lovely to see! He snatches her ankle. I don't myself comprehend how he braces his body where he is. But he hauls her back from the final quietness. I shout shaken thanks which are lost in the rain and wind.

It soon becomes clear she's hysterical, in no shape to proceed. He assists her back to the trail. No doubt she pleads for her Larry. But Larry can't come; that'd eliminate him too. Probably the rest of them squint through the quicksilver torrent at me. I continue.

First down, five to go.

I wouldn't mind having that million at my beck. It's not an unmixed pleasure, being dependent on a trust established by one's grandfather. I have sufficient intelligence and guts to admit that I have no special competence, and a lifetime of plodding through the nice secure executive suites of the family businesses holds no attraction. I made this quite plain to Father and Mother, immediately upon my graduation with gentlemanly grades. A million of my own, and I could break entirely free.

Anselmo reappears in a dwindling rain. I continue. It is good that strict concentration is required.

The descent is long.

I end on the tiny beach.

A breaker bursts around me, over me. Almost it takes me, out and out to the deeps beyond. I cut my hands, clinging to a pair of barnacled boulders while the green fury (sunlight overhead again) takes me in its teeth and shakes me.

O God, it's like that time at Copacabana, I swam too far from shore without noticing and suddenly the waves had me, threw me about, helpless, down to scrape my cheek across the sand, up for the quickest gasp before I was hauled back under. . . . I knew I could easily die. I stayed cool (I always am in a crisis) and husbanded my strength, gained what yards I might toward the beach, until the lifeguards arrived. . . . But always, always was that thunderous green peace, and at the heart of it, shining like the sun which broke through those billows, Tommy Wilson waited.

I seize my chance, crawl back out of reach, start my return. Larry Rance passes me on his own way down. He grins and gives me a "thumbs up." You're a fine opponent, Larry, when the guilt isn't yours. You ought to be a still finer one, now that that cheap cunt—

What guilt is mine? Suppose we had had a death today?

Suppose, as Julia said, I went on a peasant's budget and divided my money—at any rate, that part of it I can spend on myself—among selected families. I could, but I don't. Thus I am indirectly starving children. Or, if we assume the earth is overbloated with man, I am letting wildlife and wilderness perish that I could help save.

And likewise is every comfortable American, European, whoever has more than he needs for survival. Do they feel guilty? No. Then why should I?

I hurt nobody. I go my own way, and those who choose may play my game, but I don't force it on them.

I proceed, inch by marvelously demanding inch, to the heights.

Gayle isn't there. Doubtless she lay in the rain and mud awhile, weeping, then stumbled back to the house. I wonder why Haverner picked such a futile character. To be a tool for someone else? He's a hypnotic figure. A demon? A natural force?

I sit down in the wet grass and regain air. Sunlight slants through thinning clouds. It's from low above those hills that hump darkling, south of the Crag. Our expedition has taken hours.

Larry comes over the rim. For an instant, the light upon his bright hair under the face-shadowing solar topee . . . I thought he was Tommy, and eternity stood still.

Oh, no. Oh, no.

He joins me, puffs a prosaic minute, hauls out pipe and tobacco pouch. "Wow, you picked a mean one!" he says.

"We're not done yet," answers my throat.

(I know the theory. Schools on the English public model can breed certain traits. But nothing ever happened. Nothing except friendship, and his beauty like sun and stars, and his cruel death of meningitis at age sixteen. It's common. See Kinsey and all the popularizers in his wake. If anything, the abnormality would lie in never having felt any such emotion. I needn't cite, oh, Alexander and Hephaestion; I need merely go on with my life.

(Very well, let's go on with it.)

We have a long wait until Ellis, the last, rounds the cliff edge, followed by guardian Anselmo. Meanwhile, though the wind continues strong, clouds mostly blow away. Those that remain, eastward oversea, are tinged golden against bottomless blue clarity. The Crag looms stark, deepening minute by minute toward black.

"Congratulations," Ellis says. "On our first elimination, I mean. Now we've begun to get somewhere." Businessman, confidant of bankers, he sits beside the half-liquid trail with the same glee, open or ill-concealed, as do the bear, the spider, the woman, the ape. Anselmo gives away no feelings, but stays on his feet above us.

"The rules better allow for middle-aged shortwindedness, however," Ellis adds.

"Of course," I reply in my diplomatic voice. "We can take a few more minutes here. Then we'll go a couple of miles further, in no hurry, for my final challenge."

"What'll that be?" Matt demands. The ape, bred to a concrete forest, turns uneasy again, then sullen.

I smile and do not speak.

Larry laughs toward Orestes. "I hope you'll pick something less strenuous."

"I believe I will," he replies, amiable and impassive.

Julia smiles very faintly toward those two. She has scarcely said a word this whole day.

"All right," I tell them after a proper interval, and rise. "Shall we proceed?"

I have scouted the area and know my way. Climb further north, almost to the cedars where Julia and I had such a vivacious picnic. (Now night rises under them.) Here the ground surges inland toward the Crag; in that geological time wherein I am a drop of flung spume, this is a billow. A dimmer, narrower path which Anselmo has explained to me was made by free-browsing goats (will those *animales de Castilla* ruin this land as they ruined Greece and her isles, and will it then show forth the same skeletal comeliness?) leads from the human trail. That's a steep walk. I hear them breathe hard behind me. We cross a ridge where the wind catches at us and go down into a glen. There the air is nearly still, but shadows are heavy and it's hard to see, vines catch at feet, withes at eyes, while the sky above is burnished lapis lazuli to west, where clouds run molten gold.

What do I almost remember? I was here once before, long ago, this very place, this exact blue and ruddy hour, but somebody else was beside me. . . . This evening I remember, across many years, how when I was small I used to escape from my governesses into fantasies about the sister that Mother was always going to give me.

She never did, of course. It kept being postponed: inconvenient for the wife and social director of a bright young Navy commander, bright young partner in our century-old investment brokerage, bright young leader in worthy causes, bright young congressman, bright young senator. No doubt I owe my own existence to the fact that a child, just one, would be a substantial political asset.

I remember, I remember, I called my sister Maria. You slip among these shadows beside me, Maria, and I ache for the coolness of your hands I shall never kiss.

A second harsh ascent and: "Here we are," I pant. "Take five." They straggle to me and look around, taut as if they awaited an ax blow.

We are on the highest hill in the immediate vicinity. Westward they break against bare Crag and here-discernible bronze-hazed Peak. Grass, bent by the noisy wind, ripples beneath a ceiba, easily a hundred and fifty feet tall and more than thick to match, whose foliage makes a cave around its roots. The lower leaves roar, the slimmer middle branches creak, the uppermost boughs are thin and toss insanely, silhouetted on ultramarine. The sun has gone behind the hills, to leave them black athwart that streaming furnace of clouds. The east is royal purple, and a planet stands not far above the sea-gleam.

"What next?" Julia says. I suppose even her nerves are tattered. "Don't forget, it isn't safe here this time of day."

"Take five," I repeat. "You'll need them." I turn my back on her appalled gaze. Evidently she masters herself, for I hear nothing further from her.

Matt swears, trying to light a cigarette. Larry finishes his pipe. They are the only smokers. Julia told me she quit to economize; Orestes and Ellis are moderate users who abstain at present. I wonder why tobacco has never tempted me. Well, I'm austere in all things except adventure. Not that I don't appreciate good food, drink, clothing, music, art, literature. I simply don't overindulge, and I leave the unrewarding vices alone.

"Time," I decide, and say into their attention, "we'll climb this tree to the top. I've tried, and it's entirely possible, not even especially tiring when the limbs are so close together. I'll take the lead. Anselmo should be able to judge from the ground whether or not we all eventually settle onto an equivalently hazardous roost."

"Huh?" Matt yelps. "You crazy nut! In this wind? No!"

"I do not have a man's strength for clinging," Julia puts in.

"You don't need that," I tell them. "Settle into a fork. Make yourselves fast with your belts if you like. We'll stay till dark."

"And climb down blind?" Ellis protests. "No, I agree, this is madness."

"You don't have to play," I answer. "I'm as likely to have my bough break under me, or misgauge and fall to my death creeping down by night, as anybody else."

Shivers in my scrotum and out to the ends of my flesh!

Anselmo recalls me a little by saying, surprisingly, " 'Ave you forgotten, Meester Shaddock? The bats come out at dusk. Een thees weather, maybe not many, but some, and some of them 'ave the 'ydrophobia."

"That's why I urged you to bring protection for yourself, Anselmo. The rest of us must take our chances." My look is focused upward, to the flicker of blackness, green, gold, and orange, the beating heart of a lover.

"No!" Matt howls across the groans and mutters of his companions. "No, I won't you crazy summabitch. No, listen, Anselmo, you call your boss. I gotta right you should call your boss!"

"Absolutely," Ellis concurs. "Pasteur treatment is no use if you're bitten on the head, and rabies is one of the worst ways to die there is."

"Go home now, then," I retort. "Or if you have bad luck—though really, the odds are much in your favor—if you are unlucky, you may have the tablets I always carry against that kind of need."

"My religion forbids. Call Mr. Haverner, Anselmo."

Meanwhile Larry and Orestes, by threats as much as anything else, have somewhat calmed Matt. Anselmo speaks rapid-fire Spanish into the set. I hear the dry response: *"Es satisfactorio."* What gloating is Haverner's? Or does he, in horrible pathos, mourn that he is too old to climb among us?

Matt rages anew and tries to attack me. He is stopped by Anselmo, who decks him in about three motions which are hard to see through the murk growing beneath the mighty tree. He sobs where he lies. Well, well, he managed when solid rock was beneath him, but my guess is he has an acrophobia which could not endure swaying in the wind a hundred feet up.

Me, I can't wait. "Come if you dare," I say, and swarm aloft.

One by one they follow, with more or less alacrity, more or less skill; they rise, hauled on the hook of Haverner's million.

Except Matt. He tries, can't do it, worms his way back to earth and ululates vileness.

I pay him no heed. His noise is soon lost in the immense voice of the leaves. Picking my way, branch by whipping branch, muscles alive as once they lived beneath Tommy's fair smooth skin, I see sky overhead through the green darkness that encloses me. I see the first of the evening bats. Golden, the last sunlight shines through his wings.

INTERVAL FIVE

Everyone slept late the following day, except Byron. He, who had avoided a turbulent supper table, set his alarm clock in order that a couple of Tanoan youths might take him fishing as arranged earlier. Their boat cast off at dawn. Calm had descended upon the Island, cloudless clarity, dazzling brightness, slow rise of temperature and humidity.

Larry got breakfast about ten and established himself, his pipe, and a copy of *Eothen* he had found, in a deck chair at the tree-shaded east end of the patio. Flowerbeds blazed to his left. The lawn rolled solid green until it ended in the complex hues and shapes of wild brush. Far downward, glimpsed between several feathery-topped coyal palms, lay a white gleam of sea.

He was chuckling somewhat wistfully over Kinglake's reminiscences when a slither of sandals, the blotting out of sun flecks on flagstones, caught his attention. Glancing up, he saw Julia. His look remained. She was in her bikini, had obviously been in the lagoon. Drops still gleamed on bosom, flanks, thighs. "Hi," she said. "Lazy bird. You should've come with me."

"I would've, if I'd known." He half rose. She waved him back and drew another chair alongside his on the right. "But after yesterday," he said, "frankly, I figure I rate some loafing."

"Oh, I intend to do likewise." She lowered herself. "Refreshment first, however."

"Haven't you eaten? I'll holler for service."

"No, I'm not hungry yet, thanks. A cup of coffee was ample. I'll have brunch." She removed her bathing cap (unlike Gayle, she kept her armpits smooth) and shook down the dark-ruddy hair. "It's taking me a while to get my appetite back—the swim helped me more than any food—after yesterday."

134

"That was rough, for sure." Larry held eyes on her, drew breath, and blurted, "You've changed your opinion of him, then?"

She nodded. "Yes. He seemed, he was on the surface, pleasant, cultured, amusing. But what he put us to, well, I doubt his sanity. I honestly do."

He shrugged. "We survived. Two dropped out, but they weren't otherwise hurt. The game's getting stiff."

"You wouldn't have let it go that far. You didn't."

"I aim to hang on, Julia."

"Of course. Me too. But we . . . Let's say I hope to play my turn your way." She reached for the book on his lap. "What're you reading?" When she raised it, her knuckles brushed his legs, which were in shorts. "Oh, yes."

"Found it in the library here," he said. "Fun."

"The whole way through, Larry. I expect a sailor like you will get a real kick out of, oh, what happened in the storm off Cyprus. Have you come to that part?"

"No, I'm, uh, still in Servia. Serbia? No, they—"

"Ah, yes. That wonderful line—let me see—" She leafed through the pages. "Here. 'Endless and endless now on either side the tall oaks closed in their ranks, and stood gloomily lowering over us, as grim as an army of giants with a thousand years' pay in arrear.' " They laughed together.

She returned the book, caught his hand, and said, "Larry, you're my kind of people. Or better. You know, I never have thanked you properly for what you did—or didn't do—that day when you watched me in the surf."

"Aw-w-w," he began, and shifted to: "Well, a lady in distress. In a need worse'n mine, I must agree."

She sighed. "It's a gruesome situation, isn't it? Those who ought to be friends, ought to help each other, forced to fight and connive and even make danger of death."

He laid down his pipe and leaned nearer her till the scent of her locks reached him through all honeysuckle odors. "Right. Damn it, I am glad my turn's past and nobody hurt. Your shoulder is okay now, isn't it?"

"Oh, a scratch, just a scratch, Larry. The bruise you see is incidental. I bruise easy but I heal quick, to make a startlingly original remark."

"Good. I'm glad." His free hand stroked hers.

"Not everybody has to be corrupted, do they?" she asked. "Need is not the same as greed."

He fell quiet and alert.

"We . . . some of us . . . might settle for less than the entire prize," Julia said. "If we don't have to have the full amount, why compromise our honor?"

"M-m-m. Yeah, why?"

Julia disengaged herself from him with utmost gentleness, lay back, looked for a time across land and sea, and finally murmured, "Such a gorgeous world. Such fantastic beauty. So much to do out there, know, discover, love."

"M-hm."

"That's all I want. To keep my Kilby in this world." She turned back toward him. "And you, am I right, you want to live in the whole world yourself, fully, a free man."

He nodded.

"I'd like to hear more about your plans," Julia said. "What few hints I've gotten sound fabulous." She straightened. "Tell you what," she continued eagerly, "let's dress for a walk, have 'em pack us a lunch, and—if you don't find the associations too bad—I know a real little paradise above the Iron Cliffs."

Orestes chose to read on the veranda.

Ellis and Matt exchanged a few words in a corner. Subsequently, at different times, they announced they wanted a stroll and left in different directions. They returned likewise, a couple of hours later.

Gayle woke in the early afternoon, came downstairs, inquired about Larry, fled in tears when a servant informed her that Mr. Rance and Mrs. Petrie had long since departed.

Byron arrived in high spirits. He had caught a tarpon. Rather than sit in the living room after his shower, he took a gin and tonic through the north door and found Orestes absorbed in his book.

"*Buenas tardes,*" he greeted.

Orestes smiled. "You wish to join me," he answered. "Do."

Byron sat down beside him. "Care for a drink?"

"No, thank you, I will wait until evening."

Byron studied the smooth swart countenance. It gave him nothing in return but that faint, changeless good humor it had carried this whole day. "I hope," Byron said, "you aren't too furious with me."

"No. You took the same risks. It is true I am happy there were no casualties and that I, in particular, was not eliminated."

"What a strange feeling," Byron mused. "Having that experience—not the action *per se,* that wasn't so special, but the people, my influence on their lives—having that behind me."

"Did you look forward to your turn?"

"As a sportsman. Believe me, not because I wanted, ever wanted power over anybody else. In fact, that's the strangeness, that I have had the power, that I have changed lives."

"We each do that, simply by existing, no?" Orestes lit a Santa Anan cigarette. Sulfurous yellow drifted on the simmering air. "It is the fallacy in Buddhism that one can escape responsibility by staying passive. The question is, do we influence for good or evil?"

Byron frowned. "No doubt you'd rate me under evil."

"Not your intentions. And to speak the truth, I enjoyed your challenge. No, I think I like you, Byron Shaddock, and regret the waste of a potential in you which may be very great. Let us talk, if you wish. I am curious about your milieu, and you perhaps would be interested if I took you behind some of the clichés about mine."

"Thanks. Yes. I would be." Byron drank. The ice tinkled in his glass; the chains of the porch swing creaked. A servant padded by, immaculately white-clothed, dark-skinned and blue-eyed.

"And I could take *you* behind a cliché or three," Byron offered.

"Let us not argue politics," Orestes said. "Let us get acquainted as two men."

"Okay." Byron plunged. "How do you feel about your turn tomorrow?"

Orestes chortled deep in his throat. "That would be telling." His mirth drew a disconcerted stare, and he proceeded quickly. "We might begin, if you want, by you describing what you have seen of my country."

Larry and Julia returned when the sun touched the hills. They were dusty, sweaty, and merry. On the steps she released his hand. "I've got to beat everyone else to a bath," she said. "If I stood around indoors, smelling myself, I'd keel over."

"I wouldn't," he answered. "If I were smelling you, that is."

She grinned at him. He stood where he was and looked till she was gone.

Gayle came around the hog plum tree. "Larry!" she exclaimed. Her voice was still scratchy from last night's sobbing in his arms. The swollenness had not quite left her eyes nor the blotchiness her cheeks.

"Oh. Hello," he said. "Feel better?"

She stopped before him and stared through the long shadows. "Why didn't you call me when you got up, honey?"

"I figured you needed the sleep."

She tugged at his sleeve. "Come onto the patio. Let's sit and talk. I've missed you so, all day."

He resisted. "I have to go wash."

She forced a *moue* and a finger-wagging. "Oh, poof! I know you. What you want first is beer."

He gave in and let her draw him around the house onto the flagstones. Light dwelt tawny on grass, among leaves; it seemed to fill the air, which had relaxed into warmth. A hummingbird was busy at a nearby jasmine bush; a mockingbird made sweetness against the remote yells of homebound parrots, the muted noise of surf.

"Sit." She pushed him into a chair. "I'll get your brew."

She pattered off. He scowled, drew forth his pipe, stuffed and kindled it. She came back with remarkable promptitude, bearing two frosty Pilsener glasses on a tray. "The first'll go down fast," she said in uncertain gaiety, gave it to him, put its mate on the deck at his left and herself into the seat on the right which had been Julia's. Her thighs squashed out from her shorts.

"Thanks," he grunted.

One hand sought his arm. Being occupied, neither of his made response. "I'm sorry you didn't call me," she said. "Maybe I did need the sleep. But I need you worse, Larry."

"I felt restless." He looked into foam, gulped half the glassful, breathed deeply. "Aaah! That does go good."

"Can't take much beer along on a hike, can you? Where'd you go, . . . you and Julia?"

His head gestured. "To the Bight."

She winced. "There? I'll never be able to again."

"I won't ask you to."

Silence followed until she stirred and said, "Okay. I was beaten. I'm out of the game officially. But that Byron —he's got to be out of his gourd, don't you think? It wasn't just what he did, it was how. It's awful knowing anybody can be like that. That's how come I, well, I guess I panicked a little afterward."

"I thought I soothed you." Nothing else had happened between them last night in her room. His consolations, spoken and stroked, had been mechanical.

"But Larry." She rolled onto her left hip so that her right hand also could seize him. "You don't understand. When you came back and I learned what he'd made *you* do, that's what threw me. I could've lost *you*."

"By the time you learned, we were home safe," he snapped.

"But—"

"Look. Competition's escalating. We knew it would. Please belay telling me over and over. I'm tired."

"We're partners, Larry." She clutched.

He put the pipe between his teeth and pried her grasp loose. "Ouch," he said. "Watch those fingernails."

"I'm sorry," she whispered.

"Tomorrow," he said, "I go back on the line. God knows what Orestes is planning."

"I can help you, though! We agreed! I can help you from the sidelines! Just tell me what to do!"

"We talked about the possibility," he said. "Nothing else."

"We agreed! You swore—"

"I didn't swear one mucking thing except that we'd see if we could maybe help each other, and make a fair split if things happened to work out that way." The words rapped from him. His eyes glittered at her. "Well, how the devil can I tell what tomorrow will be like?"

She cowered in her seat. One arm lifted as he rose. "Larry, you can't, you promised, you—"

"Pipe down. I let you off once, didn't I? Maybe we can still work together somehow, but I'm finished carrying freeloaders, you savvy? And I'm tired. I've got to get rested. You leave me be tonight."

He strode from her and the beer she had fetched him.

"Well, well," Haverner murmured. "A full company at supper, eh? How delightful."

He made no comment on the changed seating arrangements. Julia remained on his left, but she had entered early on Larry's arm, he thus taking Byron's former place. Gayle had beaten Ellis to his usual chair at the foot of the table. After an exchange of glances, the latter settled at Haverner's right, Byron beyond him. Orestes and Matt were as before. They appeared the most self-possessed, the Santa Anan affable and unreadable, the Chicagoan sober and watchful. Byron's ongoing exhilaration made the wineglass shake in his grasp; Ellis's mouth occasionally twitched sideways; Julia and Larry kept joining looks, and their cheer of the day had yielded to a stiffness; Gayle, who had drunk a considerable amount in a corner by herself during cocktails, stared muzzily now at her plate, now at the prints hung on the north wall.

"I must confess, however, I found yesterday evening's conversation more animated," Haverner said.

"Damn Byron Shaddock," the New Englander laughed in a high voice. "Damn everybody who won't damn Byron Shaddock. Damn everybody who won't sit up all night damning Byron Shaddock."

Matt's fingers closed around the silver of a knife.

"There was bitterness, for sure," Ellis said.

"Me, I kept still," Larry told Byron.

"And I . . ." Julia waited till he must look at her before she smiled and finished. "I was not ungrateful for being shown something of what to expect from you. And from the remaining players, of course."

"How about that, huh, Orestes?" Matt said. "C'mon, be a sport. What you got lined up?"

"Wait and see," was the mild reply. "I promise you this, it will be a quiet game."

Gooseflesh stood forth on Julia's bare shoulders. Gayle giggled.

Following the meal, the silence of which had been filled mainly by Larry's and Byron's carefully-not-overdone tales of past experiences in odd corners of life, she was first to leave. "Brandy and soda over ice," she told the butler. "Easy on the soda. And the ice." She cast herself into a corner armchair and groped on the end table for a cigarette.

"I beg your pardon, Mrs. Thayer." Ellis had appeared. He detained the butler. "Could I suggest coffee instead?"

"What's this?" Gayle flared. "Who do you think you are?"

"A middle-aged man who's been through a wringer," Ellis answered. To the butler: "Coffee for two." Getting no spoken contradiction from her, the Islandman went off. Ellis took one of the chairs that had been used in her attempt, drew it close and said, "I've been hoping for a chance to let you know how sorry I am you didn't make it."

"You? Sorry?" Gayle threw back her head and stretched her lips. "That's a laugh!"

"We disagree about a lot of things, true, but that doesn't mean I can't sympathize. Do you mind if I smoke a cigar?"

"No, I guess not." Defiance: "But you mind what I smoke."

"Do I?" Ellis raised his sparse brows. "Not necessarily. You young people jump to so many conclusions about my generation. Ever stop to think you could be wrong about some of us at least?"

"Well." Gayle regarded him for a while. "Yeah, maybe I do want coffee."

They chatted about neutral matters, places they had mutually visited, chances of the baseball teams, for a pair of cups each. It went more easily than might have been expected. Elsewhere in the room Byron and Matt had found a television program in common, a suspense movie. No others were present.

"Maybe we—you—better turn in soon," Gayle said at length. "Orestes wants you here at seven, doesn't he?"

"Plenty of time," Ellis replied. "He's visiting his, ha,

proletarian friends. And Julia and Larry are out admiring the night scenery, I guess."

"What're you hinting?"

"How about a breath of fresh air?"

When they got to their feet, Matt glanced in their direction. Ellis shook his head a trifle. Matt nodded as inconspicuously and stayed put. Ellis conducted Gayle outdoors, down a path between rosebushes.

Dew glistened heavy upon these. Stars in their hordes seemed to match the absent moon. The world reached silver-gray and black, darkly ashine where the sea lay. Insects stridulated. The air was motionless, gently warm, tinged with growth fragrances.

Ellis pulled on his cigar till its end rivaled the fireflies. "I don't often wish I were young again," he said. "But this kind of place—"

"Listen, I don't feel, you know, sociable," Gayle warned.

"Ha! I hardly expect you would, lady. Nor do I, not that way. No, what I mainly wish is that I didn't ache all over from what I've gone through and didn't have to dread what that damned Commie's plotting for tomorrow."

Gayle nodded. "I thought that was what you were getting at," she said in a harder tone than hitherto. "Okay, Ellis, let's not bullshit. Tell it like it is. What do you want of me and what am I offered?"

"You're really a very practical girl under that hippie act of yours, aren't you?"

"I've got to be. Nobody else is about to look out for Gayle Thayer. I thought different . . ." Her voice dissolved but soon recrystallized. "Seems like I was wrong. Unless something new happens, I'm finished here."

"Maybe something new could happen."

"Like what?" Anxious animation broke through. She stopped and swung around to face him. He halted too. They were at the botanical garden, as if having sought the concealment of its overshadowing wall.

"Well, now," he temporized, "that's hard to say when we've no idea about how matters will develop."

Gayle stamped her foot. "Look, man, do you want my help or don't you? It's not for free. Win, lose, or draw, I demand honest pay."

"For honest work. Ye-e-es." He streamed smoke across

the gloom. "A retainer. . . . All right. I've got traveler's checks along, ready to endorse over to you. A flat payment for joining my side. A second payment if I call on you to do something for me and you try your best but I don't make it. Everything'll have to be played by ear, you realize, and you'll have to stand ready to jump at my command, or my straw boss's command, with no questions asked.

"If I win the whole million, that second payment, added to the first, will be enough to give you the full sum you want. If I have to share the prize with other players, the amount to you will be prorated.

"We'll discuss the exact figures later. Right now, though, are you agreeable in principle?"

She pondered.

"Suppose I do try hard on your account, but you wash out anyway," she said after a time. "Who's to decide if I really did try?"

"Matt Flagler. He's joined me on similar conditions. He'll be your straw boss that I mentioned." Dryly: "I'd like you to keep him honest in turn."

"I won't . . . do just anything, Ellis. Got to draw the line somewhere."

"I can't force you," he said almost uninterestedly. "What I can do is refuse to pay you that second part of your wage, and it'll be a lot bigger than the first." With a quick sharpness from which she recoiled: "Whether or not you join me, whether or not you stick it out with me, you'll keep everything you may have seen or heard secret. Starting from this minute. Get me? Blab, and you're in bad trouble."

"I . . ." She made fending motions.

His cigar traced a genial gesture. "Don't be scared, Gayle," he said easily. "That wasn't a threat. Let's just say that you won't ever—how do they put it—won't ever spill your guts to the fuzz. Not even if you don't quite like what you know."

She gulped and nodded, a motion barely visible.

"Anyhow," he continued, "we hope we won't have to get too tough, you and Matt and I. We'll fight as fair as the rest, or fairer. Only if someone turns really mean— well, in that case, it says in Ezekiel, 'Ye have plowed wickedness, ye have reaped iniquity.' "

"You got a cigarette?" she asked in a tiny voice.

He took a pack from his jacket and followed it with flame. She appeared to draw strength from the smoke, which presently she mingled with his while she said, firm once more, "Okay, it sounds pretty good, but we'll have to get some reality on it first. Like, what kind of money are you thinking about for me?"

The tub in Haverner's private bathroom was an antique in itself, claw-footed, long and narrow as a coffin. He stretched out and felt water rise warm around him.

Awake earlier than usual, he saw the first sunlight in a window above. It brightened the dimness he had let remain here, but not much as yet, except on the swirling surface of the water. There its gleams formed what might have been the changeable sketch of a face, just over his withered loins. Gush from the faucets and splash beneath them might have carried words.

"You do not intend to miss a minute of today's drama," Samael said on a note of mockery.

"Of course not," Haverner replied. "It will be the best so far, won't it? And a playback hasn't the same excitement."

"It will be the last, if Cruz gets his way," Samael warned.

"I know, I know. But I also know about contingency measures that a certain player has developed. Do you?" Haverner gibed.

"Therefore you will allow Cruz's game. You will permit events to take their course, whatever that may prove to be?"

"Oh, yes. Don't you agree?"

"The show must go on." Samael chuckled.

Haverner laughed aloud. To possess this power over lives and deaths was like being young again.

ORESTES CRUZ

Now why are Matt and Gayle here? They have no reason left to get up for a dawn breakfast. Curiosity, I suppose. It must be intense, considering how they watch me out of the same drawn faces as the rest. (Collusion? No, I think not. Julia, deceived in Byron—it would be interesting to know what happened between them—has deftly cut Larry out of Gayle's herd. Matt, this past couple of days, has been clumsily trying to be cordial to everybody; yes, also to nigger me. That may be camouflage for a partnership with one of them. . . . No matter. Today this grisly thing will end.)

"We are going down to the beach, please," I command, and give out a big teeth-baring smile before I turn my back and lead the way.

How odd that I don't hate them all. Only Haverner the shark, Nordberg the hagfish, Flagler the poisonous drifting Portuguese man-of-war. The rest are likeable enough and, in their different ways, pathetic. They have little or nothing to do—directly—with cold gringo calculators in the offices, ruttish gringo sailors on the streets and in the brothels of Ciudad Vizcaya, or with that white rapist my grandfather.

(Did he exist? The mirror tells me of many a thrust into terrified female flesh whose skin did not happen to be white. But that anguish could be further in the past. I really know only that my father was a black man. Doubtless he stemmed from one of the Caribbean Islands, since there are no other stemmings of black men in Santa Ana: son or grandson of one of the dark multitude who came to help put asunder what God had joined together by the Isthmus of Panama, and afterward, rather than return to the starveling archipelago, trickled north and south into neighbor republics. One evening after work in the canefields he met an Indian girl by the side of the road, and he stayed a few days or weeks. . . . So she told me, I think. It's barely at the edge of memory. I scarcely know about her either, having been quite small when she invested her capital in a bolt of bright cloth and a new axhead and moved on in the general direction of her native village without me, since blacks were not wanted there. . . . I feel certain there have been white rapists on both sides of my "family.")

I step off the veranda and am careless. The sun, low above a molten sea, catches me in the eyes. Good morning, sun. Your image chases across dew-steaming grass, listless leaves and blossoms. Already we breathe in warmth. Before long it will be heat. Not a cloud, says my clearing vision, and my feet are jubilant on the downward path.

How does the Latin go? *Sol Invictus!*

The beach is wide, smooth, raked. But nothing can tame the fieriness of those sands. Capes on either side, pier-supported steel net stretched across its mouth, mark off Haverner's part of the lagoon. In this slant sunlight it's like sapphire, hardly a ripple across it. But beyond, surf tumbles and booms, exploding on rocks that will tear the bottom out of any boat whose pilot forgets them. Nor has Haverner really made these inner waters his. Do what he will, he can't rub out the ages before man that lie beneath, that gave slow birth to the land and in their own good time will claim it back.

At the end of the path, on the shore edge of the beach, is a kind of summerhouse: straw-matted concrete floor, shading wooden roof and latticework walls, separate dressing cubicles for the oh-so-nice white rapist and his white woman whom only white hands may touch. Above it are sheer bluffs, red granite a-sparkle with mica flecks, crowned by saw grass, palmetto, bamboo thickets, the Island wilderness that presses in on your estate, Sunderland Haverner, the same as the forces of history do.

"Well?" It's Iron Man Ellis whose question sounds shrill. "What're we going to do?" Your turn next, isn't it, Nordberg? You have everything computed and scheduled, like a bombing raid on a village, no? Too bad that villages fight back.

They cluster around. Their dark glasses remind me of

their skulls. Anselmo keeps aside by the television camera, showing neither interest nor boredom. His right hand rests casually on his revolver, his left holds a cigarette. He too is wearing loose, full white garments, canvas shoes, broad hat, Polaroids. A shame, those Polaroids. I'd like to watch his eyes. They are so alive in that terra cotta face.

No matter. Triumph makes my throat feel swollen. I can't make my announcement as lightly as I meant to. But I try.

"I promised you a quiet game, Mrs. Petrie and gentlemen. You shall have one. No exertion, no deprivation of any kind. You may move about freely, talk, sleep, send for food and drink, whatever you wish." I had wanted to pause and enjoy their waiting; but when I see how Julia's teeth catch her lip and her fingers try to break each other, I must hurry on. "We merely stay here on the beach in full sunlight. Nude."

Silence roars over us like the surf out yonder.

Gayle makes the first shriek. Silly little chicken, she's already failed. Larry clenches his fists. Byron crows what may be a laugh. Ellis shouts above Matt's obscenity, "No! I protest!" Julia freezes where she stands.

"What is impossible about removing your clothes?" I ask chalky Nordberg in a rush of joy. Fish belly. Fool. White lord of the earth. Die.

"The . . . you . . . you're a breed; you got the skin to last us out—" He whirls on Anselmo. After a second, Larry joins him, and then Byron. Matt officiously shoves his voice in among theirs.

"I am sorry," Anselmo tells them. "The challenge ees fair."

"Call the old man," Larry says.

"Yes, do," Byron adds. "If he didn't let me take people into water that not everybody could swim—well, we're not equipped for the tropics the way Orestes is."

"I am sorry," Anselmo repeats. "I do not deesturb Meester 'Averner for notheeng. Sr. Cruz 'as asked 'eem and 'e say okay."

That was a short interview, three days ago, but I came from it trembling. Why did he find my proposal such cause for amusement, when it's sure to end his game? He is a Hitler, no, stranger even than that, and he frightens me more than the system that brought him to being.

147

Matt fumes. Anselmo drops hand back to gun. "You are not een play, Meester Flagler," he says. "Be quiet, please, or I send you away."

Again they fall silent. I remind them that they can resign.

Julia comes near. "Oh, but my little girl . . ." she cries.

Her sentiment is genuine, but sentimentalism doesn't become her. I stiffen myself to answer. "I have seen too many little girls made slaves of, or sick, or dead and rotting, Julia. I fight for all of them."

And it's true, it's true. I saw them tend mosquito-tortured baby brothers when their own legs, encrusted with sores, had scarcely begun to walk. I saw them, not much older, join their mothers to toil in the canefields, beneath that unmerciful sun which I have today turned on the gringo. I saw their bellies puffed up by hunger or shriveled by dysentery; I heard them cough tubercular blood. When I'd come to Ciudad Vizcaya, it was the little girls who first made me know that life in the stews was not all fun, the little girls, their maidenheads not yet fledged, brought crying in; yes, and now and then their little brothers.

"The game begins," I say, cast off my hat and start to unbutton my shirt.

Julia stares at me an instant before she snarls and follows my lead.

Each of them does. I am surprised. "Be warned," I say. "Heat stroke can be fatal. Or . . . We shall be here until nightfall if necessary. Tomorrow you may have no skin left."

"Maybe you'll drop dead, Orestes," Byron retorts with an ugly grin.

"Or we can try to talk you out of this insanity," Ellis says.

"Spare your breath." I can't help myself. "Be careful of your eyes. No sunglasses either. Retinal damage is possible from reflections off sand and water. Blindness? I do not know."

"You'll burn us alive, then?" Larry seems shocked.

"No." I reply. "You will do that to yourselves, if you stay. It is the napalm that gives no option."

"Or the slave labor camps in your workers' paradises,"

Julia snaps. But at once she turns to Larry, for consolation, I suppose.

Anselmo collects their garments and lays them neatly in the summerhouse. They may watch that cave of shade as long as they choose. (Out here, shadows are blue.) "If you want anything," I say, "tell him and he will call the house for it to be fetched. I forbid only lotions or burying yourselves to the neck, or whatever else may reduce your exposure."

The five of us look upon each other's nakedness. Byron is the most sightly of the men, trim and tanned. (I find my own color more pleasing, alive, human, but my knobbly frame is nothing to boast of.) He should last longest of them. Our gazes clash and he grins again, on the right side of his mouth. Ellis is hideous, though spindle shanks and bulging paunch may be age more than neglect. He seems to take regular exercise, but he's worn himself out in the course of wearing out earth and man. Fungus white, he'll soon redden and blister. Good! Larry is burly, shaggy, heavily hung; he has large muscles but he's let a good deal of fat grow over them, and his torso and legs are pale.

Julia . . . Beneath that Scythian head is a Grecian body, tall, supple, faintly sun-colored except where two thin strips of ivory outline neat small-areolaed nipples and the black silkiness further down. I feel a stir of desire; it's been long since my last woman. To keep them from seeing that I too am flesh, I haul out memories to put between me and her.

My references are confused. What Enrico Brunner said was, "In Christ Jesus there is neither Jew nor Greek," and he explained, "neither black nor red," "Scythian nor Barbarian," and explained, "latino nor gringo." I was pleased to learn this; no doubt it was the first germ of my social consciousness. Of course, by age twelve I'd grown less pleased to learn that—evidently— in Christ Jesus there was also to be neither gaming nor wenching, dancing nor cockfighting. Yet I continued to stay and to listen. It was more than the certainty of bread and watered wine when I could scrounge or steal nothing elsewhere, a floor to sleep on among the leather and kerosene smells of the cobbler's shop. . . .

. . . After my Jamaican foster mother married that Bay Black who said, "Me no gweyn wuk give nyam Panya b'y," I'm not going to work to feed a Spaniard's boy, and "Mama," shed an easy tear, gave me a baked plantain, a clean shirt and the words, "You mus' be de God pickney now, me no see you more. . . ."

. . . No, I had learned my basic survival, but the old man who saw me through to that stage had much else to teach me, and the main thing that he taught me was to *want* to learn. He did it with hugs and bribes; he did it with scoldings and canings and lockings out, but he did it. So I let him teach me to read, write and cipher; I let him straighten out and build on that warped foundation of English I had from my foster mother and her kind; I devoured his books and sat cross-legged at his single foot and his peg leg to hear, as other children heard tales of heroes and demons and ghosts, his ramblings on about Petion and Boyer and Garibaldi and Juárez and Henry George and Aesop and Madero and Haya de la Torres and . . .

Tío Rico, Tío Rico, I never ran away from you. Never. I only wanted a change, and to try my luck in the city. Listen, I was just fifteen years old by then, and you had taught me that a whole world reached beyond our dust and canefields. I knew I would be back inside a year to bring you a fortune I had won and my love. It's only, Tío Rico, that somehow I never did win the fortune, and other things came to me, and I never quite found time to return even for a visit, and finally our infrequent letters stopped. Yours first. Did you die, Tío Rico? Did a stroke crash through your brain while you sat alone in your shop at night? I should have written to the priest and asked, but he's barely literate himself and anyhow I was so involved in the Party. . . .

Gayle is speaking to Larry. "I'd help you if I could, honest, but I've got to get out of this sun. There in the summerhouse. I'll wait for you. Or can I bring you something?"

"No," he says. His attention is on Julia, and he begins to show what I was about to show. Desperation breeds hankerings.

"Or me," Matt puts in unexpectedly. "What can I do?"

"You can stop embarrassing us," Ellis clips. "Both of you. Please go back inland and wait." With curious emphasis: "Do what seems best. Only not here."

I don't quite read Matt's expression, his stance. (These

people remain alien to me, as I to them, however many I've dealt with, begged from, run errands, shined shoes, and pimped for, all the while sharpening my command of their harsh language till at last I was the interpreter in that secret meeting between our Santa Anan Fidelito and the influential North American professor.) But he says, after the slightest pause, "Sure. I get you. Come on, Gayle."

They trudge upward and out of sight. Ellis straightens as if their absence from his nudity takes a weight off him. Byron demands salt tablets and plenty of iced lemonade. The rest second him. Anselmo sends the order on his walkie-talkie. A servant will bring it down. I hope he won't be too shocked by what he sees. They have a charming archaic morality, the Islandmen.

Anselmo, the mainlander, is he more akin to me? I'd like to know. I move over and ask him for a cigarette. He obliges. "You may as well sit in the shade," I remark in Spanish.

(Light raves around us. Even to my horny soles, the sand is growing hot. I hear Larry advise Julia to sit down before it becomes impossible. They do so together. Scant sweat shows on her sleek skin. The air drinks it straight out of her, greedily as a child might suckle, or I her lover. Sand fleas hop; a fly bumbles gold and bottle-green; a small land crab scuttles in fear of my shadow. Gulls cruise, waiting, vultures of the shore. The sand is fine, gritty, scrunchy under my step. Not every shell, fishbone, kelp strand, dried polyp has been combed away by Haverner's hirelings; not every whiff of life and clean decay has been abolished.)

"That would be no courtesy when you cannot, Sr. Cruz," Anselmo says.

"Oh, nonsense!" I snort. "Come, take a bench inside by the door. I'll sit outside and we'll talk."

He spreads his hands, barely, and does. I settle my bottom, which is a little painful for a moment till temperatures equalize. I fold arms around shanks, rest chin on drawn-up knees, and take care to keep lids squinted and vision well away from the water. Seated above me under the roof, Anselmo says, "This is a most clever game you have called, Sr. Cruz."

"It's one that nobody but I can win," I answer in a

fresh burst of glory. "Whichever of them is crazy enough to hold out till sundown may cause me a certain discomfort tomorrow, but he will die. None who stays more than two or three hours at most—at most, because the sun is low yet, the air screens off more of its rays than it will later—none who does that will be fit for anything. I'm surprised they didn't concede to me on the spot."

"Sr. 'Averner would not be happy about that," Anselmo drawls. "But he picked them well. Maybe he wants to compare how stubborn they are, if he allowed this challenge. Anyhow, they dance to the clink of his dollars."

"Like you?" I look straight at him; for I have nothing to fear in this end game of mine, and it may be that I can bring him out of his darkness. "Why are you his dog?"

He is not insulted. "It pays well. The work is usually easy, often pleasurable." For the first time ever, I see him smile. "It happens not a few times, the big Yankee men who come visit him on business, they bring along wives or daughters who discover they want to try something different. It's fun to educate them, almost like having a virgin."

(Julia—how much does she know? I think she'd quickly and gladly learn what she does not. But I may be wrong. I've never lain with any of these colorless mistresses of the earth. My girls have been many, and most of them hot and sweet, but all were earth-dark. . . . To whom will I finally commit myself, when the revolution has come and I dare take a wife before the world to bear children I dare acknowledge for me to sing and tell stories to? The daughters of the fields are simple, the daughters of the city—the city that I know—are sluts. A Castilian then, tall, aloof, refined in Paris on the rent of her father's tenants? A European? A free-souled Yankee lass, come down to help us with guitar slung over blue-denimed shoulders and straight yellow hair tumbled across it?)

Julia and Larry have their backs to me. They talk: her fist beats the sand; he gestures widely. Byron prowls. Ellis dabs at the flush on his hide, the grains that cling to his scraggly-furred legs, the fleas around his feet. From time to time he glances aloft, no doubt longing for that lemonade. Will you not surrender soon, gringos? I'm hot and I prickle.

"Have you no conscience?" I snap at Anselmo. "No thought for your mother, your sisters, the whole future of your family?"

"When I am dead," he answers coolly, "the universe ends. That is, we have only this life. If you're a proper Communist, you must agree. Then why give away a minute?" In haste: "I'm not a coward, understand. I'm not afraid to die. In fact, I enjoy risking my neck. I'm never so alive, not even in a woman. My question is, Sr. Cruz, what can your holy cause, or holy Mother Church, or anything I haven't already got here, what can it give me that makes it worth my while to lay my head on the block, or pass by one single pleasure?"

"If you don't know that," I say in full solemnity, "you have never really lived, Anselmo."

(Not that Lenin ever appeared to me like Jesus to Paul. My conversion was slow, and was bitterly resisted.

(For I had found my happiness, it seemed. In the red-light district of Ciudad Vizcaya there was always a place for a boy who could read and write and cipher, had excellent English as well as Spanish, knew when to speak or fight and when not to, was quick of eye and ear and fingers and wits. There was no snobbery, no race distinction except for the gringos we made sport and prey of, no toil except delightful hours when we spun our webs around the fat flies, no law except loyalty to one's chief and brother huntsmen, no limit except one's own daring, speed, skill, and luck. And oh, the songs, dances, laughter, music, marijuana, liquor, feasting, oh, the pungent sweat-slick girls!

(It's a pity, in a way, that Tío Rico had given me that example of compassion, that habit of studying and wondering.)

"What happened to you in prison was a piece of real life I'm content to have foregone," Anselmo says. "Be glad they didn't beat you too much over the balls, interrogating. They would have in time, I suppose, if they didn't simply shoot you the way they did your bosses of the junta."

"Not my immediate boss," I answer. "General Ribera, Minister of War, yes. But I was driver and handyman for his aide-de-camp, Colonel Ybarra, and he escaped. To Venezuela, I believe. I'm happy about that. He's a decent man in his fashion."

"Did you meet him first in a whorehouse?"

"Yes, him and Ribera both, when I was playing the piano downstairs before the junta seized power. He took a fancy to me—" I realize what I am saying and peer hard at him. "Why should I tell you this?"

Anselmo spreads his palms. "You need not. I can read the old man's dossier on you if I want to. I have already, though I don't recall every detail. For instance, you were in the Party by that time, and not unimportant, either. But when Ybarra offered you a position, they told you to accept, keep your mouth shut and your nose clean, and wait for further orders."

Anger explodes in me. "By God, does Haverner have the CIA itself in his pocket?"

I am certain it engineered the restoration of the reactionaries. Is not the thoroughness with which progressives were identified and—if you couldn't escape—jailed, proof enough? I had yielded this flesh and these bones to death, anonymous mortar in the walls of tomorrow, when that stunning "condition of probation" sent me here to Tanoa.

"He has his connections," Anselmo says. "Be glad he found you were suitable material for his experiment, after your dear Party wrote you off."

No, it didn't. Yes, I am. Glad. A million gun-buying dollars' worth of glad.

Though be honest, Orestes, it is good merely being alive, in a cosmos of light and warmth, sun and stars, salt and breath, friends and songs and Cervantes and girls and wide-eyed small children.

I love you, my people. The best thing in this day is that I am alive and thinking how much I love you.

Every last mongrel one of you . . . almost. True, you have exasperated me to fury, you on the land. You take your fate like oxen. Stone Age superstitions drone through your heads so loudly that you cannot hear, let alone understand, the truth. Someday, though, I shall take your toil-crooked hands in mine, and lead them from the machete haft to the controls of a reaping machine.

And everything I remember from the village, everything that made me what in my marrow I truly am, will die. It must. But I shall always remember, and when I am alone weep a little for the dead ways which were my mother's and my playmates' and Tío Rico's.

"Well!" Byron says. "Here come the refreshments!"

"You should take some yourself, Sr. Cruz," Anselmo counsels.

His tone is once again polite and impersonal as a jungle cat. Is that what he is . . . a creature still more archaic than peon labor, one-room palm-thatched huts, drunkenness at fiesta time, and Christ Jesus? What has Haverner brought back to dwell among us?

"Thank you, you are right," I say, and rise. Where my feet have not shielded it, the sand is scorching.

I cross toward the others, who stand in their misery, their whole souls reaching for the servant who trots down the trail with his tray. Give up, I want to tell them; keep your health, your lives; return to what you were before, which is more than you can imagine, you who have not known my people. Yankee, go home, and I say this not in hatred but in love, because *crash* . . .

INTERVAL SIX

Part One

The lank man cast arms wide apart and half spun, half lurched on the blazing ground. An instant later came the crack of the gun. His head burst. Gray and red gobs flew out of his bush of hair. He fell beneath the second delayed noise.

Anselmo's automatic had soared into his hand. He crouched at the entrance of the summerhouse, peering around its shelter. The bluff behind showed nothing except a glimpse of the brush on top. "*¡Aquí!*" he shouted. " 'Ere, to me!"

Get clear of the line of fire! Julia was first of the figures congealed in sunlight to comprehend. Larry pounded after her fleetness, then Byron. Ellis stood a moment longer before he trotted behind them.

The Islandman servant had vanished up the path. His yells for help drifted faintly through the still heat. From tumbled tray and glassware, lemonade soaked into the sand. The blood that pooled around Orestes was drunk more slowly. Amidst the whiteness, it looked as black as he did.

Anselmo snapped a shot. The sound reverberated painfully from wooden ceiling and concrete floor. Julia and Larry gasped and shuddered in each other's arms. Ellis clenched his fists. Byron, shivering but somehow alight, craned his neck past the Santa Anan.

There was no response from above. After barking a few words into his walkie-talkie, Anselmo darted forth. Bent, bouncing zigzag, he fired thrice more. The green tangle that crowned the granite hardly moved. He lowered his weapon and stood erect.

"I theenk the keeller 'as gone," he said. What expression he had shown departed from him. "Come out eef you want." Nonetheless he kept glance and pistol cocked as he approached the corpse. A gull, which had landed to inspect this possible meal and been frightened off by the racket, wheeled and mewed in indignation.

Ellis started donning his clothes. The rest imitated him. No one uttered a word, nor did anyone look at anyone else.

When Byron had finished buttoning his shirt, he was first to speak, his tone flat and seeming overly loud in the surf-deepened silence. "Don't go see him, Julia. It's not a pretty sight."

"I majored in biology, remember." Most of the hue had drained from her lips and irises, making them stand forth in the suntanned countenance. "It included a human dissection."

"But we knew this guy." Larry strangled on the words. Breath whistled between his teeth.

Ellis pinched his mouth together and strode to join Anselmo. Byron followed. Red and white flowed over him and he likewise breathed hard. Presently Julia more or less dragged Larry along.

They surrounded the dead man. He sprawled on his back, covering the entry holes of the two bullets. One, emerging on the left side of his chest, had opened a crater in the flesh. Yellowish splinters of bone stuck forth. The next had gone straight through the cranium and left little of the upper face. An eyeball, shocked loose, lay amidst bloody mush; the other, still in place, stared out of the wreckage. His jaw was intact but fallen to show a tongue that was gray and already dry.

Flies were gathering.

"Oh, no, oh, no," Larry moaned. "Oh, that's bad."

Byron's look flickered about. "Somebody wanted him murdered," he said. "Specifically him, Orestes Cruz. That was a high-powered hunting rifle, with telescopic sights, I'll bet."

"But we players were all here," Ellis objected.

"Conspiracy—"

Julia clutched Larry's hand, met their gazes and said, "Okay, let's be honest. This, what's happened, was our last hope. I'm sorry for Orestes. He was a better man than . . . most of us. But I'm not sorry my daughter has a chance to live. Don't any of you tell me you don't feel the same kind of relief."

"The game's done!" Larry shouted. "It's got to be!"

"Does it?" Ellis replied quietly. When he turned his head, sunlight, reflected off the Polaroid clip-ons he wore above his glasses, made two blank circles.

Anselmo pointed to the path. " 'Ere comes 'elp Meester 'Averner sends."

Six chairs, drawn in an arc in the living room, confronted the chaise that held the old man. Behind him stood Captain York, somehow gone small in his nautical garb, not quite able to keep his mouth from twitching or his feet from shifting. Behind the visitors, arms folded, imperturbable, waited Anselmo.

Haverner surveyed them. On the right sat Larry, next to him Julia, their fingers intertwined. Byron, legs crossed, his own fingers bridged, did not seem to notice how Gayle clung to his forearm. Matt, on her left, glowered now at her, now at the room in general. Ellis, stiff at the edge of his seat, hands on knees, had reclad himself in tropical suit and dark tie.

Dimmed against noonday, the room felt cavernous. For a while only the air conditioner had voice. The coolness it gave did not stop sweat from standing forth on the skins of the six.

Haverner made them wait before he creased his parchment visage in a smile, leaned his skull a little forward on the scrannel neck, and said, "Ah. A sad occasion. But urgent. We have decisions to make, ladies and gentlemen. I hope you are not too shaken to make them, and in realistic wise."

"What d'you mean?" Larry croaked. "What decision? Murder's been done. What do we do except call the police"—he let go of Julia, half rose, twisted around and stabbed a forefinger at Matt—"and put the murderer in irons!"

"Huh?" The Chicagoan was tense but controlled. He sat where he was and grinned into Larry's trembling. "You mean me? Come off it, buster. What'd I want to do the nigger in for? I was washed out, remember?"

"B-b-bribery—" The big man's glare staggered among them, searching.

"Where'd I get a gun? Anyway, I got a witness. Gayle here."

The woman whimpered and leaned against Byron. He pulled back to observe her. She released him, buried face in hands, and wept.

"She's rattled, naturally," Matt said. He drew forth a pack of cigarettes, extracted one, tapped it on his thumbnail. "But she'll bear me out. Her and me went back like we was told, and decided to take a stroll along the blufftops. It's shady under the trees and we felt, you know, restless. First thing we heard about the killing was when one of the servants come running and found us, maybe a mile north of the beach."

"Is that true, Gayle?" Larry demanded. He strode past Julia and Byron to stand above her. "Look at me, damn you! Is that true?"

"Larry, Larry—" She kept her gaze on the floor, which she probably could not see through the spurting tears, but groped blindly for him. "Larry, darling, help me."

He struck her hands aside. "Answer me!" he roared. "Is that story true?"

She raised her head long enough to scream, "Yes, you

mother! Yes!" Matt offered his arms and she collapsed into them. Across her shoulder he gave Larry a smirk.

The latter growled, or groaned, and returned to his seat. His fist smote his knee again and again.

"I can corroborate that Mr. Flagler ordered no weapons from me," Haverner said. "As for his baggage . . . Captain York, you have inquired of the butler and chambermaid, have you not?"

"Yis, sir." The Islandman could barely be heard. "No gun in anybody's room, no, sir."

"You'll swear to that?" Byron asked sharply.

York drew strength from somewhere. "No, sir, not me Boible oat', because I have not inspected for meself, sir. Not my vork. But I vill svear I have known bot' Benbow and Philpotts for many years. If dey had noticed a gun, dey vould have told me, yis, sir."

Byron nodded. Ellis declared, "Well, I'll insist on a weapon for my own protection, when a killer is loose." Larry jeered wildly, "Think you could hit a hippo's ass at five paces, dad?" Matt gave him a stiff look. Gayle went on crying. Julia sat still.

"We might bear in mind," Haverner said, "Sr. Cruz did not come from nowhere. He was a political figure, associated not merely with the late junta, but with the Party, with backwoods guerrillas, city terrorists, connections to Cuba and the Tupamaros. The present government considered him dangerous. I had to apply a great deal of pressure as well as, ah, reimbursements, in order to have him sent here on probation. Were it not for me, he would surely have stood before a firing squad."

He paused. "And therefore?" Byron challenged.

"It is possible that some, shall we say, overzealous officials decided he should be eliminated lest he get away from Tanoa as Bonaparte did from Elba. They would not wish to offend me by acting openly. But assassination is a well-developed technique in this region."

"And in his case, I can't say it was a bad idea," Ellis stated. "He wasn't just our opponent in a contest. He was the enemy."

"No more than you," Larry retorted.

Byron lifted a hand. "Wait. Please. Let's think. Mr. Haverner knows this country inside out, we don't know it at all. We'd better be guided by him. Sir, if this was a, uh, an impersonal murder as you suggest . . . maybe we shouldn't lean on the local police. Am I right?"

Haverner nodded. "It could cause difficulties."

"You mean, don't report this, ever?" rattled from Larry. "What happens when they find out we didn't?"

"Nothing," Haverner answered. "Because I will, of course, report it myself. Not to any local imcompetent, but by radiophone to a more appropriate person in Ciudad Vizcaya. He will instruct both me and the *comandante* in the North Port as to what we should do. I can tell you in advance, he will—if I request it—deputize me to conduct what investigation I see fit. If I report no result, the case will simply and quietly be closed. He and I have a mutual understanding, do you see, and violent death is nothing extraordinary to a mainland Santa Anan."

York rocked on his heels.

Julia took the word: "Let me get this straight, Mr. Haverner. Are you saying we have a choice? That we can either sweep Orestes's killing under the rug with the connivance of a government that's quite happy to be rid of him and maybe did the job itself . . . or we can send direct to North Port for the gendarmes and raise a stink?"

"Correct, Mrs. Petrie, even to the literal meaning of the word 'gendarmes.' The military garrison doubles as the constabulary. If you choose to invoke them, it may become a little awkward. We will probably have to terminate our game."

"What?" It was odd to see that Ellis too could be hit.

"Publicity, you know," Haverner said. "From my viewpoint, the game is an experiment; and experiments require controlled conditions. If you don't play isolated, we get too many variables." He raised his brows. "However, if your desire is to stop here, so be it. That in itself will be a significant datum."

"No!" Julia said.

They regarded her. She flushed in the humming shadowiness and defied them. "I liked Orestes. I did. But he's gone. My daughter isn't, yet. We can't help him; I can help her. Let's shovel him under and get on with our business."

"Right," Ellis said at once.

"Agreed," Byron added.

"But . . . but you're crazy," Larry stammered. "A man's been killed. And the killer could be one of us!"

Byron half smiled. "I don't want to sound callous," he said. "It's certainly a terrible tragedy that's happened. But the fact you mention—let's be frank—does add a certain spice, doesn't it?"

From Matt's smug embrace, Gayle watched them in horror.

"I fear you are outvoted, Mr. Rance," Haverner said. "I will obtain magisterial authority from the capital itself, immediately, that legal forms may be observed. Among other things, I can then order a closed coffin made here, and the body taken to the North Port for burial before sunset. With no coroner, and in this climate, that will be entirely proper. And no inconvenient questions will be asked. The Island has come to accept the fact that outré things sometimes happen here, as it accepts the value this establishment has to its economy." He gave a dry spasm which may have been meant as a chuckle. "I fear Sr. Cruz would not have appreciated the religious ceremony that will accompany his interment. But we must not flout local mores."

"You're crazy!" Larry yelled. "You're—" He groped for the word. "You're *cruel!*" He looked like an outraged schoolboy. Leaping to his feet, he stormed from the room.

A while later no one was in sight on the grounds. The staff had withdrawn to their posts in the mansion or to their cottages, hiding from the incandescence around, or from the body laid out in a locked shed? The house loomed huge and white, the lesser dwellings huddled small and bleached-pastel, amidst mowed grass, trimmed flowers, motionless leaves from which the sun smashed all real color, alien shapes rearing higher than the wall around the botanical garden. Above them the sky reached wan, without depth, empty save for a cruising vulture. In the forest to northward, which seemed like a cardboard cutout, a woodpecker drummed and a macaw shrieked, over and over, endlessly. From one of the cottages, several voices, male and female, droned a capella, *"Ve vill rest in de arms of Jesus. . . ."* A lizard panted.

Larry stopped. He was breathing equally hard. His

shadow lay in a puddle at his feet. He swung his head from side to side.

Abruptly he gathered himself and sprinted. As quietly as might be, he passed through the row of servants' quarters, across a narrow road covered by pipeshank still faintly redolent of the once-living coral, to the long stoutly timbered building where that road ended—or began. Its several sliding doors were closed but not secured. They gave on chambers used for various kinds of storage. The roadway indicated which was the garage.

Larry entered. He needed a moment for his vision to adjust to the gloom within. Beneath a corrugated iron roof, the place was a furnace. Three pickup trucks, a station wagon, and two automobiles waited like bulky cats at a mousehole. He poised himself awhile, inhaling shallowly because the air here was so vicious, and looked them over. The wagon was a utility vehicle, likewise the Buick. He'd started out for town in the latter before he fell sick. The Mercedes was reserved for Sunderland Haverner and extremely special guests.

A grin of sorts crossed Larry's lips. "As well be hanged for, et cetera," he muttered. "Besides, she's got more legs than anything else."

By now he could see reasonably well if he kept his glance from the open door. He found a workbench and tool rack. The Mercedes wasn't locked. If it had been, a piece of stiff wire would have corrected the situation in short order. Larry had never worked for an auto repossessor; he claimed it was immoral for banks to pick on some poor devil down on his luck. But he had known, and watched in action, men who claimed it was immoral to be a deadbeat.

Hotwiring the car took a few minutes. It purred to life. He got behind the wheel, touched the gas pedal, eased the machine outside, stopped to let his pupils contract again.

A man, who must have heard, popped from a cottage. "A'oy!" he called. "Vhat you doing, sir? Dat Mr. Haverner's, dat is!"

Shell spurted from tires and Larry was off. Past the service building and landing strip, his road led to the North Port. Dust whirled pallid behind him.

Sunderland Haverner appeared to find humor in the news. "Doubtless our impetuous friend has gone to seek what he imagines is the police," he said. "Well, I presume he's a good driver who will take care on those treacherous curves."

"But won't you try to have him stopped? Intercepted?" Ellis asked in an appalled tone. "He could bring an end to the game!"

"I think not, Mr. Nordberg," Haverner replied. "I rather think not."

Gayle, stretched belly-down on her bedspread, stirred at a knock on the door. Midafternoon flamed beyond drawn blinds. An air conditioner labored noisily to maintain coolness. Distantly came the hammer falls where a carpenter worked on a coffin. "Who, who is that?" she called.

"Lemme in," ordered the Chicago voice.

"No. No, please. Please go away."

"Lemme in, I said. We got a lot to talk about, sister."

Gayle rolled over, sat up, plucked at a button under her throat. "No," she begged. "Later, Matt. Honest."

"Now. While we got the chance. Quick! Or do I have to tell you-know-who you've ratted on us?"

She moaned but rose, passed through the disorder of the room, turned the knob. Matt slipped through and refastened the door behind him. "That's better," he said.

They stood, he staring down and she up, for half a minute. Her arms were crossed, fists drawn against breasts. Air shuddered in and out of her. His blue-shadowed face bent in a laugh. He chucked her under the chin and said, "It's not that bad, sweetheart. Relax. We just got to get a few things straight."

She couldn't answer.

"Now's the chance," he continued. "Larry's off on his Boy Scout mission. Don't worry about it. Byron's in the library; Julia's gone for a walk—in this weather, can you imagine? We won't be snooped on, except maybe by Mr. Haverner, and he don't care."

"El-Ellis . . . Nordberg?"

"In his room. But we don't worry about him either, do we, sweetheart? It's you we got to get squared away. Come on, siddown, let's talk." He urged her to a chair and took the other, directly opposite her, reversing it so he sat astraddle with his arms laid over the back.

163

She reached to the table and groped in the cigarette box. "Me too," Matt said. She gave him one. "Light," he commanded. She put the fire to his before her own.

He sucked smoke. "Ahh! Good, huh?"

She gathered courage until she could say in a rush, "Matt, listen, I didn't know what I was getting into. I never expected . . . And then the shock, you know, like I was numb. I couldn't think, I was scared and went along, like I was programmed, you know? But now— no, I can't."

"You can, baby, and you will." He transfixed her from between squinched-together lids. "You're in this every bit as much as me. Or you're dead, understand? Maybe worse than dead."

"But I never—I mean—" She strained backward into her chair. "I thought we'd cooperate, you and Ellis and me, but I never—"

Matt gave an elaborate sigh. "Listen," he said. "Listen close, because I don't feel like repeating.

"Ellis and me got this here signal. He says, 'Do what seems best,' and that means anything goes. He gave it to me down there on the beach, right before you and me left the scene, Gayle. Remember? 'Do what seems best.'

"Okay, so we walked a little ways into the woods on the blufftop. And I said you should wait, and ducked into that bamboo thicket, and there was a couple of shots, and I come out and hustled you on along the trail."

"You . . . had a gun in your hand—" Her voice broke. "You *killed* him. You're a *murderer!*"

"And you're the accessory, sweetheart. You were willing to string along with me and Ellis, weren't you? He must've told you this game is for keeps. How much were you worth to your precious Larry Rance, baby, when he saw a better partner in Julia after she'd given up on Byron? Huh? Think about it."

His words smote her. "Okay. Ellis ordered the gun. Old Ha—Mr. Haverner doesn't care. He only wants to see what we do. Well, Ellis hid the gun after they handed it to him in Mr. Haverner's office. He turned it over to me later. Idea was, if a situation looked too tough, he'd pass me the high sign and I'd cool the leader." He laughed anew. "I told him I'd never done that sort of thing before. I don't know if he believed me, but it helped jack up my price. Hell, I lost *that* cherry at age twenty-one. So I stashed the rifle where it'd be handy, and today I told you to give me an alibi—"

"I was stunned," she pleaded. "I was scared. You threatened—Ellis'd threatened—I didn't know what I was doing. Now I see: we murdered Orestes."

" 'We' is right," he answered sardonically, and shook ashes off onto the floor. "You're in it over your scalp, kid. You didn't see exactly where I hid the weapon and ammo along the trail. I didn't let you watch that, but you know I've got 'em, and I'll use 'em again if I have to."

She trembled so much that she dropped her cigarette. It scarred the hardwood before going out.

Matt reached around his chair to pat her thigh. "Take it easy, Gayle." His voice turned soothing and his smile beguiled. "Look, ask yourself exactly what did happen. You were out of the game. You'd been booted out by dear Larry, too. Nothing was ahead of you except back to the same old nothing. Remember? This way, you still got a chance, a damn good chance, to be a winner. To be your own boss, for the rest of your life. How's that sound?

"Okay," he went on into her sobs. "Too bad about Cruz. That's what you say. Me, I don't think he's any loss. He was ready to fry those people alive, wasn't he? But however you think, dead's dead. You got no way to bring him back, do you? Okay, why not make the best of it? You got nothing to be scared of. You're covered. All you have to do is stand pat. Right, Gayle, baby?"

She shook her head. Still she wept. He stiffened. For a while he glared at her. At length he rose, kicked his chair aside, seized a handful of brown curls, hauled her face up and slapped with his free hand. They were hard, loud blows, which rocked her where she sat. She made a tiny noise, and afterward none, while he hit her.

When he stopped, both cheeks were livid in the yellow dimness of the room. She stared at him, mute and slack. He grinned.

"That's better," he said. "Now listen, you stupid bitch. I don't want to have to say it again.

"You're in this thing. You got in of your own free will, but there's no way out. If you squeal, you lose your money, and maybe I'll cool you, or maybe you'll go to jail here in Santa Ana. You know what a Santa Anan jail is like? Killing-hard labor. A dish of dirty beans and a dirty glass of water, once a day. No bath, no toilet; down the hall, a hole to squat over when they let you. No lights in the cells, no radio, no TV, no books, no cooling system, half a dozen women crammed together and the guards . . . well, I won't say they'd use you, they might, but they're for sure quick with a whip or club. You saw Cruz's bare back, didn't you? And rats, roaches, lice. They lose a lot of prisoners to typhus and such. You might come out alive, baby, but if you do, you won't be the same gal who went in. Uh-uh. You'll be *no* use to yourself.

"Better you stick with me and Ellis. We got protection for you, and money, and the freedom you always wanted. Right?"

Her lips moved. "Answer me!" he demanded.

"Right," she whispered.

"Good." Matt relaxed. "I knew you weren't dumb."

He finished his cigarette, tossed it in the ashtray, leaned down and took her by the elbows. "C'mon," he directed. She obeyed. They sat down side by side on the bed. He started to feel her.

"We're partners, you and me, hm, Gayle?" he breathed in her ear. "You want to keep me happy, don't you?"

She sagged. "I've got a choice?"

"No," he admitted. "You don't."

Tlat, tlat, tlat went the carpenter's hammer.

He laid her down and unbuttoned her blouse. "I like it in special ways," he told her. "I hope you do too. Because that's how it's going to be, baby."

The North Port has a curiously New England look. When the visitor takes thought, this is not curious after all. Some of those weathered-gray houses were built when Massachusetts was being colonized, and the rest are in much the same style. Furthermore, homes, the general store and café, the ship chandler's, the church cluster on a hillside which descends to a bay where fishing boats, the packet, an occasional trading schooner, a rare yacht lie along the wharf and its sheds. There the stevedores are young boys, light-haired and in calf-length trousers; they all look like Tom Sawyer.

But if the visitor takes further thought, the illusion is gone and the marvel is that he ever had it. That water and that sky are too blue; the land behind is too green; coconut and coyal palms rustle near the remains of groves whose wood was once precious; trumpet vines cloak the pillars of porches; yams and plantains grow in cactus-fenced backyard gardens; orchids flare in the foliage of enormous ceibas whose "cotton" the Arawaks brought to the first Castilians. The streets are unpaved: winding dusty lanes where children play, dogs and chickens wander, horsecarts are common and automobiles scarce. The people are loosely clad, usually barefoot, easy of gait, free with their laughter; they are a brown folk, half British, half Negro, half Indian, for that kind of arithmetic makes sense in this part of the world. And the flag above them is not the Stars and Stripes nor the Union Jack, but the red and gold of Santa Ana.

That staff rises over the Cabildo, which the Spanish erected in one of their several takings of possession two hundred years and more ago. It is still a foreigner in town; the brick wall around it seems to expect Moors or Cid to come and thunder at the gate, while the building at the middle of a flagged courtyard is pure Criollo. Most of its rooms stand empty these days, and none are in good repair.

A fat *comandante* blinked across his dusty desk in the dusky refuge he called an office. First he blinked at the large Yankee, then at the two soldiers who had escorted this person in to him, back and forth, back and forth. He took a comforting drag on his cigar. Spanish torrented from him.

"Uh, uh . . . *pardón, Señor,*" Larry Rance stumbled. *"No comprendo."*

More Spanish. *"Yo no—"* Larry tried. "I mean . . . *un muerte en la casa de Haverner* . . . no, damn it, that can't be right. . . . *¿Hay un hombre que habla inglés?"*

Words ripped past him. A soldier slouched out. His Garand rifle (military aid or surplus sale, three decades back? slapped the jamb as he went through. The *comandante* thought for a minute, issued an order, and waved Larry to the chair the other soldier brought.

They stared across the desk, face into unlike face, till the dispatched mainlander returned with a chance-found Islandman, a youth nervous and unhappy. (The garrison had an annual quota of smugglers to apprehend for six-month sentences to road gangs and similar jobs.) When he saw the newcomer, he beamed with relief. "Ah, sir, you are de guest of Mr. Sunderland, not so?" he exclaimed. "Villcome to Tanoa! How can I help you?"

"You can interpret," Larry said. "I want to report a murder."

"Vhat?" The youth was taken aback. "But sir, ve got no murders on Tanoa. De Sponyard, yis, he kill plinty. But here ve got only six of dem, in de Nart' Port, and I can tell you, sir—"

"This was at the Big House." Larry rose to tower above everybody else. "I saw a man shot from ambush, three, four hours ago. And nobody aims to do anything about it!"

"But Mr. Sunderland, sir, he vould newwer—"

Larry grabbed the speaker by the shoulders and shook him. "Tell the chief here, damn you! Tell him what I said. There's a man laid out with the brains blown loose from him, and Haverner wants to cover it up! Tell!"

He let go. The boy stepped back, gaped at the officer, broke into accented but rapid-fire Spanish. The body behind the desk contracted in its shabby uniform, then abruptly swelled. The answer was fierce.

"He . . . he say you mus' be wrong, sir," the Island-man told Larry. "He say you make a mistake. Mr. Sunderland, he wery big. He vould not kill anybody." A puzzled grin. "Vhy vould he need to? He wery vell off, him."

"I didn't say Haverner did it," Larry grated. "I said he allowed it . . . for that horrible project of his . . . and the killer's gonna get off scot-free unless . . . Don't you *care*? You're supposed to be a Christian, aren't you? Don't you care that a man got shot from behind?"

"Please, sir." There went more dialogue which Larry couldn't follow. The *comandante* tinkled a bell. Two additional mestizos entered, armed.

"You see, sir"—the Islandman waved his hands, anxious to be tactful—"dis is a wery serious t'ing you say. No insult, no, sir, but maybe you saw wrong. People not used to de sun here, dey get feewers in de head. Maybe you lay you down, bide a bit, you soon feel better."

"But," Larry said. "But. But."

"Hush, please."

The chief had evidently made up his mind. He took an incongruously modern telephone off the base, but dialed only a single digit. Conversation traveled. He put in a request which was granted, for they caught a hint of Sunderland Haverner's parched voice before the chief squeezed the receiver to his ear.

At the end: *"Sí, Señor. Sí, Señor. Immediamente. Mucha' gracia'. Para servir Usted, Señor. . . . Adio'. Adio'. Mucha' gracia'."*

When the phone was back together, the *comandante* became very businesslike indeed. He issued a curt order, and suddenly Larry had a man gripping either arm, while a third aimed a gun at his midriff and a fourth scuttled close bearing a set of handcuffs.

"You isn't to be afraid, sir," the Islandman said. "Nobody vill harm you, no, sir. Ve understands about sunstroke here. Dey vill take you back to Mr. Sunderland, your host, and he vill see you gets a good rest. He is not angry, not eewen about his car. He is a foine gentleman, you see."

"Immediately" turned out to mean "shortly after siesta." Thus Larry spent some hours in a cell, unable in his manacles to scratch most of the resulting fleabites. The truck that brought Orestes Cruz to his final resting place carried a driver for the Mercedes. But the *comandante* insisted on returning his prisoner personally in the garrison's Ford, though that weary machine could barely climb the hills. Haverner received him with a good cigar and a sealed envelope, and sent him home. Thereupon Haverner interviewed Larry in the office. It didn't take long, but the younger man emerged shaking, blood gone from his cheeks, and fairly ran upstairs. Having bathed, he retreated to his room, where his supper was brought him.

He did not miss much dinner-table conversation.

Sundown gave the benediction of a breeze. Captain York said, "Dis heat go'n' avay now, ve vill be more comfortable tomorrow," as if the fact held some mystic significance.

Larry gulped at his food and slipped out while the rest were in the dining room. He walked far. Matt retired early, beckoning Gayle to follow him. Byron and Ellis played gin rummy awhile longer. Julia said she wanted to take a stroll.

She was in the botanical garden when Larry returned from his own journey. He noticed that the gate, ordinarily shut at sundown against stray animals, stood open. Entering in a nearly random fashion, he found her.

Again the night was magical. City folk forget how radiant stars and natural sky-glow can be. Even here at sea level, it seemed as if there were more stars than there was clear blackness between them, constellations were hard to make out in that multitude, which finally melted together in the great river of the galaxy. Fireflies flitted and blinked by the hundreds among flower-bush fragrances. The air was cool and singing; the surf replied to it clearly but drowsily.

The garden within the bamboo walls seemed likewise enchanted, though some would have thought of witches or trolls. Paths wound narrow and intricate among stands of saw-toothed palmetto, needle-bristling prickly pear, high gaunt saguaro, yucca like spiky dinosaurs, and things more strange than this to a Northern eye, crouched or rearing, gray among shadows. It was as if Haverner had wanted to bring together all the weirdness he could find.

Julia rose from a bench whereon she sat. She wore a short, sleeveless yellow dress, whose color was lost but whose lightness stood forth. "Larry," she called low.

He stopped. She came to him. "Where were you?" she asked. "I was beginning to get afraid."

"Around." His tone was rough and his bulk stood rigid.

"You always want to be alone in your grief, don't you?" She took both his hands, unresponsive though they were. Luminance pooled in the eyes she raised to him. "Have you ever thought your friends might like to help you?"

"What friends? Connivers at murder?"

"What a man of conscience you are. I've not forgotten what you did for me, the day it was your turn. I never will forget."

His mouth twisted. "Oh, God, Julia, when you too went along with this thing—"

"I understand. How absolutely cut off you must have felt! But Larry, dear, won't you try to understand also? If human life means that much to you, won't you help save a good little girl? She's only six, Larry."

"Yeah." He eased the tiniest bit. "I kept trying to tell myself that."

"You must meet Kilby. She'll introduce you to her kitten. He's named Very Squashable and sleeps on her pillow. She makes up long stories about the adventures of Very Squashable. He travels around with her teddy bear, Winston P. Sanders, and . . . I think they're hilarious." Julia sighed. "Oh, I'm bragging, of course, and no doubt she is somewhat spoiled. But we can't help it, her father and I. She's so heartbreakingly patient about pain and confinement and those terrifying times in the hospital. We can't help it."

"I s'pose not." He hesitated. "Kid of my own, by an ex-wife. I don't see much of him."

She tightened her grip on him. "You're a lonely man, Larry."

He gave back the pressure. "Sometimes. Not always."

She let go, slowly, took his arm and guided him toward the bench. "Don't think I want to let Orestes lie unavenged," she said. "No, never. Should I win . . . I could see devoting some of the cash to tracking down the killer and bringing him to justice. But don't you see, at present we're helpless. We can surrender and go home, or we can dance to Haverner's tune—till we have his money. Then it may be a different story."

"M-m-m . . . you know, that angle hadn't occurred to me."

They sat down and watched the restless goblin lanterns. Their arms remained linked. "Do you mind telling me what he said to you?" she asked.

"He didn't say a lot." Larry's tone wavered afresh. "Didn't act mad. Warned me that if I queered the game, I'd earn the, uh, hatred of the rest of you. Reminded me I'm still in the running myself. I said no, I resign, but he told me to think that over before making it final. And then he dismissed me. The hardest thing to take is, he doesn't *care* what we do. Anyway we behave, it's an item for his notebook. Like rats in a maze." Louder: "Rats in a maze!"

"Worse," Julia replied. "Experimental animals put into a situation scientifically calculated to drive them insane."

Her free hand reached across both their laps to clasp his. "But we're more than rats," she went on. "We don't have to submit. We can choose to keep our decency— you and I, at least—can't we?"

He regarded her for a space, their faces quite near, before he murmured, "Are you proposing a partnership?"

"Yes," she said frankly. "Whatever happens, we two needn't stab at each other's backs. And you know, we could maybe do a bit of detective work together, try to learn who the killer is and who put him up to it . . . if nobody suspects we're a team."

"Ellis has the next turn." His words crawled.

"No telling what he'll do. But if we come through that . . . or one of us fails but not the other . . . An outside helper . . . It's even within the rules."

"What do you plan on calling, Julia?"

"I . . . haven't quite decided. We can talk that over. But later. The question right now, Larry, is, are we going to swear partnership? If so, we'll split whatever prize either or both of us may make, right down the middle." She drew breath before adding most softly: "Though that's less important than our being two people—two human creatures, maybe the only ones on this hell-haunted island, who can trust each other."

"I've got to say this," he forced out. "What does Byron think about your trustworthiness? Or Gayle about mine?"

"Byron turned on me, not I on him. I'll tell you what happened if you want. Gayle . . . well, you needn't bare your past to me. She's certainly been quick to take up with that loathsome Matthew Flagler. Am I right, Larry, you and she never made any formal agreement?"

"Uh, ye-es . . . yes, I suppose you could say that."

"Well, I, on the contrary, I offer you my word of honor and ask for yours."

"How do you know mine's any good?"

"Or you mine?" She leaned closer yet. "People discover such things, Larry."

He took her to him. She was wholly alive.

". . . Larry," she said as the kiss ended, "my dear, it's been hard for me. And Malcolm, yes, him too, worry and sorrow and . . . But he isn't here. I am. And . . . oh, doubtless I've not been what I ought to be with him. We're together, and I can't forget Kilby, and . . . often that's too much for him, too. Lately he's stayed away a lot of nights. He says it's business, but I think he's found another woman, and I can't honestly blame him. But Larry, Larry, it's lonesome!"

She kissed him again. "C'mon, boy," she whispered while she blew in his ear.

"The rooms—" He hesitated. "Bugged."

"To hell with that." She sprang to her feet and tugged at his hand. "Tonight we take a vacation from reality!"

Part Two

In the master's bedroom stood a grandfather clock. He had acquired it years ago as part of his program of restoring to the house as much of its heritage as might be.

Incapable of sleep, he opened his eyes and saw the clock against the wall, beyond the foot of his equally old four-poster, by the starlight that seeped in through uncovered windows. Glass-glimmery, its face was vague, half human. The pendulum swung like a long, emphatic arm. The ticking seemed louder than usual, sufficient to carry a whispery voice.

"Well," remarked Samael, "we got our melodrama in full measure today, didn't we?"

Haverner moved his head around the pillows in search of more comfort than they were giving his weariness. "I was mostly too busy to enjoy," he complained. "*You* need only be a spectator."

"The object of the game is not entertainment, it is the study of personality disintegration," Samael replied; he sounded almost academic. "A detached observer is necessary."

"If you are that. You never tell me anything that happens away from the spy gadgets."

"No. Think back, and you will see that I have always made you learn and do things yourself. You are a partner, not a puppet. In Machiavelli's phrase, I would not deprive you of that share of glory which belongs to you."

"I remember. Machiavelli said it about God vis-à-vis man. Are you claiming to be God?"

"Not exactly." The tone suggested that the face grinned.

"Satan, then? In which case you'd lie about your intentions, and whatever else suited you."

"We've been over this ground tediously often, Sunderland Haverner. Let me repeat that if you do not believe in God, which you claim not to, it is inconsistent to believe in devils. Not strictly illogical, but inconsistent. Please spare me your usual next question, whether I am an extraterrestrial being here to study or to torment humankind."

The old man lifted his head a little. His hands reached out into darkness, but remained empty. "What do you want?" he pleaded. "Never mind what you are. I realize you won't tell me; I simply can't help asking again sometimes. But what do you want? You guided me to where I am, all these years we've been together, but never told me more than that it interested you. What else? Why does it interest you?"

Dik . . . dik . . . dik, said the clock.

Haverner shivered. "Is what's going on here—the

game—was that your purpose from the start? Have I just been your means to this end?"

"Means and ends are not separable, you know," Samael answered, as if being patient. "You have enjoyed yourself along the way, have you not? You are enjoying yourself keenly as the game happens, true? Why look further?"

Haverner sank back. His hands dropped onto the coverlet and lay still, exhausted. "Part of the time, yes, it is a tremendous experience," he agreed.

"Schadenfreude with respect to the soul, eh?"

"What? Oh. Maybe." Haverner lay listening to his flimsy heart. "Yes," he murmured after a while, "if I can no longer create, I can destroy, and that makes me sure I'm still alive." He drew a sharp breath. "Only *can* they be destroyed?"

"Explain," invited Samael, though presumably aware of what the response would be.

"Thayer, yes, she seems bound for the abyss," Haverner said. Even now, his vocabulary bespoke that long-ago excellent education. "Shaddock . . . problematical. But Flagler and Nordberg—are what they have always been, and their partnership is winning the game because of it. Rance and Petrie—well, she has become an adulteress, but they don't take that too seriously in her circle, and she sees herself as doing it for the sake of her child, and mainly, those two are finding strength in each other. And Cruz, why, he was merely killed, unchanged, undefeated to the very last."

"He got off free," Samael admitted. "But as for the rest, let us wait and see what becomes of them. I think it will prove more satisfying than you, at this moment, expect."

Part Three

Byron and Ellis happened to share a breakfast hour. They exchanged wary good mornings and sat down on opposite sides of the table while making a mutual, slightly hopeful inspection for sunburn. But—apparently like everyone else—they had not been exposed so long that, given prompt and continued applications of cold vinegar, they showed anything worse than a redness which might or might not peel later on.

Leaf shadows flickered on the patio outside. Small cottony clouds ran before a wind that made rushing noises in the trees. Coffee and bacon perfumed the mild air. Neither man appeared to notice.

"I keep thinking you're our glorious leader tomorrow," Byron remarked with a somewhat strained laugh.

"I wish I were today," Ellis said impatiently. "Yesterday felt a week long. I'm sick of this place, this unwholesome atmosphere. And I do have work at home."

Byron considered him. "Aren't you worried? You may be the killer's next target."

"My turn won't be outdoors, and I've spoken to Haverner about security."

Byron consumed a mouthful before he waved his fork and said, "Simply getting through your day needn't make you safe, my friend. Suppose you don't eliminate everyone else. Then you're a potential sharer in the grand prize. Unless you're disposed of."

The look through the spectacles was careful. "You mean the killer was a torpedo for a contestant, don't you? In that case, his boss is Rance, or Mrs. Petrie, or me, . . . or you."

Byron nodded and took a sip of coffee. "It implies, besides, the actual murderer is Matt Flagler. I scarcely think Gayle can shoot, though she does act as if she's somehow tied to him. Of course, the contestant may have bribed an outsider, maybe one of the staff here, maybe a North Porter or a garrison trooper. But that seems unlikely."

"I favor Haverner's suggestion. It was a political job. Those Red terrorists live by the sword, and they perish by it."

"Still," Byron said, "no harm in keeping rather close tabs on Matt, is there?" His gaze hardened. "Or whoever has anything special to do with him."

"If you like," said Ellis. With unaccustomed wryness: "Thanks for the warning."

"No thanks necessary. Nor have I made any accusations. But I'd as soon arrange matters so nobody can put anybody up to bushwhacking me."

Again Larry and Julia took a box lunch, a bottle of wine, and this time a blanket north to the Bight and their place above the Iron Cliffs.

On the way, he worried. "If we're together like this, won't people guess we're, uh, allies?"

"No great harm if they do," she replied. "Except, as I said before, it might interfere with our possibly learning who's behind the murder. I've a few ideas about that."

"What are they?"

"Later." She hugged him. "We've so little time, darling, and this day is so gorgeous."

"Allee same you," he answered willingly, and when they reached their goal they started by making love.

Afterward they resumed their clothes, for in spite of the air being warm, a brisk wind whooped from the sea toward the Crag. In a slight haziness, that height floated half real above the rolling emerald west. Pines stood around them, a verdancy which somehow matched the sky, rough-textured ruddy trunks. Sunlight struck between branches, and the amber-hued mat of old needles drank it and gave it back in a warmth that felt like touching a living animal. Darkling, the precipices dropped straight down to the wrath among the reefs. Beyond, water was a million shifting diamond-dusted blues, and southward the curve of the shore was as lovely as the curve of Julia's flank.

"You know something?" Larry said. "You're a hell of a good lay."

Her lashes fluttered. "Thank you, kind sir. You inspire me."

"I hate to think how in a few days—"

"Then don't. Make with the corkscrew while I unwrap the sandwiches. . . . M-m-m, look. Feta cheese and marinated tomato slices, Italian salami and cucumbers, roast beef and horseradish on sweet-buttered pumpernickel, Greek olives and those magnificent pears."

"Plus a magnificent woman." He laid his face against her breasts. A hand roved over her buttocks.

She rumpled his hair. "Sensualist! Let's eat."

They took their time and talked much. She spoke mostly of Arizona, and of one unforgotten summer in Europe on a bicycle during her undergraduate years. For her, he remembered Japan, sans a girl named Suiko, and an unaffectedly bohemian houseboat community on Lake Union in Seattle, and scrapes he had been in that made entertaining stories; for himself, he recalled boats he had sailed, and finally he told her about *Morgana le Fay*.

"What a wonderful dream," she murmured, and stroked his cheek.

"Maybe you'd like to join me in it?" Having finished the meal, he sat leaned against a bole, smoked his pipe and nipped at the last of his wine. She knelt before him. The wind made ripples in her locks.

"No, darling," she said. "I have my damned duty. But every time the breeze blows in from the sea, I'll think of you."

"I was hoping for more." He leaned forward. "Julia, this's turned out to be not just a romp for me. After we get back to the States—"

"We have to do that first. Get back, with what we came here for. Otherwise nothing is any good."

"If we do, though, you and me?"

"We'll think about that then."

He set down his cup and reached for her, but she avoided him. "Please, not now," she requested. "We have serious business."

He sucked hard on the pipe. "Okay," he said dully. "You're right, I suppose."

"We're a working partnership as well as . . . what we've become since last night." She settled herself crosslegged. "We've a jungle, no, a nightmare to win through. A man has already died. I can't bear to imagine the next might be you."

"Or you." The paper cup crumpled as he snatched at it. Claret ran over hand and wrist. "Judas priest! Let's get busy."

"I've thought a lot about this. Maybe deeper than you. You've reacted. I . . . Well, they do say women are the practical sex. I have some ideas."

He tensed himself to listen.

"We dare not assume Orestes was killed by an outside enemy," she told him. "Because if that's wrong, our guard would be let down against the real murderer. Anyway, how plausible is the notion? Why would a political assassin choose that exact moment? He could operate easier, safer, at practically any other time. I'm convinced this was an inside job. One of our group arranged it."

"Or Haverner?" he exclaimed. "I've been wondering. He could've paid a hireling off—to keep the game going, and to see how we'd react."

She tugged her chin. "That hadn't occurred to me." After a few seconds, tossing her head: "Not too reasonable, however, if only because I doubt any of those nice Islandmen would go along."

"He could've bribed Matt."

"Or a player could have done that. Three possibilities there."

"Huh? You mean four, don't you? Or, no, wait, two."

"Three. If you were involved, Larry, and afterward registered the kind of shock you did, you wouldn't be needing a million dollars. You would already have made them, on stage and screen. But I can't be eliminated on those grounds. I even did have a confidential talk with the old monster."

"What about?"

"Equipment for my game. Never mind now. You'll simply have to take on faith that what your partner asked for was not a rifle which she later slipped to a trigger man."

"I believe," he said gravely, before he smiled a bit. "Logic, too. Your only possibility in that line would've been Matt, and you've been mighty cold to him."

"We could have reached a working agreement, he and I, while keeping up a pretense. In fact, two such collaborators would make a point of not seeming especially close."

"Him and Gayle—" Larry frowned. "Something funny there."

"Gayle knows what she isn't telling . . . probably doesn't dare tell." Julia nodded. "But let's continue our list. Ellis? He's egoistic enough to arrange a murder. Byron? He's crazy enough." She shivered. "What he made us do . . . Ellis wants the money, Byron wants the thrills. Both have the means on hand to pay for a killing. I know Ellis held a private talk with Haverner. Byron could doubtless have done the same when nobody was looking."

She paused, until she added in a wintry voice, "We'd better admit a further possibility. Crime is contagious. If TV reports a liquor store holdup, next day there are three times as many as usual. Or shootings or bombings or whatever. Well, we've all been under a terrific strain. And Byron is *not* stable."

He lowered his pipe. "What're you driving at?"

"Even if he was innocent yesterday, the example . . . Didn't you notice how he wallowed in the excitement?"

"Not really. But . . . m-m-m . . ."

"I got to understand him a little, Larry, when I thought he might make a good ally. Under that smooth surface, he's racked by demons. I'm pretty sure he's impotent. In any case, think about his career. He's had to keep proving he's a real man. And . . . 'the most dangerous game.' "

Larry grunted as if kicked. "Haverner, Flagler, Nordberg, Shaddock. We can't watch them all."

"No." Julia spoke crisply. "But we don't need to. Haverner would scarcely act unless his torture chamber gets threatened again with premature breakup. Ellis is no physical menace. He's far too cautious, besides being on the wrong side of forty. That leaves Matt and Byron.

Matt's under suspicion, therefore under close surveillance by everyone. He might give them the slip regardless, but hardly in the near future. Which brings us to Byron. He could be neutralized."

"How?"

Her gaze dwelt on him. "You're a strong man, Larry. You're gentle with me, but I can feel your strength underneath."

"Wait!" He sat bolt upright. "You mean I . . . But Julia, we don't know if he's ever dreamed of harming a soul!"

"Dare we take the chance?" She returned to her kneeling position, grasped his shoulders, said quickly and intensely, "You wouldn't kill him, nor seriously hurt him. But you could, I know you could leave him unfit . . . for a while . . . to be a menace."

"Or to play against us." Larry's voice came thick.

She dipped her head. "True." She raised it. "He doesn't need any share in the money. He's here for nothing except competition—excitement—and he can buy as much of that as he wants around the world. How big a break does he deserve?

"Hush." She laid a palm across his opening mouth. "Let me finish. If I last out tomorrow, whatever Ellis is hatching in that cold brain of his, I'm certain of a share in the loot, because of course I won't call a game I could lose myself, the way you did, dear chivalrous Larry. The question is, how large a share? I'm not necessarily able to eliminate anyone else. Suppose I don't, and the pot splits four ways. Then you and I each have a quarter million, two hundred and fifty thousand dollars, to play with. Sound like a lot? Think. It might buy you your ship, but what about supporting her for a lifetime? The interest on it, if Malcolm and I make the right investments, will maintain Kilby, but we won't dare touch the principal. It won't liberate us from debt, from the damned middle class; and you, you who don't carry my burdens, can you imagine how I want to escape that pen after these past years? How I want, how I need money to be something that's simply there, like air or sunlight?"

She barely caught her breath before hastening on. "Now say you alone drop out. We're partners. So we split one third of a million, which is one-sixth apiece, worse than before, not sufficient at all. A hundred and sixty-odd thousand. I've lain awake nights with those figures, Larry, and wretched company they are!

"If I'm broken tomorrow, but you aren't, the contest ends, because I'll have forfeited my turn. Same situation. One-sixth apiece for us.

'But a three-way split at the finish, you, me, and Ellis—I say Ellis because he doesn't seem to have buttons we can push—that's three hundred and thirty thousand plus. Too little for his purposes, and we can grin at that, but not bad for ours.

"And if Byron's forced out, and I last through Ellis's game, and he doesn't last through mine . . . Larry, you and I will each walk away with half a million. Five hundred thousand tax-free dollars to spend however we please. You could take half of that to build and supply a *Morgana* like you've never dared imagine, and invest the other half for a good income the rest of your life!"

"If Byron's forced out," he rasped.

Her face was flushed, eyes brilliant, lips parted over ice-white teeth. "Yes. If Byron's forced out."

Presently she added, "Don't think of it as greed. Think what you and I could do for the world that he or Ellis would not. You mentioned the Salvation Army a while back that seems like ages. Or what about some genuine oceanographic work? Or—more my department, perhaps—getting into politics, helping elect a few of the right officers for Spaceship Earth?"

Her mouth stretched wide. "Oh, unmerciful God, Larry, I'm so sick of being helpless! Aren't you?"

The tears came, and he held her close and promised everything.

Gayle kept to her chamber, uneasily napping.

Ellis, in his own, sought the news, especially Stateside, on the radio.

Matt watched television and drank bourbon in the living room. Eventually he passed out on a couch. He was to wake about midnight, grope his way to bed, and snore on.

Byron went fishing. He had no luck.

Returning at four, he sauntered up from the dock. His white sport clothes were no longer immaculate.

Following a shower and change, a gin and tonic would go well. The crew stayed behind, cleaning the boat and battening down. Thus he emerged on a wide sweep of lawn, trees, flowerbeds, altogether alone.

No—from the brush, to the right, a murmur: "Byron."

He turned. Julia stood on the trail, gesturing. Her tall form was clad in shirt, slacks, walking shoes, to which a few pine needles clung. When he joined her, palmetto and bamboo screened them from the grounds, and from the beachward path itself after she had drawn him around a bend. Stalks and fronds rustled dryly amidst wave-boom and gull-cry. It smelled green here, and the light was unrestful, a shadow-stippled yellow.

"Hi," he said tentatively. "What's the occasion?"

"I've been wanting to talk to you, Byron." Her manner was shy. "In private, I mean."

He stiffened. "Oh?"

"About what happened—that night before your leadership."

He bit his lip and regarded his toes. "I owe you an apology. But, well, next day—day after my turn, that is—I felt awkward. And then came poor Orestes's death." He swallowed. "All right. I'm sorry I slapped you. I was overwrought."

"That's what I wanted you to know," she told him. "That I do understand. Or think I do. In fact, the mistake, the fault was mine."

He reddened under the sun-scorch and ran fingers through his limp brown hair. The long chin quivered. "I must have, well, misinterpreted what you said."

"You didn't. It was me who misinterpreted you." Her hands fell briefly onto his waist. She caught his glance and did not release it. "They call you a playboy. I knew that wasn't right. Don't you remember? I told you you're a terribly serious person. But I suppose enough of the 'playboy' label stuck that I didn't quite see you're more principled than I am."

He cleared his throat. "Everybody to their own principles. Very well. Two-way confusion, and under these unnatural conditions . . . Well, I'm glad you took the initiative, . . . Julia. I do like you."

"And I you, Byron. I couldn't let that wall stand between us." She sighed. "I wish . . ."

"What?" he was forced to ask.

"Oh, nothing. Everything's too ghastly mixed up." She looked away. "Who do you think killed him?"

"I hesitate to make possibly unfounded charges," he said.

"Of course. But we can't help wondering, can we? Especially when the killer might . . . I'm scared, Byron. Less for myself than for my daughter. If I never come home . . ."

He touched her shoulder. "Stick close to me if you want," he offered.

"I'm not sure I can," she said forlornly.

"What?" He showed surprise. "Why not?"

"Well . . ." She filled her lungs. "Okay, I'll tell you. It's Larry Rance. You must have noticed how he was kind of paying me court. And how desperate he was, yesterday after the thing happened. Well, I was too. I showed it less, but I was. He and I . . . gravitated together? . . . But he's almost a paranoiac. He thinks anybody may have done the crime, or instigated it. So he trusts nobody. He spent this whole time today, that I'd hoped could be an escape for a few hours, he spent it haranguing me. . . . Oh!"

The big man stepped into their sight.

He halted and glowered. "Hello," Byron ventured.

"I warned you, Julia." Larry's voice was flat. "You're lucky to be alive."

Byron attempted a smile. "Do you mean I might be the one behind the murder?" he responded as casually as possible.

"And maybe ready for a do-it-yourself project," Larry said.

"Ridiculous. Why on earth should I?"

"Because you can't stand to lose," Larry jerked a thumb over his shoulder. "On your way, charlie."

Byron tautened a notch further. "See here, Rance, I'm willing to make allowances, but I don't concede you the right to order me around."

"Come over here, Julia," Larry said. "I don't want you out of my sight. It isn't safe."

She caught Byron's arm. "No. You're wrong." She sounded frightened.

"You heard me. Both of you."

"Hey, wait just a damn minute," Byron erupted. "It's *you* who's begun acting dangerous. Julia, would you like me to escort you to the house?"

"Please." She could barely be heard.

"We both will." Larry moved closer. He donned an unpleasant grin. "Not that you need be afraid of losing your virtue . . . to him."

Byron stood dead motionless. A jay cawed off in the fallow shadows.

"Larry." Julia slipped halfway behind Byron. "Please."

Byron stirred. "That'll do, Rance." He spoke as if hands were around his throat. "Leave us. Immediately. Or must I give you a lesson in manners?"

Larry cocked his fists. "Care to try, pansy-boy?"

Byron looked suddenly tired. "I'm sorry, Julia," he said. "Stand clear." He advanced.

He moved in boxer wise, bent-kneed, slightly crouched, left arm on guard, right fist held low and back. Larry waited.

As the attack came, Larry slipped aside, caught wrist and elbow, used momentum to whirl his opponent around. Byron recovered and threw a punch at the stomach. Larry chopped the blade of his left hand down to deflect. With his right, he struck at the neck. Byron staggered. Larry closed. His knee drove upward. Byron shrieked and lurched back. Sweat spurted forth upon him. Larry pursued, blow after blow to the now defenseless body. He grunted as he smashed them home. Byron toppled and lay curled in the dust, half-conscious, hugging his agony.

Larry stood above him, gasping nearly as hard. Julia plucked his sleeve and hissed in his ear, "Kick him a few good ones."

Larry shook his head as if to tear it loose. He walked stiff-legged away. Out on the lawn, beneath the sun, he mumbled, "Christ. I could puke. He expected I'd fight fair."

"Did the engineer of Orestes's murder?" Julia retorted.

"Who's proved that was Byron?" Larry half turned. "Look, I've got to go back and help him."

"No. He'll manage. You didn't do any permanent harm." Julia embraced Larry. "I know. It was an ugly thing. But you had to do it. You had to. Come on, darling. Upstairs, bring a stiff drink for both of us, and I'll soon have you feeling better."

Only they and Ellis dined with Haverner that evening.

"I trust the breach between you and Mr. Shaddock can be repaired, Mr. Rance," said he at the head of the table. "Would you care to tell me how it came about?"

Larry stared at his plate. "A mutual misunderstanding," Julia said. "Each near the point of breakdown. I'll try to make peace between them."

"Good, good," Haverner answered. "Mr. Shaddock is resting in his room under sedation, however, so I doubt the advisability of speaking to him before morning."

"Will he be in shape to compete?" Ellis inquired fretfully. "I don't want my turn postponed. No disrespect, sir, but I have to get away, get home as soon as possible."

"That depends on what you have in mind, Mr. Nordberg."

"You know what I plan. Nothing physical."

"But pain and the aftereffects of shock may be too heavy a mental handicap. I think, in fairness, we shall have to ask Mr. Shaddock tomorrow if he himself feels able to participate."

Ellis scowled. "I believe he will," Julia said. Further talk was desultory.

They went back to her room right after the meal. Unlike Gayle's, it was of almost military neatness and held a minimum of feminine gear. Two pictures of Kilby stood on the bureau; she had put Malcolm's in a drawer. Some books, paperbacks she had brought and hardcovers she had borrowed from the library here, were on a bedside table. They included a couple of mystery novels, de Voto's *The Course of Empire,* a Kipling collection, an anthology of modern verse. Both windows stood open on the duskless tropical nightfall. Stars and fireflies were coming forth, as if racing to see which could finish first. The wind had died, leaving only surf, and warmth and forest odors drifted in.

Larry closed the door. "Are we being too obvious?" he fretted.

"Nobody seems to be paying attention," Julia answered. Her tone was indifferent. "They're wrapped in their personal troubles and fears. I've noticed for a long time, even in ordinary life, how few people are really aware of what happens outside their own skins."

Larry glared at a wall. "Haverner, though. His electronics somewhere behind that pretty paper, recording for him to listen. I don't like that."

"Nor I. But we can't do much about it, can we? And after all, it's his whole purpose in bringing us here. To observe. We won't hurt our cause with him by furnishing him data. I don't believe the information will go any further."

"Is what you just said a data too?"

Julia laughed. "Yes. And by the way, dear, the singular is 'datum.'"

"Okay," Larry said. "Here's another datum for you, Haverner. You are a turd."

He cast himself into a chair. His neck drooped; his shoulders slumped. "The worst is," he mumbled, "I've become the same."

"No, Larry. Never." Julia came to stand beside him. She stroked his hair. "What happened? You beat a man, a younger man, in a fight. He was ready to hurt you, wasn't he?"

"I picked that fight. You helped. We planned it."

"For Kilby. For *Morgana le Fay* and the saving of the oceans. And maybe for survival. I tell you, Byron Shaddock is dangerous to more than our pocketbooks, quite likely to our lives. Or he was, till you cut him down to size. At worst, if I'm mistaken about him, he took an undeserved beating. He'll soon recover. Innocent bystanders always suffer in war, and this is a kind of war we're in, isn't it?" Julia laid hands along his jaw and raised his face. "Lord, Lord, Larry,' she breathed, "how lucky that you're strong!"

He reached to enfold her waist and lay his cheek on her belly. "I need you worse'n you need me, Julia." But when he tried to unzip her dress, she stopped him.

"Not yet. You've something left to do this night."

"What?" he asked, weakly dismayed.

She sat down in the second chair and captured his gaze. "We're not through. You want justice for Orestes, don't you? And safety for us. That means finding out for certain who shot him, and why, and where the gun is."

His countenance tightened. "Yeah."

"We haven't eliminated Matthew Flagler. In fact, he's the likeliest of the lot, at any rate as the actual killer."

"What'm I supposed to do? Give him the same treatment? I'm pretty sure he'd pull a switchblade if the gun wasn't handy."

"There's Gayle. They have a relationship going."

"I wondered—"

"I didn't. I knew from the start. It's obvious. Equally obvious is that it's his idea and she's frightened and miserable."

Larry winced. "Poor kid."

"You two were making beautiful music together for a while, weren't you?" It was hardly a question.

"Well, uh . . ."

Julia stroked his arm and smiled. "I'm not jealous. You're mine now, and that's what counts. But I'd like to see Gayle made happier."

"Hey, wait!" Larry cried.

"If you went to her, right away, while Matt's downstairs in his drunken stupor, and treated her kindly, she'd tell you what she knows."

"But . . . no, *darling,* you can't mean it."

She fended off his hands. "Can and do, lover," she snapped. "It's absolutely necessary to us, and it'll help her. You can go to her, and I'll wait for you here. Or you can go, but not to her, and you needn't bother coming back. Take your choice."

Larry regarded her for an entire minute. The window was now full of stars. Against the light in the chamber they showed small and cold.

Julia gentled with a slow smile. " 'The female of the species is more deadly than the male,' " she said low. "Conceded." Then, urgent once more: "But will you concede that deadliness is the name of this game?" She got him to his feet, kissed him at length, smacked him between the shoulderblades. "On your way, lad."

Gayle had asked for sandwiches to be brought her, had eaten them and fallen back into troubled sleep. The soft knocking hauled her from it. She sat up amidst tangled sheets in darkness and called, "No, Matt. Please. Tomorrow. Please. Please."

"Larry here," came the muted answer. "Let me in, will you?"

"Matt—" She shuddered.

"Passed out. He won't count for anything till morning, I'm certain. Gayle, I've got to talk with you."

She switched on the bedside lamp, made an uneven way to the door, and admitted him. He shut it as soon as he was through and turned the latch. For a space they stood breathing. He was still in sports clothes. She had the same nightgown she wore when first she sought him; but it was crumpled and there were stains on it.

"Julia throw you out?" she asked shrilly.

"I, uh, I've missed you," he said.

She collapsed into his embrace. He led her to the bed, sat down and held her till she had finished sobbing.

Finally she blew her nose, dabbed at eyes gone red and puffy, said with a forlorn giggle and several hiccoughs, "Oh, my, I bet I look like billy hell."

Larry grimaced above her head and hugged the plump shoulders. "You'll always look good to me, Gayle."

"L-l-let's share a joint."

"Fine. Thanks."

They took chairs and passed the twisted cylinder back and forth. At each exchange their fingers brushed more lingeringly, and she pressed her knee against his. Before long the room was full of the harsh smell, and a measure of peace had come upon her.

"Sweet Jesus, I've been scared, Larry."

"Why?" he insisted.

She squirmed. "Well, Matt, he's, he's a scary type. I mean, well, he wants what he wants, when an' how he wants it, an' he'll hit you, an' wave that knife o' his around, if you don't . . ."

"Bad, huh?"

She took a long draught. "What he makes me do, well, sure, I don't believe God'll punish us or anything, but most of it I don't like—I'd throw up if I dared—and some of it hurts." She gave him the reefer. "Oh, Jesus, how glad I am you're back!"

He was not inhaling the smoke, a fact unobservable from outside. "Why do you stand for it?" he demanded.

"You could come to me or—or Haverner himself—and ask for protection."

"Well, I, I . . ." She sucked frantically on the roach. It burned her. She dropped it.

He leaned forward, laid hands on her thighs, and said, "I want to help you, Gayle. We could become partners again, maybe." He swallowed. "Well, at the very least, I want to help you out of this swamp you've fallen into. But you've got to cooperate. Understand? You've got to trust me."

And the story spilled from her.

In Julia's room he concluded bleakly, "I told her to play along for the time being. Do no good if we came straight out and accused El—Nordberg and Flagler—would it? They'd deny everything, and Gayle's life wouldn't be worth a second mortgage on Haverner's soul."

"Right." The tall woman nodded where she stood athwart the midnight in a window. "Did you tell her to try wheedling from him the hiding place of that rifle?"

"No. I didn't think of that."

"Probably just as well. She's no actress. He could see through her and . . . We'll have to do something. I'm not sure what. But if they were prepared to commit one murder for the prize, they won't stop at a second or third."

Julia shook back her hair, came to him, took his hands and brushed her lips across his. "Good work, though, you lovely boat bum," she said. "We know who the enemy is, who to beware of, and that's a long forward step. Your doing!" She paused. "Now we'd better get some sleep. We have to be fresh for Nordberg's test. He said breakfast at nine, and it's almost two."

"I s'pose," he muttered.

She cocked her head. "Troubles? You've done marvelously. And there's a way of getting sleepy, you know, the best in the world."

He shook his. "No. Thanks."

"Too tired? How understandable. Never mind, dearest. Tomorrow."

His voice plodded. "Not that. I mean, I did have to convince Gayle I'm on her side, didn't I? It turned out that involved screwing her."

Julia's chuckle was tender. "I'm glad. She needed to be screwed by someone who cares how she feels."

"But I'm not used up," Larry said. He stood passive in her presence, in the night. He might almost have been a small boy trying to explain to his mother how he had come to do wrong. "It's that . . . proceeding straight on to you . . . would make things worse. I don't know why, but it would. I'm going after a drink, and I'll take it to bed with me—my bed—and hope it'll relax me till I can sleep."

He turned from her. Gripping the doorknob, he said, "I'd feel better, Julia, if I hadn't been able to make it with her tonight."

ELLIS NORDBERG

Therefore wait ye upon me, saith the LORD, until the day that I rise up to the prey: for my determination is to gather the nations, that I may assemble the kingdoms, to pour upon them mine indignation, even all my fierce anger: for all the earth shall be devoured with the fire of my jealousy.

Who'd have thought to hear words out of Zephaniah from the pulpit of a barebones church on a forgotten island, or expected majesty like that in the dialect of a half-breed preacher? That was a good sermon he gave on the text, too. He really laid it on the line. I wish I could have gone to hear him again this Sunday.

I truly do, Lord. You know I don't often miss a chance to attend divine service. If the chances come kind of seldom these days, why, that's because you keep me busy. You want me to prosper, for an example of your mercy and to become able to do your work in this world.

For that which I am about to receive, I thank you, Lord, in the name of Jesus Christ our Saviour. Amen.

You understand why I can't say grace aloud at the table of the heathen. You read it in my heart, every meal. I am a miserable sinner and not worthy, of course, but you are always with me, you deliver me from evil, because I am your servant.

Light sheens off the silver coffeepot as the waitress pours for me. I'm first at breakfast. It's sunny outside, Sabbath quiet, most of the staff gone to chapel in town. I don't do wrong to take my turn on Sunday, do I? You made those cards come up the way you wanted them. It's actually a sign that my day is yours, isn't it?

A clatter. Blast it, can't people be decently quiet in the morning? Gayle Thayer comes in. "Hello," she says. I only nod. That wanton doesn't rate courtesy; still, I'd better stay polite till I can figure how to get rid of her. Matt could doubtless handle it, but that'd make him still more of a problem in himself. . . . They deserve each other, those two, the hairy swine and the fat sow, honeying and stewing over the nasty sty. (Funny how that line of Shakespeare sticks in my mind. Mainly he's overrated, a windbag.) The wicked shall feel the wrath.

She looks happier than she did, these past days. Maybe because he was too besotted to come to her last night? Or—she simpers when Rance appears. "La-a-rree-ee!" What's been going on?

He doesn't give her more than a grunt. He brushes past her, prowls to the French doors, stands looking out. I can see how tense he is. Well, me too. My heart flaps and my ribs prickle. This is my day. It is, isn't it? Unless that miserable Shaddock puts things off.

Here he comes, limping. From Glamor Boy to Wounded Hero. You can practically hear him creak, though no injuries show. He stops cold when he sees Rance, who turns about. Silence stretches and stretches between them.

Julia Petrie! I don't believe she arrives at this exact minute by accident, that witch. She lays a hand over Shaddock's. "How are you, Byron?" Oh, she really knows how to sound concerned, that cunning, cunning harlot. She doesn't want any delays either. So we're on the same team right now, Julia. I'm rooting for you as hard as x many men have rooted in you.

"I'll live," Shaddock says with his Errol Flynn leer,

"in spite of not being terribly enthusiastic at the prospect."

Rance clears his throat and shuffles his feet. His mistress (I'm not blind) maneuvers for him. "That was a dreadful thing yesterday," she says. "Can't we make it up before it festers worse?"

"Well," Rance says, and he must have rehearsed his lines with her, "I'm sorry it happened, Byron. We both flew off the handle, right?"

"*I* tried to observe a few elementary decencies," Ivy League tells him.

"Well, I wasn't sure. I mean, a fight to me's not a, uh, sporting event, it's something to get over as fast as may be. I suppose I should've realized you might see the matter different. I tried not to hurt you badly." Rance is not an experienced hypocrite. But he's learning.

The Petrie woman is in charge anyway. "I'm afraid I owe you both an apology. I lay awake the whole night, or so it felt, [like fun you did, sister!] trying to figure out what went wrong, and the more I thought, the more it seemed my words, my actions, provoked you both. Before God, I'd no such intention! [The Lord will remember how you take his name in vain.] But there the horrible result was. Must we fall apart?" she whines. "Can't we be civilized human beings again? No prize is worth what we've been doing to ourselves."

So she gets them to shake hands, and she sits down between them, opposite me. Larry, by quick footwork, puts himself on her right, next to Haverner's empty place. That way he avoids having to sit by Gayle, who's at the foot of the table as usual and watching him like a . . . a brat outside a candy store, I guess.

But I can't hold back. "Do you feel up to playing today, Byron?" I ask. My heart bumps.

He rubs his forehead. "Pretty woozy, I'm afraid."

"That needn't make any difference," I say. Julia's glance crosses mine. She knows better.

"If you possibly could, Byron," she oozes, "it'd be one day less for us all."

No doubt she composed Rance's line. "Don't lean on him, Julia. Frankly, in his conditon, I doubt if I'd be man enough to play."

Shaddock flushes (under the sunburn that Commie

bequeathed to us. Mine still feels hot, and it's begun to itch, and I hope you enjoy yourself, Orestes Cruz, looking up from hell). She soothes him. After a minute or two of wheedling, he yelps, "All right! All right!" She kisses his cheek, the she-Judas.

York escorts Haverner in. I'm the only one who's not surprised at this first breakfast appearance of his. He must have figured out what's coming and wants to witness the confounding of mine enemy.

We rise while he is seated. What a head he's got! If you think of him as human, he's pretty hideous, but you mustn't. Inhuman, he's beautiful, like an eagle, the eagle of John; and the computer inside that skull . . . !

I gather he's not a Christian. Nevertheless the Lord has seen fit to make him mighty upon the earth, even as Cyrus was made mighty to free Israel, as Augustus was so there'd be a Roman peace wherein the words of our Saviour could be heard. My Cyrus, my Augustus. "Good morning, Mr. Haverner."

If only he'd join me in some projects, once I have his million, once I've shown him what I can do. He never had children, did he? Is he maybe sifting men in search of a worthy heir?

Since everybody's here, except for Matt who's sleeping it off, the servants take our orders and bring us our food. "You will be playing today, then?" Haverner asks.

"Yes, fortunately," I say. "The material I wanted is on hand, isn't it?"

"Indeed. At your disposal."

The three rivals I have left grow tight where they sit facing me. "When do we start?" Rance wants to know.

"Directly after breakfast," I tell him. That's when we start. And that's when you finish, Rance.

None of them eat or speak a lot.

After my third cup of coffee, I say, "Does everyone feel ready?" May as well be polite. Julia can't quite hide the stiffness of her nod. "Where do we go?" she says.

"We stay here for the first round," I reply. "Mr. Haverner?"

He signals to York, who goes out.

Triumph beats in my temples. "I've planned a couple of very simple, fair games," I hear myself announce. "Nothing that you can't do if you put your minds to it."

York comes back and sets a bowl in front of Haverner. (The Islandman still looks shocked. I wonder how he can be religious and not rejoice that we're afflicted with one less godless Communist.) The bowl is full of assorted nut meats.

"Help yourselves," I invite.

Rance jumps nearly out of his seat. "No!"

"That's the first round." I meet his eyes and know I am his master. "Each of us eats a one-fourth part of this dish."

He collapses back into the chair. For a minute Julia is as horrified as him. But she's quick to mask her feelings, except that she caresses his arm, shameless before us all. Byron doesn't get the idea at once, he's dull-witted and pain-distracted for sure, but he's grimly pleased to see his rival shaken. Gayle puts hand to mouth and squeaks, "Larry, honey, what's wrong?" Haverner—who can read Haverner?

"You son of a bitch," Larry whispers.

He whirls on our host and bawls, "I can't! I'm allergic to nuts! This bastard knows it. He . . . yes, he must've slipped some grated nut meat into my eggs, a week ago, to test—I wondered—it's not fair!"

"You made me risk my life in the surf," I remind him, and smile, because I've already gotten this test approved. "Youth and experience were on your side then. If chemistry [and the Lord, the Lord] is on my side now, you've got no complaint coming."

He babbles at Haverner. Adulteress Julia takes his part in a more reasonable style. But of course the eagle head shakes; the desert voice answers, "It is legitimate. You would not be fatally stricken, would you, Mr. Rance?"

"I'd be out of shape to do anything the rest of the day!" His fist hits the table, a thump that rattles the china.

"Same as you planned for me, eh?" Shaddock jeers.

The air goes out of Rance. He slumps. Finally he groans, "Okay, I'm licked. I quit."

Julia grips his hand. They trade a long look. It seems to encourage him. It proves they have an arrangement, those two, beyond simple lust. If I don't beat her today, I'll have to be almighty careful. I wouldn't put murder past them.

Rance moves his chair to a corner, lights his smelly pipe and fumes away. Gayle joins him. He ignores her. I guess he's not sulking—yet—so much as he's trying not to cry. We three who are left go through the solemn farce of eating the nuts.

Afterward Haverner excuses himself and I lead them —the two spectators as well—into the living room. Anselmo is there. Good man, that; wish he were mine. Clipboards and pencils have been provided. On a table stands a locked box. I confront them and explain.

"We'll have a little arithmetic session today, folks. Nothing but problems any grade-school kid can do: adding, subtracting, multiplying, dividing. I haven't seen them myself. At my request, Mr. Haverner kindly ordered a computer to prepare the test, and the printouts were flown here in this box, which I'll ask Anselmo to open." I lift a hand to forestall Julia's objection. "Yes, I know people have different talents. You can't blame me for calling a contest I'm strong in. But you'll have ample time for the work. Till tomorrow sunrise if you want. What you must do is get every problem right. A single wrong answer means you've lost. The solutions are in a sealed envelope which we'll check when we're done."

"Suppose *you* make a mistake?" Rance says spitefully.

"Well, then Mrs. Petrie and Mr. Shaddock are home free." I can afford to laugh. Me make a mistake with numbers? I live by them! Arithmetic was always easy for me—in school they called me phenomenal at it, though they never appreciated me properly otherwise—and the years in business have only sharpened my skill.

Shaddock glowers. Julia's stare is cool. Oh, you're a sly bitch, all right, you.

Everybody is startled at the size and number of the long sheets that Anselmo passes out. Everybody but me. I specified things like fifty figures to add together, ten-digit long division, stuff that'll twine around in their heads like worms.

"You can send for coffee, food, tobacco, whatever you wish," I say benevolently. "Only get Anselmo to lead you when you go to the restroom, so we'll be sure nobody peeks at somebody else's—ha—exam."

Julia sighs and settles in. The pencil shivers in Shaddock's fingers. He'll never make it, and knows that, and knows I know it, and from time to time his bloodshot eyes reach over to hate me, but he won't quit.

I get busy myself, seated straight in my chair, clipboard on lap. It's pleasant work—automatic after a while. There's no sound except the scratching of pencils, the rustle of paper, an occasional muttered oath from Shaddock. Before long, Rance rises, stretches, says a sullen "No spectator sport, this, hunh?" and slouches out. Gayle patters behind him. I wonder if they'll pass the time fornicating.

How is it to fornicate with Julia?

Imagine her naked on a bed of flowing numbers. I'm sure she's better than Gayle, besides being better-looking. Gayle has that in-heat quality, doubtless she's more experienced, the little tart, but Julia projects this aristocratic image, like she always knows exactly what's she's doing, and—

Hoy! Almost carried a three there. It's a four, actually.

Julia's doing well. She goes confidently ahead, then checks and rechecks each result. I'm afraid she'll last the course. Shaddock's pencil wobbles.

A mighty good secretary was lost in you, Julia. Should I offer you a job? No, you'd be too clever about looking after Number One. Everybody does, yes, but I have to make sure my employees are less smart than me. You, I'm not sure but what you're my equal, in your underhanded female way.

It'd be good for you if I got you in bed. Bring down your pride. If I made you do exactly what I wanted, you'd see that you are less than dust in the sight of the Lord.

Suppose you last out this day; you'll have something diabolical cooked up for me. Only, suppose I got Haverner to lend me his recordings, photographs, micro-camera movies. . . .

Well, Julia, here's the proof. You wouldn't like your husband to know you've been rutting with that Rance beast, would you? Unless you cancel your own game, resign in my favor. . . . Ah, yes, I understand about your daughter's problem. We can work something out. In return for *that* favor . . .

No, better' not. It is a sin. Besides, I might fail in bed,

which is embarrassing. I admit to myself, because you want me to be honest, Lord, I admit the reason I domineer over my wife, and find endless fault with her, is so I won't have to try copulating. Of course, the real blame is hers, the way she's let herself get unattractive.

No gratitude in her. I've done my duty. I'm still doing it. She has a fine home, the best food, her own car, a fantastic clothing allowance, doesn't she? And two sons, who are good boys at heart, I hope, though I worry about Bob, his long hair and wild clothes. He could go the hippie route. . . . How did I fail him, if I did? Was I too merciful? Dad never had pity on me. It was up before daybreak to milk the cows and swill the pigs before walking a mile to the schoolbus stop, and after school the same, and summer vacations were because we really had hard work to do, and as for Sundays, Dad considered our pastor too lax.

(Even so, why did he christen me Elias? Elias Nordberg! How many hours altogether did I waste, explaining I was not a Jew?)

How we struggled to hang on to our flat gray piece of South Dakota, and how I hated every minute and swore over and over to myself (teen-ager's tears in a haystack, a cornfield, a stinking chickenhouse that must be cleaned) that I would break free, and how good for me the discipline of it was!

1,287,416.

Matt Flagler shambles in. Anselmo shushes him and eases him out. On the way, he gives me what he imagines is a significant look. He hasn't shaved and I catch a stale whiff of him. The creature.

The problem. He did prove to be a reliable executioner. (Farsighted of me to take him out in the woods, well beyond earshot, and make him demonstrate on targets that he really is a good rifleman.) But that was his only value. As blabbermouth or blackmailer he's dangerous.

Should I have him get rid of Gayle Thayer? She knows too much herself. But she's timid. I'm reasonably sure she can be frightened into silence. And however richly she deserves death for her sins, Lord, you know I am a merciful man who doesn't like it, who didn't even like it when I had to arrange about those gooks in Korea.

Matt, however . . .

Well, I'll string him along for a while, anyhow, and then decide. Julia's my next hurdle, if she doesn't fail today. I'm afraid it's a pipe dream that Haverner would release the evidence he has of her misbehavior, to me. Haverner and the Lord help those who help themselves. Now the Lord can't possibly intend for her to get half a million dollars—or the whole sum, and I nothing, nothing—as the reward for her adultery.

The wages of sin. Yes, probably Matt and I will be having us a little talk this evening or tomorrow.

Lord, I'm sounding like a gangster movie, aren't I? But you know I'm a righteous man. I'm not perfect, I know better than to believe I'm perfect, but when I fall from grace, my repentance is sincere, and I really don't think my church could carry on without the contributions I make.

A good master rewards good service. By what you have given me, Lord, I know I have found favor in your eyes. *Blessed shall be thy basket and thy store.* Oh, my ramming virile Jaguar! Oh, my enthroning to come in my own executive aircraft!

That's where it's at, Bob, my prodigal son. Your brother understands (though he seems to feel I owe him a cushy job in the company), why can't you? This is the atomic age. A bunch of eco-freak old women of both sexes want to take us back to a nature that never was. Well, I've got news for them. If we tried it, we billions, it'd be famine, pestilence, war, and death on his pale horse. We've got no place to go but ahead. The machine is our destiny. Sure, I like nine holes of golf as well as the next man. I'm the one who appreciates nature, not those Sierra Club bastards. I want to help the human race by developing the land so the ordinary man can drive there and enjoy it at a price he can afford. Those lock-the-door-and-throw-away-the-key wilderness bastards, they're the snobs, not me. Me, I work to make more energy available. Power. Power. Power.

And is not the laborer worthy of his hire?

I have toiled long in your vineyards, O Lord. I have borne meekly the troubles, disappointments, frustrations, betrayals, unjust hostility and outright paranoia, with which you have tested me. Now comes the day of my reward.

It must.

A million. One lousy million. That's all I need to start my empire.

Shaddock blinks; his head rolls downward; he jerks it upright and struggles on. But he won't make it. Rance did too good a job on him, and the harvest is mine. We've hardly been at this business an hour. The computer has given us a full day's work for me, more for anybody less gifted.

I'm afraid the Petrie woman will last the course, though.

Think. Between me and my reward, me and the deeds which will make me remembered a thousand years for my prophet's vision . . . nothing except her. That whore, that slut, that bitch, that tramp, that abomination in the sight of the Lord.

INTERVAL SEVEN
Part One

Larry and Gayle stepped out onto the veranda. When he halted at the rail, she did too. Beyond the screen, the grounds sloped upward to wildwoods and the Crag beyond, downward to beach and pier. Grass seemed like a newly washed rug, its woven-in flower patterns almost garish beneath the sun. Trees were the ponderous furniture, but a fuchsia and a hummingbird were playing together. Waters sparkled, heaven reached dizzily high. The air lay mild, scented, full of an enormous quietness.

"Oh, gosh, Larry," she attempted. "You lost. Your boat, your dream. I'm so fucking sorry."

He grunted around his pipestem and did not look at her.

"You're sure taking it bravely," she said.

"No use bursting into tears, is there?"

She leaned against him and stroked his hair. "Hey," she murmured, "how 'bout we go upstairs and console each other? You know, last night was wonderful. Like being born again. Larry. Lover."

"No." Observing her dismay at his curtness, he turned to her and went on in a low, hard tone, "The game's not done. Can't you get it into your fluffy head, you're involved with murderers?"

"Oh, sweet Christ." She shrank back against the wall. Terror stormed her countenance. "I know, I know. But what can we do except run?"

"That's no solution. Listen, unless Julia fails today, and I don't think she will, she's in awful danger. . . . Okay, okay, you're thinking you don't care what becomes of Julia. Think again, doll. Let Ellis win, and what're you to him and Matt except a nuisance claim? What if they decide not to risk your blabbing to the fuzz, or the press, or whatever? . . . Damnation! Don't pass out on me! Here, here's a swing, sit down if you feel faint, but listen. Julia—as winner—Julia won't have any reason to threaten anybody. In fact, if we can help her, maybe save her life—you follow me?—she'd show her appreciation."

After an effort Gayle could whisper, "What . . . should . . . I do?"

"Work on Matt. Jolly him. If you possibly can, learn where he's hidden that rifle. But sugar-talk him, at least, distract him, try to drop hints that may drive a wedge between him and Ellis. Get the idea? Can you do that?"

"Oh, please, Larry, please, no. I hate that pervert, and I'm scared for my life—"

"You didn't mind Orestes losing his," he rapped.

She cowered. The swing creaked to her trembling.

"Don't hide from the fact." His words fell angrily; his pipestem chopped. "You may've gotten sucked in, not letting yourself foresee the consequences. But later you alibied a murderer, Gayle. Only you can scrub yourself clean of that. Or do you want more killings? Do you want to stay Flagler's slave . . . ?"

"Larry, I thought you were gonna rescue me! You said!"

"Till he slits your throat? Look, I'll do what I can; we're working together, but you've got to pull your share of the load. I can't be our agent in the enemy camp, can I? That's you. My job's to stand by for your protection, receive what information you can get me, and, at the right time, strike the blow that sets you free. But you'd better prove you're worth saving!"

"Yes, yes, yes," she wailed. "I will, honest, I will. I love you, Larry. I will."

"Good. See that you do. Be careful about contacting me. We'd better not keep together like this the rest of the day." He departed.

She stayed to weep, and had not recovered enough to seek Matt when he found her. "What's eating you now?" he demanded.

"I, I . . . oh, Matt, I'm miserable. I'm t-t-terrified and . . ."

He nudged her sprawled form to make room on the swing and sat down beside her. His gaze was bleared, blinking, and yet intent. "Who've you been with? I went out the back way, walked around the servants' quarters and—Holy mother, can't I let you out o' my sight for thirty seconds?"

"Matt, I, I, I—oh, please!"

He shook her. *"Who were you with?"*

The teeth clattered in her jaws. She coughed and moaned. He let her go. Bristles on his chin scraped beneath a stroking palm. "Rance, of course," he muttered. "Who else? Well, what'd he say to put you in this uproar?"

"Nothing . . . we weren't . . . we . . ."

He rose. "Come on."

She cringed. He heaved on her left wrist. "Come on, I said. We're going for a stroll in the woods."

She stumbled under his force. They followed the trail for a silent half-mile, until he shoved her ahead of him past a tangle of banyan. Beyond was a space, clear save for moss and punk, walled and roofed by leaves. Sun-flecks touched its gloom, unmoving in a breathless warmth.

Matt gave her a stage leer. "Ah, my proud beauty, at

last ve are alo-o-one. You can tell me whatever your heart desires."

From behind her lifted hands, the puffed and reddened face, words torrented. "Yeah, sure, Matt, honey, sure, Larry and me was talking. It was his idea. He b-b-browbeat me. Wanted to know if I'd told you anything about, about it. He was real mean, a bully; he scared me out of my gourd, no wonder I started crying."

"What'd you tell him?"

"Nothing! The, the same thing . . . we said before—"

He yanked her warding arms aside and slapped her, a rhythmic right-left-right-left. The blows smacked loud. A parrot screamed. Gayle only begged him to stop. "You lie, you stupid cunt," he answered, "you lie, you lie. What'd you tell him? Let's hear the truth before I really get mad."

"No, nothing, nothing—"

Matt stepped back and sighed. It was constructed as a weary sound, but he could not hold back all the eagerness. "Okay. Take off your clothes."

"What? Here, Matt?" Her question was dazed.

He showed her his switchblade. She hurried to obey. Slowly, he unfastened his belt and ran it between his fingers. "We'll have some correctional therapy till you get less stubborn," he said voluptuously. "Bend over."

"No, no, oh, please."

The leather lashed across her calf. She gasped. "Let's see your ass," Matt ordered, "or you'll be sorry."

He worked on her with skill that rarely got out of hand and left few marks. She didn't hold out long.

Afterward he stood, staring down at her where she lay huddled, and drawled, "So you let him in last night, soon's my back was turned, huh? So you agreed today you'd be his spy, huh? I ought to kill you."

"Oh, God, no, please, Matt," she yammered into the earth. "I'll do anything, I—" The rest was incoherent.

"Well, I'm not such a bad guy." He sank down next to her. Sweat glistened on his forehead and stained his shirt; its smell filled the little glade. "Make me happy, and I'll let bygones be bygones. Here. Right off. You know what I like."

She crept to do his bidding.

Some yards away, crouched beneath a tall, scratchy,

insect-laden bush, Larry Rance hesitated. For a moment he hefted a dead branch that looked as if it would make a serviceable club. But the wood was rotten and crumbled in his grasp. He released it and, taking the same elaborate precautions as he had used when tracking the others, sneaked back toward the house.

Larry borrowed a boat and fishing tackle, but spent most of the afternoon swimming.

When they returned, Matt and Gayle went to his room. He used a bathrobe sash to secure her ankle to the bedpost, told her that he expected to see the same knot when he awoke, and fell asleep. Eventually she did likewise, on the carpet.

Downstairs, the game continued. About three o'clock Byron cursed, threw away his pencil, and shambled off to his own bed. Julia and Ellis exchanged careful smiles.

He finished in time to dine with Haverner, which no one else did. Well after dark, she, who had called for a sandwich, squared her shoulders and said stiffly, "That's it. Check the answers."

When hers, like her opponent's, proved correct, she drew a single breath and fled upstairs.

Larry knocked on Julia's door and was admitted. He snatched her to him. Joy blazed from his countenance. "Congratulations!" he roared, and kissed her thoroughly.

But when his hands started to travel in earnest, she resisted. "Not tonight. Please, darling. I'm worn to a skeleton."

He let go. Slowly, he nodded. "Yeah. I s'pose. All right."

"You're sweet." She returned to her bed, fluffed a pillow against the headboard, sat demure in her pajamas beneath the thin blanket and regarded him with eyes that tonight were like onyx. The lampglow burnished her hair. Through an open window could be seen stars and fireflies, stippling a darkness that the ear found quiet.

She stretched her arms. "What a relief! For you too, no?"

"I'm sorry he beat me," Larry pushed out.

"He hasn't, yet. You still mean to deal with him and his hired killer, don't you? Oh, you'll earn your share of my guaranteed half-million." Her voice could be said to gleam. "Or my whole million. I've got hopes."

Larry drew a chair to the bedside, folded himself into it, fumbled with tobacco. Julia wrinkled her nose slightly at the sourness—he hadn't cleaned his pipe nor exchanged it this day, and it had seen furious use—but spoke no complaint. Scowling at his match flame, he didn't notice.

"We do have to watch out, and then some," he warned, and went on to relate his encounter with Gayle and hers with Matt. "They're onto us, Flagler and Nordberg. They know we know. Your life's in danger. Mine too, maybe, but yours for sure. Did I goof?"

She stroked his bare forearm. The hairs rose beneath her fingers. "No, Larry. You did magnificently."

"Poor Gayle."

"Well, she *is* an accessory to murder. If she suffers no worse punishment than you witnessed, she'll have gotten off lightly. As for you, what you've accomplished— I've read a bit of information theory and strategic analysis. It sounds confusing, but the fact is that knowing what they know about what we know is a tremendous asset for our side."

"Never mind theory," he growled. "What do we do?"

"We plan how to convince Haverner that Matt must be made harmless."

His laugh rattled. "Do we actually need to approach him . . . tomorrow?"

"We'd better." Julia grew intent. "Let me think a minute."

In the morning, when they applied to Captain York, he said, "Yis, mah'm, sir, yis, he been 'specting you. Please, dis vay," and ushered them into the office.

The master sat at his rolltop desk. The subtle machinery hummed around him and the otherwise sterile air seemed to have a tinge of odor: blood, sweat?

"Good day," he greeted. His manner was downright genial. The perfection of false teeth shone from a withered smile. "How are you?"

They refrained from observing that he must know precisely how they were. "Uh, okay, sir," Larry said, unable to meet that stare. Julia, who could, responded, "Fine, thank you. I hope you're the same. Is everything ready for my turn?"

"Yes. Certain equipment came yesterday while you were busy, and is in the main shed under lock and key. It will be installed and checked out this night. Meanwhile I've worked out a program which I trust will prove suitable."

Julia could not altogether repress a shiver. Larry gave her a troubled glance. She had not yet revealed to him what she had in mind.

"I have, of course, followed your progress, like everyone else's, as closely as I have been able to," Haverner said. "I pass no moral judgments. Do remember that: no moral judgments. I am an observer, an amateur scientist, an ancient in whom every passion has burned low except a certain curiosity about this ridiculous species to which we belong—I too, I too. I am most obliged to you for the generous supply of data. Believe me, they will remain confidential. I have no particular interest in publication."

"Then you'd better take steps to make sure we can keep on performing," Larry said in a rush.

"Eh? Explicate, please."

"You know. You've recorded everything we talked about."

"True. But I prefer to hear you out *viva voce*. More data, you see."

"Well, we've learned that Nordberg hired Flagler to kill Orestes when Orestes called a game only he could win. I . . . don't suppose . . . you objected seriously, . . . sir."

"Do you imply I might have connived a trifle at the event, dropped a hint or three, instructed my subordinates to look into the middle distance, in order that my experiment might continue?" Haverner's cheerfulness was unruffled. "It's conceivable. Further than that, deponent sayeth not."

"Now," Julia stated, cooler than her escort, "we've a single challenge left. Mine. You told me it fascinates you. But what happens if I'm killed before Ellis and I play? They, Flagler and Nordberg, they know we know about their guilt. Quite aside from the prize itself, can they afford to let us go back to Ciudad Vizcaya

—to the States? We may not have courtroom proof, but we could make things pretty damn awkward for them. If you want your game played out, Mr. Haverner, you'd better take steps to protect us."

"I've got a responsibility to Gayle, also," Larry put in. "I can't leave her in the claws of those vultures."

The old man arched skeptical brows at that but made no direct comment. He did ask Julia, "What do you propose?"

"That we stow Flagler where he can't do any further damage," she replied. "You still have your magisterial commission, don't you? Not that anybody in Santa Ana would ever question your right to the high, the low, and the middle justice on your fief, I'm sure. Well, arrest Matthew Flagler on suspicion of murder. Hold him locked up till, um, day after tomorrow. Then turn him over to the authorities."

"That—the prospect of eventual official investigation— might unduly perturb Mr. Nordberg, might handicap him vis-à-vis you," Haverner said. "He deserves his fair chance."

Julia stamped her foot. "What about me?"

"Indeed. I have given thought . . ."

For a long while silence filled the room. The two who stood, since they had not been offered chairs, grew visibly more nervous.

Finally the one at the desk continued. "It's certainly unfeasible to call in the constabulary or, for that matter, try to deputize such peaceful retainers as Captain York to confine Mr. Flagler. Gossip, if nothing else. Your threat to 'make things awkward' upon your return home is idle, I fear. Think. You yourselves don't want publicity. So much of what you have done here could be misinterpreted." He snickered. "Or interpreted, as the case may be.

"Furthermore, we do have an experiment going, hence a need to control the variables, to restrict the number of persons who significantly interact. My focus is upon this select group. To bring in outsiders will interfere with my objective, which is to observe the behavior of my chosen people. You must concede me a few rights, Mrs. Petrie. A million dollars, even in an age when Caesar finds it convenient to advance under the banner of egalitarianism, a million dollars of one's own money ought to buy a certain privilege, ought it not? I would be sorry to call off the contest at this late stage, Mrs. Petrie."

Larry inhaled a lungful. Julia asked flatly, "But you do agree something has to be done about Flagler?"

"Yes, provided it can be kept within the family, so to speak."

"What, then?"

"Well, suppose I give you *carte blanche*. Within reason, of course. We must not scandalize my staff unduly, or otherwise risk a plague of officials. But if, say, you confine Mr. Flagler under citizen's arrest until the last game has been played out—on a clear understanding with Mr. Nordberg that the eventual disposal of the case will not publicly embarrass him—"

. "I guess we'll have to work some kind of deal," Larry said at the end of his report to Byron. "Be hard to send Matt up for murder without involving the guy who hired him, and so all the rest of us."

"You mean they go free? But we protect ourselves from them by demanding signed confessions which we stow in the traditional safe deposit box with the traditional instructions to open in case of our sudden deaths?"

"Yeah, something like that. Wish I could think of something better." Larry kicked the gravel. "I hate to let murder go unpunished. It's not right!"

Byron barely smiled. "Rightness, fairness, justice are human artifacts. Lies—gallant or cowardly, depending on how you look at it—lies we tell ourselves, the same as God and immortality and love. Quite irrevelant to a universe estimated to be ten or twenty billion years old and that many light-years in radius and mostly hollow."

"I dunno." Larry scratched his head. "I'm not a believer, exactly, but it doesn't make sense that there isn't any . . . Hell! Why am I arguing metaphysics?"

"I take it you want my help in confining Flagler."

"Yeah. He's got to be confined, or we won't be able to bargain at all, and he may kill again—maybe back in the States, even, as a precaution. Haverner won't stand in our way, but neither will he deputize any of his men. The business will have to be handled strictly among us white rats."

Byron nodded. They walked on in a minute's silence along the roadway to the landing strip, a path they had picked arbitrarily to get away from possible eavesdroppers. No one else was visible beneath the sun of early afternoon. Elms lining the way gave scant shade at this hour against gathering heat and glare. Flies and bees droned; ants scurried past scrunching shoes; a hawk dipped and soared on watch overhead.

"To be frank," Byron said at length, "I'm rather disgusted. What you've told me—perforce, almost everything—is altogether sordid."

"Sure, you can be smug if you want," Larry rasped. "You're out of the running. Go ahead, relax, watch us twitch, watch us die." He paused before continuing more quietly. "Sorry, I didn't mean it that way. And I beg your humble pardon for what happened between us earlier. But I need your help. Two women need it worse, and that kid away off on Long Island."

"Hm. You don't think you could take Flagler by yourself?"

"I could try. I will, if I have to. But he'd have a better than even chance of slashing me to pieces." Larry went red and swallowed. "Or he could escape, and somewhere out in the woods is that loaded hunting rifle.

"Actually, Byron, you're in this too, whether you want to be or not. You too know more than he likes. You knew it even before we had this talk.

"The pair of us ought to be able to handle him fairly safely."

The younger man's eyes glistered. "All right!" He laughed. "I could protest that I'm crippled from what you did to me, but the truth is I'm back in fair shape and— All right, Larry, you bastard. If you'll put on the gloves when we come home and let me trounce you according to Queensberry rules and afterwards buy you a drink, I'll help you today."

"Good guy!" They clasped hands. "I think he's in his room," Larry said. "Let's go for him before he does any further damage."

But instead they met him on their way to the house. He was crossing the lawn from the row of cottages, where he had been boasting to a young nephew of Captain York.

Larry and Byron stopped and stiffened at the sight. "Hey!" the first called. "Hey, uh, Matt, wait up."

"Yeah?" The quarry obeyed. But as they trotted close, he squinted at them and tensed. "Wha' d'ya want?"

"Oh, a, uh, discussion." Larry started to sidle around, to get at him from behind.

Byron frowned and gestured. Matt edged from them both. "Hey, what is this?" he protested.

Larry pounced. Matt dodged. "Hold on there!" Byron cried. "Stay where you are. Matt, we have business with you."

"What kind?" Matt poised himself on his toes. "Don't come no closer. Don't." The switchblade went *snick*. "I'm warning you, you mothers. Stand back."

Byron grinned and slipped near, ready to dance clear of a thrust. Larry moved again to Matt's rear.

The lone man saw. "No, you don't!" he screamed, broke past and ran.

Larry and Byron swapped glances, the first grim, the second rueful. They lined out in pursuit. Astonishingly fast, Matt distanced them and vanished in the northward jungle.

"He's gone for that gun," Larry panted. "Should we follow?"

"We'd better!" Byron loped on. Larry clenched his fists and accompanied him.

Feet whispered behind them. Armed, white-clad, Anselmo Gomez drew alongside and matched their speed in an effortless cat-pace. He gave them a minimal smile. "I weel go along," he said. The walkie-talkie was slung across a shoulder.

—And in the old house, Sunderland Haverner said to a part of the wallpaper whose pattern suggested a face, "You were right, Samael. They are behaving just as we hoped."

MATTHEW FLAGLER

Branches like claws. They scratch after my eyes; they grab my ankles; they jab at my balls. Christ, it's gloomy in here! And hot and stinking. Nature, shit! That's what this woods is, shit and death. The trees crowd around; the brush fights me and snaps, rustles, yells where I am.

Like the graveyard at night, a few pus-yellow street lamps far far off, and red sky-glow, but the church, the warehouses and tenements crowd close, the damn graveyard's a black well and it's past midnight, quiet like a corpse waiting underground to reach up and grab me and haul me down to him in his coffin, and I'm seven years old and Bull Brannigan'll beat me if I don't stay here the whole night through, my punishment for goofing that errand he gave me. Oh, Mother Mary, oh, Saint Matthew, Saint Patrick, help me, don't let a little boy go down into the grave!

Stop that. Stop where I am. Think. Maybe the jungle does remind me too much, but that's its way of tricking me. If I let the jungle paralyze me with fear, it'll have won. *They'll* have won, the smug rich motherfuckers chasing me.

Stand still and think.

Don't breathe loud. Strain out the laughing of that damn bird, somewhere off in these thick shadows. It hates me too. Well, I hate right back. I'll whip you yet, you Island, you sons of bitches.

Figure. What do they want to do? Lock me up. Maybe kill me. They're afraid of me, that's what they are. Suppose I promised . . . But they wouldn't listen. I suppose old Haverner gave them his okay. He doesn't care what happens to human beings, the creepy crazy mummy. Jesus, he scares me! He ought to run away if I make the sign of the cross, that vampire, but he won't. . . . Stop. I've got to think hard.

(Ellis said, "His only interest is in watching us. He looks on us as animals. If he has any preference about how we behave, it's that we keep his show going as long as possible. Get me, Matt? If it seems like somebody's about to make a clean sweep of the field and end his fun, . . . why, he'll be grateful, in his way, to whoever fixes that."

(And I did, Haverner. I shot that godless Communist who'd've walked off carrying your whole million bucks. You know I did. You haven't said anything, of course, but you know, you know. I did you a good turn. Then why are you letting them treat me like this?

(Why aren't you helping me, Ellis? I helped you.)

Think, think, in the damn damp shadows.

He's got no gratitude, Haverner, no conscience. He'd as soon turn me over to the Santa Ana cops . . . and God, those kids and niggers back home that whine about police brutality, they've sure never seen a Santa Ana jail! Or a Santa Ana firing squad; that's what a murder rap can mean. Gimme a Chicago flatfoot anytime, and I know what I'm talking about.

Oh, God, Chicago! Civilization! Let them whine about smog and pollution, too. I'll trade them this tropical paradise for it, even-Steven, quicker'n a whore can roll a drunk. Hell, after these heavy stinks around me, exhaust would smell good, clean car fumes, and the same for piss in the cheapest pool-hall john, and stale cigar smoke, oh, I love you, I love you. Cars . . . me behind the wheel of a Cadillac, steering her under flashing neon, over pavement where nothing worse lays around loose than old newspapers, dust, chewing gum wrappers, maybe an epileptic bum. . . . I'll take your winters too, Chicago, sooty snow, overcoat dragging me down, wind like a wolf off the plains and frost-howl from the wheels of the El train. . . . What'd I ever do that they made me spend this past six years in hell?

I'm going back. I can go back. If I think.

Haverner—I don't expect Haverner gives a damn what happens to me either way. If I can take care of myself, that's all right by him. I've always had to take care of myself. From the beginning. Father a drunk working stiff, mother a drunk slob, eight brothers and sisters crowding me in a tiny apartment, at a skimpy table—what could

I do but hang around street gangs, damn near from the first time I could walk, and run errands for them and try to pick up a little money or . . . ? Nobody ever looked after me except myself. Nobody ever helped me.

Not Ellis either. I don't kid myself he cares about me. If I can't do this one more job he wants, and it looks like I can't, why, he'd be just as glad to have *me* cooled, because of what I know.

Or, no, not exactly that. Let me prove, here, today, that I'm tough and smart enough to be worth his while and . . . He did talk about putting me on his payroll.

So. What I've got to do is last out the game. And like a free man, not a prisoner that they can do anything they want with. One more day to go. After that, well, I have my return ticket, or at least a ride back to Vizcaya. (The rich motherfuckers go to the States.) And Ellis did for sure promise me more if he wins, and he'll keep his promise—he'd better—if I stay free.

Especially if I help him against the Petrie dame. We should talk that over more, this night. We didn't get a chance to make real plans. I wouldn't mind putting a slug in her belly, the snotty bitch. No, sir. But Haverner might get mad if I spoiled the last match. Maybe if I caught her alone and beat up on her or something. . . . Well, Ellis and me can talk about that. What I've got to do right this minute is make a chance for us to talk.

Okay. If Haverner doesn't care about me, he doesn't care about Rance or Shaddock either. They're both out of the game anyway. (Why are they persecuting me, then? Because the Julia cunt put them up to it! Why else? She laid them and bribed them. Oh, how I'd like to get you alone, Julia!) If I kill them—well, hell, plain self-defense. A man's got a right to defend himself. They attacked me when I was walking along minding my own business, me that never did them any harm and even saved their bacon that day on the beach.

Besides, if I chill them, that'll be two less possible stoolies for Haverner to worry about afterward. He ought to appreciate that.

Hold on. I'd better not get too ambitious. Don't borrow trouble. I've got plenty of that in my own name. Hang loose, play cool.

The main thing is to defend myself. Okay, I've got

to have my rifle. After that, maybe I'll hole up till dark, or maybe I'll walk straight back and dare them to come near me. Anyhow with a weapon I'll be safe, I'll be on top of things.

These stupid trees all look alike. How am I going to find the hollow one I moved the rifle to?

Well, I know the landmarks from the path above the coast. And I can find the path by plowing straight east. And I can tell east by those sunbeams that cut through the leaves into the shadows.

But Rance and Shaddock may be on the path. . . .

Help me, saints. I promise you a novena, a stained glass window, whatever you want; I promise you I'll believe. Oh, God, God, God, there has to be somebody in heaven who cares!

I push through the grabbing, clawing brush, under the horrible brooding trees. Sweat soaks my clothes till they stick to me like a shroud. My own stink drowns the jungle smells. I shake, I stagger, I strain for air. What have I done to deserve this?

Okay, I'm a jailbird. But I served my time, didn't I? And I was poor; I had no choice; it was a bad environment. That's what the fat sociologists are saying these days about the niggers, isn't it? Why can't they say it about me?

My mistake, okay, I'll admit I made a bad mistake. (Was it also a mistake marrying Eva Delvecchio? She's in the Family, and her old man gave me a job managing a night club, better than any other job I could have gotten after being in Joliet. But God, what a slob she is! Why'd she have to follow me down to Santa Ana after the trouble broke? I guess I'm too good for her. She said once, throwing a fit, she did say she'd been foolish enough to be in love with me. And four kids . . . I got four kids, even if they are runny-nosed yelling brats, four kids to say I'm no fairy. And plenty of other women; not just that Gayle moron.) My mistake—Papa Delvecchio, shriveled old bastard, chewing me out, calling me stupid. What right did he have to call me stupid? I told him again and again, okay, I told him, I was running a badger game upstairs, but nobody gets hit by one of those unless he asks for it—I didn't hold a gun on any customer's head and tell him he had to go upstairs or else, did I?—and if just once I happened to badger the wrong guy, why, anybody could make a mistake. You don't look down on a businessman who made a wrong investment, do you?

It wasn't fair that I had to skip the country one jump ahead of a .45 slug. My God, they yak about the death penalty being cruel and unusual punishment, don't they? They yak about equal protection under the law. Well, where was the law when I needed it?

And that's how come I landed in hell. The Family happening to own a casino in Vizcaya, and Papa making me manager. Only sheest, what a crummy operation! Chickenfeed, chickenshit. And then when the goddamn colonels closed us down, well, what could I do but pimp? I had a wife and kids to support, didn't I, and Papa was dead now and nobody else in that oh-so-loving Family would send me any more checks, and when the old government was restored I had nobody to speak for me and the Family put that Collodi turd in charge of my casino. . . .

Listen, up there. I'm due for a break. I am. I thought this would be it, when Haverner's people approached me. And instead I'm fighting through a jungle, my life in danger. It's not right, I tell you!

. . . Ah.

The trail. Thank you, Mary, thank you; you led me out of the graveyard and I won't forget you. Now, quick, which way? Take a bearing on that rock where Rance tried to drown me. . . . Yeah, it's south of here.

But him and Shaddock are coming at me from the south.

Be quick. I've got to beat them to the gun. Trot, trot, trot, never mind the sweat or my backbone jarring into my skull. I'll remember this later in my air-conditioned Chicago penthouse and be proud, like a combat soldier. (That's what I am. A combat soldier. Orestes Cruz could've become another Fidel Castro, couldn't he? They ought to pin a medal on me. Instead, I've got to hide in Santa Ana, the asshole of the world. Except maybe Ellis Nordberg can help me out. He's got to. After all I've done for him.)

The air's hot, a-boom with surf, but the sun's behind the trees on my right and I jog through shadows. My tongue's a log in my mouth and my chest hurts. Why does this have to happen to me?

There!

The big tree with the hurricane scars, my marker, my salvation. Turn off here into the jungle, but only a few yards, and here's the hiding place. I snatch into the gnawed-out trunk and my hands find the weapon.

Salvation roars. I grab that gun the way I'd grab young Billy York's cock.

(I am not queer. Ask Eva. Ask Gayle. Ask a hundred women, well, a couple dozen. Eva never guessed anything. Christ, if she had, if she'd told Papa! Suddenly it's cold, till I hug the gun to my chest.

(Okay, I like it with boys. Better than I like it with girls. Is that so terrible? Not according to the fat sociologists. I've never made a fool of myself joining Gay Liberation or anything like that. I'm just liberal, that's all. And—reform school, twice in the pen, *years* at a time— what the fuck do they expect a guy will do?

(And what's bad about it, when it's what they both want? Or about supplying horse to people that want horse, who'll go out of their heads from wanting it if people like me don't find it for them? Hell, they say cigarettes are bad for you; the government makes them put it on every package—I don't believe that, I want a smoke right now, but better wait till I'm safe before I light up, my mouth's so dry—the government says cigarettes give you cancer and then goes right ahead and lets the big companies sell them and collects taxes on the stuff. Why not horse, smack, whatever anybody wants that isn't hurting anybody else?)

I stroke and stroke my long gun. I love guns. We call cocks "guns" too, don't we? I love shooting. Both kinds.

That's another thing the do-gooders want to take away from us. Our right to be armed. To protect ourselves.

If I ever went into politics . . . Oh, I'd have them behind me, the people. They've had a bellyful of do-gooders. They're crying for a leader who'll tell it like it is. I could do plenty of good myself. The right kind of good. Make the rich motherfuckers really help the poor; squeeze them till they squeal. Solve the race problem: send the niggers back to Africa where they belong. And the Jews to Israel? No, wouldn't work, I guess. But keep an eye on them: use the good ones but don't let the pushcart types, even the millionaire pushcart types, don't let them go on running the country the way they have been. Tell the Russkies and the Chinks to toe the line or we'll blow them off the map. Tell the world that Uncle Sam is through taking everybody's shit.

Oh, I'm a realist. A guy who's been in jail will never make President. But I could work behind the scenes and really help the people. I've seen enough behind-the-scenes politics. Only that's corrupt and I'd be different.

All I need is a break. One big take. It's not even a steal. It's just getting my fair share that I never had before in my life. If I'd won Haverner's million, I'd have put it in something gilt-edged and never broken another law where anybody could notice, and maybe gone into politics and become a big name, which I deserve better than that dimbulb in the White House. What's the difference between him and me? Why does he make it and me not? Money, that's why. It's as simple as that.

As simple as this gun in my hands.

Eight bullets loaded, and here are two extra clips. I put them in my coat pockets. Their weight feels good.

I guess I'll just sashay out in plain view. I won't say anything unless they speak first. I'll just hold this old rifle at the ready, and make sure they don't jump me from behind, and walk on up to my room, and wait for Ellis to come to me, because he'll need my help against Julia; we'll have to plan something against that frigid witch. Her and her pitiful little daughter! Ha! I wonder if she even has any.

March south to the house, big man.

I round a corner that the bamboo makes blind.

Oh, God, oh, Jesus, saints, Mother Mary, there they are. *And Anselmo is with them.*

Two quick shots would take them, but the Indian's got his own gun, that S. & W., and I'd never make him fast enough—

Rance and Shaddock stop short. Then Shaddock yells, the crazy fool, and charges.

I could drop him, but meanwhile Anselmo could drop me.

Everything happens slow, slow, slow. Why am I caught in this nightmare? When will Mother wake me from it?

Run.

I'll shoot if they don't leave me alone. I will. But I'm no mad dog like Shaddock. I don't want to kill anybody. And I'm in good shape in spite of the poverty, in spite of the drinking, because I had troubles to forget. I can stay ahead of that lunatic. I did good in track, in school. It's like I can see us again, all naked in the locker room.

Him and me, we round another blind corner and are out of sight of the others. I whirl and snap a shot. I miss. O God, that wasn't fair, making me miss! But he does stop, then fades back.

I go on. They won't push me hard. Leave me be, that's what I ask, leave me be. Stop torturing me before I get mad.

The thing to do is hole up. Stand them off. Anselmo, yeah, Anselmo is Haverner's gun. He won't necessarily shoot at me. *Or will he?* I piss in my pants; it runs hot down my leg; I run; I run in the heat. What are his orders?

What I've got to do is get behind some shelter. Then I can ask him. Maybe he doesn't really mean me any harm. It's just that I can't take the chance. I've been stabbed in the back so often by people I thought I could trust.

He has his radio set along. I saw it. So through him I can talk with Haverner. We can talk like reasonable men, Haverner and me, once I'm safe.

Or does Haverner own Anselmo? Really? Like Bull Brannigan and others have owned me? Stomp hard on that thought. I'm only tired, hounded out of my skull. I only need a chance to rest. I've needed that all my life.

It's a hard uphill jog. And I have to keep twisting my neck to try and see them in the shadows. But they're keeping out of sight, the backstabbing cowards; they're slinking after me. Let me find a place to make a stand and I'll soon put them in their place, down in the grave-yard. Give me half a chance, the half-chance I never had in my life, and I'll take care of them.

Suddenly the tangle on my left opens up. There's a steep slope here where the hills stick a ridge out toward the sea. Grass, bushes, scattered pine trees, boulders, the Crag behind—but look, that sheer rise, barely a hundred yards off, and the mouth in it, a cave!

From here, the cave's a black triangle. Let me get in there, belly down, rifle butt against my shoulder, and I'll be invisible from outside. I'll pick off Rance and Shaddock, self-defense, and then I'll talk to Anselmo and Haverner and they'll see how they've misjudged me.

My heartbeat's trying to shake me to pieces.

But somehow I make it over the slope, reach the beautiful deep shadow of the cliff and get into the cleft. I throw myself down, and there's even a kind of natural threshold in front of me, a rocky ridge to shield me.

I am safe.

It takes me a while to notice how I lie in stinking mush and can barely see the clustered bony-winged things that hang over my head, barely hear them chitter in the dark. . . . Holy fuck! A bat cave! I'm sunk to my chin in batshit!

Well . . .

They come into sight, big blond Rance, slim Shaddock, hunting me that never did them any harm, hunting me for nothing except money and fun. I get Rance in my sights, right in the cross-hairs, lover-boy Rance, ah, how he'll feel when it goes into *him!* I squeeze the trigger, slow, careful, enjoying.

The gun comes.

And I've missed. The swine moved at exactly the wrong moment. (Well, he was being cautious, of course, moving all the time, not like the nigger on the beach who thought he had the whole white world in his hand.) He springs back. They all three take cover behind a couple of big rocks. Light glows on the grass around them. And me, I've got to gag on the stink of guano.

A voice: "Ahoy! Flagler!" Sounds like Shaddock.

"What do you want?" I call. "Why are you after me? I never hurt you."

"You've hurt elsewhere." Who but a Haah-vahd type would say it like that? "We can't take chances with you."

"What do you want?" I yell again, and fire another shot to keep their heads down, keep Anselmo out of the picture, hear the crack and feel the weapon come alive. Bee-eee-*yow!*

"We'll bargain," Shaddock shouts. I hear Rance argue, can't make out the words, but sure, sure, he's got a deal with Julia.

Shaddock seems to overrule him. "Listen, Matt. Turn in your gun and your knife, and I don't think we need be afraid of you. Is that fair?"

"Hell, no!" I answer. "One of me and how many of you? You could do any damn thing to me you wanted, once I was disarmed. I got a right of self-defense. I'll keep my weapons."

"How long? You're under siege, you realize."

"I am? What're you going to shoot at me with?"

When Anselmo doesn't say anything, I feel my glory.

I call to him. "How about that, Anselmo? You're just a reporter for Mr. Haverner, aren't you? He doesn't care what I do, what any of us do, as long as we do something. Isn't that right?"

Still the Indian doesn't speak.

"Do you propose to come forth, then?" Shaddock asks. "I warn you, if you come armed, we'll have to assume you're dangerous."

Think.

It must be three or four miles to the house. Anywhere along the way, a thrown rock, a mugger arm . . . "Here's how we'll do it," I say. "You'll walk ahead of me. We'll go straight to Mr. Haverner."

"Suppose we don't agree?" That's Larry. Sure, he wants to hurt me on account of his precious Julia, his daahling Gayle, his hope for a share in the loot.

"Then I stay put," I tell them. I can stand the guano, slimy softness, sharp stink, as long as they can stay crouched behind those boulders. I can wait till nightfall, when they won't be able to see me, and slip free and make my own way back to the house. I can.

I'd rather not, though.

"Anselmo, come talk with me," I beg. You and me, we understand each other, don't we? You don't really want for me to stumble home after dark, through a graveyard jungle, do you? Okay, you're Haverner's man, but even a mouthpiece can speak a kind word now and then, can't he?

"No!" Rance shouts.

Only it's Shaddock who freezes me. "Better surrender, Matt. The sooner you do, the likelier you are to live. That's a bat cave you're in. A percentage of the Island bats have rabies, you know. You don't have to get bitten.

Right now, you're in a mist from their droppings and passings, and it carries the virus. I warn you, come out and give up!"

No, no, no.

Why does this happen to *me?*

Is he lying?

Can I take the chance?

"What'll you do . . . if I come?" I holler, thin and shaky.

"Confine you. The rest can be discussed later."

Haverner—Haverner will understand. He's got to. Sunderland Haverner and Ellis Nordberg. O God, I've had so little all my life, you've got to give me a break at last, and I'll be good, I'll be good.

It squelches when I get to my feet in the horrible stink that may already have screwed me with horrible death. I hold tight on to the rifle and stagger out of the cave.

Down at the bottom of the hill, there's Anselmo, stepped out into the open. He says something into his walkie-talkie. He looks like he's getting an answer, but I can't hear. He nods a little bit and starts up the slope to meet me. I'm real careful, I hold the rifle by the middle of the stock, at arm's length. I don't want to drop it, not just yet, but they can see I'm not aiming at anybody.

What?

The automatic's in his hand. He's in range now, and somehow he's pulled his gun, and he grins. He doesn't even show any enjoyment in the grin, just an awful not-unfriendliness. I'll never bring my weapon to bear in time.

No, no, no! *Please!*

INTERVAL SEVEN
Part Two

The shot smote eardrums. Echoes of it rang back from the cliff. Startled, a toucan whirled aloft from trees beyond, brilliant and shrill.

Matthew Flagler folded at the midriff, fell, and rolled downslope. His arms and legs flopped. Anselmo padded to intercept him when he should come to rest. Squatting, the mainlander laid pistol to bulging-eyed open-mouthed head. The spraddled shape did not move, nor did blood —smeared around the curiously small hole in the breast, over jacket and shirt and trousers, in a wet line through the grass—flow further. Anselmo felt the throat for a pulse, nodded, rose and holstered his gun.

By that time Byron and Larry had blundered to join him. "Dead?" Byron croaked.

"Yes," Anselmo said. "I was not sure. I am a good shot, but the peestol ees"—he searched for a word in English—"treecky." He might have been talking about a target on a range.

"You'd . . . have . . . finished him off?" Larry asked.

Anselmo shrugged. " 'E was dangerous. A keeller, armed, no?"

"But—he'd quit," Byron said dazedly. "That rifle wasn't at the ready, wasn't aimed or anything."

" 'E should 'ave dropped eet. I called Meester 'Averner. 'E said use my own judgment."

Larry stared and stared, unblinking as the corpse, before he whispered, "Haverner said kill."

Anselmo made no reply.

"Haverner said kill," Larry repeated. "It'd be too inconvenient if Matt lived. All right for us to chase him, make a show for Haverner. Haverner was curious what we'd do. But when it turned out we'd only shut him away for a while . . . why, he might let out too much truth sometime when he was drunk, or . . ." He swung to confront Anselmo. "Sometime soon, you'd have gotten your orders to kill him. Wouldn't you? It was only that right here and now gave you a great excuse, seeing as how Matt forgot to let go of his rifle."

The least touch of annoyance crossed the broad brown features. "Why you care? 'E shot Orestes Cruz. Gave 'eem no chance."

"You didn't mind that."

"No. And why you mind about Flagler? A coward, a woman-beater, a boy-lover, and dangerous like a poison snake. 'E should 'ave been dead long ago."

"He was human." Byron stooped and tried to close those eyes. "And he'd surrendered to us."

"You like better eef 'e went before a fireeng squad een Ciudad Vizcaya? . . . *Ay,* you let me do that." Anselmo nudged Byron aside and drew down the lids in the blue face. "You got two monies?" Numbly, Byron held out a handful of coins. After he'd placed a pair of them, before he rose, Anselmo quickly signed Matt and himself with the cross.

Then he said in a brisk voice, "We go back now."

"We can't leave him here!" Larry protested. "Look, already the ants—"

Anselmo shrugged. "I weell call a'ead. Meester 'Averner weell send men to breeng 'eem een. No, wait, one theeng." He went lithely uphill and retrieved the rifle. Returning, he wore a satisfied smile. "Good piece, thees. Come." He slung it over his back, unshipped the radio, spoke in Spanish as he started toward the distant house. He didn't look behind to see if the North Americans were following him. Probably, keen-sensed, he knew they were.

Two women and three men gathered before Sunderland Haverner in the living room. Neither Larry nor Byron had changed clothes. Stained, dusty, sweat-drenched and reeking of it, those garments were a shout amidst the immaculate whiteness elsewhere, the cool Georgian hues of the chamber.

Haverner alone was seated. His mottled hands rested on a cane that stood upright between his legs. His nose curved sharply above. Light fell upon his brows in such a way that the eyes beneath were almost unseeable.

Behind him, arms folded, showing no particular signs of the chase, stood Anselmo. Captain York kept well aside, at the corner where the L-shape bent back to form a cavern of books. He wrung fingers together and subvocalized prayers.

Ellis was likewise apart from the rest, if not that far. Gayle and Julia stayed close together.

Evening shone on the lawn and leaves outside.

"This is a serious accusation you make, gentlemen," Haverner rustled.

Byron's nod jerked. "Murder is serious. Your man shot Matt down like a dog."

"That is not a bad analogy, especially if the dog is, shall we say, rabid."

"Matt wasn't threatening us," Larry grated. "Sure, he hadn't dropped his rifle yet, but the way he was holding it, he couldn't possibly have brought it into action when An—when Gomez already had him covered."

"It's understandable that you are overwrought," Haverner responded mildly. "I will pardon what you have said thus far in defamation of my trusty man, not to mention myself. But now I must insist you cease it and exercise common sense."

He lifted a finger. "How well did you see the actual situation?" he pursued. "It's notorious how unreliable witnesses are. What they think they observe in their excitement bears no necessary relationship to reality. None whatsoever. Scores of psychological experiments confirm this—and thousands of police and court records likewise."

A slight sigh. "You should also reflect that Anselmo is mortal too," he said. "He had to gauge what the possible menace was, and what to do, in a split second—when you three had already been fired on. Perhaps he made an error. If so, it is not one for which he would ever be convicted, certainly not in this republic. I do not propose to subject him to tedious legalisms.

"I will report that the murderer of Orestes Cruz, having been identified, was killed while resisting arrest. I will further report it as my belief that he did the murder in a fit of rage at having been bested for the prize, and therefore was obviously so unstable that nobody could dare to take any further risks with him. I assure you, the Santa Anan authorities will be content with that, and promptly mark the case closed."

His look was skewering. "In view of your own involvements in both deaths, gentlemen," he said, "both deaths, I repeat, inasmuch as you kept silence about the first, Mr. Shaddock, and you did the same, Mr. Rance, after your one abortive attempt to be officious, and the two of you drove Flagler into the panic which caused him to overreact and thus brought about his demise . . . In view of your own involvements, I say, you had better observe discretion, now and always." He barely underlined the added phrase, "you had better."

Larry glared around. Julia had made no sound or sign, was as masked as Anselmo. Gayle trembled and hiccoughed tears into a handkerchief. Behind his glittering glasses, Ellis wore the faintest of smiles. When he made the faintest of sounds as well, Larry pointed at him and yelled, "There's the real murderer!"

Ellis frowned. "I know some nonsensical lies have been made up about me and Matt," he said. "Do I have to stay and listen to them?"

"I believe we should terminate our proceedings," Haverner agreed. His lips gave a dry smack. A look passed between him and Ellis. "Yes, Mrs. Thayer has stated that you suborned Flagler to eliminate Cruz. At best it is hearsay evidence, worthless in law—merely a thing he told her. I do suggest, Mr. Nordberg"—again the emphasis, no stronger than was needed to make it totally unmistakable—"that it does put you in a somewhat vulnerable position. You would not be well advised to attempt, ever, coercion of Mrs. Petrie with the threat to reveal certain indiscretions she may have committed here. You also would have nothing except hearsay and conjecture. No, let the game be played out as planned."

A starkness came upon Julia's face. Larry gulped and knotted his fists.

Haverner turned his attention to weeping Gayle. "Why are you distressed, Mrs. Thayer?" he asked urbanely. "I should think you, of all persons here, have occasion to rejoice."

"I was scared of him," she strangled. "I hated him." A scream: "But he's dead! Shot down! I didn't want *that!*"

She fled from the room. After a moment, sick-looking, Byron followed with long strides.

"Julia." Larry reached for the tall woman. His hands shuddered.

"I may as well be honest," she told them. "I don't mind what happened. He's no loss; and he could well have dry-gulched me." Her glance at Ellis was flat jade-green. "Now the last contest will be strictly fair."

"I won't dignify that with an answer," he snapped.

"Julia," Larry pleaded. "I've got to talk to you. Alone."

She nodded. "Let's go for a walk, then."

"I believe dinner should be late, in order that we may compose ourselves," Haverner proposed. "Nine o'clock?"

"Okay," Julia stated. "But remember, my game begins on the stroke of official sunrise."

"Stuff your dinner!" Larry shouted. "Think I'll ever eat at the same table as you again, Haverner?"

"A matter of choice, Mr. Rance," was the reply. "Feel free to order food sent to your room while you enjoy the hospitality of this house."

Larry spat on the carpet and rushed out. Julia lingered a moment. "I think I'd better calm him down," she said to Haverner.

Sudden avidity passed through the skin and bones of him. "Do you think you could do so, . . . for instance, . . . in the summerhouse on the beach?" he whispered.

She bent her lips upward. "It's bugged, hm? Well, I'll try. I do owe you a lot, sir." With a fresh stare at Ellis: "After tomorrow I'll owe you twice as much." She left.

"And lead us not into temptation," Captain York implored, "but deliver us from evil."

The sun was not yet under the curve of the planet, but it was behind the mass of the Island and the light lay violet across the waters and inside the little shelter. From there, one saw the bluff as a featureless wall, the sand a wan road, the lagoon polished metal across which ripples passed. Beyond the shark net burned the sea. Radiance dripped from a gull asoar in blueness. Surf noises moved like the same wing beats. The air was cool and salty.

Julia guided Larry by the hand. "Let's sit here," she said.

"I want to walk," he objected, "wear myself out till I can sleep."

"Well, I don't." Her tone cut. He yielded, entered the pergola, slumped onto a bench, elbows on knees, head a faint-bright drooping. Julia joined him, though not in bodily contact.

"I can't see why you're this bothered, Larry," she said across his ragged breath. "At worst, a sneak murderer has been executed informally. Are you that hung up on the letter of the law? Thousands of people are killed every day who deserve it less."

"This was different. I was there. I saw."

"Does that change the principle? Really? Listen, Larry. Did you support the Vietnam War—the American role in it?"

"Huh?" Startled, he moved to peer at her through the dimness. "No, of course not."

"I did, as a matter of fact. I didn't think we dared let Southeast Asia go. The balance of power would tilt too badly. Then there was the moral question. What happened after the United States scuttled out? The boat people, more wars, genocide, famine—exactly what we inhuman hawks predicted."

"But . . . Julia, what's this got to do with—"

"Quiet. It has everything to do with it. Hardly anybody failed to approve of the war against Hitler and Japan. Our fathers fought in it, or did war work, or at least helped pay for the effort by their taxes and the war bonds they bought. True? Well, then, how guilty are they of the saturation bombings of Berlin and Hamburg, the senseless burning of Dresden? How guilty do they stand before Tokyo, Hiroshima, Nagasaki?

"Quiet, I said! They supported the Korean War also, no doubt. That means they supported burning human beings, whose names they never knew, alive with napalm."

"But the alternatives—" he attempted.

"Exactly. What choice had you with Matt Flagler?"

"I, oh, God, Julia, darling, I don't know, I don't know. I only know I saw him butchered and you don't give a damn."

"Why should I?" she hammered at him. "The blood of Cambodia is on your hands. Yes, wars do brutalize people, and a My Lai or a Dresden is inevitable. The question is whether the consequences of not fighting would be worse. If you thought we were doing wrong in Vietnam —okay, why did you pay your taxes? How many gallons of Agent Orange did *you* buy? And what are you doing now, you son of a bitch, about the horrors that your kind helped unleash over there? Anything whatsoever?"

"What the hell makes you so self-righteous about Flagler?"

He reached for her. She leaned away from him. When he slid toward her, she shook herself free. "No, Lauritz Rance," she said, "I want an honest answer. We're supposed to be partners. What use is a partner, in a game like this, who won't admit even to himself that he's as greedy a time-server as the rest?

"Come off your high moral horse. Recognize what you are. That boat of yours—what is it except a wish fulfillment, an escape from a world you can't handle? For a shallow dream like that, you'd put human lives in danger. You'd exploit Gayle, the way you exploited two wives till they couldn't take it any longer, and Satan alone knows how many other trusting women. You certainly didn't mind crawling into bed with me, another man's wife. And it was a thrill chasing Matt. Wasn't it? Never mind his terror and pain. You simply objected to seeing the end result.

"I don't. I'm happy that viper is dead. I'd cheerfully have shot him myself. But you—can you take a share in what you think is blood money, and ever make it with a woman again?"

He sprang to his feet. "Shut your mouth!" She did not entirely duck his roundhouse slap.

Hand on cheek, she said slowly, "That's right. Use your strength. I can't fight back. Go ahead. You hunted Matt down, but no one will hunt you."

"I'm going!" he yelled. "The partnership's done! You think I'll take anything from you?" He ran, shaken by tears.

Julia caressed the red site of his blow until the stinging faded. Then, smiling, she made her way up the path through the night that descended upon her.

She and Ellis were Haverner's only dinner guests. They

dressed for the occasion, and conversation was very civilized.

Afterward, as Ellis was about to seek his room, an apologetic voice said, "Please, sir. A minute of your toime?"

He turned in the mahogany-paneled entryroom and saw Captain York. The small man stood, dark-skinned, gray-headed, deferential in his nautical jacket and crisp trousers. "What is it?" Ellis asked.

"I have somet'ing to show you, sir."

"Me?"

"If you vill please come. I t'ink it vill interest you."

Ellis considered for a moment. "Okay. Why not?"

He accompanied York out among the fireflies. "What is it?" he wanted to know.

The Islandman, a shadow beneath stars, drew breath. "Special for you, sir. Mr. Sunderland, he not loike this, maybe. But I t'ink you vill. And soon I kvit here."

"Really? After this many years, and no pension plan or Social Security? Why?"

"I have seen too much for a Christian man, sir. And ve have relatives in de Nart' Port who vill help us find vork. . . . Here ve be. A minute, please." Captain York fumbled with the ring of keys he always carried.

Ellis scowled beneath the shed. "What're you getting at? This place is creepy enough without—"

"Vun minute, sir, vun minute only. You do not believe I vould hurt anybody, do you? Blessed are de meek." The door groaned back. York found the light switch. "In here, please."

Ellis entered, and stopped.

Matthew Flagler lay on a workbench. The litter-bearers had folded his hands, tied a kerchief around his chin, replaced the coins on his eyes, stripped and washed him upon arrival and afterward drawn a sheet across nakedness. But apparently York had folded it back. By now the measureless emptiness of his condition was upon the dead man. Desiccation had begun, making the whiskers stand forth, the skin draw back from the nails. In spite of precautions, the ants were there, up the bench legs and down again, into every bodily orifice, a red-black stream that left its pockmarks.

"Ve take him to de graveyard tomorrow early," said York. "I t'ought you vould loike to see first."

It rattled from Ellis, who had turned his back: "You ... morbid ... swine."

"I only t'ought you vould loike to see, vhen he vas your man till you had no more use for him."

"I'll report you—I—"

"I have given notice, sir."

Ellis choked and ran outside. The sound of his vomiting came irregularly back to where Captain Evans York stood at the dead man's head, in his countenance the justice of Jehovah.

Gayle entered Byron's room with him. Lamplight showed the place impersonally neat between drawn blinds, except that on the bedside table lay a few books.

"Well," he said clumsily. "Goodnight. It's been ... it's helped me a lot, walking and talking with you."

"Not half as much as it helped me." Her gray gaze dwelt on him. "From the time we left this house, hating ourselves for what we'd gotten mixed up in, right through building those sandwiches in the kitchen like we did."

He gestured at the walls. She laughed with sparse mirth. "Oh, forget the bugs," she said. "Let Haverner get his jollies. What else have you got to enjoy, Haverner? This is a recording."

Byron sat down on the bed. She joined him, and after a while quietly laid an arm around his waist.

"What did we do today, you and I?" he wondered in no loud voice. "We drifted through woods and over hills. We admitted our guilt, and that led to us telling frankly why we came here—you for money to buy a lazy life, I for cheap kicks—and somehow admitting the truth made it better. Why?"

"Maybe we got to be a little less alone." She kissed his cheek. "Even with God."

"Depends on what you mean by God."

"Who knows?" She leaned into the curve of his arm. "One thing, Byron. Our whole way back, I was trying to think how to say it."

He waited.

She drew his head around until their eyes met, and said, "We both needed somebody to, well, confess to and trust. So I want you to know, that's where it ends. I mean, I promise not to spoil it later by bracing you. Nothing about how you're a millionaire and I'm a poverty case and I only need a few bucks. I'm done with that. It hasn't even gotten me anywhere."

"You certainly have been shabbily treated."

"Well, I had it coming. Larry used me, didn't give a damn about me, right? But what was my attitude? Sure, I enjoyed him screwing me, but I myself started that affair because I wanted to use him. Matt—well, I was scared and uptight, but still a tiny bit hopeful—of a cut in the money, or something. If it hadn't been for that, I'd have tried, really tried, to get free of him.

"This afternoon, under the easy tears, I saw I was glad he was dead, and mainly glad because it saved me the trouble of sloughing him off somehow. I'm guiltier than Anselmo. At least he never laid his victim."

"No, you mustn't feel like that," he urged.

"Yes, I ought to. Not to ruin my life with it or anything, but—don't you see? It was a kind of shock therapy. I owe it to Matt and, and Orestes, to make sure it doesn't go wasted." She dropped her earnestness and nestled more comfortably. "You're helping no end, Byron. You give me a kind of, of absolution."

"Me?" He turned rickety laughter into an equally fragile smile. "Hardly. But the thought makes me a bit less unhappy." He stirred. "Well, I suppose we'd better say goodnight."

"Why?"

He flushed. "If nothing else, no privacy."

"Never mind that." Her voice thinned. "Please, Byron. Finish helping me. I swear again, I don't want money from you. We'll go home to our different coasts, if this horror ever ends, and that'll be that. But don't take away the hand you've reached me—not yet! Don't leave me alone with myself—not till I'm stronger."

"Eh? You want to, to spend the night?"

She kissed him long and unsteadily, getting little response.

"Well, if you . . . yes, of course you may." His face grew still fiercer. He stared straight before him, hands passive in his lap. "However, don't expect—I mean, you know, a hard day, a terrible experience, not to mention awareness of being spied on. I'd scarcely be up to, uh—"

She cast herself across him. "Oh, you poor lamb! Do you think I care what happens, as long as it's us two?"

According to her wish, they undressed; according to his, they turned off the light. They lay for an uncounted while in each other's arms, hardly stirring. But then she began to caress him, slowly, undemandingly, but more and more intimately. "What?" he whispered. "It's just my way. You mind?" she answered in endless gentleness.

"No—no—sure, Gayle, whatever you want—"

There was no haste. She had never been one to hurry things, nor to insist on any particular outcome of them. She only lay against him, fondling, sleepily purring a little. At last he began to fondle her in his turn.

There was not even any exact moment when she took him into herself. When they were done, he lay with his head between her breasts and wept for happiness.

And the hell with Haverner.

The master grimaced. "Disgusting," he muttered to himself.

He switched off the receiver, leaving the recorder on in case he later wished to know just what had happened next. Quite likely he would not; he had never approved of pornography. If only Shaddock and Thayer had had a fight, like that beauty which Petrie maneuvered Rance into . . . !

Seeking refreshment before he retired, he went to a window. It stood open on a mild night, so that he heard the surf afar, like a voice that whispered to him. Above the distant heights, some starlit pieces of cloud hinted at a face.

"You are disappointed," Samael said.

"Well, yes," Haverner admitted.

"Why? Was our objective not to discover what the subjects would do under these extraordinary circumstances—whatever it might be?"

Haverner sighed. "I suppose that was, is, your aim. Mine . . . Very well, I thought of this experiment as a testing to destruction."

It was as if the face smiled. "That will probably come tomorrow."

"We'll see. You did have some excellent suggestions."

"Which you will get to watch enacted in person, if you like."

He gnawed his lip. "Unfortunately, no. The real action will take place inside their heads, where I cannot go."

"I do not think," said Samael, "that tomorrow even you would want to go there."

JULIA PETRIE

Dawn stands white over the sea. It nearly drowns a sickle of dying moon. Westward, where the land rises in formless black tree-masses, the sky is still purple and a few stars linger, tiny and icy. Birds have begun to twitter here and there. Lawns and flowers are one glitter of dew. A breath of salt air brings surfsong and coolness to clothe me.

Look, look well. Inhale the odors, taste the wind, hear the gravel beneath your striding feet. Feel that motion, the infinite subtle interplay of nerve and muscle. Gather in all the reality you can, to take down where you are bound.

The veranda is shadowy, but windows are aglow in the house. My time is almost come. I go around to the patio and enter the dining room by its French doors. (Smells of coffee and bacon, purity of linen and silver, startling orange of an egg yolk.) Sunderland Haverner is there, Ellis Nordberg and nobody else. Surprising. I expected Larry would sulk, ostentatiously avoiding me, and that that Gayle slattern would oversleep, whatever her intentions. But isn't Byron interested?

"Good morning, Mrs. Petrie," says the terrible old man. "I hear you rose two hours ago."

"Yes, I wanted a walk," I say, not telling him why, though doubtless he knows. Exercise, wide-open senses, the right preparation for what waits. Or so I think.

"You have breakfasted, then?"

"Yes." (It is best not to have much undigested food in

the stomach under the conditions I plan.) I slipped the help a substantial tip for making them begin early. Well, I can afford it. Regardless of what happens, I've half a million dollars, free and clear.

Ellis, primly dressed, wets his lips. A faint film of sweat stands on his forehead. Good. The more ill at ease he is, the better. I give him my most poisonous politeness. "You've said you needed the entire sum for your purposes, Mr. Nordberg. That's become impossible. Do you want to resign and save yourself trouble?"

The look I get! Technically it's nonsense that eyes have expression; it's the tissue around them. But blanched blue hates me from behind its glass. "No," he forces out of his mouth.

I knew beforehand. Half a million is better than none. Besides, he wants to impress Haverner. You'd like being pilot fish to our great cold shark, wouldn't you, Ellis?

"Don't blame me for any consequences, then." I trust he understands what I am really saying: You are a murderer, Ellis Nordberg; two men are dead because of you; I mean to whip you, and I hope to do you harm in the process.

Glancing at my watch, perhaps too elaborately, I tell them, "In ten minutes, gentlemen. The living room. I'll be there."

Anselmo already is. He surprises me by rising from his couch and bowing. " 'Ow do you do, Meessees Petrie?" His smile actually seems to have warmth. Why? Well, he knows what my game will be. He knows better than I do. Doubtless he likes me not only for staying the course, but for deliberately invoking horror at its end, when I could have decreed something nominal and taken my safe five hundred thousand. I've shown him . . . What's the female equivalent of *cojones*? We're equals of a sort, this huntsman and I.

I see the slim black box on a table beside us. I know what's inside, and my heart stumbles. Almost convulsively, I take his hand. "Wish me luck," I say.

"*Vaya con Díos*," he answers low.

Can you go with God into hell?

You can into heaven. Maybe. Can I force this journey of mine to be in that direction? Do I dare? No, it's practically certain that'll be impossible anyway. I asked Haverner to design a hell for us, and he's good at that.

Light strengthens in the windows. Haverner's cane replies to my heart. He limps in, nods, settles himself where Anselmo was. I don't imagine he'll stay for more than the beginning of our battle. Or will he? I can imagine him hovering over us like a vulture over two corpses. . . . Stop it, Julia! The one place he cannot follow you is into your head, where all the hells and heavens are.

Ellis, entering behind him (of course), stiffens to a halt. His eyes seek mine, recoil, rush about. "Well?" he barks. "Well? What's your game? Let's get started. Sooner we get started, the sooner we can end this fool"—remembering Haverner—"this experiment."

I savor each word. "It's quite simple, Nordberg. And quite scientific. You're in favor of science and technology, aren't you? Here's a little applied chemistry."

His look finds the box and is caught by it.

"Open that, please, Anselmo," I say. The brown hands snap back the lid. Two loaded hypodermic needles lie on red velvet. Does Ellis guess the truth at once? He chokes on a breath. I feel enough glee at his discomfiture to cover —almost—my own fears.

"Choose your weapon," I say. "Either of those, loaded with a thousand-microgram solution of lysergic acid diethylamide. You've heard of it under the name LSD."

"What?" He throws his hands aloft before he whirls on the devil to whom I have sold a part interest in my soul. "Mr. Haverner, no!" he yammers. "What is this . . . I mean, an illegal drug, a dangerous *drug!*"

Haverner does not condescend to explain once more that here the law is his whim and nothing else.

Red and white mottle Ellis's face beneath the scraps of peeling skin which are Orestes's *memento mori* to him. "It's not fair! Some hippie like her, used to those things."

"Hippie?" My jeering is calculated. The worse his mood when he begins, the better for me. "Have you forgotten I'm a suburban housewife who favors the Conservative Party? I've never touched any psychodrugs but alcohol in my life [reasonably true; a couple of incidents with marijuana don't count; mere curiosity, and nothing happened, probably because I never have been an inhaling smoker] and I don't mean to do it ever again after today." Now I wish I were an actress, to load my words with grue. At least I can speak slowly, emphatically. "I've been a psychiatric nurse, you may recall. I've seen what those materials can do."

"The dossier on Mrs. Petrie gives me no reason to doubt her," says Haverner, playing the fish. "She discussed her idea with me some time ago, and I decided it was entirely acceptable. True, her background gives her more information about this substance and its effects than most rivals could be expected to have. That is an advantage. However, I believe it's counteracted by the fact that both of you will receive identical dosages and you, Mr. Nordberg, have the greater body weight." He yanks deftly to drive in the hook. "To be sure, you may elect to forfeit the contest."

Ellis's head swings from Haverner's faint geniality to Anselmo's impassivity to whatever is in me. He has to wet his lips twice before he can ask, "What's the plan? What do we do?"

"You will receive your injections," Haverner says. "This is to make any cheating impossible, as might occur if the drug were taken by mouth in the usual way. Going directly into the bloodstream, the chemical has almost immediate effect. It will peak in about four hours, thereafter declining. Most persons get back to normal in twenty-four hours or less from the start."

I wish he hadn't felt it necessary to tell the snake that. Knowing roughly what to expect can be a help. I add, "You should be warned, Nordberg, there may be recurring hallucinations for several days. And there's always the risk of permanent damage."

Haverner frowns. "Rare," he says, "at any rate in subjects who are not habituated. The chances are excellent that, by this time tomorrow, you will be yourselves again." Damn him, he is being fair.

"Then what—" Ellis rallies, squares his shoulders, flings out a nearly self-possessed question. "What's the purpose? She can't just mean for us to sit around giggling."

What a relief! Haverner forgets, or (does he ever forget to do anything?) does not see fit to say that the outward signs of LSD are much more controllable than those of alcohol. Some who came to us at the hospital showed no traces whatsoever; they only told us that demons were loose in their skulls, and pleaded for help in curiously flat, objective voices.

People tend to act out their expectations. If Ellis expects to become the maundering maniac of popular mythology . . .

"No," says Haverner. "What she asked was for me to devise ways to make this a, ah, a difficult time. After all, the commonest reaction to LSD is a sense of ecstasy, mystical awareness, childlike marvel, or something else equally absurd. Mrs. Petrie wanted me to try to assure a bad trip, as they call it. Needless to say, she has been given no hint of what I have planned."

"That is," I put in, "Anselmo's more our leader today than I am. Or, m-m, Mr. Haverner himself if he chooses, but I guess mostly Anselmo. We do whatever we're told. Only we mustn't speak. The first one who balks, or asks for help, or passes out, or screams, or otherwise shows he can't stand the gaff, loses."

Ellis replies like a lash. "Does that include you?"

Ouch! "No, certainly not. I'm just giving you your chance at half the prize."

And myself the chance of punishing you, murderer, and of denying you the money you'd use to buy further evil, or the closeness to horrible Haverner you might also gain. Haverner's empire mustn't have an heir, it's got to die with him. My banner is flying; my sword is aloft. If I've had to do dishonorable things, it's been for an honorable end that includes more than saving my little girl. . . .

Oh, yes, true, it also includes that independence which the additional half million will nail down for Malcolm and me. He could do so much, given this; and I—I could do whatever it may be I desire.

Whip my enemy onward! "Take off your coat, Nordberg, and roll up your sleeve. The game is beginning."

He glares, I hear his raw breath for seconds before he yells, "All right, harlot!"

Oh, my, oh, my. I *have* got him going, haven't I, if he starts off on Bible language this early in the morning?

I, in a loose comfortable dashiki-like gown, lift a fold of cloth to bare my own left arm. Anselmo glances from Ellis to me. "Either one," Ellis rasps. "Damn you." With a slight, amused shrug, Anselmo picks up a hypodermic and glides to me.

His left thumb and forefinger pinch the flesh. It is a virgin needle that enters me. I hardly feel the prick. Anselmo is skilled at this kind of shooting, too. My heart bangs. Suddenly, well-nigh overwhelmingly, I'm aware of him, his sinewy clasp and the smells of leather, gun oil, man.

He lets me go. Through an east window I see the sun come out of the waters, one enormous blaze. "Remember," I say, "we follow orders strictly, and we don't make a sound unless we're told to."

Ellis stares away from the needle while he's injected. His fists are clenched as if to rip the skin across the knuckles. "I'll outlast you, you bitch," he vows. "The Lord is with me."

I could declare that that cost him the game. But no, Haverner would surely overrule me. How hard Ellis tried not to flinch when he was penetrated!

My skin tingles a little. Am I really getting disoriented, or is this simple nervousness, hyperventilation, my frightened body at war with itself?

Be at ease, Julia, be at ease. Sit down, since nobody has forbidden it. Never forget, the anticipation of a bad trip is a powerful factor in bringing one on. Remember, you told Haverner not to subject us to anything physically dangerous. You did. Didn't you?

No matter. It's cool in here, and faintly murmurous from the sea. Or the air conditioning? No, must be the sea, the Mother, singing to me. Have I ever heard Her in this room before? Well, LSD does open the perceptions. Feel the couch underneath my shoulders, back, buttocks, thighs, cradling each last least muscle in a softness like Kilby. See how yonder sunbeam slants gold through a window, dust motes dancing in it that are stars, stars and planets dancing in the radiance of God. (Call It God until It reveals Its true name.) Nordberg has taken a chair. By rolling my head in time with a star, I can thrust both him and Haverner out of sight. Anselmo passes across my view with his panther gait.

I smile at him. His return glance is appreciative. Okay, I enjoy displaying myself to him. Wish I'd specified nudity today. No harm in that. My sex life was lousy, this past couple of years, till I came here. It should become good again when I return in triumph, but I don't kid myself that everything can be healed overnight. Let me strut a tiny bit before that handsome stud.

Larry—

No. You're done with Larry Rance. You eased him out quite neatly.

You might cop a feel on me as you go by, Anselmo. I wouldn't mind.

He passes from sight. Oh, well, probably for the best. Adultery may be addictive. You've done what was necessary, Julia. To do more would be the real unfaith. Though Malcolm—

Watch the world, Julia, while you can, before you enter your madness.

That's what it is. Even (the more rational) regular users admit that what LSD creates is either schizophrenia or the next thing to it. A thousand micrograms is a heavy dose; let's see, I had it figured out as thirty-five millionths of an ounce, didn't I? Less than that will jam the circuits and scramble the programs of this ten-million-million-unit computer we carry around in its bony box to love and grieve and declare, "I am." Well, it doesn't take a very much heavier blood clot in the right place to dam off every reality.

Careful, careful. You're hoping Ellis Nordberg will have more brittlenesses than you do. But don't strain yours. You've planned this. You know a few techniques. Relax. Think happy thoughts. Watch the music billow golden through the sunbeam. See Anselmo again, off to fetch something. The sun is in him.

Golden, golden. Whatever happens, half a million dollars. (Unless your mind breaks . . . No! It won't! I feel *good*. I begin to see why acidheads do.) That kind of sum you don't put in a savings bank for a pittance of interest; it commands a return that stays well ahead of inflation, and it hires experts to minimize the taxes. No problem about having Kilby's machine at home, with extra equipment and a specialist standing by. She'll be so much happier—less unhappy?—so much happier. I hear the machine happily humming in the sun.

Malcolm, our financial monkey off his back and a chunk of investment in capital in hand, should soon be making even better money than that, of course. He won't sit idle. Dear earnest Malcolm! I miss you, sweetheart. Why are you wearing Larry Rance's head?

Or Ken's? No, it isn't Ken who's touching off the soft little flames that dance across me and in me, red, red, and gold. Not really. I told you, Malcolm, in honesty, I told you I was no virgin, that I'd lived with one other man before we met, you and I. What I never told you was how much I was on the rebound from the final disaster of it. Ken and I, we weren't a possible pair; I learned the hard way that bronze curls, clean profile, and football player's muscles aren't enough, but sometimes, Malcolm, I've closed my eyes and pretended you were him.

Shall I now? There he is, right in that picture frame. No, that's Larry. Hang on, hang on. Stop crowding them out of the universe, Larry. There's room for everybody in the singing. It *is* everybody. You've got to be out there somewhere, Malcolm.

Whoever you've been making love to in Manhattan, have you sometimes pretended she was me? Go screw with Larry, you girl, and let me have Malcolm back. Where is he?

We can repair what we've had. Can't we, Malcolm? We're intelligent, unprejudiced, realistic adults. We're joined by Kilby, and by those further children we may have, and by the joy we used to find in each other and will again, again, again, children around us, a tide of children; we're drowning in them but where's Kilby? Kilby died!

No. No. Julia, you mustn't cry out to her poor little corpse. Go, Kilby. Go away with that silent, silent, silent ocean of children Julia has not had.

Anselmo's come back. Has he? He talks Spanish with Haverner. Spanish? Eyulatl, the language of the Those. It rises and falls in a high fever-whine. The screen, when did he set up the screen, it ripples, it foams, waves roar past the bows of Larry's ship as he hounds the sunset.

Why Larry? A bum, not particularly young or handsome, why him? Why did you never pretend he was somebody else? Use this immense clarity and insight that you are, while Its immortality lasts.

Think words. Think causes. Romanticism that you

should have outgrown. A certain resemblance to Ken and, yes, Dad.

Dad's no sailor, though. Nor does he really belong in a jerk-water college, in snitty academic infighting. No, Roger Fenn, your people who are mine found their land of sagebrush heights and infinite heavens almost a hundred years ago, and possessed it and were possessed by it. You should never have become a professor of English, who happened to marry a woman who would always be homesick for New England; you should have been a range rider, a bronco buster.

At least Uncle Joe has a ranch, where your daughter could spend her summers in a young girl's love affair with horses.

They smell warm, horses. Their noses are velvet. Come off with your little girl, Dad, here where she is. She'll make it that you did become a cowboy, in this place where she wasn't ever begotten, and we'll go off together on our horses.

Dawn at Espada Canyon! The depths brim with twilight blue, and then while we crouch over our fire, teeth clapping in a Fimbul wind off the mountains, crags and buttes come into shape down yonder, and color waxes in them, and at last, slowly, slowly light and shadow steal across the Gothicness of them, and I am day.

Larry wouldn't settle down with us away from the sea. He's obsessed. Hear the mermaids singing to him, but they have shark teeth.

Not that he'll ever make it. Poor futile dreamer, he'll continue drifting from job to job, woman to woman; he'll drink harder, smoke more pot, maybe serve time on a bust for that; he'll grow creepingly old and fat and puzzled about where his hopes went. See him bloat. See Kilby, puffed and rotting in her grave. No. Dad. No. Dad, where are you? Where've you taken our canyon? The sunbeam is black.

No. Shades drawn. Only shades drawn. Whirr-r-r-r-r-r-rrrrr, "Please watch the film," says the god who makes flies of us for his sport, ah, movies, something to watch, something for the self to cling to.

It's exactly a film. Cling to that. A film, not a transcendence, hastily put together out of what clips his agents could find out of those he thought would most terrify and torment us.

The shapes! They whirl! They rush devouring from the end of infinity! I am whirled; you fall flaming from heaven and sunder the world in your crashing; it lies in the shards of the world and its horse is a stallion that crushes it under his weight and tears its flesh with his teeth and rips it bloody with his battering hugeness and *I must not scream.* They're stacked to heaven, the corpses of Buchenwald, hell groans beneath their weight, where's Kilby, Kilby, Kilby, Kilby, in whirling and roaring, flashes and thunders and God feasting on the souls of the newly dead, where are you, Kilby, what are you, Kill-ll Bee-ee?

Bad trip. Remember. Bad trip. You knew there'd be terror. Ride it out. Cling to Larry.

Nauseating copulations spout across the screen, or is this just a penis of the mind? Come, let me clutch thee.

Tell Larry I'm sorry, Larry. We had some lovely times; she never came with Malcolm, quite, the way she came with you. It was like Ken . . . except she understood from the outset, we were rivals, you and I, Larry.

We needn't have been. I did mean to share with you. But after the callous way you used Gayle, that last night, you deserved casting off, like an outworn snakeskin.

Orestes hardly cold in his grave, too.

Ahhhh! There he lies dead! Is it in the film, or is it in me and therefore forever? You feel the wind whistle through your mouth; she feels the sweat start forth on her flesh. He glares, dead on the sand, and it that betrayed Larry the betrayer is altogether alone with him.

Steady. Endure. For half a million extra dollars, and coming home with Kilby's life in my purse.

As for that Matthew Flagler thing—

But she did not deal fairly with Larry, and so he's gone from it, and Dad and Ken and Malcolm; it's by herself in the whirling and flickering and hate.

What's fair? Who else rates five hundred thousand dollars, that none but I will have wrung out of Ellis Nordberg's body and brain?

Where is he, anyway? How's he taking it, these war films, if that's what he's seeing too, where fire from the sky sticks to the living flesh that it burns off the fleeing bones, where bombs smash cities and machinery to chaos?

These scenes must be meant for him. Hang on, Julia. Find a hillside forest and silence. Ignore the voices that drone on and on, accusing me in a language I do not know. See, you can call up a hawk to fly overhead, and sunlight like molten gold upon his wings.

Don't let Matthew Flagler come running in terror for his wretched existence. Don't let the voices swell to a hymn about God's vengeance.

Twenty-four hours. You can endure that, Julia, lass. You must. Only twenty-four quadrillion years.

So hold Larry to you. No, he's gone. Malcolm, please, please come through this storm and ruin, to me. I've got to spend the rest of my life at your side. Help me now.

There is no help. There is Nothing.

Crouch on the infinitely thin skin stretched above Nothing and do not scream.

Anselmo raises the blinds. He carries a scythe. White birds toil past the window. "The feelm ees feeneesh'," he says. Echoes of his voice roll off the canyon walls of eternity. *Consummatum est.*

Haverner-God-Nothing takes her arm. "Come," he says. His flesh is dust and cobwebs, whirled around and around the bones, which are not human bones; they are the hollow bones of birds, and the wind of Nothing that whirls the shadow-gray powder skirls in them. "Come." O-oh, come, come, come, come, come. . . .

Ellis Nordberg shambles on Anselmo's support. What is his reality? You can at least walk through yours, Julia, erect, showing none of the horror, not even asking what time it is. For time is not. That is the secret of hell. It goes on.

We cross the lawn. The sun howls around us. Heaven opens. The God of her childhood (her parents made her go to Sunday school for cultural reasons, though they themselves never set foot in a church), Who is a huge man in a sky-blue business suit and storm-gray fedora, leans forth above beach and jungle and old, fat, futile Larry Rance whom she has made what he is, to demand of her, "What precise sum does the child that is born unto us require?"

"Shall a maker of murder have any share in it?" she yells without lips.

The shattered head of Orestes says, "You have your share."

Matt runs through the woods, fighting brush and snake-like vines, screaming into endless hot silence, alone. From your winged station you see Anselmo on his track. He has a hard on. For you, when he has slaughtered Matt. Your blood still runs from the wound the stallion left.

Larry collapses into a dead man's decay.

Byron leers through the stench. He's very thin, an ascetic whom she did not succeed in seducing; yes, he wears a monk's brown robe and carries a flagellant's whip. O Byron, please don't bring back the films!

Flash. Flash. Flash.

Its heartbeat is shaking it to pieces.

A rat will live in its skull.

Malcolm, you're the lawyer, tell me, what should drowning I do?

Call off the game? Right this minute of eternity? But she can't. At most, she can beg for help . . . after Nord-berg does, because half a million dollars would be power in the hands of a man who buys murder and I owe you that much, Orestes, Matt, don't I?

The gates of hell are opened unto me.

"Pass through," says the mummy. "Walk in my garden."

We enter, and the cactus throbs in and out, in and out, needles flame-hot, death-cold, they will inject us again and again and again, we will never more be in the world. The tropical blooms make mouths at me.

It's cactus, only cactus and flowers and such, Julia, that you loved when you were a girl on horseback, before you turned into a thing your big clean father cannot possibly have begotten. Cactus, cactus, cactus. Peyote, mescaline, chaos stabbed into me while the voices roar and the sky burns and *Ellis screams.*

I see him run. Matt, Orestes, and Anselmo pursue him.

"Congratulations, Mrs. Petrie," Haverner sneers across the gulf. After a glance at his watch: "Almost precisely four hours. The peak effect, evidently, and more than he could take. How are you doing?"

"Go away," I hear. His real face, if that is his real face, is coming back, measurelessly more ghastly than what was before. "Let me be."

He sketches a bow. "As you will, Mrs. Petrie. I daresay you will do best to be at peace for a while, in pleasant surroundings, after the stimuli you have experienced. If you change your mind, or want or need anything the house can supply, do come there and ask for it." A pause, no longer than the interval between the Crucifixion and the Nativity. "I must go observe Mr. Nordberg. He's giving Anselmo quite a struggle, isn't he? In a bad way, I fear. But then, according to those works I consulted, cacti are often a fear symbol in hallucinogenic states. Especially to him, who wouldn't be used to them as you are." He lurches off.

What strangeness did you have planned for me, Haverner? I don't ask. I don't want to know. I sag onto a bench and am alone.

The cactuses still pulsate, the sun keeps time in great waves of impossibly rich scarlet, gold, emerald, sapphire, ultraviolet, and baal, but the voices are fading to a mumble and, though the world is still hollow, one can look away from Nothing. She counts the drops of sweat that roll out of her, down her; she knows their exact iciness. But she does not shake. The shivering is all inside her muscles, where the sea wind makes them ring like harpstrings.

You have only to wait now, Julia. The madness is ebbing. When it's quite gone, or nearly gone (because I fear there will always be a haunted place in my skull), you can decide how to spend your million.

Yours and Malcolm's, you mean. No, by God, mine. What had he to do with gaining it?

Shall I, who have stared down Nothing, flinch from asking myself while this clarity lasts, whether or not I really want Malcolm hanging onto me until death do us rot?

It's not as if you needed to be an alimony leech. Think. If only the numbers didn't twist around in that jungle where a man runs forever alone! Grab a number by the tail. No, the head. You mustn't let it bite you. The fangs are venomous.

Annual income on a million, and you are taken care

of, dear elfin trusting presence whom I wish I could see before me. And plenty is left over. Taxes . . . No, arrangements can be made. Haverner will help me if I ask. He delights in legal fictions. What good is it to have made a pact with Satan if you don't get some work out of him?

Well, let's play safe and suppose I will have a reasonable net income, after expenses, for the rest of my life. What am I going to do with that life? Be the bland suburban appurtenance of a prominent attorney?

Oh, Matt, stop screaming. At least quiet it a bit, can't you? You had no mercy on Orestes.

But if it weren't for you, Matt, I'd be home already, in the same debt and despair as before. You cleared the way for me, Matt.

Sure, I've been ruthless. Survival. Not my own survival—

Though what will I do, given my money-like-sunshine (the sun is brazen and hammering on dead Matt where he runs from dead Orestes) freedom?

Travel? Yes, certainly. We'd do that in any event, Malcolm. (Malcolm, where are you?) My one summer, me nineteen years old and on a bicycle, youth-hosteling it along with Gloria and those chance-met boys and girls who'd join us for a few days, that lanky whimsical Norwegian, that unutterably charming Giacomo. . . . No, be damned, Larry's right, we've not been given much life and to spend it in a single place is lunacy.

But a prominent attorney must keep himself available. At most, he can take a few careful weeks off per year.

It's likewise lunacy to sit here and let dreadfulness roll through my head. When there's so much beauty, so much joy.

Larry, come to me through the jungle. Hold me. Fuck me. If I'm hallucinating, which I am, make it be your South Seas, your *Morgana* white-winged before the wind, and you.

Why should you come, after what I did to you?

Call up what strength you have left, Julia. You fought for your little girl, and won. Now you must fight for yourself.

Sunset rises. Eternity draws to an end, losing itself once more in time. Occasionally the sights, the voices and the

Nothing come back, but always fainter, always less often. I sit in the world and its peace, victorious.

"Well, let's go eat, then," I say, and wish I hadn't laughed aloud. That's too high and ragged.

Stars blossom as I cross the lawn. Fireflies answer them. It chirrs, it soughs, it murmurs everywhere around me, and it smells of life. Never have lighted windows glowed so deep an amber as welcomes me.

But they block off the living world. When I have crossed the threshold, night is infinite in the glass.

Someone enters the hall before me. It is Anselmo Cain, followed by Haverner. On the arm of Anselmo leans Ellis Nordberg. He can barely shuffle along.

He doesn't scream. If only he would! Anything's better than that mummy mumble out of his bitten and bleeding mouth, that Nothing in his eyes. The dead men have taken him, and no one can shake them loose.

"Ah, good evening, Mrs. Petrie," says Haverner brightly. "I trust you feel better than our poor friend here? He seems to have had a rather precarious hold on sanity, and to have suffered a complete psychotic break."

That is my final damnation.

Am I too still back there in the dark, or do wings truly follow me?

Me, the avenging goddess who mainly wanted half a million more dollars all to herself.

What grabbed my running foot and threw me down the stairs? Blood drips from my chin. I crawl, hands and knees. The hall above, unlighted, is full of shadows.

Somehow I raise myself. The knob of his door feels like a bone.

He sprawls on bed in a foul gray fog of pipe smoke. A bottle of whisky stands by for his use. "Heard you won," he says, not even deigning to hate. "Congratulations. What do you want?"

I fall again, before him. "Larry," I cry, "help me!"

FAREWELLS

As folk came down for a late breakfast or sent after it, the servants announced that Mr. Haverner would meet them on the patio at noon, and when business had been settled his plane would fly them back to Ciudad Vizcaya.

Four sat beneath the hog plum tree to confront the Ramses head and skeleton body in the blanketed Morris chair. Their hands were interlocked, Larry's and Julia's, Gayle's and Byron's. Fruit glowed like lanterns in the darkling foliage, but no one ate thereof. The sun smote pitilessly on English lawn and flowerbeds, bleaching them; it was a hot day again, and growing worse. Odors were of tropical forest, and though the air never stirred, the noise of surf somehow came loud.

"Well." Haverner hefted a notebook. He smiled. "We come to the end of a most intriguing half month." (The moon stood horned and pale above the house.) "My felicitations to our winner, Mrs. Petrie. My condolences to the rest—who are, anyhow, richer in experience—and my thanks for providing a huge amount of unique psychological data." He intercepted Byron. "Rest assured, nothing will be published. And I trust you yourselves will observe discretion in relating what happened during our experiment."

"Think so?" It was Gayle who spoke, shrill with anger. "Do you imagine we won't do whatever we can to bring you to justice?"

"Well, well." Haverner was untouched, save for amusement. "Has the recent stress converted you back to bourgeois values, Mrs. Thayer? Here is an offer: I will pay one thousand dollars for a letter from you, a year hence, stating your philosophy as of that time."

Appalled, she turned toward Byron, whose free arm reached around to give her a brief caress.

"As for your somewhat melodramatic resolve," Haverner went on, "I personally do not care what you do. This whole affair has taken place in the jurisdiction of the Republic of Santa Ana, whose authorities are satisfied with the report I have made to them. I simply advise you, for your own sakes, not to create a sensation that could ruin you."

"I'm afraid he's right, Gayle," Larry said. Julia nodded. Byron leaned forward. "What about Ellis?"

"Mr. Nordberg is far from well," Haverner answered. "What're you going to do?"

"I think he had best remain here awhile, under the care of a physician whom I shall send for. I've already instructed my agents to notify his family and ask for their agreement to this. I expect to get it. Psychiatric treatment at home would be costly, and . . . his dossier indicates he is not overly precious to his wife or sons. Let us hope that treatment, rest, and recreation will restore him. However that goes, he's a fascinating clinical study."

They sat altogether still, those four.

"Well," Haverner said after a minute, "since you're obviously eager to return, I shan't detain you much further. I do need to know how you wish your prize awarded you, Mrs. Petrie."

"The money will be paid?" Byron asked in scorn.

"Indeed. Indeed." Wattles under the chin swayed as the knaggy head nodded. "I am, irrespective of your opinion, an honest man. You might also consider the fact that my failure to keep a promise like this would inevitably become general knowledge and thus discourage volunteers for what future experiments I may want to arrange."

Gayle shivered.

"It is a question of technicalities," Haverner explained. "Legal forms must be gone through. You do not wish trouble with your government, I am sure, Mrs. Petrie. So the instrument must be carefully drawn. I will direct you to a gentleman, resident in Ciudad Vizcaya but an American and expert in these matters, who handles such affairs for me. You'll doubtless have to stay there a few days till he's finished, to be available for consultation and the like. But it's quite a picturesque city." He ran tongue over lips. "And you need not lack for companionship, need you?"

"Get this thing over with," Larry snapped, "before I forget Anselmo and his gun are on call."

"Yes." Julia let go his hand, folded both hers on her lap, sat rifle-straight in the rattan chair and said fast, out of a white countenance, "There were seven of us. I want a seven-way split." For the first time in more years than the four had been on earth, Sunderland Haverner was seen to be astounded, even shocked. "That is, of course Kilby must have what she needs. I am taking half the million home with me—but that includes both my seventh and Matt's, since I don't intend to reward murder. As for his wife and children—now that he's out of the way—if I know anything about the . . . the Family, they'll be taken care of." Julia drew breath. "So, for the rest of the players, one hundred thousand each. Ellis's people can use his share if he's incapacitated. And if Orestes hasn't left any kin that can be traced, whatever village he came from can have his portion. I'm sure they need it."

Gayle gasped and burst into weeping. Byron held her close, and the inner happiness which had shown on him this morning before the meeting now resurged.

Julia turned to Larry. The smile that passed between them was tender. "Whatever I have left from my own winnings," she told the group, "will go toward the Morgana le Fay Oceanographic Research Foundation."

He kissed her, lightly but in front of everyone's eyes.

"Can I buy into that outfit?" Byron asked.

"And me?" Gayle gulped through her tears.

"No, hold on awhile, sweetheart," Byron counseled, "till we see how things work out . . . for you."

She laid her head against his breast. "But, but I know they will."

"What is this nonsense?" Haverner demanded.

Then, slowly, his mouth quirked. "Interesting," he breathed. "No, fascinating."

SUNDERLAND HAVERNER

Night leaps over the horizon and engulfs us.

Us: myself and the muttering madman in this office with me, him drugged half-unconscious to hold the dead men at bay. I thought it would be worth observing him as the sedation wears off, but he merely lies there, empty-faced, in the chaise for which my own weary bones are longing.

I press the button that summons York. A brandy would lessen this unreasonable interior cold. The machines stare and stare, like Nordberg. Well, let's start that final set of tapes going; let's learn what happened yesterday after they needed no longer follow the leader. The information should help explain that scene they played out this noon. Not that it was anything more than half-hysterical reaction. Too bad I won't be able to collect the details of how they will repent and seek to squirm out of their pledges.

A knock. "Come in." Anselmo. Oh, yes, York left today! Where am I going to find another factotum as competent? What drove him?

"¿Señor?" Anselmo inquires.

"A-a-aguardiente." Why do I stammer? "Una botella."

He asks who should bring it. He won't, of course; that is beneath his dignity. We discuss the matter of York's replacement. Am I imagining things, or does Anselmo's gaze despise me?

What difference? Don't let it make a difference. He's my hireling, isn't he?

My hands shudder so that it's hard to set up the playback. How long do those dogs need to fetch me a bottle? And strange how I crave a smoke, after ten years of abstention. I must resist. The doctors have warned me. They warn too much, too officiously, which is why I don't have one on the premises. Nevertheless, this dwindled heart, these papery arteries . . . I can buy death, but I cannot buy Death.

All right, then, you young swine! Perform for me! I bought *you*, didn't I?

The brandy comes, and the first double shot slides into my bloodstream, hot as the bodies of Indian girls whom I can no longer recall. I smile at Nordberg. "Care for a show?" His response to it may be significant.

He doesn't give me any. He is too lost in his darkness. Well, the video brings hardly a thing, from rooms where the lights were turned off. The sound is excellent. It fills this chamber.

"Don't you understand, Gayle? I love you. I want you to marry me."

"And don't you understand, Byron? After these horrors . . . I'm through chasing money. I am."

"Do you blame me for being rich?"

"No, of course not, silly. But, well, a couple of nights, when we were both feeling scared and guilty and desperate, what do they mean?"

"They mean everything to me, Gayle. Someday I'll tell you precisely how much. I love you. I need you. I'm as, as adoringly thankful to you as—I don't know. I haven't the words."

"M-m-m . . . you're sweet. I'd no notion how dear you are, till now. But a lifetime together? We're damned different, Byron, honey. Sooner or later, the crunch will come."

"We can last that out. If we try." Humbly: "If you want."

"I do want, I do want! But I will not use you. Listen. They'll call it a shack-up, but screw them." A giggle, warm in the dark. "I mean, screw me. We'll try for a year or two. No promises on either side. No legal claims if it doesn't work out." She stops his words with what I, amplifying, identify as a kiss. "Don't talk for a minute yet, Byron. Only listen. This is the way it's going to be, or I'll have no part of it. Can't you see, I've got to become something I can respect. I've got to make sure I'm worth—not your money, but your time, your life—before I can take a promise from you."

"Oh, Gayle, Gayle, Gayle."

Sickening.

Did she mean what was said? Did he? Obviously, the Petrie woman's decision today came as a surprise to them both. The Thayer slut didn't know she'd get that sum. Therefore, last night she was showing a measure of psychological independence. As for him, he finally met a woman, experienced but not unduly expectant, who was at the same time in real need of him as a person. Naturally, he's delirious about that.

Well, a permanent cure won't come fast or easy, Shaddock my friend, and you can seek a more appropriate partner after you have some idea of what to look for and how. Or she may well find you delightfully gentle and cultured at the moment, but in time that can pall.

Then *why* did they go to my airplane hand in hand? Could the ludicrous romance conceivably last?

Never mind those babes in the woods. Jam Rance and Petrie into the machine.

The recording indicates she was in a very bad way. Pity she didn't crack.

He disbelieves her at first, but soon changes his mind. Why, the big baby joins his tears to hers. I speed up the next hours, during which together they exorcise the demons, in search of something more coherent. Ah.

"I love you, Larry. I've been fighting it every step, but here at the end of that road, I love you."

"Same here. What're we going to do about it?"

"Nothing."

"Julia!"

"Hush, darling."

"But—"

"Oh, we'll have a little, little while to carry us through the years. Then will come the hardest time—because I'm going to help you with your boat, Larry, and we'll have to make practical arrangements. You'll be our house guest off and on and we your guests on her shakedown cruise. I don't pretend that'll be easy."

"Julia, no."

"Hush. Listen. But kiss me first." Stillness for a minute. "Larry, believe. I want you to have your boat, not because you need her, though you do, but because the world needs her. Do you remember telling us half the oxygen we breathe comes from plankton? And the oceans are already loaded with chemical fallout? We have our children to think about. Go learn what we need to know."

"Missing you every second?"

Low laughter. "Oh Larry, you know better. All my days I'll love you, and hope you do me. But does that keep us from finding new loves? You will, I'm sure. A sailor girl from Australia or Polynesia or Asia to bear and rear your sailor sons. Or we go back to old ones, Larry. Me to Malcolm."

"Why not to me?"

"Please, darling. Malcolm because of Kilby, and because he has my oath, and because I think I've come to realize what I was to him and that it's never really died and we can light it again. You—" A sigh. "You're stronger than he is. I found that out this night. Therefore it's you I must say goodbye to."

Silence again, until she ends. "It's a terrible responsibility, isn't it, being loved?"

My finger smashes the switch down to STOP.

No more, no more! Tomorrow I destroy every last record.

But what can I do to forget this man here beside me, who was broken not by weakness but by a buried honor?

I stand among my machines. Like none of the seven, living and dead, I alone have always been alone. I always will be. The knowledge is unbearable.

"Samael," I cry in my need, "help!"

And Ellis Nordberg turns his dead face toward me, and his mumbling somehow also carries words. I lurch back, hands held out as if to fend off this last manifestation.

"Have I not helped you enough, Sunderland Haverner, helped you to where and what you are?"

From some unknown place comes the strength to confront that which is here and to say, "I did your will all these many years. Didn't I? Now, your part of the bargain, whatever you are. At least tell me I was right."

"Right about what?"

"About what's real. About the way things are. That those . . . those white rats of ours . . . were nothing more, can't ever be, are as worthless as—"

"As yourself?" asks Samael quite softly. Then out of Nordberg's throat comes laughter. "Why, how do you know that my entire purpose was not their salvation, and that I did not begin my work before they were born? Can you be certain that the sacrifices made toward that end are for eternity?"

"What?" I scream.

Once more Samael laughs. "To be sure, there remains the possibility that they have simply been my experimental means for testing you to destruction."

My body will not bear me up. I sink to my knees.

"I am not going to answer any such questions, of course," Samael continues. "I am not even going to tell you whether my silence comes from cruelty, or indifference, or mercy."

Sternness: "You shall carry out your promises to the players. You shall trouble them no more in their lives. Otherwise, you will not like the way in which I return."

Terror grips me by the heart. The pain forces me down onto all fours. I can only nod my head again and again and again.

"For I am leaving you," Samael goes on. "You have, as you said, served my purposes. In what few years remain to you, seek your own.

"Farewell, Sunderland Haverner."

The madman sinks back into his hell. I lie on the floor and weep.